The Magnolia Ball

The Magnolia Ball

A Southern Novel

Rebecca T Nunn

Writers Club Press
San Jose New York Lincoln Shanghai

The Magnolia Ball
A Southern Novel

All Rights Reserved © 2000 by Rebecca Tebbs Nunn

No part of this book may be reproduced or transmitted in any form or by any means, graphic, electronic, or mechanical, including photocopying, recording, taping, or by any information storage retrieval system, without the permission in writing from the publisher.

Writers Club Press
an imprint of iUniverse.com, Inc.

For information address:
iUniverse.com, Inc.
620 North 48th Street, Suite 201
Lincoln, NE 68504-3467
www.iuniverse.com

All characters are completely fictitious. Any similarities to any persons living or dead are purely coincidental.

ISBN: 0-595-14209-5

Printed in the United States of America

In honor of Spike and Ashley and in memory of Fay Gulley, a North Carolina debutante, and my biggest fan.

Foreword

For the Southern family, particularly the matriarch, the selection of a daughter to formally bow to society is one of the most coveted of honors. The seemingly antiquated tradition is alive and well today below the Mason-Dixon Line.

Prologue

The Magnolia Ball is one of the longest running debutante balls in the South. It began as a birthday party a local tobacco and cotton farmer of some wealth gave for his daughter in 1892. He lived near Montiac in Dorchester County, South Carolina, which is located between Hilton Head, South Carolina, and Savannah, Georgia. Mr. Beecham owned several hundred acres of land and employed many servants as well as the hands who worked in his fields. He owned a large center hall colonial house, stocked with furniture shipped from England. The shipment traveled first to Savannah and then was transported by barge to his estate.

On the rolling front lawn of Mr. Beecham's estate, "Beechland," stood a perfectly shaped, seventy-five foot magnolia tree. People came from miles around to gaze upon the splendor of its flowers that bloomed each summer. Every year during the Christmas holidays, Mrs. Beecham used the perfectly shaped magnolia leaves to decorate the fan she braided from grapevines. She then placed a large pineapple in the center and surrounded it with red apples. The festive decoration hung majestically over the marble fireplace in the great room through the holiday season.

Mr. Beecham's daughter, Celeste, who resembled her father, was a plain, homely girl with a hooknose, a lantern jaw, and she was none too bright. She was nearly eighteen and unmarried—an old maid! She had never had a gentleman caller or been courted by a gentleman. As far as anyone knew, she had never had a male head turn in her direction other than to snicker and point.

Celeste (despite her lack of beauty) was a special child. She had been born on Christmas Day. As her eighteenth birthday approached, her parents fretted over a way to get Celeste safely married to anyone, whether he be old, ugly, or poor. Their only requirement by that time was that he be white.

Mrs. Beecham, a beautiful woman who was from a family long on background and short on cash, had consented to marry the rather unattractive Mr. Beecham, a gentleman to the manor born, some twenty years prior. While Mr. Beecham was dull and quiet, Mrs. Beecham was imaginative, perky and garrulous. One day, she was on the front lawn gathering the leaves for the Christmas fan. As she was admiring the tree, she noticed Celeste gazing out of the second story window. Because of the direction the sun was shining, the shadow of magnolia leaves seemed to form a band across Celeste's head, framing her face. For a moment, Celeste looked almost regal, as if she were wearing a crown. Her daughter did have a confidence about her that showed in her straight posture and the way she held her head so high. Mrs. Beecham was suddenly struck with an idea.

She and Mr. Beecham were going to have a Magnolia Ball for Celeste's eighteenth birthday party. All of the young men for miles around would be invited. The highlight of the evening would be when Mr. Beecham proclaimed Celeste "Queen of the Magnolia Ball" and crowned her with a tiara of magnolia leaves Mrs. Beecham had woven.

Mrs. Beecham planned to make Celeste an absolute confection of a gown in pure white to attest to her virginity (as if there were any doubt!) She would curl Celeste's hair, pinch her cheeks for color and add a touch of berry stain to her lips. She remembered the belladonna that she would drop into her blue eyes to dramatize them. Celeste would also wear the family heirloom pearl choker and drop earrings that would put the finishing touch on her masterpiece. Celeste would certainly look presentable. And when some of the young men drank sufficiently of Mrs. Beecham's potent eggnog, maybe, just maybe, someone might become inebriated enough to ask Mr. Beecham for Celeste's hand in marriage or at least to dance!

Mrs. Beecham dispatched a house servant to find Mr. Beecham and bring him to the house. She continued to pick magnolia leaves while she plotted and planned. When Mr. Beecham arrived, she told him of her idea. She shared all of the details with him except how much bourbon she planned to pour into the crystal punch bowl the evening of the ball. Mr. Beecham excitedly agreed. This would be a chance to show off his wealth and his beautiful wife. He had longed for the day he could display to the neighbors his expensively furnished house with his stocked larder, impressive wine cellar and liquor supply. He thought how impressed they would be when they saw his stable of thoroughbred horses and his two new buggies.

Christmas night of 1892 arrived. Tables were laden with food in the huge dining room, the library, the parlor, the great room and the center hall at Beechland. Servants wore new uniforms and carried sterling silver trays filled with flutes of French champagne and Mrs. Beecham's "high octane" eggnog. Beechland was decorated as never before. Garlands made with magnolia leaves draped the mahogany staircase in the center hall. They hung across every doorway. Mrs. Beecham felt her best idea was to bathe the entire house in the light of tiny tapers rather than large candles and gaslights. They gave the house a lovely, festive glow. The soft lighting also enhanced the presentation of Celeste by not showing her every flaw to its greatest disadvantage.

The best families came from fifty miles around. The prospective suitors, unaware of their roles, eagerly arrived. The least attractive girls of the surrounding three counties had been invited. All of the spinsters from twenty-two to thirty-five years old were in attendance. Celeste, conveniently, was the only girl between the ages of sixteen and twenty-one; the field was wide open.

The Magnolia Ball

At the stroke of nine as the string quartet's music faded, Mr. Beecham presented to the guests Celeste, his beloved daughter and the birthday girl. She looked resplendent in an off the shoulder, white satin gown with a gathered skirt and white satin heels. The heirloom choker and earrings and white elbow length gloves complimented her gown perfectly. Pure white cotton was stuffed into the top of her corset to replace what the Lord had forgotten.

Celeste, in all of her radiance, with her hair waved and curled and her perfect posture descended the mahogany stairs. The flickering of the tiny tapers cast just the right amount of light on her imperfect countenance. By the time she reached the bottom step on her father's arm, the guests had begun to applaud. As the quartet struck up a Strauss waltz, Mr. Beecham took his daughter in his arms for the first dance of the evening. At that moment, the French champagne and Mrs. Beecham's eggnog took effect. A young man cut in on Mr. Beecham, and then another, and another. Celeste was in heaven and the Magnolia Ball had become a legend in its own time.

Part One

The Committee: 1991

1

Celestine

Celeste, the first Magnolia Ball queen, did not meet her husband-to-be the night of her eighteenth birthday party. However, at the age of thirty, when the Beechams had given up all hope, Celeste became engaged to a Mr. Edmonds, who lived ten miles away on his own large plantation. An older man and recently widowed, Mr. Edmonds began to call on her. A year after his wife's death, Celeste became the lady of the Edmonds' manor.

At thirty-two, Celeste bore a daughter Margarine, who in turn married and bore a daughter, whom she named for both of them—Celestine. The granddaughter of the first Queen of the Magnolia Realm married into the illustrious and prestigious Piersall family and served on the Magnolia Ball Committee. The committee's most important function was the selection of the young ladies to be presented each year at the Magnolia Ball. They also planned the Ball and decided the theme. They made arrangements for a local florist to handle the decorations and wrote the society articles for the *Montiac Minutes*, the sole local weekly newspaper and Bible to most of the inhabitants of Dorchester County. They held the first tea for the debutantes the Saturday after Thanksgiving at the local Country Club, and rehearsed the young ladies for their presentations to society. Serving on the Magnolia Ball Committee was a great honor in Dorchester County and a very coveted position.

The Magnolia Ball

Celestine Piersall was attractive, unlike her grandmother. She was the pampered daughter of Margarine and Jonathan Batterson. She attended the proper Country Day School and later St. Agatha's School for Young Ladies in Savannah, Georgia. She then attended Sweet Briar College in Virginia. She made her debut at the 1952 Magnolia Ball in Dorchester County, where she was escorted by her future husband Jamison Piersall IV. At the Ball, she was crowned "Queen of the Magnolias" as her mother had been before her. Active in all of the proper charities, a gracious hostess, and winner of the treasured blue ribbon almost every year at the Dorchester Garden Club show, Celestine was a model citizen, a pillar of society and a paragon of virtue.

In addition to her many charitable activities and volunteerism, Celestine spent a great deal of her time in the tradition of many Southern ladies—planning her funeral. It's never been clear as to why Southern ladies delight in planning their funerals, but like so many other members of her social group, Celestine knew exactly what she "wished to be laid out in." The details of her plan would change from time to time as she outlived a particular favorite in her wardrobe, or as the styles changed. She sat for many hours at her Victorian secretary and planned the music that was to be played at her funeral. Her choices would be magnificently played on the massive pipe organ in the old, socially prominent Episcopal Church in Montiac. The processional was to be "Onward Christian Soldiers." During the service the priest was to read Alfred Lord Tennyson's "Crossing the Bar," followed by the choir's rendition of "In the Garden." The recessional of "Lead on, O King Eternal" was to be sung by the entire congregation. The pipe organ was to have the trumpet key engaged. The pallbearers, another ever-changing list, would carry Celestine in her casket covered with a blanket of red roses and magnolia leaves down the aisle to the cemetery at the old historic Episcopal Church, her eternal resting place.

Even with all of Celestine's duties as a member of the Magnolia Ball Committee, for she entertained at a huge breakfast each year after the

Ball at Beechland where she and Jamison resided, she also headed the annual cancer drive in Dorchester County. She made all of the arrangements for the Heart Fund's annual "Cardiac Arrest." This was an event where prominent citizens were "arrested" and taken to "jail" in a local restaurant. "Bail" money of one hundred dollars per "felon" was donated by friends of each of the participants, and the proceeds went to the Heart Fund. Celestine was a member of the local library board and a volunteer at the library. She was an active member of the historic Episcopal Church in Montiac, served as chair of the Altar Guild, and also as a docent for the tours given at the Church. She was a member of the local Art Society and the Little Theatre group. She supported all artistic endeavors within the community. Celestine also found time to play bridge twice monthly once on the first Wednesday of each month at the Woman's Club Sandwich Bridge (so called since each of the members brought her own sandwich to eat during play.) On the third Thursday of each month Celestine played duplicate bridge at the country club's "members only" luncheon.

An average golfer, a fair tennis player, and an adequate bridge player, Celestine was well liked and highly regarded. She never gossiped or allowed anyone to gossip to her. With all of her breeding, background, and money (for her husband Jamison was the owner of an insurance conglomerate) Celestine was that rare individual who alienated no one.

The one great sadness in her life was her inability to produce a child. She and Jamison had tried for years to provide an heir to the Piersall fortune. They had visited numerous doctors and tried every suggestion made to them short of witchcraft.

Finally, after thirteen years of marriage, Celestine became pregnant. Both she and Jamison were ecstatic! Celestine's numerous friends gave a deluge of baby showers, luncheons, dessert bridge parties, coffees and teas for her. At one of the functions, her good friend, Jesse Earnest, presented her with a handmade two-and-one-half foot doll. It had big, blue eyes and a shock of red hair. Jesse had dressed the doll in short, blue pants, a white shirt, red tie, black shoes and white socks. She told Celestine that the doll was to be a friend for the new baby. Celestine was absolutely smitten with Jesse's gift. She named the doll Anthony after her great uncle and placed him on a specially made shelf in the newly decorated nursery. Often, as Celestine went to the nursery, either to admire the lovely room or to place new clothing in the chifferobe for her awaited bundle, she would talk to Anthony about the forthcoming event. It wasn't long before Celestine affected a high, squeaky voice for Anthony so that he could respond to her many conversational tidbits. Often, Celestine sat for sometimes an hour or more carrying on "conversations" with Anthony.

Two months prior to her due date and with no previous complications, Celestine went into labor. The doctors did everything they could to stall the delivery, but all of their attempts failed. After hours of straining and pushing, Celestine gave birth to a perfect baby boy with the umbilical cord wrapped tightly and hopelessly around his tiny neck. Jamison was inconsolable. Celestine's friends feared for her sanity. Celestine, while depressed, seemed otherwise philosophical about the death of her long-awaited child. She told the doctor that she wanted to go home as soon as possible. The doctor agreed, thinking that perhaps the maternity ward where Celestine was exposed to new mothers with their babies might be the worst place for her at the time. He allowed her to leave the hospital on her promise that she received complete bed rest. Jamison collected her and drove her home. He helped her up the winding staircase of Beechland to their bedroom and made her comfortable in their king-size canopied bed. Afterwards, he went downstairs to tell Izonia, the maid, what to prepare for Celestine's lunch. While in the kitchen, he heard footsteps from the second floor. He raced up the stairs to see what was so important as to make Celestine get out of her bed. Why hadn't she rung for him or Izonia? There he saw Celestine in her bed with Anthony in her arms. She was crooning and talking while rocking the doll back and forth.

Anthony became Celestine's "son." She made him an extensive wardrobe and changed his clothing daily. He had riding clothes, suits, a bathing suit, sports outfits, Madras Bermuda shorts and even a tuxedo. To anyone arriving at the Piersall home from that day on, Anthony was introduced as "my son," by Celestine and guests were encouraged to talk to him. In a high-pitched voice, Celestine spoke for Anthony and carried on conversations as if he were actually speaking.

Occasionally, when chatting with a guest, she would suddenly say, "Oh, excuse me," turn to Anthony, who was always sitting nearby, and speak to him as if answering his question. The situation, even though sad, became laughable. But Celestine seemed perfectly fine in every way except for the "Anthony thing," as people called it. Jamison apparently coped with the situation, although he didn't converse with Anthony to anyone's knowledge.

Celestine and Jamison were accompanied each year to the Magnolia Ball by Anthony, who was always handsomely attired in a tiny tuxedo, black, patent-leather shoes, a ruffled, formal shirt complete with bow tie and cummerbund, oiled hair and a miniature rosebud tucked in his tiny lapel. Anthony drank only milk at the Ball, however, since he did not mature beyond the age of twelve.

2

Bonita

She sighed, wrinkled her nose, and tapped the black gardener on the shoulder. He looked up from the mounds of cellulite between her thighs. "I must get dressed now, Alphonso. I have a committee meeting. Today we're selecting the girls. I have one little bit of unpleasantness to take care of at the beginning of the meeting and then we will begin the selections."

"Yes'm," said Alphonso as he stood and wiped his mouth on his sweat-stained, shirtsleeve.

"Ah, the committee meeting." Thoughts of the committee always filled Bonita with a warm glow. To think that she, Bonita Roberts, was in such a seat of power with so much authority and clout. Her "yea" or "nay" could make or break a young lady's social success in Dorchester County.

Bonita raised her hulk from the pink chaise and waddled slowly to her luxurious master bath. The mounds of fat between her legs rubbed grotesquely against each other as she felt a trickle of Alphonso's saliva run down her left leg. "Whoever said blacks don't know how to go down was crazy," she giggled to herself.

Tipping the scales at over three hundred pounds, her ugliness threatened to break mirrors into which she frequently gazed. She surrounded herself with feathers and velvet, ribbons and lace, and tiny, twinkling lights. Her house was covered with deep pile carpets, her bed with Porthault sheets and filmy, chiffon negligees trimmed with marabou hung flamboyantly throughout her bedroom. She was a sight to behold. Her face was made up with false eyelashes; dyed, black eyebrows and pale pink lipgloss lined with vivid red in the shape of a Cupid bow. Regardless of what color outfit she wore, Bonita always used fluorescent, blue eyeshadow smeared from her eyelashes to her eyebrows. Her silver hair was teased and sprayed and her pink fingernails were held in place with acrylic glue.

Bonita started the water for her bath. Tepid—not too cold, not too hot—just the way she liked it. She added a handful of scented bath oil beads from a pink vase next to the pink, sunken tub. While the tub filled, she inspected her chin in the wall-to-wall mirror above the pink marble lavatory. With her tweezers, she delicately pulled two black hairs from the large mole on the right side of her massive jaw. As her pink negligee fell to the floor, she inspected her huge, pendulous breasts. Holding her left breast in her hand and pulling it closer, she again reached for the tweezers and removed one hair from the aureole surrounding her left, teacup sized nipple. The right breast had three hairs today. No doubt the progesterone Dr. Nyland had prescribed to accompany her estrogen tablets was causing all of this ghastly hair to grow.

Bonita wafted over to the pink, throne-like Johnny and lowered herself onto it. She daintily reached between her legs and then placed one of her sausage-sized fingers in her mouth. "Exquisite," she thought to herself, as she tasted her essence mixed with Alphonso's saliva. Having donated a large quantity of urine to the pink throne, she flushed and moved to the tub. There she lowered her huge frame into the scented bath.

Lying back, feeling the water relieve tensions and relax her, Bonita let her thoughts wander to the committee. Bonita, the chairperson of the Magnolia Ball Committee, would be in her glory today. All of the committee members were to submit names of unmarried ladies who were eighteen years of age, in their first year of college, and of prominent or moneyed families. They were to be daughters of Bonita's friends or of other committee members', or of clients of committee members' husbands. Then Bonita and her two carefully selected members, Nancy and Blanche, would secretly select the young ladies to whom this year's honor would be bestowed. The young ladies selected would become the season's debutantes to be presented at the Dorchester County Magnolia Ball of 1991.

Bonita had already decided on several young ladies that would not be asked, especially Sandy Hibbert, Trudy Waltham's daughter. It was all so perfect! She had all the power, but the committee met in secret. No one else knew the inner workings, so no one ever contested the selections or got angry with her. Not that it would have mattered if they had. Bonita was so firmly entrenched in the social strata of Dorchester County that her word was law. She was unimpeachable. The only person with equal clout was Celestine Piersall, but Celestine never made any waves.

Bonita thought back to the little girl who covered her ears with her hands to try to blot out the grunting sounds. Every night it had been the same; the horrible noises went on for hours. The nine-year-old Mexican girl had endured these nightly grunts, groans and shrieks every night for as long as she could remember. Lying on her mat, the little girl was sandwiched between her older sister and her younger brother, both by only a year. Twin sisters slept sprawled at her feet. The "ughs" and "ahs" and "ohs" became intolerable. It wasn't just the noise, but the heat was debilitating. The mosquitoes gnawed at every part of her exposed little body adding to her agony. The child felt her sanity slipping, but she knew better than to get up, cross the dirt floor and go outside for fresh air. She had gotten up once before, and suddenly the grunts and groans had ceased. She had turned her head just in time to hear a loud crack as she saw stars before her eyes. Her father had slapped her on the side of the head and said, "You getta back on you mat—whatsa matta wif you? You know you donna get up after you been put down."

"Yes, Papa," she had whimpered as she dragged herself back to her mat. Her head had hurt for days. A big bump had swollen at the site of impact. She would not risk the pain again. From then on, no matter how hot or how many mosquito bites she felt, or how much she might need to relieve herself, she stayed put on her mat.

The rutting sounds her parents made in the night were horrible, but not nearly as bad as what took place in the light of day. She awoke early one morning with a pain in her stomach. She heard the noises and glanced over to the only bed in the two-room house. There were her parents, naked. Her father was on top of her mother. He was holding her hands against the rickety old headboard. He slammed into her mother so violently that the child thought he was going to kill her. She saw blood on the dirty bedcover. The sight of the blood frightened her so much that she thought her father had hurt her mother badly. Then another noise had made her look at the floor next to her parents' bed. There, lying on a dirty towel, was her squealing baby brother. He had been born only the day before.

She was one of eleven children ranging in age from ten on down. She had a ten-year-old sister, an eight-year-old brother, twin seven-year-old sisters, six-, five-, and four-year-old brothers, three-, and two-year-old sisters, and a one-year-old brother. Her groaning mother, into whom her father pounded, was pregnant again. Her mother worked in the homes of wealthy white people in Brownsville, Texas. Her father, Roberto, an excellent carpenter (when he worked), was an alcoholic.

The house, constructed of wood, had one door and a dirt floor. The stove was made from a barrel with a pipe that went through the roof. There was one bed, six unstable chairs and a table. Facilities included a well outside and an outdoor Johnny house. The thirteen occupants sweltered in the hot Texas summers and froze in the often bone-chilling winters.

Her ten-year-old sister, Felicidad, took care of the younger children, while her mother worked and while her father drank. The little girl was miserable. She hated her life. A twelve-year-old girl who lived down the road had married a boy last month. When things became unbearable, the child daydreamed. "That's what I'm going to do. In only three more years, I'll get married. Then I'll get away from here. I won't have babies every year. I won't let my husband do those terrible things to me. I'll work for a rich white lady, and my husband and I will have a house and a bed all to ourselves."

She slowly removed her hands from her ears. "Gracias! They have finished and gone to sleep." Then all the child had to do was ignore the steady hum of her father's snoring and that of the mosquitoes. As she tried to fall asleep, she thought, "Maybe tomorrow it will rain, and at least there will be some breeze. Maybe the rich white lady will give Mamma some ice to bring home. Maybe God will kill all of the mosquitoes. Maybe my father will be too tired to do that to my mother tomorrow night; maybe I'll be…" and she mercifully fell into a fitful sleep.

Bonita gave a start and realized that she had been about to drift off in the cooling bath water. She hurriedly finished her ablutions. As she left the tub, she reached for a plush, pink bath sheet. After drying herself, she made her way into her bedroom where she began her long process of making up and dressing for the committee meeting.

The little girl whom Bonita had thought about in the tub had grown into a beautiful, full-figured young woman who drew stares and catcalls wherever she went. Boys and men were always after her when she went out to do chores or walked into town to try to get a few essentials on credit for her parents. Her hair was long and wavy and so black that it had blue highlights. Her almond-shaped eyes were fringed with lush lashes. Her mouth was full with pouty lips. A dark beauty mark accented her right lower cheek, and she needed no cosmetics to enhance her beauty. Her high, full breasts were complemented by her small waist and gently swelling hips. Long, shapely legs completed what men considered perfection.

Although she was aware that she was attractive, the girl had never realized the dazzling effect she had on men until she was walking back from town one day. She stopped to watch a camera crew filming a scene on the side of the road. Marvin Hammond, a Hollywood director, was overseeing the shoot. Just as he yelled "Action" for the twenty-first time, the girl came into his view and he yelled, "Cut!" Upset at first that yet another take had been interrupted, Hammond, known for his tempestuous nature, was about to throw another tantrum. His eyes focused on the girl. Immediately, he approached her and asked her name.

"Maria," she responded.

"Not anymore," said Hammond. "Maria is much too common a name for someone as lovely as you. How would you like to go to California with me? I'll make you a star."

Maria didn't have the vaguest idea what Hammond was talking about. She had never seen a movie and had no idea what a star was. However, she had heard about California. She knew it was where everything was beautiful, including the women and the men, where everyone was rich, and where all of the houses were mansions.

"I have to take these things back to my mother and then I'll be ready to go."

Hammond asked how old she was.

"Fourteen."

Hammond was concerned that her parents would not let her go, but Maria assured him she would be back. She went home and told her mother she was leaving for California with a man who wanted to make her a star. Her father yelled that she wasn't going "nowhere", that she was needed to take care of the children and help around the house. But Maria's mother told her she loved her and to go quickly. As her father lurched across the room to stop her, Maria dodged out of his way and ran out of the house and down the road to her new life: the camera crew, Hammond and Hollywood.

Hammond asked her where her luggage was. Maria didn't know what he was talking about. "Your clothes?" he asked.

"I only have this dress, and one other, and it's too short and besides, it's torn."

He left the last few details of the shoot in the hands of his assistant. Hammond's driver took him and Maria to the airport and Hammond flew with her to Hollywood. He ensconced her in an apartment of his home and instructed his secretary to take her shopping.

In the following months, maids drew her baths and laid out her clothing. Cooks fed her whatever she wanted to eat. Hairdressers arrived to cut and style her hair. Voice coaches gave her speech lessons. She was instructed in ballet. A modeling coach taught her how to walk and sit. She was taught the proper way to eat using the correct utensils.

For over a year, Maria was schooled or coached everyday with no breaks. For some it might have been a lonely existence. She saw only Hammond or various teachers and coaches. For Maria it was better than any daydream she had ever experienced.

The day arrived when Hammond thought she was ready for her screen test. She was fifteen. Hammond brought Maria a script. Coaches worked with her. She learned her lines quickly and was ready in a short time. Perfectly groomed, coifed and gowned, Maria tested. It was less than Hammond had hoped for, but not terrible. He immediately cast her as the ingenue in his latest film. The movie bombed.

Hammond tried Maria in several more features, and all were disasters. The girl could not act and the pizzazz, that extra something needed for the silver screen, although she possessed it in person, was missing on film. Finally, after two years, Hammond told Maria that he had made a mistake. He said that while she was a beauty, he could not make her a star. He explained that he would pay all of her expenses back to Brownsville, Texas. She could take all of her clothes, jewelry, etc.

Maria was not going back to Texas. She took the money and the plane ticket and thanked Marvin Hammond. She kissed him on the cheek as he put her into the cab. She told the cabby to take her to the Beverly Wilshire where she checked in and tried to figure out what to do. That evening she dressed in a designer gown and went to an elegant restaurant to have dinner. As she walked into the room, every male and female head in the place turned. The men leered, and the women fumed. Maria asked for a table for one. She was there for only a few minutes when she was approached by a handsome gentleman. She accepted his invitation to join her at her table and as they dined, he listened to her story. As he walked her back to her room, he told her he would take care of everything. In the next several weeks, he sent her roses daily. He paid all of her expenses at the hotel. He took her to famous restaurants and clubs. He seduced her and then told her of his plans. She could make thousands of dollars a week, continue to live in the Beverly Wilshire, and not have to go back to Texas and poverty.

Maria, under the tutelage of Enrique Dubra, became the highest priced call girl in Hollywood. She slept with directors, producers, set designers, and anyone else whom Enrique brought to her door with the thousand-dollars-an-hour fee that her beauty and bedroom techniques demanded. She serviced them all without regard to color, social status or gender. She entertained lesbians, couples and groups, in addition to her regular clientele. Maria found that the very thing she had vowed she would never let a man do to her was in fact her favorite thing of all. Maria, the harlot, became known all over Hollywood by one name. That name was Bonita.

For twenty-five years she plied her trade in the luxurious Beverly Wilshire. She awakened around four each afternoon, at which time her maid served her croissants with jam, orange juice, and chamomile tea. After partaking of a late breakfast in bed, Hannah, the maid, drew Bonita's bubble bath where Bonita languished for an hour. Her bath was followed by a massage. Hannah lavished Bonita's ripe body with a multitude of silky and fragrant oils and perfumes. Bonita dressed for the day at eight in the evening. Her working day began an hour later, when Enrique's first caller arrived.

Often Bonita entertained a gentleman caller for the entire night at a thousand dollars an hour. When this occurred, the gentleman was expected to leave by eight in the morning. She then bathed again, ate an enormous dinner of either lobster or Porterhouse steak with a baked potato or rice, a large salad, and green beans (the only vegetable she could tolerate.) After a calorie-filled dessert and champagne, she retired to her bed on which Hannah had arranged freshly washed and ironed Porthault sheets. She slept for the next eight hours.

Bonita worked six days a week. She elected to take Saturdays off. Enrique protested that it was the best night of the week for her profession, but Bonita was firm. No work on Saturday. On that day she arose at noon, and, after her bath and breakfast, she hired a car to take her to Rodeo Drive where she spent the afternoon shopping for beautiful "at home" gowns, peignoirs, designer dresses, jewelry, and Gucci shoes and purses. Bonita had a fetish for shoes and owned several hundred pairs of pumps, sling-backs, mules and slippers.

Many of her callers became regulars and brought her expensive gifts. Occasionally she traveled with some of them, but she never developed any emotional attachment. Her manner was seemingly loving and affectionate, for it turned out she was a rather good actress after all. She was able to convince the gentlemen that she sincerely cared about them, but inside felt nothing.

When she celebrated her fortieth birthday, Enrique began to worry about her longevity in the field. Younger and more beautiful girls were working in the Hollywood arena. Although she still commanded her high fees, and business had not yet slowed, Bonita was beginning to gain weight. Gravity was making itself known. The once proud breasts sagged a little; the voluptuous hips were spreading and the waistline was thickening. Whenever Enrique mentioned these things to Bonita and suggested cutting back on the food, she laughed and said he had nothing to worry about.

But Enrique's concerns soon were realized. Various regular clients failed to call back, and when Enrique contacted them, he found that many of them were hiring younger women. By this time, Bonita was only working two or three nights a week, and there were no longer requests for her services overnight.

When it seemed that Bonita's career was all but over, one of Enrique's regulars contacted him about a friend seeing Bonita. The friend was sixty-five years old and having an impotency problem. The regular had experienced the same problem a few years prior, and Bonita had "cured" him, or at least he thought she had. The regular made an appointment with Bonita for his friend, Joshua Roberts, owner of a large New York publishing firm.

Roberts arrived at Bonita's suite at promptly nine o'clock in the evening in an extremely nervous state; although he had played around most of his married life, he had never paid for the attentions of a woman. When he saw Bonita, Roberts thought she was attractive. But he was interested in a younger woman and feared that Bonita was not the antidote to his problem. What he would soon find out, however, was that Bonita had learned a great deal in her twenty-five years of prostitution. In addition to being wild in bed, she was very seductive and a brilliant conversationalist. With her ministrations, Roberts rose to the occasion three times that evening.

Roberts became a regular, one of the few Bonita still entertained. He even began spending entire nights with her on occasion. He took her with him on business trips and sent her gardenias, her favorite flower, almost daily. He also gave her trinkets from Tiffany's and Cartier's. To put it bluntly, Roberts fell head-over-heels in love with Bonita. She felt nothing for him, but when Roberts asked her to marry him, she remembered Enrique's warning: her working time was limited. Bonita reminded Joshua of what she had been doing for the past twenty-five years and asked if that would bother him. Roberts said that it would not. This was true, for what Bonita didn't know was that after his first session with her, Roberts had found, through trial and error with numerous women, that Bonita was the only one who could entice him to maintain an erection long enough for penetration. Roberts also genuinely liked her. He knew he could mold her to fit into his world. She was very attractive, and she was polished, knowledgeable, and dressed with style.

Bonita discussed the proposal with Enrique, and while he was sorry to see his forty percent of her earnings disappear, he knew that she didn't have many years left. She had never given him trouble in their twenty-five-year arrangement. She had not taken a day off, even during her period, and had never gotten pregnant or had a sexually transmitted disease. In all, Bonita had been a pimp's dream. Enrique released her with his blessing.

Roberts flew to Mexico and divorced his wife of forty years. He married Bonita in Reno the following week and took her to his Fifth Avenue penthouse in New York where, as Mrs. Joshua Roberts, she became the toast of Manhattan. Bonita Roberts was to all of New York a Spanish countess who had lived for a time in Mexico. She had made a few movies in California. She was married to a sickly gentleman for fifteen years. Consequently, no one asked questions about why they had not met her previously in their jet-set world.

Bonita settled in with Joshua Roberts and loved her new life. While Hollywood had been fine, this new life surpassed her wildest dreams. She could hardly remember the nights of mosquitoes and the grunts and groans—her miserable life as a child.

In 1972, Joshua Roberts had a massive coronary followed by a series of mini-strokes. Bonita was at his side during his recovery. When Joshua was well enough to converse again, he told Bonita that they needed to move to the country away from the hustle and bustle of New York City. She was willing to go with Joshua if that was what he needed. He had visited an aunt near Hilton Head Island when he was a young man and had always remembered the beauty and tranquillity of South Carolina. He sent two of his trusted business associates to find a house in Dorchester County.

The executives found the perfect home for them, a small thirteen-acre estate on Danzer Creek. The home was antebellum and was lovingly preserved. It had huge public rooms downstairs, a lovely master suite, and three bedrooms on the second floor. It had servants' quarters, a runway for light planes, a boathouse suitable for a large yacht, and stables. Joshua and Bonita bought Creekside Farm in 1973, moved with their entourage of servants, a nurse for Joshua, and forty-six trunks of Bonita's clothes. Her shoes were shipped separately.

During the first Christmas in their new home, Bonita and Joshua held the most fabulous party Dorchester County had ever witnessed. Engraved invitations were sent to the "creme de la crème" of Dorchester society, and Bonita spared no expense. The fresh Beluga caviar was flown in the day of the party. The plane taxied to within fifty yards of the Roberts' front door. French champagne was flown into Savannah Airport. Alphonso, a local black that Joshua had engaged to help around the estate, picked up the bubbly in the Roberts' maroon Rolls Royce that he drove into the city.

Hannah, with the help of a troupe of local caterers, carved mammoth sugar plum fairy ice sculptures, and around them, arranged pounds of Louisiana shrimp and Maine lobster. Both had been flown in earlier in the day. Fresh anthuriums had arrived by plane from Hawaii the previous week. Local florists worked for three days decorating the mansion's foyer, ballroom, and the mammoth tent Bonita rented. Latham, Bonita's florist from New York, was on hand to arrange the flowers the day of the party.

"Les Brown's Band of Renown" found their way to Montiac by four in the afternoon and checked into the Dorchester Grand. Everyone in the county was in a titter. Why, a band of that reputation didn't even play at the Magnolia Ball! The giant tent Bonita had erected included a closed entranceway from the ballroom, complete with a dance floor. Diamond-chip earrings and diamond-chip cuff links rested at each place setting. Bonita spent days on the placement of the guests. The attire was black tie, of course. She had left Joshua in the hands of his nurse on two occasions for her fittings with Oscar de la Renta in New

York for the white silk column trimmed with ermine she planned to wear that evening.

In short, Dorchester County was "blown away" by the spectacular event. Joshua was "blown away", as well, for several days after the party, he suffered a debilitating stroke from which he never fully recovered. He didn't regain his speech and was relegated to being moved from here to there, either in a wheelchair or on a rolling chaise lounge. Bonita spent time with him each day, but the bulk of her time was spent attending social functions throughout the county. Since moving to Dorchester County, she had tactfully let people know that she had been a starlet in Hollywood and had been in several movies. She also made them aware of her compelling contralto voice.

The following Christmas season old Mrs. Woodward, who had served as the grand dame of the Magnolia Ball for eons, came down with bronchitis two days before the Ball. Bonita was asked by the committee to emcee the presentation of the debutantes. Mrs. Joshua Roberts was delighted, and the rest was history. She was splendid in her role. With her talent for giving parties, her "royal heritage," her reputation and social status, and her sophisticated appearance, Bonita had planted the seedlings that would firmly entrench her as not only the mistress of ceremonies at the Magnolia Ball, but also as the committee's chairperson.

Bonita became the most socially prominent and powerful person in all of Dorchester County, with the exception of Celestine Piersall. The only person in all of Dorchester County (or on the East Coast for that matter,) other than the faithful Hannah, who knew her humble beginnings and what her life's work had been, was her husband. And he was unable to make a sound, and his right hand was too shriveled to write.

Bonita took her duties as society matron very seriously. She never made passes at any men. As Roberts withered away, she grew tired of her vibrators and began to look around for something or someone to interest her. One of her favorite clients in California had been a very wealthy black man, and Bonita had been particularly attracted to his generous amount of hardware.

Recalling her black client, she told Hannah to send Alphonso to the master suite. Hannah replied, "Law, Miss Bonita, I don't think that would be proper. You should talk to him downstairs in the parlor, not up here in your bedroom. He might get the wrong idea."

"When I need your advice, and I often do, Hannah, I will ask you for it, but for right now, please send Alphonso up, and I promise you he won't get the wrong idea. When I have finished explaining to him what it is I desire, I am sure he will have exactly the right idea," answered Bonita.

"Oh, Miss Bonita, don't go startin' somethin' here. You knows how much I loves you, and that I been with you since you was a mere slip of a gal, and I seen it all and heard it all, and even if my fingernails was to be ripped out, I wouldn't tell nothin' I knows. You been far too good to me. I wouldn't never tell, but you don't know what that Alphonso will do. We's 'come-heres.' He's local. We don't know him. We don't know where he goes or who he talks to. You can't be trustin' him. S'pose he was to tell?" fretted Hannah.

"Hannah, please go downstairs and send Alphonso up. Why don't you make some of your delicious petite fours for dessert tonight? That will be all, Hannah. Thank you."

Hannah went downstairs and sent Alphonso up. Bonita explained to him that he was about to have his salary doubled for a little extra evening work. Alphonso couldn't believe his good fortune. He thought Miss Bonita was a mighty handsome woman, and he was more than happy to accommodate her. Fortunately for Bonita, he knew when to keep his mouth shut. He never told anyone about the kinky things he did with Bonita in exchange for his greatly enhanced paycheck.

Bonita had it all. Alphonso, with the proper guidance, became a talented and compassionate lover, and his hardware was something to behold. She was able to convince him to go down on her, an act that black men are not known to particularly relish. Alphonso relished and pickled and radished. He took advantage of the entire banquet Bonita frequently offered to him.

Bonita continued to eat her lobsters, steaks, baked potatoes, and rich desserts. And gravity continued to pull and tug. By 1991, at the age of sixty-four, Bonita was tipping the scales at over three hundred pounds. She proceeded to have designers "tent" her in gowns that would have looked fantastic on a size sixteen, but looked ridiculous on her. Still, even though she grew obese and ugly, with fleshy jowls and hairs growing from the mole that had once been called a beauty mark, her social position was maintained. She held on with a firm grip to her scepter as Queen of Dorchester County.

3

Milicent

Reed-thin, perfectly coifed, silver-haired Milicent Pritchard hurried home from her August teachers' meeting prior to the school year. She showered, changed, and raced out to her car. She couldn't be late for the selection meeting.

As a young girl, Milicent had been extremely slender and reasonably attractive. A Nakes by birth, she was a member of a very old, very prominent and very political family. She lived with her parents, Lem and Sadie, wealthy landowners in Dorchester County. She was their only daughter. As a high school student, Milicent had fallen in love with a man by the name of Harold Bauer, a young man she adored and one whom she felt her parents would readily approve.

The Nakes were not gossips and had sheltered Milicent from the randy goings-on (and there were many) in Dorchester County. The only words Milicent had ever heard about the Bauer family were kind. When Milicent related to her parents her love for Harold, Lem hit the roof and forbade her to see him again. He subsequently dispatched Milicent to Raleigh, North Carolina, to spend an extended vacation with her maiden aunt. Milicent was devastated and had no idea why Harold Bauer's name had aroused such fury.

Lem did not tell Milicent why he had reacted as he did. There was an old Southern tradition or habit of which the Nakes did not approve, the interest many Southern gentlemen took in what were referred to as "high-yellows." These were female Negroes of light color. Mr. Bauer, Harold's father and the brother of U.S. Senator Willard B. Bauer, had a definite affinity for "high-yellows," so much so that he had impregnated one. She had a son.

Less fortunate than his mother, the son was not light-skinned but very dark. Shortly after the child's birth, Stafford Bauer, as the child was called, was orphaned. After his mother died, Harold's father had his maid rear the boy. Stafford, Harold's half-brother, attended the one-room schoolhouse with white children. This was unheard of at that time. He lived in the Bauer household and was accepted as a magnanimous gesture on the part of Mr. Bauer, although everyone knew that Stafford was really Mr. Bauer's son by the "high-yellow."

By most people in Dorchester County, Stafford's heritage was overlooked. Lem Nakes was not one of those people. Weaknesses of the flesh, and especially weaknesses of the flesh with what Lem considered to be an inferior race, could not and would not be tolerated. Lem also ascribed to the theory, "Like father, like son," and his Milicent was not going to be placed in the position of having a husband who might someday embarrass and humiliate her, as Harold's father had done to Harold's mother. Thus, Milicent was banished to North Carolina.

Heartbroken, she remained in Raleigh for two years and went to Normal School, an educational institution for aspiring teachers. She barely fulfilled the requirements, but she managed to obtain her certificate. Two days after graduation, she received her weekly copy of the *Montiac Minutes*. It was the Dorchester newspaper and the Bible to most Dorchesterians. She read in the "Social Notes" of Harold Bauer's nuptials to Vivian Lenox on Saturday last.

Several months later, she returned to Dorchester County and took a position teaching in the Montiac School. Lem and Sadie insisted she live at home with them. They never mentioned Harold Bauer. Each night, after coping with the twenty-eight beastly little hellions in her class, Milicent cried herself to sleep.

Harold's family, the Bauers, also were members of a very old, very prominent, and very political family. They lived in the town of Montiac in Dorchester County, a very old, very prominent, and very political town in the very old, very prominent, and very political state of South Carolina. His name was Harold and her name was Vivian, which was insignificant. Their last name was Bauer, which to anyone who lived in Montiac, Dorchester County, or even the state of South Carolina, was extremely significant. He was average looking and part owner of a successful butcher shop. She was average looking and a housewife, but politically well connected and a member of the Lenox family. They lived on Willowoak Street in Montiac in an old, white, three-storied Victorian house which boasted wrap-around front and side porches with four large pillars spanning the front of the house. Wings attached to the sides made the Bauer home one of the largest in Montiac. Carefully maintained shrubbery and lush green lawns completed the picturesque property.

Harold and Vivian had a daughter, Pauline, and a maid, Queenie. They were entertaining six members of the South Carolina House of Delegates on a particularly warm evening in 1930. Harold, the nephew of U.S. Senator Willard B. Bauer, also a native of Dorchester County, had called this auspicious group together to discuss the state's politics for the upcoming legislative session. Although he held no elected office, Harold was the power behind many thrones.

Queenie served a delicious dinner of Southern fried chicken, turnip greens (which had been cooked all day, as Southern vegetables are), with a streak of lean (as opposed to fatback, which is for the poor and underprivileged) topped with cornmeal dumplings made in pot liquor. They had home-cured country ham; sliced fresh cucumbers, tomatoes and spring onions swimming in vinegar, salt and pepper; hoecakes, biscuits the size of saucers; and slabs of hand-churned butter stamped with the Bauer seal. Dessert was Apple Brown Betty, a concoction made from apple slices, stale bread, butter, cinnamon and sugar. The beverage was sugared, minted, iced tea (called Sweet Tea in the South). The gentlemen were sated and retired to the parlor for after-dinner brandy and Havana cigars.

The parlor of the house displayed an ancient, threadbare Oriental carpet passed down through many generations of Bauers. The fact that it was threadbare made no difference to the homeowners or to their six guests. The Bauers, as everyone knew, were above being concerned by what other people thought. (Besides, everyone below the Mason-Dixon Line knew that an Oriental carpet became more valuable as it got older and more threadbare.)

Two faded, rose, damask Victorian sofas and two overstuffed, ivory-brocade wing chairs, complete with antimacassars crocheted by Vivian's mother, sat upon the ancient rug. Elegantly framed photographs of the Senator, Harold, Vivian, Pauline, and various other members of the Bauer and Lenox families graced the walls. There were several Chippendale tables. The room had only one entrance, and that was from the huge center hall.

Parlors in the South were used only occasionally, most often when a family member died and the corpse was laid out for viewings, for important guests' after-dinner cigars and brandy, when the preacher came to call or when a gentleman was courting an eligible daughter of the household. Other than on those rare occasions, the room was kept tightly shut. The heavy-lined draperies remained drawn to prevent the furniture from fading. Parlors were traditionally opened once a week to be dusted and cleaned.

Queenie had been with "Miss Vivian" since she was a child and had "practically raised her up single-handedly," according to Queenie. Black servants in the thirties, forties and fifties in the South were often outspoken. Many of them had reared the daughter of a well-to-do family and then gone with her when she married and became the lady of her own house. Such was the case with Queenie. Just as Queenie did, many servants often ran the house and usually the people in it. They were more authority figures than servants; they voiced their opinions, ordered family members out of "my kitchen," instructed "poor white trash," in their "opinions," to use the back door, and generally managed the household.

While the gentlemen conversed in the parlor, Vivian instructed Queenie to help her set up a huge metal wash tub in the center hall just outside the parlor door. As Queenie's large brown eyes rolled, she loudly protested and questioned what on earth "Miss Vivian" was doing.

Many servants of this ilk and era were, in fact, the children or grandchildren of slaves who had been owned by the same white family's grandparents or great grandparents. Their ancestors had been freed but had refused to leave and remained with their white families as paid servants. A large number of them still lived in a tradition that may have continued except for the advent of the welfare programs of the late sixties.

Queenie, daughter of Princess Aurelia Jones and granddaughter of Jesus Jones, had worked for the Lenox family all her life. She considered herself a member of their family. Her mother Princess Aurelia had worked for Vivian's parents throughout her lifetime. Queenie's grandfather, Jesus, had been Vivian's grandparents' house servant, the highest rung on the social ladder of servitude. Jesus had originally been a slave, who upon learning of the Emancipation Proclamation, asked to remain with the Lenox family rather than leave to make his way in an unknown and alien world.

Vivian shushed Queenie. She told her to fill the tub with buckets of hot water suitable for a bath. Queenie filled the tub muttering to herself, as she knew trouble was brewing. "The menfolks is in the parlor and now 'Miss Vivian' wants bath water in a tub right outside." (Queenie thought that the combination of tubs and bath water in the center hall was as strange a combination as hen shit and lemonade.)

Once the tub was filled, Vivian returned to the center hall. Nondescript in appearance, "mousy" as some may describe her, Vivian was of mediocre intelligence. She had never in her life done or said anything above or below the established line of normalcy. One might say that she was so quiet and uninteresting that she would be easy to miss in a room filled with unforgettable people.

Vivian proceeded to the door of the parlor. Without knocking, she opened it and graciously invited the gentlemen into the center hall. Harold was annoyed at the interruption, but he rose and invited the gentlemen to accompany him. Once everyone was gathered in the hallway, Vivian proceeded to remove her dress. Underneath she wore nothing. Harold quickly moved to Vivian's side, took her by both arms, and attempted to steer her towards the stairway. Horrified, he begged the other gentlemen's pardon. Vivian screamed obscenities at him, and with what appeared to be superhuman strength, she pushed him aside. With shrieks of laughter, she immersed herself in the tub where she began to scrub herself and sing a bawdy song about "Mabel whose hands were tied behind her and whose tits were nailed to the table."

4

Milicent's Husband

He pulled into the one-horse town of Montiac, Dorchester County, in his brand new Willis. Three ferry rides had brought him from the big city to this, the last left-hand turn before the end of the world. Maybe this little excuse for a town would be different. He had barely enough money to last another week. He definitely could not make his car payment unless he sold some insurance. And he had to sell it fast. He passed the first block of business buildings and saw in the center of the second block the only hotel in town, the Dorchester Grand.

Walter Pritchard parked the Willis, checked into a seedy room, and washed his face. At the restaurant downstairs, he ate a bowl of vegetable soup, the only item on the menu he could comfortably afford.

Sammy, a small greasy man of unidentifiable foreign birth and the owner of the Dorchester Grand, was sitting in a booth when Walter entered the restaurant in the uncomfortable hotel. Sammy, a small-time hood and gambler, was always looking for a little action, so he struck up a conversation with Walter. Before long, he had bought him several drinks (served in coffee cups since Prohibition was at its height and the sale of alcohol was illegal). Sammy had convinced Walter to sit in on a poker game later that evening. Before the evening was over, Walter had won seven hundred dollars, a small fortune in 1930.

Tuesday morning, feeling better than he had in weeks, he proceeded directly across the street from the hotel to the post office. He mailed his overdue car payment to the bank in his hometown of Macon, Georgia. Realizing he was hungry, he spied Ben's Restaurant next door where he ate ravenously. Ben's was decidedly better than the restaurant at the Grand. Walter had a Southern breakfast of three sunnyside-up eggs, a slab of bacon, grits floating in melted butter, orange marmalade, drop biscuits, sausage gravy, home fries smothered in cheese, hand-squeezed fresh orange juice, and chicory-flavored fresh brewed coffee, with a side order of fried tomatoes topped with cinnamon and sugar.

As he prepared to leave Ben's, Milicent Nakes walked in. She sat in a booth and ordered a cup of coffee. Walter was impressed and walked over to introduce himself. Milicent was horrified! This kind of behavior was totally foreign to her. Strangers were suspect in Montiac. She had already labeled herself an old maid, and had given up hope of finding a man, but here, standing in front of her was the most handsome, dashing man she had ever seen. He probably even owned that new black Willis she had seen parked in front of the Dorchester Grand.

Walter began to court Milicent. Milicent never told Lem and Sadie about her romance, but suddenly began to regularly attend night meetings at the school. Walter traveled to other towns up and down the South Carolina and Georgia coasts selling insurance, but he returned every night to Montiac and Milicent's willing arms, legs and other bodily regions.

After six months of traveling, selling, and making mad, passionate love to Milicent every night on the "less-than-pristine" sheets of the Dorchester Grand, he proposed. Walter, with the gift of gab, gleaned from his many client contacts that "poor Milicent-the-schoolteacher" was anything but poor. He discovered that she was the only daughter of one of the wealthiest families in the county. He also learned that she was in line to inherit from various other relatives. Apparently Lem and Sadie were the only members of each of their respective families who had produced offspring.

In marrying into the Nakes family, Walter saw a way out of his financial problems. He could finally own The Willis outright and get rid of those horrid monthly payments. Milicent would provide enough money for him not to have to worry about selling insurance. Best of all, Walter knew that once he and Milicent were married, he could leave this God-forsaken, God-forgotten place. Although she never told him why, he knew that she also wanted out of there.

Walter went to Appleby's Jewelry Store on the left of the post office facing the Dorchester Grand and bought, on time, the biggest diamond ring the store had to offer. He was able to do this since he had now lived in Montiac for six months and was no longer a stranger. (He could live there for sixty years, but since he was not a native, he would still be referred to as a "come-here".)

That night he took Milicent to dinner at the Elms, one of Montiac's finest restaurants, where he requested a secluded table. Milicent thought it was very daring for her to be seen in public with him without a proper chaperone. But she felt that this might be the "big night." Walter ordered two coffee cups of champagne, and, while Milicent was in the ladies' lounge, he dropped the magnificent engagement ring into the bottom of her cup. As she was finishing the champagne, she discovered the diamond, and knew it was the most romantic moment she had ever imagined.

After meeting Lem and Sadie and undergoing a thorough interrogation by her father, Lem granted Walter permission to marry Milicent. They were wed in the old, historic Episcopal Church in Dorchester County, the only place where the socially prominent were married, and Walter was presented the huge dowry.

Upon returning from their honeymoon to Luray Caverns, Virginia, Walter bought Milicent a car. The Prichards became the first two-car family in Montiac. After Walter ensconced Milicent in a suite at the Dorchester Grand, he set off to Georgia to attend a business convention and to find them a suitable home. Milicent was unable to accompany him, as she could not take more time off from school that year: however, she had already given her notice that she would not return to teach in the fall.

Walter Pritchard was never heard from again; however, the following month, Milicent received a bill from Appleby's Jewelry for the diamond ring and a bill from Darlton's Ford for her new car. The Dorchester Grand bill also had to settled.

Milicent fortunately was reinstated as a teacher for the forthcoming school year. She couldn't divorce Walter because she was not able to find him. She continued to wear the huge diamond and went by the name of Pritchard rather than Nakes. Miserable, she went back home to live with her parents, who presumably paid for the ring, the hotel fee, and the car.

When the county schools consolidated in the late fifties, Milicent had to drive to the little town below Montiac to teach the elementary school brats, heirs to the very old, very prominent, and very political families of Dorchester County. Being a member of one of those families herself, Milicent busied herself with teas, bridge, luncheons and shopping excursions when she was not teaching.

In 1958, an exciting event occurred in her otherwise dull life. She was asked to serve on the Magnolia Ball Committee. A former debutante herself, having been presented at the prestigious Ball, (at least it was perceived to be such by the inhabitants of Dorchester County) Milicent accepted immediately.

5

Milicent and Harold

Five years had passed since Walter Pritchard left town on the same night that Vivian Bauer took her famous bath in the center hall of the Victorian house on Willowoak Street. After apologizing, bidding his guests good evening and ushering them to the door, Harold called the doctor. Poor Vivian had lost her mind, plain and simple, as had her mother and grandmother before her. (A defective gene, no doubt.) She was not sent away to the state hospital or to a private institution, but was kept at home under Queenie's supervision and watchful eye. From that day on, she never left the house, nor to anyone's knowledge had another caller other than the occasional visit by her doctor.

Harold had never really loved Vivian; he married her on the rebound after Milicent had left town. He had also married Vivian for her social and political connections. He had simply felt respect for her, but now he was lonely and trapped in a marriage that he could not escape since Vivian was crazy as a loon. She was however physically healthy and would probably live for many years. She did.

Harold's thoughts eventually turned once again to Milicent Pritchard, his high school love. He didn't know why Milicent had suddenly gone to North Carolina, but after two years of not hearing a word from her, he had married Vivian. On occasion he had seen Milicent in town, and sometimes she had purchased meat at his butcher shop. She had simply been civil toward him. Once or twice he had come from behind the meat counter and tried to engage her in conversation, but she had always cut him short. He never really understood the entire situation with Pritchard, but the word on the street was that Milicent had been deceived by a con man.

It was destiny. Harold couldn't divorce Vivian, but she was a wife to him in name only. Milicent couldn't divorce Walter since she couldn't find him, even though Lem had hired several detective agencies to track him down. Harold offered his proposal, and Milicent agreed to the arrangement. They saw each other every Wednesday night for the next forty-nine years.

Milicent would drive her car down Main Street and make a right turn on Willowoak Street and park one block down from the drug store. Harold would come out of the back door of the butcher shop, walk down the alley, to her car and get into the passenger seat. They would drive to the end of the street, which was about a mile away, to a little creek that emptied into the Savannah River, where they would park and make love in the back seat.

This arrangement continued until they were well into their seventies. Every school child in Montiac over the age of twelve knew about the tryst. They would often hang out to watch Harold get into the car. As the children moved into their teenage years, they would sometimes follow Milicent and Harold to the creek, and some would even be so bold as to watch the old farts "do it" in the car.

Milicent always remembered, however, that she was a Nakes. She attended church services every Sunday morning at the historic Episcopal Church, the only church that the very old, very prominent families attended. She never missed a cocktail party, a woman's club meeting, a Magnolia Ball Committee meeting, or any of the annual debutante events held each year from Thanksgiving through the Christmas season. Everyone knew about her and Harold and accepted it. Eventually, no one gave it a second thought.

Milicent took care of Sadie after Lem's death, taught school, "helped out" on weekends at an exclusive boutique and met Harold every Wednesday evening until 1984. That year, two mammoth events took place in the lives of Harold and Milicent. Sadie died. One month to the day later, Vivian passed away. Milicent was seventy-four and Harold seventy-nine.

Vivian's funeral was held on a cold, rainy day. Prior to the service, her remains were removed from the parlor into the center hall (the site of her unforgettable bath routine). As Harold followed, they were carried in a bronze casket down the front steps of the Victorian house. As they were descending, Harold slipped and broke his leg. With the help of two of the pallbearers, Harold, since he was a Bauer and certain things were expected of him, attended the funeral and went to the gravesite. Vivian was buried in the hallowed ground of the old, historic Episcopal Church, the only suitable final resting-place for members of very old, very prominent, and very political families of Dorchester County.

After the funeral, Harold was taken to a local doctor where his leg was set. Where to put Harold to be taken care of until his leg healed was the burning question on his son-in-law's mind. Queenie had long since met her Maker. Pauline, the only daughter of Harold and Vivian, had married when she was twenty-six and had not married well. She also inherited a trait from the Lenox side of the family: she, too, was crazy as a loon. With the help of Harold's money, she spent at least half of her time in Westbrook or Tucker's, two private mental institutions for the well to do in Richmond, Virginia.

Pauline obviously was unable to take care of her father since she was practically incapable of caring for herself, much less for the two children she had brought into the world. Milicent, genteel Southern lady that she was, never missed a funeral (for in the South, funerals are very social occasions, always followed by extravagant luncheons often resembling cocktail parties. Mourners become as competitive as yuppie mothers do about their little darlings' birthday parties always trying to outdo the last one).

Milicent approached the son-in-law and offered her services to take care of Harold. Harold moved into Milicent's house that very day. They lived together from then on, although Milicent was quick to point out that Harold slept downstairs and she upstairs.

Harold and Milicent proceeded to attend all social functions together. They grocery shopped and attended church together every Sunday (you know where). When Harold went to sleep in Jesus' arms, Milicent was listed in the *Montiac Minutes* obituary with the survivors as "Harold's good friend, Milicent Pritchard."

(Some people in Dorchester County wondered what Milicent did on Wednesday nights after Harold died, since old habits are hard to break.)

6

The "Come-Heres"

They rolled into the little town of Montiac on August 15, 1991, in a yellow Ferrari. She was French and her name was Lalique. No last name, just Lalique. He was from New York City and his name was Hunter Quarrels. They stopped the sleek machine in front of the first of thirty-one real estate offices the little town had to offer. Hunter went inside to inquire about the rental of a large estate on the water.

It just so happened that Jimbo Taylor had such a property on the water for rent. It had become available only the day before. Jimbo couldn't believe his luck; he thought he would never be able to rent out the mansion on the creek belonging to the Walthams, who had fallen on hard times. William Waltham had given the listing for Walthome, the home place of a long line of Walthams, to Jimbo and told him that he wanted six thousand-a-month rent for the house, grounds and dock. "Who in the world would rent that rundown old place, even though it is big and beautiful, for six thousand a month?" Jimbo had wondered.

"Well you sure are lucky, Mr...?" Jimbo said.

"Quarrels. Hunter Quarrels. You have a place?"

"Yes sir, I sure do. It's an eleven-room hacienda about four or five miles from here. Beautiful grounds, dock, mean low water of five feet. House isn't furnished and is right old, but she's a beauty," Jimbo said as he smiled. He thought he was quite the real estate salesman extraordinaire.

"How much?" Quarrels asked.

"Well now, it's a mite steep on the asking price for rent, but I think if you was to be sincerely interested, we might could negotiate that price down some," Jimbo replied.

"How much?" Quarrels asked again, a little more impatiently this time.

"They want six thousand a month, but as I said…"

"What water is it on? How far is it from the mouth of the river and the ocean? I like to fish," said Quarrels.

"It's on Nassa's Creek which empties into the river, about six or seven minutes by speedboat, and then it's about twenty minutes or so from the ocean in a fast outboard," Jimbo replied, realizing that Quarrels had not batted an eye when he'd told him the rental fee.

"Fine. I'll take it. I'll want it for at least six months, so that'll be thirty-six thousand, right? I guess you want a security deposit, too?" Quarrels asked as he started out the door.

"Yes sir. Thirty-six thousand, plus six thousand security deposit for a total of forty-two thousand, but don't you want to take a look at it first?" asked the stunned Jimbo.

"Yeah. I'll get your money; then you can show me where it is," said Quarrels as he reached into the trunk of the yellow Ferrari and took out an alligator briefcase. He opened it, took out a stack of money, and walked back into the real estate office with the gaping Jimbo fast on his heels. Quarrels then proceeded to count out forty-two thousand dollars in fifties and twenties to the now speechless Jimbo Taylor. He handed him the money. "Now show me my new place."

"Yes sir, right away," Jimbo replied while he stood there with wads of cash in his hands, not knowing quite what to do. "Just let me put this er—in the safe."

Quarrels looked at him and said, "Aren't you going to count it?"

Jimbo stopped, turned, and said, "Well, I reckon I ought to. Yes sir. I'm going to count it. That's what I'm going to do." And Jimbo began to count more money than he had ever seen at one time all in one place. When he was finished, he put it into the safe. Swaggering past the receptionist of the Waterfront Galore Real Estate Company, he casually announced that he had rented the Waltham property for six months for cash, plus the security deposit, and that he was leaving the office to take his client Mr. Hunter Quarrels to the property. The receptionist barely looked up from her *National Enquirer* and said, "Right, Jimbo."

Jimbo got into his VW bug and pulled out onto the main street of Montiac with Quarrels. The yellow Ferrari followed. Jimbo usually took a right on Bank Street when going in the direction of the Waltham mansion to avoid the two stoplights in town, but this time he went right through town. Never having seen a yellow Ferrari except in a picture, he knew everyone on the streets and in the shops would notice the beautiful automobile.

Fortunately, both lights caught Jimbo and the yellow Ferrari. The town fathers of Montiac had never seen fit to synchronize the stoplights, which were exactly one block apart. Jimbo was ecstatic; everyone would see that yellow car and wonder who it was. Later, as people were talking about the car and the strangers in town, Jimbo would have the perfect entree to let people know that he not only knew who was in the yellow Ferrari, but that they were his clients. He would say he had rented them the Waltham mansion (on the market for less than twenty-four hours) for six months, and that Mr. Quarrels had paid the rent plus the security deposit, a total of forty-two thousand dollars, in cash with *fifties and twenties*. He would recall that Mr. Quarrels was an avid fisherman and that he had taken the property without looking at it first.

Jimbo turned right at the second light and proceeded down Dorchester Road. They drove down to the little town of Hanover and took a right turn onto an unmarked country lane. Two miles further down, Jimbo made another right turn. They pulled through the gates of the black, wrought iron fence encircling Walthome. The drive meandered to the front of the old Mexican-style hacienda with its red tiled roof and Porte' cochere. Jimbo stopped his car and jumped out. Mr.

Quarrels got out and walked around to the passenger side of the Ferrari and opened the door.

Out stepped the most exquisite creature Jimbo had ever laid eyes on. She was about five-feet-eight-inches tall with a fabulous figure, long, coal-black, hair and huge, blue eyes. She wore black stretch pants that left nothing to the imagination and a hot-pink halter-top. Jimbo squinted and then looked away "Cuz it was obvious that the creature didn't have anything on under the halter," he explained later.

Quarrels and the creature walked over to Jimbo. "This is Lalique," Quarrels said. He didn't give a last name, and that was the end of the introduction.

"Howja do, ma'am?" Jimbo said.

She merely nodded.

Jimbo got the key out of the box above the front door, opened it, and led the couple inside. He had just started to walk away from the foyer into the large living room and give them his spiel when Quarrels said, "Thank you, Mr. Taylor. We'll find our way around. Is the electricity on? The water? That's all we really need to know."

"Yes sir, she's ready to go. Family fell on bad times and just moved out a few days ago. 'Course I reckon you'll be wanting to stay in a motel or hotel tonight cuz there ain't no furniture."

"Thank you, Mr. Taylor," said Quarrels as he turned and showed Jimbo the door.

"Don't you want me to show you how she's laid out? Take you down to the dock or something?" questioned Jimbo.

"No, thank you. We'll be fine," replied Quarrels as he steered Jimbo toward the door.

"Mr. Quarrels, you haven't signed the rental agreement yet," Jimbo whined.

"No, I haven't, but you have my money. I'll be up to your office tomorrow morning to sign it. Good-bye," said Quarrels, as he closed the door abruptly.

Jimbo got back in his car and headed for town. He shook his head in wonderment. First of all, this was the biggest rental he had ever had. It was the largest commission he had ever made. In addition, he had never known people to dole out forty two thousand dollars in twenties and fifties. The people didn't have any furniture, rented that great big old house, and, furthermore, they didn't want him to show them around. It was the easiest ten percent Jimbo had ever made. He was already planning what he was going to do with his thirty-six hundred dollars. But something wasn't sitting just right with old Jimbo. Although he didn't have a great deal of formal education and looked, talked, and acted like a hick, he did have a modicum of common sense, or as it was called in Dorchester County, "horse sense", and something was wrong about his deal. But he couldn't quite put his finger on exactly what it was.

All of this aside, he couldn't wait to tell someone about the strangers in the yellow Ferrari, and he put his foot to the floor as he sped back to town. He kept his eyes peeled for any of his cronies so that he could pull over and tell them the story, but it was a hot day and no one was stirring. Jimbo remembered another appointment, so he went straight to his office.

The couple from Savannah was waiting for him. They had come down five weeks in a row and had looked at everything Jimbo had to offer. They rode in Jimbo's car and always suggested lunch, a snack, or dinner at Jimbo's expense. Once again, they were waiting for him to drive them around and feed them.

"Lookers," thought Jimbo, "Gawd, how I hate lookers!"

Taylor wasn't about to give them the heave-ho, however, because there were thirty other real estate offices in Montiac just waiting to squire the couple around, and one could never take the chance that they wouldn't buy from a competitor after all of his hard work. Jimbo pulled into the gravel parking lot and pasted a big smile on his face. He opened his car door and waved.

After three hours of showing Mr. and Mrs. Gillum property after property and stopping at the local pub for a few highballs, the "lookers" told Jimbo they wanted to think about some of the properties they had seen. They would be back in touch with him the following week.

"Feel free to call anytime, and if I can be of any help to you folks, just let me know. I'll look forward to hearing from you soon," said Jimbo with a smile as the Gillums departed. He watched them leave and got right into his car and drove home. He couldn't wait to tell Lillie Mae, his wife of thirty-five years, the good news about the Waltham rental.

Smelling the frying chicken as soon as he opened the door to his modest bungalow, Jimbo called, "Lillie, have I got some news for you!" She stood perspiring over the large iron skillet, her frying hand in a metal funnel contraption with a fork sticking out of it. (Lillie Mae burned herself often when she fried chicken, and the grease always spattered up on her hand and arm, so Jimbo devised a contraption combining a fork within a funnel to prevent burns from the grease. It was strange looking, but it worked. When she had shown several of her friends the creation, many wanted one also. Consequently, Jimbo started a side business selling the funnel/fork gadgets, which he made at night in his garage).

"I've already heard your news, Jimbo Taylor. You're a rich man tonight, aren't you? Strangers in town in one of them fancy foreign sports cars, yellow, wasn't it? Girl is French and a fine looker. Man is older and needs a shave. Rented the Waltham place for six thousand a month, paid cash for six months, plus a security deposit. Took the money out of an alligator briefcase in the trunk and paid it all in twenties and fifties. That's forty-two thousand dollars and your share is ten per cent of the rental fee, which is thirty six hundred dollars. Congratulations!" All of this spewed out of Lillie's mouth in a single stream. She never looked up from her chicken turning.

"How in the hell do you know all that?"

"I called you at the office earlier to ask you to bring home a can of Crisco, and Denisa, the one who's always reading the *National Enquirer*, told me everything."

"Well, you sure could have fooled me. I didn't think she ever knew what was going on unless it was in one of those scandal sheets," responded Jimbo. "Where you reckon those folks got all that money?"

"Drugs. That's where anybody with big money gets it these days. 'Specially when it's in small bills like that and in an alligator briefcase. You're going to have to report this, Jimbo."

"Report it. Report it to who?" asked Jimbo.

"To the sheriff. That's who," said Lillie Mae.

"And what is that four-eyed dumbbell going to do about it?" yelled Jimbo.

"Nothing, but that doesn't make any difference. You've got to report it. Then you're out of it. If the money is from drugs, you've done your duty."

Jimbo crossed to the phone and dialed the sheriff at his home. "Hello, Sheriff. Jimbo Taylor here. What's that? Yeah, that's right. Twenties and fifties. From the trunk. Yep, a briefcase in the trunk. Just wanted to let you know in case there's a problem. No, no furniture. Guy said he likes to fish. No, I don't think they're married, but then they might be. I don't know what her last name is. He just said her name was Lilac or something like that. Yeah, you heard right about that. She's real pretty. Just about as pretty as a spotted puppy in a brand new red wagon. Yeah, I have the money in my safe at the office. All right, Sheriff. I'll see you tomorrow. No, I won't deposit it 'til you have a look see. All right. You have a nice evening yourself. Good-bye."

Jimbo turned to Lillie Mae, "Well I did my duty, but it seems I didn't have to. Denisa must have put the word out to everyone in a twenty-mile radius. People probably knew everything that happened while I was still at the Waltham place."

"Come on to the table, Mr. Rich Man, your fried chicken is ready and I mashed potatoes for you and there's sweet peas fresh from the garden, and salad and cornbread and plenty sweet tea."

Jimbo washed his hands at the kitchen sink, "A meal fit for a king, Lillie; I really am a rich man."

7

Trudy Hibbert Waltham

Trudy Waltham was like the little snake hissing around the pit. When his mother asked him what he was doing, the little snake responded, "I'm just hissing around the pit."

His mother said, "Well, little snake, you have to stop hissing around the pit because I have to clean the pit now. You go over to Mrs. Pott's pit to hiss."

So the little snake went over to Mrs. Pott's pit to hiss. Shortly thereafter, Mrs. Pott came out and asked the little snake what he was doing.

"I'm just hissing around your pit," replied the little snake.

"Well, I have to clean my pit, so you go back to your own pit to hiss," said Mrs. Pott.

The little snake returned home and was hissing around his pit when his mother came out.

"Little snake, what are you doing?" she asked.

"Just hissing around the pit."

"I thought I told you to go over to Mrs. Pott's pit to hiss," said the little snake's mother.

"I was over at Mrs. Pott's pit hissing and she told me to come back to my own pit to hiss," answered the little snake.

His mother said, "Isn't that something? Why I knew Mrs. Pott when she didn't have a pit to hiss in."

Trudy hardly had a pit to hiss in anymore, either. She and Bill Waltham had fallen on hard times. It has been said that it's easy to go from poverty up, but very difficult to go from riches down. Trudy had not minded the trip up, but the trip down was proving to be extremely difficult to swallow.

Born to illiterate parents, Trudy was the older of two children from a county about one hundred miles from Dorchester on the other side of Savannah. Her parents eked out what some might call a living by doing sharecropping whenever they could find anyone who needed help, and whenever Trudy's daddy was well enough (her father suffered from nerves, according to her mother) to plant a few seeds here and there.

Trudy certainly wasn't what one would call a beauty, and her brother was even more homely than she. He had the added disadvantage of a severe speech impediment caused by a cleft palate, which Trudy's parents were convinced was a sign from the devil. They had no money to have it corrected, even if they had known such an operation existed.

Trudy hated her life as a young girl. She despised her parents for their poverty and lack of intelligence. She hated her brother who was a constant reminder to her, with his horrible, guttural voice and mispronunciations, of the futility of her existence. All she wanted was a better life and she didn't want to take any of her family with her.

A neighbor lady took pity on poor Trudy when she was fairly young and taught her to read. Unlike the rest of the Binsons, Trudy had an average IQ. She caught onto reading pretty quickly. The old neighbor woman lent her books, Sears' catalogues, and magazines. Trudy Binson quickly realized that there was another world out there and longed for a better existence than the one in which she was captive. Once she learned to read, she took great interest in the neighbor lady's patterns, for the old woman was a seamstress for some of the wealthy women in the county near Savannah. Old Mrs. Squiggs gave Trudy scraps of material and taught her to make little dresses for the pictures of the models that Trudy cut from the Sears' catalogues and used as paper dolls.

Trudy rapidly learned the rudiments of sewing and soon was pestering Mrs. Squiggs to teach her how to make a dress for herself. Several of the ladies for whom Mrs. Squiggs sewed always brought her an abundance of fabric. Mrs. Squiggs helped Trudy make a simple dress and a few skirts and blouses.

When Trudy was thirteen, she went down to the stream near her ramshackle old house and bathed herself as best she could. She then went into her parents' room and rummaged through the drawers in the dilapidated old chest. There she found a piece of a comb and combed her dark hair. Trudy's mother always made her keep her hair short with bangs, so Trudy did as well as she could with what she had. Dressed in one of the skirts and blouses Mrs. Squiggs had helped her make, she went into her mother's closet and took her one pair of high-heeled shoes. She put the rest of her clothing, which consisted of another skirt, a blouse, a dress, an old flannel shirt and a pair of her father's pants (which she had cut off) into a piece of fabric that Mrs. Squiggs had given her and started walking to the nearest town.

Once there, Trudy rinsed her feet off in a puddle near the major street and put on her mother's shoes. She placed her knapsack under some branches on the side of the road and walked to the single block of stores. Three stores down, she saw a sign in the window of the drug store that read "Help Wanted." Trudy went right in and convinced the storeowner that she was eighteen and showed him how she could read and write and do figures. She got the job and was to start the next morning.

She left the store, took off the shoes, and walked back to her knapsack. She crept off the roadway about twenty-five yards and undressed. She put on the flannel shirt and pants and laid down to wait for morning. On the way to town, she had picked up a few apples that had fallen from a tree near the highway. She ate one and soon fell asleep.

The next day Trudy started her job and did exceedingly well. Everything went fine, except her feet were killing her in those heels. The owner suggested to her that she not wear heels to work, and Trudy explained that she didn't have any other shoes. The owner told her that she could go barefoot until she got her paycheck, as long as she stayed behind the counter.

Trudy slept outside and worked for a week until her first paycheck. Then she got herself a room at a boarding house and a pair of flat shoes and continued working in the drug store for six more years. She never missed a day. Her parents didn't come looking for her, though she did see her father and her brother walking down the street one day through the drug store's front window.

Still an avid reader, Trudy spent every extra cent she had on magazines, patterns, and fabric. Mrs. Johnson, the owner of the boarding house, had a treadle sewing machine and allowed Trudy to use it in the evenings. Trudy managed, through her frugality, to put together a decent wardrobe. Still wearing her hair in the bob with the bangs, she brushed it each night until it shone. She bathed regularly and used the lotions she read about in the magazines. Men had never shown interest in her, because she certainly wasn't striking, but she was clean.

On a sunny Thursday, when Trudy was washing the lunch dishes, a thirtyish man entered the drug store. She went over to help him, and he ordered lunch. She fixed him a chicken salad sandwich with chips and a pickle and fountain coke. They passed the time of day for a short while, and the man paid his bill and left.

Every Thursday for the next six months the man came into the drugstore and always ordered the same lunch. Trudy became so accustomed to his visits that she would start making the chicken salad sandwich as soon as he entered, without even waiting for him to order. She had learned quite a bit about him. He was an accountant. He lived in Montiac in Dorchester County. His name was Doug Hibbert. He was single and he and his brother had opened an accounting firm only a few years before. Doug came to Nesting, the town where Trudy worked, once a week to take care of his accounting clients there.

After six months of chicken salad sandwiches and many chats, Doug asked Trudy to go out the following night. He said that he had seen where the volunteer firemen were going to have a dance in Nesting the next evening and he wondered if she would do him the honor of being his date. Well, Trudy almost died! She had never had a date, and certainly never been to a dance. She didn't know how to dance, but she liked Doug, and she was accustomed to him from seeing him every Thursday for so long and making him so many sandwiches. Before she knew what happened, she told him that she'd love to go to the dance with him.

"What time shall I call for you and where?" Doug asked.

"What time does the dance start?" asked Trudy.

"Eight o'clock."

"Then I guess you better come get me at ten minutes to eight. I live at Mrs. Johnson's Boarding House on Blount Street. I'll just meet you at the front door at ten to eight. All right?" said Trudy.

"That'll be fine," answered Doug, "I'm really looking forward to it."

Trudy raced to her room after work and got out a piece of blue velvet and a pattern for an evening dress. She banged on Mrs. Johnson's door and asked if she could use the sewing machine that night. Trudy stayed up all night making an exquisite dress.

The next morning she was at the drugstore early, and later, when she was on her fifteen-minute lunch break, she did something she had never done in all the years she had worked there. She left the drugstore during working hours. Rapidly running to the shoe store, she bought herself the most gorgeous silver shoes she had ever seen.

Doug picked her up that night at promptly ten of eight. He was a little shocked by her attire since dances at the firehouse were not formal. But he had come to like the girl, so he didn't comment except to tell her that she looked very nice. Trudy felt ridiculous once they arrived. As she looked around, she realized that she was the only one in a long dress. She told Doug that she wanted to go home. Doug, from one of the better families of Dorchester County, would not hear of it. Neither he nor his date would be made sport of; he told her again how nice she looked and that they were staying. When Doug asked her to dance, she admitted that she had never learned. Doug calmly escorted her onto the dance floor and taught her the basic box step.

Throughout the following months, Doug continued his Thursday ritual at the drugstore, but he also came to Nesting several evenings a week to tutor Trudy in proper English, correct attire for certain occasions, literature, etc. In short, Doug created the Trudy he wanted. Never a popular young man with the ladies and one, who hadn't dated very much, he relished his role. As he helped her, she began to idolize him. She couldn't wait for his visits.

Once Doug was satisfied with what she had become, he asked her to marry him. Trudy was astonished. He instructed her to give two weeks notice at her job and to tell Mrs. Johnson she would be moving out of the boarding house.

On the appointed day, Doug drove to Nesting and bundled Trudy and all of her worldly goods in his Chevrolet. They drove to Fayetteville, North Carolina, where they were married. He then took her to a motel near Lumberton, North Carolina, where they spent their honeymoon weekend.

On the way to Montiac, where they would settle into their new home, Doug began Trudy's most important lessons of all. He told her what she was to say about her background. Although Doug knew the truth, he knew his family and particularly his mother, Rachel Hibbert, a stalwart Dorchester society matron, would not be pleased to hear of Trudy's lack of formal education and her meager beginnings as a sharecropper's daughter and soda jerk. Trudy was to tell Doug's family and everyone else in Montiac that she was an orphan who had been reared by her aunt, a seamstress, after both of her parents were killed in a steamboat accident. Trudy was to say that she had attended school in Kentucky and she and Doug met while she was in Nesting visiting distant relatives. She was not to mention that she had been employed, but was to say that for the past few years she had been a companion to an elderly relative in Louisville. Trudy listened and absorbed.

She was not prepared for the large and stately home where Doug stopped the Chevy. The big brick house looked like a castle to her. As he reached her side of the car, she was already halfway out. Doug reminded her that she was always to wait for him to open the car door for her. She nodded and smiled. They entered the house, and Doug introduced Trudy to Rachel.

Rachel instantly liked her. She believed everything Trudy told her about her background and congratulated Doug on his excellent choice in a wife. Rachel's only disappointment was that they had eloped and she had not been able to splurge on a large, important wedding as the mother of the groom (preferably held at the old, historic Episcopal Church in Dorchester County). She did hope that Trudy was an Episcopalian, or that if she were not, she would convert. Rachel immediately planned a party to announce Doug's and Trudy's wedding to her friends.

Eventually Trudy and Doug bought a house and had a daughter. Trudy learned to play golf, smoke Marlboros and drink martinis. She joined the woman's club and mingled with the right people in Montiac.

As time passed, Trudy was basically happy, except she was bored. Doug, who felt he no longer had anything to teach her, was only interested in figures. Even when they went to the many social functions, to which they were invited, he was dull, uninteresting and uncreative. Trudy accepted this, however; any place was better than where she had been.

At a bridge luncheon, Trudy caught Bonita's eye. Bonita hoisted herself across the table and said, "Trudy, a few other committee members and I have spoken about you. Celestine Piersall speaks very highly of you. We have decided to ask you to serve on the Magnolia Ball Committee."

Trudy thanked Bonita. She said she would have to discuss the matter with Doug and would let her know of her decision later. Bonita was aghast! She had bestowed this major honor upon Trudy, and Trudy had to talk it over with that insipid Doug? Because she was so flabbergasted, Bonita didn't comment. She merely nodded.

That evening Trudy waited until after their daughter had gone upstairs to do her homework and said, "Doug, before you get all engrossed in your figures tonight, we've got to talk."

"All right, Trudy, what is it?" he replied.

"What's a deb-u-taint?" Trudy asked.

"You mean a debutante, don't you, Trudy?"

"Well, I don't know. Is that how you say it?" she asked.

"I'm quite sure that is how it's pronounced, and I'm very surprised that you don't know what a debutante is. We've been going to the Magnolia Ball every year since we were married."

"I know we go to the Magnolia Ball, and I know we see the girls with their daddies in their long, white dresses when they're presented to society, but what is a debutante?"

"Trudy, the girls who are presented at the Ball are debutantes. That's what the Magnolia Ball is. It's the debutante ball," said Doug. He realized that he had left out a very large segment of what Trudy needed to know.

"Oh, well, I never made the connection. Anyway, when Bonita Roberts said something about a debutante—is that right?

Doug nodded.

"A debutante today, I didn't know what she was talking about."

"Dear God, you didn't let her know that, did you?" whined Doug.

"Of course I didn't, Doug. You've taught me well. You told me never to ask questions until I get home and ask you."

"Why was Bonita talking to you about debutantes, Trudy? Was she mentioning Sandy's presentation when she's eighteen?"

"No, she asked me if I wanted to be on the Magnolia Ball Committee."

"Oh, my God! What did you say?"

"I told her that I would have to think about it and discuss it with you."

"You what? Trudy, to be asked to be on the Magnolia Ball Committee is a privilege, an honor. Only the most prestigious women in the community serve on that committee. There are people who would kill to be on it. What did Bonita say when you told her you would think about it?" asked the incredulous Doug.

"She just nodded," Trudy responded.

"Well, you call her right now and tell her that you have discussed it with me and that you would be delighted to serve on the committee. Dear God, I hope she hasn't given the spot she was offering to you to someone else because of your rudeness," Doug said.

"I wasn't rude. Shouldn't I want to think about it? I didn't even know what that debu-thing was."

"For God's sake, Trudy, do you know what being on the committee would mean? Do you know the power that committee wields?"

"What do they do? Decorate for the Ball? That's what the social committee at the club does," asked Trudy.

"No, they don't decorate for the Ball. They select the girls! They select the girls who are to be the debutantes, the ones who make their debut and are presented to society."

"Oh, I thought any girl could do it. Why can't any girl do it if she wants to?" asked Trudy.

"I want to apologize to you, Trudy. I never realized that I had neglected such a large hole in your knowledge. This is really important. I will explain it all to you, but for right now, please go and call Bonita and tell her that you accept and don't say anything stupid to tip her off that you don't know what you are accepting," Doug ordered.

"Have I ever messed up before?" Trudy said petulantly.

"No, my dear. You haven't, although there've been some very close calls. I never even considered the Magnolia Ball Committee. It's beyond my wildest dreams. Mother will be so pleased. Why, even she was never asked to serve on the committee."

Trudy called Bonita and accepted. Doug taught her all there was to know about old money, new money, prestige, why only select young girls had the privilege to debut, and why the committee was so powerful. He even regaled her with the history of the Magnolia Ball. Before the evening was over, Trudy knew all there was to know about "deb-u-taints."

Despite his knowledge and booming accounting business, Doug had neglected one area. He had never taken out any life insurance. Because Rachel was still alive and well, he had not yet come into his inheritance. Furthermore, because he thought he was in perfect health, he had not made out a will. All of this neglect proved to be disastrous for Trudy. Two years after her appointment to the Magnolia Ball Committee, Doug fell over at his desk and died almost instantly of a massive heart attack.

Rachel helped Trudy and her granddaughter financially, but Rachel kept her own agenda and certainly didn't care for Trudy and the child in the same fashion Doug had. Trudy was forced to go to work! (According to Southern tradition, it is perfectly acceptable for a lady to "help out" in a dress shop or boutique, a gourmet shop or at a resort. These situations are not looked upon as common labor, but as diversions for those who are bored or have extra time on their hands.) As befitted her social status, Trudy took a position as the Dining Room Hostess at a resort in nearby Hilton Head, South Carolina.

The Walthams had been social acquaintances of Trudy and Doug. Bill Waltham, a pillar of Montiac society, had inherited his father's various businesses and the beautiful Walthome mansion a few miles outside of Montiac. Satin, Bill's wife, had been paralyzed from a diving accident several years by the time of Doug's death. Bill was the perfect husband and companion to her. He took her everywhere, even though she had to be strapped in a wheelchair in order to sit upright.

Satin died thirteen months after Doug's heart attack. Trudy bore a striking resemblance to Satin prior to her diving accident. Less than five months after Satin's death, Bill Waltham, heir to more money than Doug handled with all of his CPA accounting, asked little Trudy Binson, sharecropper's daughter, for her hand in marriage. Trudy immediately quit her job and began planning a wedding extravaganza. She and Bill were married, of course, in the Episcopal Church.

Trudy moved to Walthome, the Mexican hacienda, with Bill. Where Doug had created her, including her background, she now made up a much more glowing past. She began telling people of the various schools and finishing schools she had attended. Anyone who would listen was given all of the details about her debut in Louisville, Kentucky. She had learned the right things to say. Now she mentioned all of them in connection with her past. She had not learned that such statements could be checked on, however, and that there was always someone who would do that in a community like Montiac. She also did not stop to think that someone from her birthplace might one day recognize her.

Trudy was making calls one afternoon for Bonita about the upcoming selection meeting, when the phone suddenly went dead. She summoned her maid and told her that she would return shortly. She drove her new Cadillac convertible down the long driveway out through the wrought-iron gates to the neighboring estate to use their phone to call repair service. When she informed the small, local phone company that she was Mrs. William Waltham of Walthome, she was assured a repairman would arrive promptly. She went home to wait.

Within fifteen minutes, the telephone repair truck came down the driveway. Shortly after the doorbell rang, the maid came to Trudy and said, "Mrs. Waltham, I'm real sorry to bother you, but I can't seem to understand what the phone man is saying. Would you mind coming and speaking to him?"

Annoyed at having to deal with a lowly workman, Trudy stomped into the foyer of the lovely home and said, "My phone doesn't work. I was making calls and it went dead. Fix it."

"Ahm pliannin' ta fis it wenna yos tillse whar is," responded the repairman.

Trudy blanched. It had been over thirty years since she had heard that speech pattern, but she knew right away that there was only one person who talked like that.

Trudy called to the maid. "Show him where the phone is, Essie. I have to lie down. My head is splitting." She raced up the stairs hoping that her stupid brother, whom she had not laid eyes on for thirty years, had not recognized her.

Rudy had not only recognized her; but he had also remembered how ugly she had always been to him. He recalled how she had left one day after stealing mamma's only pair of dress-up shoes, and how she had never been heard from again. Now here she was, living in this great big house where that nice Miz Satin used to live, and here she was yelling at her maid and at him just the same as she used to do. She was acting like she was Miz Asterpoop. He wondered how she had gotten here. The maid showed Rudy where the phone was, and he fixed it. He didn't see anymore of his sister Trudy that day, but he knew he would see her again. He planned on it.

Trudy was relieved when Essie came up later and told her the phone was working. "Where's that repairman?" she asked.

"He left, Mrs. Waltham. He came into the kitchen and told me the phone was fixed and he left."

"Good," was Trudy's reply as she began her calls once again. *He didn't recognize me,* she thought but she was nervous. *What was he doing here? What if I run into him somewhere? What if he heard my first name? What if his stupid brain can figure out who I am?* She couldn't tell Bill. She had concocted a past that did not include dull Rudy or her wretched parents. Actually, nothing she had told Bill was the truth.

In the next few weeks, Trudy forgot about Rudy and went on with her extravagant lifestyle. She thought Bill had all the money in the world, and she proceeded to spend it as if he did. Nothing was too good for her. She chartered jets to fly her and a few friends to New York to shop at the haute couture houses. Little baubles from Cartier's became almost mundane. She enrolled Sandy, her daughter, at Marymount in Arlington, Virginia. One entire day each week was spent at Tresses where she got the full treatment. Once a month, she had her chauffeur drive her into Savannah for a full day at Elizabeth Arden. Her purchases included a full-length sable coat, a chinchilla and a stone martin. Most of the committee activities and the actual deb season took place in the winter months and one had to be properly attired. She had read in one of her Dominick Dunne novels about the old money in New York, about how they have the florist-of-the-moment come to their homes to arrange flowers. She made arrangements with the most expensive florist in Savannah to send one of their floral designers weekly. They brought hundreds of flowers and arranged them tastefully throughout her home. When Bonita heard about that, she contracted with the same florist to come to Creekside Farm and create her weekly arrangements.

Meanwhile, Bill, who was not the businessman his father had been, spent most of his time on the golf course and in the Sweet Treat, a local drive-in eatery with an illegal gambling casino in the rear. Bill wagered heavily on his golf games and heavier at the Sweet Treat. His and Trudy's spending and his failure to attend to business affairs began the downward plunge to bankruptcy and a poverty not unlike the one from which Trudy had arisen. This time, however, everyone watched the couple squander the Waltham family fortune.

Bill, the compulsive gambler, always believed that the next card or the next golf stroke was going to be the one that would bring all of the wealth and riches back to him. He didn't tell Trudy to stop spending, for he was a generous man who was foolish with his father's money. His father had more money than Bill thought he could ever spend. Bill had always lived well and planned to continue living that way. Unfortunately, when the money ran out, he began to write bad checks.

On the same day Bill was approached by the sheriff to cover his checks, there was a horrible thunderstorm. Bonita's phone went out. Rudy was the repairman dispatched on the service call.

Rudy arrived at Creekside Farm and rang the bell. Alphonso showed Rudy the phone. As Rudy began to work, he noticed a photograph hanging above the phone; it was a picture of the members of the

Magnolia Ball Committee. There, staring right at him, was Trudy Binson Waltham. Rudy continued to work. When Bonita entered the room, she said, "Oh, hello. That was quick. I'm glad you came so soon."

He answered with his usual gibberish. Bonita, started a conversation, fascinated by his speech pattern and the fact that his cleft plate had not been corrected by surgery. When she was unable to understand him, she asked him to speak more slowly, to round out his words. Soon Bonita was able to understand almost everything he said She could tell that he talked as little as possible, but she attempted to draw him out.

Before long she and Rudy were chatting away. Rudy told Bonita his life story. He even told her about his sister, Trudy Binson, who was now Trudy Waltham. Bonita thought that she must not have understood him, for she knew that Trudy had been to fine schools and had made her debut in Louisville. Before the repair visit was over, however, Bonita realized that she had on her precious committee a sharecropper's daughter who had run away from home at thirteen.

There was nothing else to be done except to remove her from the committee. One with such a background could not serve in such a prestigious position. Anyone who found out about this would be horrified! The committee members selected the debutantes from all of Dorchester County and neighboring areas. Trudy had said she was from Kentucky. Now, here was this poor speech-impaired repairman telling her that Trudy was from a little shack near Nesting. Oh, it was horrid, but Bonita would make it right. She would remove Trudy from the committee immediately and she would remove Sandy's name from the debutante list. Bill Waltham was from a fine, old, moneyed family, but it was unheard of to present the granddaughter of a sharecropper at the Magnolia Ball.

It seemed that Bonita did not remember, as she began to throw stones, the Texas rock pile from which she had emerged.

8

The Lesser Committee Member Darlene

Darlene was born one of seven children in the West. Her family was not old nor prominent, political nor social. She attended a public high school and a Methodist Church in the great state of Oklahoma. Cute and petite with large brown eyes and dark curly hair, she had a Mexican look about her. More than one of the ranch hands working for her parents had eyed her with lustful thoughts as she grew to womanhood.

In high school, she was a majorette and gave only an average performance academically. Her one major accomplishment, however, occurred when she traveled to Denver with a younger sister one weekend. On a whim, she entered a pretty foot contest. Darlene won the contest for having the daintiest and most beautiful foot. Her younger sister, Charlene, came in second. For her beautiful podiatric bent, Darlene won four pairs of shoes and a year's supply of Dr. Scholl's footpads and corn plasters. Her name and her picture were in the Colorado newspaper.

As much of a struggle as high school was, she did manage to graduate. She went to a small Oklahoma college where she made quite a name for herself in the early sixties by sleeping with almost every guy she dated. Fortunately, she avoided both pregnancy and all but the most minor of sexually transmitted diseases. Even though Darlene was having a super time socially at college, she still was not academically inclined. She left school in the middle of her sophomore year to return to her parents' modest ranch.

Daddy was not pleased that she dropped out of college. He gave her an ultimatum. Either she was to return to college the next semester or get a job. Darlene decided to get a job and see the world.

She landed a job in San Antonio, Texas, where her aunt lived. Mamma and Daddy supported the move if Sylvia, Darlene's aunt, would keep an eye on her. (Sylvia soon realized that she had about as much chance of keeping an eye on Darlene as the tourist in New York City has of keeping his eye on the pea in the shell game on the street.)

At any rate, Darlene began working as a receptionist during the day. She spent her evenings working the bars of the Alamo City. In the modern vernacular, she was "hanging out in bars, looking for guys to pick up." It didn't take her long. Lackland Air Force Base is in San Antonio, and men were plentiful there. Consequently, Darlene soon met Joe, who was a second lieutenant on the Base.

Joe was born in the West also—the western part of Virginia. He was from Bristol, a city that lies both in Virginia and Tennessee. Certainly not as prestigious as Dorchester County, it, nonetheless, had its own brand of society.

Joe was one of five boys born to a well-known, respected doctor, Dr. Joseph Moreland. Joe, the eldest son, completed his undergraduate education at Washington and Lee University. He had applied to numerous medical schools to please Daddy, but had been rejected by all to which he had applied. Now he was fulfilling his two-year stint in the Air Force paying his dues to God, home and country.

Two years of patriotism seemed the right thing to do at the time. Joe had attended the "proper" public high school in Bristol and two years at Woodbury Forest before going to W&L. He had played tennis at the Bristol Country Club, escorted various debs to the local debutante functions, scrupulously washed and waxed his Austin-Healey every Saturday, worn Weejuns with tassels, faded Madras trousers, and Gant shirts.

Now he found himself in God-forsaken, God-forgotten Texas—hot, dusty, humid and full of wetbacks. On a fateful Thursday night, he walked into Rosalie's Bar in his crisp uniform and spotted Darlene. Joe was instantly smitten. Dark, tall, and reasonably handsome, he was immediately taken with the petite, "stacked" beauty. Besides, she had the prettiest feet he had ever seen.

Darlene wore gold-hoop earrings, a tight skirt, chain belts, bangle bracelets, an off the shoulder black jersey top, and string sandal heels. She was very different from the girls he had dated in Virginia. They had looked like they all belonged to the same club in their Villager blouses, John Meyer skirts, Madras cummerbunds, tasseled Weejuns, scarab bracelets, watchbands and circle pins. They had all carried the same purses—a ring made of wood, with a piece of Madras hanging on hoops. Their hairdos were flipped with thin pieces of grosgrain ribbon tied in bows on the tops of their heads. All were very conservative. Here was this doll with wild curls, giant hoops in her ears, and string heels. Wow!

Darlene was also smitten with Joe. After ranchhands, college boys in Oklahoma, and a few jerks she'd picked up in San Antonio bars, this handsome officer in his white uniform was gorgeous. She could also tell he had class—his fingernails were clipped and clean. They talked, and danced; they drank and smoked Marlboros (this was 1964).

When they left together, they necked and petted; and, of course, they went "all the way." Darlene was not one to waste time.

Unfortunately, Darlene's luck had run out. She became pregnant. Joe, meanwhile, was about to finish his service career. He had wisely applied to chiropractor school and been accepted. Doing the honorable thing, he asked Darlene to marry him.

Darlene and Joe went to Oklahoma. Darlene's parents were speechless when they met Joe. He obviously had good breeding. Chiropractor school was almost as good as medical school, and his father was an honest-to-goodness real doctor. To top it off, the boy drove one of "them" snappy foreign sports cars.

Mrs. Moreland in Bristol was not as thrilled as Darlene's family when introduced to Darlene. Joe had always dated such nice girls from such good families. She pointed out Darlene's dark skin to Dr. Moreland. She was sure there was some Mexican blood in her.

Nonetheless, the wedding took place. The Morelands insisted on having it in Bristol, and neither Darlene nor her parents put up any argument. Darlene's parents weren't able to come since the wedding coincided with the largest yearly cattle auction in Oklahoma. Dr. and Mrs. Moreland also offered to pay, which pleased Darlene and her family too.

The wedding went well for the most part. Darlene looked adorable in her Seal Chatan poie de'soie gown. She and Mrs. Moreland had only one major disagreement. When Mrs. Moreland prepared to purchase the lovely white poie de' soie pumps to complement Darlene's wedding gown, Darlene insisted that she was going to wear white string sandal heels. Mrs. Moreland was horrified. She explained to Darlene that it was simply not done. She did think Darlene had pretty feet, however, so a compromise was made. One of Darlene's gifts from her mother-in-law was a pair of gorgeous satin mules with ostrich feathers for the honeymoon.

The reception at the Bristol Country Club was lovely. The only disruption took place when, during one of those silences that always occur when large crowds are gathered, the waiter placed a fingerbowl in front of Darlene. Looking at the bowl, she exclaimed, "Oh, Joe, look! Lemon soup! We never had lemon soup in Oklahoma!"

Mrs. Moreland immediately experienced a serious attack of the vapors. That condition, common to genteel Southern ladies, is better known today as a hot flash.

Darlene and Joseph left for a two-week honeymoon where Darlene found that Joe, when he was not in his handsome, white uniform and surrounded by his sports car and his family's money, was rather dull and boring. Joseph decided that Darlene was quite possibly a nymphomaniac. She constantly wanted to go to bed with him. She also looked at every other man she saw. He began to view the way Darlene dressed as tacky. She looked like a whore. He hated eating out with her, for when they entered the restaurant at the Bermuda resort hotel, he was forced to watch all of the men in the restaurant swivel around to watch her sashay across the floor to their table. The attributes that had drawn Joseph to Darlene were now attracting looks from other men. Simultaneously, she was turning Joseph off. He also dreaded going out to the beach with her. She wore a bikini that resembled two Band-Aids and a cork; it consisted of two of the skimpiest pieces of fabric Joseph had ever seen anyone wear. His fervent prayer was that his mother would never see her on a beach.

Darlene certainly was not intellectual. Joseph knew this; however, in San Antonio, he hadn't been interested in conversation. Now with his aching penis, for Darlene never got enough, he tried to guide her into conversation. Since they really hadn't known each other very long, and since in about six months Darlene was going to become the mother of his child, Joseph wanted to get to know her better. Darlene's topics of conversation were clothes, shoes, and movie stars. She also talked about who looked at her, and what they said to her when Joseph wasn't around.

Whenever they went out, Joseph had to make sure he used the bathroom in their suite prior to leaving, for he dared not leave Darlene alone at dinner. If a man, regardless of who he was or what he looked like, approached her to dance, Darlene was immediately on the dance floor shimmying and shaking. If the dance was slow, she wrapped around her partner, fitting to his body like the matching piece of a jigsaw puzzle. Darlene was a constant source of embarrassment to Joseph in Bermuda. He couldn't imagine what life was going to be like at chiropractic school where he would actually know people. He was not looking forward to the days that he would have to leave Darlene alone when he attended classes.

After their honeymoon, they moved to Charlottesville, Virginia, where Joseph attended the chiropractic school at the University of Virginia. He and Darlene found a small apartment and began searching for baby furniture. Darlene began regular sessions with the obstetrician. Joseph felt a little better these days, because Darlene had gained a great deal of weight and was not interested in going out, since she didn't get the attention to which she was accustomed. She was content to sit at home, eat, and watch the morning talk shows and the afternoon soap operas on television.

Darlene was dressing for her monthly doctor's appointment. She felt fat, gross, and disgusting. She had already gained thirty pounds and was only in her seventh month. Halfheartedly, she reached for an orange maternity dress, a 'blimp bag,' as Joseph called it. She hated it when he referred to the dresses that way. It only made her feel more unattractive. She hated being pregnant and couldn't wait to be small and trim and pretty and desirable again. Slipping the horrid old rag over her head, she began to pull it down. It wouldn't fit over her colossal belly. She couldn't believe it. The dress was only three weeks old. She tried on the blue one. No better. *Well, I guess I'll have to wear the red one,* she thought, *Even if it is dressy.* She tried the red one. It barely made it over her abdomen.

"This is awful," she said aloud. "I can't go out in any of these. Why don't they fit?"

In desperation, she put on a peasant blouse and a pair of black slacks with the creepy elasticized stomach area. At least her feet weren't huge. She bent over with much difficulty, picked up her black sling-back heels and slipped her feet into them. Grabbing her purse, Darlene headed down the three flights of stairs to the corner bus stop. She wished Joseph would let her drive the sports car, but he always took it to school.

"Well, Mrs. Moreland, you've gained seven more pounds this month. Dr. Henderson isn't going to be happy with you," purred Samantha, her doctor's nurse.

Screw Dr. Henderson, thought Darlene. *Does he think I like feeling and looking like a beached whale?* Instead she replied, "I don't know how I could have gained seven pounds. All I eat is lettuce. I feel like a rabbit."

Darlene was telling the truth. She hardly ate at all and sometimes felt faint and weak. She was actually trying to diet during her pregnancy, as she had heard the horror stories about trying to take off weight after having a baby.

Samantha showed Darlene into the examining room, which in Darlene's opinion should have been called the "chamber of horrors." Since her mother had never taken her to a gynecologist, and hadn't bothered to explain the facts of life to her, Darlene's first visit had been quite an experience. She went behind the screen, took off her clothes and slipped the paper robe over her head. Some protection! The robe came just above her pubis and was slit on both sides. Then she sat on the table at the edge, hopefully close enough, so she wouldn't have to slide down while lying on her back for the doctor. She took the second piece of paper, the "blanket," and put it over her lap. She looked at the table near her. On it was the dreaded speculum, a huge piece of cold metal. The doctor must keep it in the refrigerator overnight. He often inserted and wrenched it into her to further open the vaginal area, probably so that if he couldn't find what he was looking for with his fingers and then his whole hand, he could conveniently insert his head also. There were the Q-tips for the pap-smear test, (which to Darlene looked two feet long) the rubber gloves, and the KY jelly, (a lot of good that did when it came time for the speculum). Next to the wall was the spotlight, which the doctor always put so close that she got a third-degree burn on her ass, and numerous other torture devices.

Dr. Henderson and the disgustingly thin Samantha entered the examining room. (Darlene couldn't help but feel that the more pregnant she became, the slimmer everyone else, even obese women, seemed to get.)

Dr. Henderson said, "And how are we doing today, Mrs. Moreland?"
I hate that "we" shit, thought Darlene. "Fine."
"I understand from Samantha that you have gained seven pounds since your last month's check-up."

See how fast the "we" shit ends. He didn't do any weight gaining, only I did. "We" were doing fine, but I gained all the weight.

"Yes, I have. I don't know how I could have gained that much weight. I eat hardly anything."

"Now, Mrs. Moreland, just lie back and relax." (Ha!)

"That's good," said Dr. Henderson. He sat on the stool beside the spotlight and peered inside her body. "Oh, Mrs. Moreland, you're going to have to slide forward a little."

Of course I'm going to have to slide forward, thought Darlene. *I could have sat suspended in mid-air with only my rear-end touching the damned examining table and I bet when I lay down I would have had to slide forward,* Darlene thought as she began to slide down.

"Oh, just a little more." Another slide on her back like a giant oyster. "Yes, that's good."

Darlene thought, *Gynecologists must have learned in medical school to always make a seven-month pregnant woman lie on her back and slide forward; what a gruesome way to get one's kicks.*

"Now, Mrs. Moreland, or would you prefer that I call you Darlene? Just slip your feet into the stirrups, please."

The humiliation was complete. She lay there like a cow with her feet in stirrups. (It seemed to Darlene that they were at least three feet higher than her body.) The "blanket" was at knee level, so her entire body was exposed. The good doctor now moved to the right side of the examining table and ripped the paper robe. He began palpating her right breast while asking questions that Darlene thought were really inane. He asked, "Well, what have 'we' been doing the past month? Have 'we' had any problems? Any indigestion? Edema?"

As Darlene lay there, she thought, *How in the hell am I supposed to carry on a normal conversation when this sadist is squeezing my breasts and while my feet are up in the air? I know my vagina is exposed to the window and now I see ropes and a scaffold. Any minute, the window washers will be at eye level for the perfect view into my uterus.*

The good doctor went behind her head and ripped open the robe to begin on the left breast. Then he proceeded to the piece de resistance. He began the internal pelvic examination while pushing hard on her ovaries and uterus, saying, "Does that hurt? How about this? Any discomfort when I press there?" She didn't say a word.

"Uh-huh." Probing. "Uh-huh." Twisting. "Uh-huh." Speculum time. "Uh-huh. Now let's listen to the baby's heartbeat. Uh-huh. Good. Good, uh-huh. My apologies now, Darlene, for the final part of the exam."

And then Dr. Henderson did the unspeakable. He was one of the rectum checkers!

"All right Darlene, you can get dressed now and I'll see you back in my office," the doctor said with a smile as he left the room. (Darlene understood that the doctor could ask her every question in the book, but she couldn't ask any questions until she was in his office. That's so he would be close to his medical books in case she stumped him with a real zinger).

Samantha handed Darlene a wipe and said, "Just go into the doctor's office when you're dressed." The wipe was the size of a single-plied cocktail napkin to get off half a tube of KY jelly.

Darlene dressed and entered Dr. Henderson's office, where she sat and waited for fifteen minutes while he examined and probed another unfortunate, fat, pregnant woman. There was interesting reading material in the doctor's inner sanctum, too, with titles like "The Seven Symptoms of Ovarian Cancer," "Breast-feeding the Easy Way," (Darlene wondered how many ways could there be.) "Do You Suffer from Post Menstrual Syndrome?" *No, but I wish I did. Anything would be better than being pregnant,* she thought.

Henderson entered the room smiling. He told Darlene why she has been gaining so much weight, and why she could expect to gain even more. Then he gave her the news he knew would elate her: "Darlene, I heard two distinct heartbeats today. You're going to have twins!"

Darlene fainted.

She gained a total of forty-seven pounds and the last ten days she couldn't get out of bed without help. She delivered two boys after twenty-seven hours of labor. During this time, she screamed, cursed and vowed that Joseph Moreland would never get near her again.

Fortunately for Joseph, the twins took most of Darlene's time. She discovered that she had maternal instincts. The next three years, while Joseph learned to contort his patients' bodies, Darlene changed diapers, mixed formula, potty-trained the boys, and made an occasional jailbreak to go to the grocery store while Joseph baby-sat. She didn't bother fixing herself up to go out any longer because she was so tired. She didn't care that she rarely received an admiring glance from a man these days.

Joseph finished his training, and he and Darlene moved out of the cramped tiny apartment. He had researched several southern states in which to start his practice. He certainly wouldn't practice in the North. He found an area near Hilton Head, South Carolina, which he thought might be a good place to work. Dorchester County looked like a nice place. The income there was substantial among those with new money, and the old money was legendary.

Darlene, Joseph, David Beauregard Moreland and Daniel Farnsworth Moreland moved to Montiac. They rented a series of homes before finding their own brick rancher several miles from town, where Joseph ran a thriving practice. The boys, upon reaching the age of six, attended the Country Day School. Darlene spent many hours each week at Tresses, the local beauty boutique. She regularly had her ringlets styled, her nails manicured and her legs and bikini line waxed. With the help of Dr. James Nyland's magic diet pills, she became adorable and sexy once again.

Darlene learned to play bridge. She learned how to mix a martini and how to talk about subjects other than movie stars. She hired a decorator, and put away her cheap home-accent pieces she had won at Tupperware parties in Charlottesville. While she learned to shop at the right stores, she also hired a personal shopper to assist her in building her wardrobe. She became one of Dorchester County's respectable young matrons.

In the sixties, some of the Dorchester young men, upon completing high school, went to college. They then made their way in the world, returning to Dorchester County only to visit their families on holidays or an occasional weekend. Those who completed high school and did not go on to college generally stayed and followed in the footsteps of their fathers. They became either watermen or farmers and they married local girls. These girls worked at the five-and-dime, the drug store, restaurants, or various other local businesses.

Very few young people the age of Darlene and Joseph lived in the area, and certainly not many young professional men. Therefore, Darlene and Joseph were quickly taken into the Montiac social fold.

As luck would have it, the Magnolia Ball Committee, at a very recent meeting, had discussed the need for new, young blood. The new members were not to have any power, but would be useful for functions such as the debutante tea that was organized at Thanksgiving. They would write newspaper articles for the *Montiac Minutes* and the Savannah papers. Addressing envelopes and assisting the florist with the decorations would be among their duties.

Darlene reminded Bonita of herself as a young woman. Bonita decided that the wife of the young, successful chiropractor, who was from an excellent family in Virginia, would be an appropriate addition to the venerable committee. Thus, the little rancher's daughter from Oklahoma with the pretty feet and the round heels became a Montiac socialite.

9

Adele Hayes Callaway Dressler

*A*dele rewound the tape and watched the beauty pageant again. Even though many years had passed, watching it always gave her a boost. Besides, it gave her something to do while her facial mask and her nails were drying. She had to look perfect for this afternoon's committee meeting. Hitting the play button, she and watched again and leaned closer to the screen when the announcer said, "And the new Miss Louisiana 1945 is Adele Hayes."

As the former titleholder placed the jeweled tiara on her head, Adele knew that from then on, the only way to go was up. After her two years of secretarial school, Adele had taken a position at the naval base near Baton Rouge as a clerk-typist. She had plenty of suitors, but all of them were enlisted men. Adele, a distant relative of Governor Adele of Tennessee, was interested in bigger fish than enlisted navy squid.

Her trek around the state as the reigning beauty of 1945 had been exciting, as was her selection as one of the ten finalists at the Miss America Pageant in Atlantic City, New Jersey. There, handsome army pilots escorted the finalists. Adele and her captain hit it off right away and began to date, although the relationship was geographically undesirable, since Captain Rod Callaway was stationed at Fort Hamilton, New York.

Love and chemistry persisted, however, and finally prevailed. Three years later, Rod and Adele were married in a lavish military wedding in

Baton Rouge and went to live in Fort Knox, Kentucky. Theirs was an idyllic marriage blessed with a beautiful daughter and two handsome sons. Adele was popular, pretty, and a wonderful hostess. All went well until Rod, now Major Callaway, received his orders for Korea.

Adele spent the first six months after her husband's deployment taking care of her children and home. She played bridge at the Officers' Club and continued to attend the Officers' Wives' coffees, teas, and luncheons. Even though she did all of the right things, she was restless. She was accustomed to having her handsome husband around, and she missed male attention.

On a Saturday evening, her phone rang.

"Major Callaway's quarters. Mrs. Callaway speaking," Adele answered.

"Adele, this is Madeline. Susan, Esther and I are going to the 'O' Club for drinks and dinner. Care to join us?"

"Oh, I don't think so. Rod warned me to stay away from the 'O' Club while he was overseas," responded Adele, but she really wanted to go.

"We're not going to Happy Hour. We're only going out to dinner and it's cheaper than any place in town. Surely Rod wouldn't object to your joining us for dinner."

"I don't think I can find a sitter this late," Adele replied.

"My Jenna can sit for you. She's thirteen and has a lot of experience."

"Well, I guess it would be all right this one time. What time are you going?"

"In an hour. I'll drop Jenna by and pick you up."

"Okay, I'll see you then. Bye." Adele hung up the phone.

She raced to the kitchen door, called the children in from the yard and told them to wash up. She boiled some franks, opened a can of beans and set the table. While her brood was eating, she hurried to her closet to select an outfit. She showered, washed her curly blonde hair and carefully applied her makeup, a little foundation on her already perfect skin, bright red lipstick, a few strokes of blue eyeshadow to emphasize her china-blue eyes, and a slight hint of rouge on her high cheekbones. She dressed in her Playtex living bra, de rigeour girdle and stockings. She turned to check the seams in the mirror and realized that it had been a very long time since she had been out in the evening without the kids. She took the blue jersey dress, trimmed in white mohair from its garment bag, and slid it over her head. Perfect! She weighed the same as before she had the children, and she was still very beautiful. Her light blue pumps and matching purse completed the ensemble. She heard the doorbell ring just as she put on her button pearl earrings.

"Hi, Jenna. The children are in the kitchen," said Adele with a smile as she opened the door for the sitter.

"No problem. I'll clean the kitchen and them up. What time shall I put them to bed?"

"Nine o'clock," said Adele. "But I'm sure we'll be home by then."

"Okay, but I'll plan on putting them to bed. Mom usually stays out later than nine."

"Bye, kids. I'm going to the 'O' Club for dinner with my girlfriends. I'll see you before bedtime."

"Bye, mom. Jenna, wanna go in the basement and play?" yelled Suzy as Adele closed the door and headed for the car.

"Wow, you're really gonna bowl'em over," gushed Susan when Adele got in the car.

"Bowl who over? This old thing?"

"This old thing," Esther laughed, "I've never seen that old thing before."

At the club, the four were seated in the main dining room and had a drink before ordering dinner. During dinner, a small band played dance music in the lounge. Adele was really glad to be out with other people. She felt pretty, and enjoyed the music and laughter in the background. Nothing could be wrong with this. Rod must have been mistaken to think an innocent outing could lead to trouble and talk on the post.

Dessert and coffee behind them, she glanced at her watch and saw it was ten minutes after eight. "Well, this has really been fun, but now it's back to kids and baths and bedtime stories." She started to rise.

Esther put her hand on Adele's, "What's your hurry, Adele? Let's go over to the lounge and have a few drinks."

Adele protested halfheartedly, but soon was sitting behind a frozen banana daiquiri holding another Lucky Strike. She had only tasted a few sips of her drink when Hugh Rollins, a captain and a handsome bachelor that she'd seen at the club a few times before when she'd been there with Rod, stepped up with a slight bow and asked her to dance.

"Oh, no, thank you, Hugh. We're here for dinner," she declined.

"What's wrong with one dance?" Hugh persisted.

"Nothing's wrong with it. It's just that I'm here with my friends for dinner."

"Fruit diet, I see," he said, glancing at the daiquiri.

"Well dinner, and then a drink," laughed Adele.

"But no dancing, huh?"

"Dance with him, Adele, for heaven's sake," Madeline shouted across the table. "No one's going to care. You know Hugh. What are you afraid of?" And so Adele acquiesced.

She wasn't at home to put her children to bed. In fact, she arrived home shortly before her children awoke on Sunday morning. Adele's Saturday night fun group had begun. As the old saying goes, once one slice of bread has been taken from the loaf, it doesn't matter who takes another. Adele slipped down the ladder of morality and fidelity at a rapid pace and soon was paying Jenna a large portion of her monthly allotment check as she joined a Monday to Saturday fun group and went out practically every night with all levels of personnel, from captains to cooks.

She became a laughing stock. Her reputation was destroyed. Her activities became common knowledge, and her behavior attracted the attention of Rod's senior officers. Finally Adele received a call from

Colonel Dressler's striker to come into the Colonel's office. Not knowing why in the world he could want to see her, she dressed carefully in a navy-blue suit and matching hat with a white, silk blouse tied at the neck and went to her command appointment. When she walked into the office, the colonel was immediately taken by her beauty. This was going to be tougher than he had expected.

"Mrs. Callaway, it has been brought to my attention that you, on occasion, have fraternized with the troops," began Colonel Dressler.

"I beg your pardon, Colonel?" Adele smiled.

"Your husband, Major Callaway, is in Korea. Correct?"

"Yes sir. I miss him very much, and our three children can't wait for their father to come home."

"I can understand that, Mrs. Callaway. Being a military wife and mother is always difficult, but it is especially so during wartime. However, military wives are expected to conduct themselves in a certain manner."

"I know, sir," Adele said. She flashed her prettiest smile and cast her baby-blue eyes downward.

"Enough said, then?" Colonel Dressler concluded.

"Oh, yes sir," said Adele as she rose to leave.

She cut down on some of her nighttime activities, but never going out was so boring. She hated it.

A few months later, after the kids left for school, she gazed out the window while downing her third cup of coffee and smoking her seventh Lucky Strike of the day. She was about to get dressed to see a new major she had recently met on one of her Saturday night forays, when an Army vehicle pulled up in front of her post housing. She watched as Hugh Rollins stepped out.

Adele ran to the bedroom to brush her hair and to put on some lipstick. She and Hugh had parted ways, but she assumed he wanted her back. He certainly wasn't concerned about what people thought, as he parked the army vehicle right in front of her house and walked up to the front door in full uniform. The doorbell rang. She rushed to the door and opened it.

"Hugh, what a pleasant surprise!" Adele said. Hugh looked serious.

"Good morning, Adele. May we come in?" asked Hugh. For the first time she realized he was not alone. The post chaplain Father Swain was with him. She began to shake.

Hugh guided her to the sofa and said, "We regret to inform you that Major Rodney Callaway has been killed in action. His plane was shot down at 0600 yesterday. He died a hero."

No, this wasn't happening. Not her handsome Rod. There's been a mistake. Why was Hugh doing this to her? She said nothing. She only continued to shake.

The chaplain mumbled something, and Hugh talked about arrangements, but Adele never said a word. All that she could do was sit there and shake. Finally, after what seemed a long, long time, Hugh and Father Swain left.

People came to the house. Someone brought the children home from school. Food arrived. Flowers were delivered. Her in-laws and parents came. Phone calls were made and received. Adele sat. She didn't cry. She didn't talk. She sat and stared into space.

There was a funeral. Taps sounded. A flag was folded and handed to her. Rifles were fired. It was over. Adele went back to her post housing and her bed, where she remained for days. She heard the doorbell from a distance ringing over and over again. She staggered to the front door. An officer told her that she had thirty days to vacate the house and move off the post. Adele went back to bed.

Two weeks later she heard the doorbell ring constantly. This time it was Colonel Dressler. He talked to her about moving, about finding some place to live, about how he had felt when he had lost his wife of twenty-five years, and about his upcoming retirement in two years. It was all a fog to her. He mentioned her behavior when Rod had been in Korea. He mentioned what a hard time she was going to have making ends meet. He put his arms around her and rocked her back and forth comforting her. He took her into her bedroom and rocked her back and forth with great passion. Colonel Dressler told Adele he would take care of her. He would arrange her move. She was not to worry.

Shortly thereafter, Dressler was promoted to Brigadier General. The moving trucks came to her house, packed her household effects and put them into storage. She and her children were moved to General Dressler's quarters.

The garden wedding was held in the evening at 1800 hours. All of the post brass attended. No one looked askance at Adele. Hugh was there and treated her wonderfully. The cooks, many of whom she had known intimately, were deeply respectful, and all addressed her as Mrs. Dressler. Adele had gone from the ranks of round heel and post joke, to Mrs. "General" Dressler. Now she could go to the 'O' Club every night, but on the arm of her general, a nice-looking man, even though he was thirty years her senior.

General Dressler, as a young boy, had spent many of his vacations with his family at Hilton Head, South Carolina, which is only slightly north of Dorchester County. Upon retiring, the general told Adele he would like to settle near Montiac. Piling the three children and themselves into his new Mercedes, the group set out for Dorchester County. They found a charming old fixer-upper overlooking the water with the help of Jimbo Taylor. Adele worked on the house and made numerous visits to Montiac with an ear to the ground. She quickly learned who and what to know there.

Within months Adele was a member of the Magnolia Ball Committee. She had regaled the society matrons with the thrill of being "Miss Louisiana of 1945," her own debut in Baton Rouge, her kinship to Governor Adele of Tennessee, and her frequent references to "the General," as she now called her husband.

The tape finished for the third time. Adele turned off the machine, tested her nails to make sure they were dry and then moved into her master bath to remove the mask. She began her final preparations for the committee meeting. Today they were to select the young ladies who would make their debuts.

10

Lalique and Hunter

Lalique didn't have a beautiful body simply because the gods had smiled on her. She was a workout queen. She walked for miles, rode her bikes, both stationery and a ten-speed, and spent eight hours a week swimming and doing aerobic exercises.

She did not intend to stop her routine of strenuous exercise because she was in this hick place. The day after their arrival, Lalique drove the yellow Ferrari into Montiac and purchased a Raleigh ten-speed bicycle from the Western Auto Store. She paid the three hundred fifty-dollar ticket price in cash. This, of course, was doled out in *twenties and fifties*. She waited for her ten dollars change and one of the store clerks to put the bike in her trunk for her. On the way back to Walthome, she stopped at the local workout club, "Mod Bod," and signed up for two classes, one in high-impact aerobics and one in body sculpting. Total cost of the package was four-hundred-eighty-dollars, and again Lalique paid in cash. She spent an additional bundle of *twenties and fifties* on various warm-up suits, tights, leotards, headbands, jogging suits and sweat socks.

Monday morning she was at the eight o'clock aerobics class at Mod Bod, which incidentally was frequented by some of the powers-that-be of Dorchester County. All brown, blue, green, and hazel eyes in the class were on Lalique's gorgeous frame, and all of them were slowly turning emerald green with envy as Lalique went through all of the contortions—jumps, leaps, bends and lunges—without popping a bead of perspiration.

The instructor soon realized that she had a winner in the class. Lalique did not moan and groan as the other matrons did. She didn't feign a problem with her bra strap or a sprained ankle, nor did she run to the water fountain every three minutes. She did the routines easily and seemed to enjoy exercising. Soon Lalique was at the front of the class demonstrating for the other ladies at the instructor's request. Though extremely beautiful, she was also very personable and intelligent. As she demonstrated, she smiled and went to individuals to assist them in doing the exercises correctly. She was kind, gentle, and helpful; therefore she made friends quickly.

After class, Lalique stripped in the middle of the ladies' lounge area. There were almost audible gasps when the others viewed her shapely body from the corners of their eyes. She showered, washed her hair and came out in a towel. Without a speck of makeup on her face, she was still one of the prettiest women the ladies had ever encountered.

Celestine picked up her bag, and as she was leaving, said to Lalique, "Thank you so much for helping us out today. You really are lovely, and your body is so firm. You're a real incentive to the rest of us to continue our classes."

Lalique responded, "Oh, I enjoyed it and all of you are doing really well. I've just been at this for a long time. I can't eat a thing that doesn't turn to fat, so I have to work at it all the time."

"Where are you from?" asked Celestine.

"California originally, but now I live about three miles outside of town."

Celestine looked puzzled and asked, "Where?"

"We're renting a house on Nassa's Creek. It's called Walthome. We moved here four days ago."

"Oh yes, Walthome, Trudy's house. Is your husband in business or will he be going into business here?"

"He's in the cellular telephone business. He's planning to build a tower in the area. He's been in the business for about three years now. Cellular telephones are the wave of the future, you know." Lalique responded.

"Why yes, they certainly are. Well, welcome to Dorchester County. You and your husband must come over for cocktails. What is your husband's name?" asked Celestine.

"His name is Hunter, Hunter Quarrels, and we'd love to. Just name the time."

"Will you be here for Wednesday's class?" Celestine queried.

"Yes, I will."

"Well, then when I go home, I'll check our schedules and get back to you with a time on Wednesday morning. Will that be all right?"

"That will be fine." Lalique smiled.

"Good, I can't wait for Jamison, my husband, and Anthony to meet you. Anthony's my son. (Anthony did not accompany Celestine to her aerobics classes; she thought the ladies might not like a young boy watching them going through their routines). I'm going right home to tell him about the lovely lady he's going to meet."

Lalique continued to smile and said, "I'll look forward to meeting him, and Jamison too."

And so Lalique and Hunter were invited to Celestine's, and then to Bonita's and Darlene's and to Adele's, and, before long, Lalique and Hunter received regular invitations to the cocktail, dinner, and yachting parties of Dorchester County. They reciprocated by entertaining the socialites at various restaurants in the area.

"Four Eyes," the name the locals called their sheriff to his face, called on Jimbo Taylor at the real estate office the day after Hunter and Lalique arrived to check out the money in Jimbo's safe. He copied serial numbers and even took some samples for the FBI lab. Jimbo was duly impressed with the sheriff's diligence.

Although Walthome was a large estate surrounded by a wrought-iron fence, the front of the main house and the circular driveway were visible from the highway. Natives, always a little suspicious of "come-heres," began to notice that there were often cars at the main house, some for several days. Yet, none of the friends that Lalique and Hunter made locally were invited to the estate, nor were they introduced to any of the houseguests there.

About a month after Hunter and Lalique arrived, an enormous sailboat was delivered by truck to Walthome. Everyone saw the huge yacht. Traffic had to be stopped for the truck and boat to make a ninety-degree turn at the second stoplight in town. The sailboat was a new, fiberglass, sixty-foot-long Morgan. In this land of water sports and numerous yachts, the arrival of the *Diamond Jim*, the name painted on the stern of the craft, was an event! It was worth well over a million-dollars, and everyone ran out of shops and stores along the route to watch the slow progress of the delivery. Some teenagers got into their cars (the same ones no doubt who followed Harold and Milicent on Wednesday nights) and followed the boat. Then they raced back to tell everyone that it had gone to Walthome.

Within days of the arrival of the *Diamond Jim*, neighbors along the shore and across the cove from Walthome began seeing several people walking down the dock and boarding the sailboat late at night. However, the boat never left its mooring. No one went on board in the daytime, but each night the boat's lights were always ablaze.

Meanwhile, when Hunter and Lalique were invited to various homes and asked about their new yacht, they responded modestly. They said that they would be inviting their friends to take a sail soon, but the boat needed a lot of work, which the boating enthusiasts thought odd, since it was obviously new. No one could imagine what repairs or renovations it could possibly need.

Hunter never seemed to try to interest anyone in the cellular phone tower, but he did buy rolls and rolls of plastic from the local wholesaler. Locals were curious about the Quarrels. However, there were other people in the area who lived well, yet had no visible means of income. So people decided Hunter must be from money. At the moment the Quarrels were the toasts of the town.

Old Four Eyes got his reports back. The money wasn't stolen or counterfeit and didn't have any traces of cocaine or marijuana on it. Four Eyes took Jimbo's four fifty-dollar bills and two twenties back to him and told him that everything was on the "up-and-up."

A few months later, Charlie, the practically illiterate town cop, was parked in front of the hardware store where he sat each night on his midnight to six in the morning shift to keep an eye on the Main Street businesses. A car ran through a red light, screeching as it turned onto Main Street, and sped away. Charlie started his engine, turned on his siren and gave chase.

About two miles outside of town he pulled the car over. The driver presented his license and registration, both from Pennsylvania. There were four occupants in the car drinking beer openly. Charlie ran a check on the license and registration. The driver had been arrested seven times for marijuana possession with intent to distribute, but had never been convicted. Charlie went back to the car and asked the driver what he was doing in Montiac. He responded that he had been at the home of Hunter Quarrels. He and his friends were investing in Mr. Quarrel's cellular telephone business. Charlie asked to see the identification of the other passengers. When he had their licenses, he went back to his car to run another check.

While Charlie was checking, the car quietly drove away. By the time Charlie managed to figure out the information he had received, he realized that the car was gone. He hadn't noticed it leave.

Charlie raced after them, but couldn't catch up. His jurisdiction didn't extend past the town limits, so he headed back to his post at the hardware store for the remainder of the night. He did, however, remember to call into headquarters and tell them about the incident and give them the license number of the car. (Charlie, of course, never thought to do this while he was chasing the car. It was too difficult to drive and talk on the radio simultaneously. Besides, headquarters was in Charleston, South Carolina, over fifty miles away. Charlie didn't see how they could be of any help.)

At six the next morning, Charlie went to see Four Eyes and told him about the incident. He showed him the three drivers' licenses. Charlie told him the driver's story. Four Eyes decided the time had come for him to take action.

He called the Narcotics Bureau of the State Police Department and reported Charlie's findings. He also told them about the cash Hunter and Lalique were liberally spreading throughout the county. He explained that no locals had been invited to the estate since they arrived, though there were usually visitors' cars parked there. He mentioned the *Diamond Jim* and the activity aboard her at night, and how she never left her mooring. The state boys went to work.

Within a matter of days, on authority of the State Police Department, Rudy, the telephone repairman, (who went to ostensibly check on the phone lines since trouble had been reported there before), tapped the phones at Walthome. Rudy reported to the police—and the townspeople—that there was no furniture in the place, and champagne bottles and plastic glasses cluttered the rooms. Rudy didn't tell anyone he had tapped the telephones. The police had sworn him to secrecy, and Rudy wouldn't dare go back on his word, especially when the police were involved.

The adjoining acreage to Walthome was vacant; the owner lived in New Jersey. The South Carolina Police Department got permission from the owner to use the property for surveillance as long as they promised not to disturb the grove of trees or the underbrush. The cops began a twenty-four hour watch on the activities at Walthome. Their surveillance spot gave them a perfect view of the *Diamond Jim*. Surprisingly enough, no locals learned about either the phone tap or the surveillance.

Strangers continued to come and go at Walthome. The nightly forays to the *Diamond Jim* went on. Only one new element had been added to the mix. Now, the police recorded every move.

11

Dee

Dee removed the two loaves of zucchini bread from her new wall oven. She loved her new, ultra-modern kitchen, with its avocado appliances; dishwasher, two wall ovens, and counter-top range and hood. She even had a garbage disposal in the three-compartment sink. The appliances were complemented by dark cherry cupboards and avocado-flecked, Formica counter tops.

Dee had the American dream. Reared in Illinois, she was the younger of two children. Her older brother had been a football star, and Dee had been the captain of the cheerleading squad at her high school. Petite, blonde with big, brown eyes, she was the all-American girl.

After high school, she attended the University of Illinois, where she met Marshall the first week of college. He pinned her with his diamond and pearl Kappa Alpha fraternity pin in their sophomore year. Two weeks after graduation, they were married in Dee's hometown of Bloomington. Dee wore her mother's wedding gown and had her reception at the Woman's Club Building on Woman's Club Drive. Dee and Marshall moved to Baltimore, Maryland, where he sold pharmaceutical supplies. She took a position as an editor with a large publishing firm.

As of today, she and Marshall had been married for twelve blissful years. They had elected not to have children and were totally happy and completely in love with each other. She kept a spotless home, and Marshall spent weekends keeping the yard and flower gardens in tip-top shape.

The Magnolia Ball

On Friday or Saturday nights, Dee and Marshall usually had another couple over for gourmet dinners and then played cards or charades. Sometimes they were invited to someone else's home for a similar evening. On Sunday nights they often went to a play, a concert or the movies. Both were avid readers. While Dee was a gourmet cook, Marshall built handsome shelves and cabinets to further enhance their already lovely home.

As Marshall had risen up the sales ladder with his company, Dee had moved into new areas of responsibility with her firm. On a Monday in 1972, after one of their idyllic weekends, Dee had gone to work as usual. A friend and co-worker, Marcia, was celebrating her thirty-fifth birthday and invited Dee to lunch with two other friends from the office. The four female junior executives selected The Pier, a fashionable Baltimore restaurant, to celebrate.

Dee, Marcia, Colleen and Karen arrived at The Pier in Marcia's Mark III Lincoln Continental. As they stepped out of the car, the valet took the keys and gave Marcia her ticket.

"I always feel so elegant when I come here to lunch," said Marcia, "If you're ever depressed or having a fat or ugly day, this is the place to come. Not only is it swish, but also the waiters are all gorgeous, and they're so attentive. We're going to have a great time, gals."

Marcia had made a reservation, and the ladies were immediately seated by the handsome host. While the waiter was taking the cocktail orders, Dee glanced up from her drink list and looked directly into the eyes of rugged, dark-haired man with olive-skin and black eyes, who was staring intently at her. She flushed as she turned to the waiter and ordered, "A pink squirrel, please."

"Very well, Madame." The waiter left. Dee turned back to her friends.

Colleen said, "My goodness, Dee, look at that man. He looks all rugged and handsome just like I imagine Rochester looked in **Jane Eyre**." Dee surreptitiously glanced in the direction Colleen indicated, and there he was, staring at her again. Dee quickly looked away.

The girls chatted about the office and their weekends until the waiter returned with their drinks. "Here are your cocktails, ladies, and David will be your server today," the waiter announced as he took his leave.

"Thank you," Marcia said. She gave him a wink.

During the salad course, Dee flushed again as she caught "Rochester" staring at her. By the time the entree was served, she felt red all over. Every time she looked up, his piercing black eyes were on her. Finally, before the birthday cake was to be served, she excused herself and went to the ladies' lounge.

The man, although handsome, was really making her nervous. Things like that didn't usually happen to her. Unlike Marcia and Colleen, Dee was not a flirt. She was in love with Marshall. She never flirted, played around, or even thought about it. She delayed as long as she felt she could and then returned to her seat. She was relieved to see that the stranger with the piercing eyes had left.

The three girls at the table were in a titter, "Well, you certainly impressed someone, Dee," Karen said.

"What do you mean?" Dee asked.

"Mr. Gorgeous beat a path right over here after you left," said Colleen.

"So?" responded Dee.

"So, he asked us your name," Colleen swooned.

"You didn't tell him, did you?"

"I told him 'Dee,' not your last name."

"Oh, Colleen!"

"He asked for your phone number too," Marcia volunteered.

"You didn't!"

"No, I didn't. Well, not exactly. I told him you were a happily married woman with the emphasis on happily, but I told him I was available, and I gave him *my* work number."

"But we work at the same place, Marcia!"

"Big deal, Dee. He doesn't know that."

"Oh, right. I guess he doesn't."

A troupe of waiters appeared with a pink layer cake glowing with candles. They all sang "Happy Birthday."

The handsome stranger's name was Chet. He was forty-one, married, and father of four children. Chet was a wheeler and dealer. He dabbled in the market; he dabbled in real estate; he dabbled in venture capital. Sometimes he was flat broke. Sometimes he was flush—tip-top or flip-flop—as they said in Dorchester County. Flush was his present state.

Chet called the number Marcia had given him and asked for Dee. After appealing to a young receptionist at the publishing company to help him, because he didn't know Dee's last name, he was finally connected. He called her every day for two weeks and invited her to join him for lunch each time. Every day for two weeks, Dee refused.

On the first day of the third week, Dee realized that she was having trouble concentrating. She also realized that she was anxiously awaiting Chet's phone call. He began each one with "Hello, and how is the beautiful lady today?" She further realized that she had been thinking about Chet not only at work, but also at home. Her final realization was that it was exciting to be pursued, to be wanted, and to be told she was beautiful. Not that she didn't get all of that from Marshall, but somehow Chet was much more exciting.

Dee had an important meeting with her boss at two o'clock in the afternoon to discuss a month-long project on which she had been working. Many long hours and sleepless nights had gone into it, and while a little apprehensive about making the presentation, she was pleasantly anticipating it. If Mr. Symons liked her idea, a promotion would certainly be forthcoming.

At ten-thirty that morning, as Dee sat scanning the presentation for the zillionth time, Chet called. Dee answered her phone and the receptionist said, "Mr. Thomas on line two."

"Hello Mr. Thomas."

"Hello, and how is the beautiful lady today?"

"Fine."

"And is the beautiful lady going to do me the honor of having lunch with me?"

Dee couldn't explain why or how it happened, but she heard her voice say, "Yes, but I have to be back at work no later than twenty of two."

"No problem. Shall I call for you there?"

"No. No, I'll meet you. Where?"

"Why not at The Pier, where we first met?" Chet answered.

"Well, we didn't meet. In fact, we've never met."

"Then we'll meet today. The Pier? At noon?"

"I'll be there," she heard her voice respond.

Dee placed the phone back in the receiver and smiled for a few seconds and thought, *What have I done?* Then she thought more importantly, *Why have I done it?* She didn't know how to get in touch with Chet to call him back and cancel. Dee thought and realized that she could call The Pier and leave a message that she was unable to meet him. No, she wanted to go.

She had to explain to Mr. Thomas that her life was perfect. She was in love with Marshall and was not available. He had to stop calling her. Besides, it was a twenty-minute cab ride to the restaurant. She'd leave at ten of, making her ten minutes late. She was sure he'd wait. Then she'd have to leave by twenty after one in order to prepare herself and calm down for her presentation. What could possibly be wrong with meeting a man in a public place for lunch?

Dee arrived at The Pier at ten minutes after noon. Chet met her in the lobby. They were seated and ordered martinis. Dee didn't eat lunch. In fact, she didn't eat until six-thirty that evening. She didn't leave by twenty after one; she didn't make her presentation at two o'clock; and she didn't call Mr. Symons and tell him that she wouldn't be there.

Dee and Chet left arm-in-arm at four-thirty that afternoon. They climbed into Chet's Jaguar and drove to Friendship Airport, where they boarded a flight to Jamaica. Dee ate a delectable dinner aboard the plane. She didn't go home prior to the flight to pack. In fact, Dee only went into her beautiful avocado kitchen in her lovely, three-bedroom home in the nice neighborhood one more time, and that was three weeks later, when she returned from Jamaica. She went there to get her cookbooks and clothes before moving into a penthouse apartment near the Baltimore harbor with Chet.

Dee and Chet lived in a state of euphoria for the next two years. He disentangled himself from his wife of nineteen years and four children. After his divorce was final, they moved to Dorchester County. Chet, still flush after the sale of the community property and a fifty-fifty split (Chet's ex-wife was a woman of some means), bought a small farm. Dee was invited to play bridge with some of the socially prominent ladies in Montiac. As luck would have it, Dee was Bonita's bridge partner.

Bonita loved Dee instantly. Since there was a vacancy on the Magnolia Ball Committee, Bonita asked Dee to serve. So, she, an unmarried woman living in sin, who had not attended the right schools, who was not from a socially prominent, very old, or very politically connected family, became a member of the all-important committee. This, of course, was the same committee that decided the fates of young, aspiring debutantes in Dorchester County—"the social Mecca of the world"—at least in the minds of the committee members.

12

Bonita's Plan for Trudy

Trudy was devastated. She had thought Bill was intoxicated, although he wasn't much of a drinker, when he had walked into the great room at Walthome with tears in his eyes. He told her that he had lost everything. They were going to have to move and put their beautiful estate up for sale. Trudy could not bear it—not Walthome!

She tried to convince Bill that things could not possibly be so bad. They certainly didn't have to sell their home. After hours of listening to Bill's confessions, Trudy finally comprehended the gravity of the situation. She was, however, able to get Bill to agree to put the property up for rent rather than for sale. Bill acquiesced, but he was sure that they would not get the ridiculous amount for rent she suggested. Soon he knew he would have to advertise the estate for sale.

They moved to a small carriage house on property owned by friends who spent summers in Dorchester County. Trudy called the couple and explained that she and Bill were going to have major renovations done at Walthome and needed to borrow the carriage house for several months. The Morriseys left Dorchester the first week in August and were not returning until the following June. They readily agreed to lend their guesthouse to the Walthams.

Trudy quickly concocted a story to tell their friends and neighbors. She and Bill did not need so much room since Sandy was now away at school. They were going to reside in the Morriseys' carriage house while looking for property to build a smaller, although lavish, home. Even though they no longer needed all of the room in Walthome or its numerous acres, they could not bear to sell the family home. They would be renting it out. What Trudy was unaware of, however, was that Bill's business affairs were already known to many in the area. She and Bill had been the subject of dinner-table conversations for the past several months.

After moving out of Walthome and giving Jimbo the rental listing, Bill visited the bank without Trudy's knowledge. He took some of her jewelry from the vault and sold it to cover the bad checks he had written. After his debt was paid, he had enough to live on for awhile. Bill gave Trudy most of that and told her it was all they had until he could get his business affairs straightened out. He encouraged her to spend it wisely and frugally.

Bill then went to the Sweet Treat and attempted to parlay his remaining money into a fortune. The other men in the back room didn't want to play with him. They tried to talk him out of getting into a game, as the stakes were often as high as several thousand dollars for a single hand. Bill insisted, nevertheless, and within fifteen minutes, he lost all that he had. He tried to play shy, but the other players would not allow it. Bill reminded them that Walthome had been rented for six thousand dollars a month, so he had the money to back up his bets. But the men would not take any more of his markers. He finally left, dejected, and drove through Montiac wondering what to do.

Driving aimlessly, he suddenly realized he had not headed for the carriage house, but was about to turn into the gates of Walthome. He'd heard about Quarrels and his cellular telephone business. *Hell, he's renting my house. I have a right to go and check on my property. I'll go and see him. Maybe I can get in on this cellular deal from the ground up and get myself out of this mess.*

He increased his speed and made the turn into the long driveway.

Bad things, however, were in store for Trudy. It was the day before the committee's August meeting. This was the day the girls' names would be submitted for the Magnolia Ball. Trudy was emotionally distraught. Sandy's name was to be submitted, and if she and Bill were in this financial mess, how in the world were they going to pay for her debut? Sandy just had to make her debut. She had heard about the Magnolia Ball all of her life, and Trudy herself was on the committee. Maybe Trudy should sell some of her jewelry from the bank vault. Bill would never have to know.

Bonita had not wasted any time in calling and informing the other committee members about Trudy's background. Adele was adamant that Trudy be removed from the committee. Adele couldn't tolerate anyone who lied about her past and tried to be something and someone she was not. She had apparently forgotten about her forays into military "society" when her first husband had been in Korea. Bonita, who as chair of the committee could only vote in the case of a tie, had obtained from Adele the first vote necessary to oust Trudy from the committee.

Milicent Pritchard felt sorry for Trudy but also respected Bonita's decision. Why, my goodness, everyone knew the members had to be above and beyond reproach! Milicent had remarked on that very subject to Harold Bauer, while parked at the end of Willowoak Avenue, on several occasions. A sharecropper's daughter and sister of that Rudy with the cleft palate—who would have thought? Yes, Milicent agreed with Bonita. Trudy had to be removed. Two votes.

Darlene, too, suffered from a loss of memory. She also seemed to forget her humble beginnings and overlooked the fact that she occasionally made up little white lies about her daddy's huge spread in Oklahoma. Darlene knew that she was one of Bonita's favorites. She also knew that to vote against something Bonita wanted would not be politically correct. Three!

Dee really didn't understand the seriousness of what Trudy had done. When Dee said she would rather not vote, Bonita explained that Trudy had lied. Trudy had led people to believe she was someone she was not. She had turned her back on her own flesh and blood by denying her relationship to Rudy. One could not serve on the venerable committee when one had made one's entire life story out of whole cloth.

Dee, who was not married to Chet, had never corrected anyone when they called her Mrs. Thomas. No one suspected that she and Chet were not man and wife. She decided to cast her vote with Bonita.

Bonita's most difficult call was forthcoming. She still had to call Celestine, who had been on the committee longer than she. Celestine really was a member of the aristocracy and did not like gossip, cattiness, or character assassination. In Bonita's opinion, Celestine was hiding something. No one could really be that nice. She dialed Celestine's number and tried to explain Trudy's unpardonable sin.

Celestine did not allow Bonita to finish. She told her she had been trying to think of some way the committee could help poor Trudy and Bill and not make them feel as if they were accepting charity. Celestine felt terrible for them and their loss, but thank God they still had their health. When Bonita continued to push the issue, Celestine assured her that Trudy certainly had not meant to lie. Everyone, at times, gilded the lily when things weren't exactly the way they wanted them to be. She was sure everyone had things they would rather not have the whole world know. My goodness, she knew that she, Jamison, and Anthony did.

Bonita gave up. Obviously, Celestine was demented. She was talking about that stupid doll again as if it were a real person. "Thank you for listening, Celestine, and I guess you want to vote against removing Trudy from the committee."

"Well, I certainly do, Bonita. That would be taking away one of the last things Trudy has to hold onto until she and Bill recover from this financial mess. Just because they have lost their money doesn't mean they've lost their good names. This is the very time that we, as their closet friends, have to stand by them."

"I'm trying to explain to you, my dear, that Trudy does not have a good name, an education, or a good background. She's the daughter of a sharecropper, ran away from home at thirteen, worked in Nesting as a soda jerk in a drug store, and then married Doug. When he died, she married Bill. She never attended any of those finishing schools she is always talking about, and she never made her debut in Louisville, Kentucky, or anyplace else. She lived in a rooming house, for God's sake!" said Bonita slightly raising her voice.

"I'm sorry, dear, I didn't hear all of what you were saying. Anthony had an urgent request right at that moment. I'm sure there's been a misunderstanding somewhere, Bonita. At any rate, my vote is nay. Thank you for calling, and I'll see you at the meeting tomorrow. Good night now; I really must tend to Anthony."

Bonita was fuming. Celestine was the only committee member who couldn't be controlled. She always stood by her high principles. Bonita would continue to campaign. Even if she didn't have a unanimous vote, Trudy would certainly resign rather than face everyone. Bonita was looking forward to embarrassing Trudy. Sadly, Bonita had forgotten her own good fortune. She had become a shrewish old biddy, eager to inflict hurt and pain on others.

13

The Committee Meeting

The committee meeting for the selection of the debutantes of 1991 was to be held at the Crest. It was a resort hotel built by a local family in the twenties. The selection meeting had been held there for the past sixty years. Prior to the current meeting, a light luncheon was served, including champagne cocktails, shrimp Louis, melba toast, fresh fruit and petite fours. The important discussion began when the members moved into the Island Room, their conversations held behind closed and locked doors. The refreshments were placed in the Island Room prior to the selection process by the staff, and once the ladies assembled, the double doors were shut. No one entered or exited again until the meeting ended.

All members were present, including Bonita, Darlene, Adele, Celestine, Milicent and Dee. Trudy was noticeably absent.

Among the members was Sarah Profitte Kirkham, daughter of a local delivery truck driver. He had worked diligently over the years, and eventually succeeded in owning the freight line for which he had once driven. He then bought into other companies including the local radio and television stations, until he became a regional success story.

Sarah had married right out of Radcliffe and had moved with her first husband, a marine lieutenant, to California. They had four children.

Twelve years later, Sarah returned to Montiac with children in tow. She was the victim of a physically abusive husband, who definitely was not one of the Corps' "few good men." Daddy built his daughter a house in Montiac, and soon Sarah began to date the recently widowed son of the owner of the Crest Hotel. Alex, the middle son of the Kirkham family, had married ten years before. He and his first wife had three children. When she passed away, Alex tried valiantly to rear his children alone with the help of governesses and nannies.

Alex and Sarah were married and moved into the old Kirkham family home with the seven children. Everyone in Dorchester Country referred to their union as a merger rather than a marriage, for the Kirkham and the Profitte empires were legally united.

Sarah was abnormally thin, rarely smiled, and had a bland personality. Alex, on the other hand, was gregarious, always the life of the party and often a buffoon. Nevertheless, because of their status and their money, they were extremely sought-after socially by Dorchester County.

Stoop-shouldered Nancy Abrams entered the Island Room in her frumpy black dress. Her pixie haircut looked freakish around her tiny face that was ravaged by the malignancy she had been fighting for several years. A nondescript little woman, she was the wife of Patrick Abrams, a bank teller, who had embezzled money from the Bank of Montiac for years but had managed to resign just short of going to jail.

Patrick was homely, fat and balding, but he had four lovely sisters. They had all married well and had summer homes in Dorchester County. The family was related to the Baldersons of South Carolina, which is akin to being related to the Rockefellers or DuPonts in the North, or the Lees, Carters or Randolphs in Virginia. Nancy could never get a word in edgewise with mouthy Patrick. She always seemed to shrink when in the company of his attractive sisters and their debonair, wealthy husbands.

Both of Nancy's daughters had been presented at the Magnolia Ball in previous years and were now members of the committee. They entered the Island Room behind their mother.

Blanche Givens, seemingly very taken with herself and her importance, waddled in and sat to Bonita's right. Her David Dow suit nearly burst at the seams as she arranged her girth in a chair. Blanche was another "come-here." Her husband was a financial advisor. She was the mother of two wild, renegade children—a son who had been in and out of jail for drug trafficking, and a daughter who had given every escort a dose of gonorrhea when presented to society at the Magnolia Ball of 1976.

Blanche was a vindictive person and spent a large amount of time dredging up gossip about potential selections and their families. Often, if there were no skeletons to be found, Blanche would create a story from her over-active imagination and spread the tale throughout the committee. Drab Nancy Abrams, her closet friend and fellow conspirator, would then swear to it. Blanche kept many a young lady from making her debut for no reason other than her dislike or her jealously of the girl, her mother, her family or their wealth.

The Bracer "girls" were in attendance. The Bracers, a long time family of Dorchester County, all had one thing in common—mental illness. It ran rampant through the female members of the family. Julia Bracer Mavis, wife of Simon Mavis, was eighty-six. She was the oldest committee member and definitely not playing with a full deck. She was attired in her wool jodhpurs and riding boots as temperatures outside approached ninety-eight degrees. Riding crop in hand, Julia strode into the room, and ladies scurried to chairs so they wouldn't have to sit near her. Julia seldom bathed and always seemed to have just come from mucking the stalls of her eighteen thoroughbred horses. Hired hands were not allowed to muck them; that was something she did every day. Julia's daughter-in-law, Dixie, followed her through the doorway.

Married to Julia's only son, who had never done much of anything and who received a monthly stipend from his father, Dixie was a high school mathematics teacher. Algebra was her specialty. It was well known that almost every student who took algebra in college after having studied under Dixie failed the course. Two of Dixie's six daughters, all of whom were debutantes, also served on the committee.

Julia's grand niece, Mary Beth, was married to a college professor whom she had met her first semester at Mount Holyoke. After her father became ill, she had returned home with her new husband to run part of her father's many businesses. Mary Beth, however, was now divorced. After four children, she had come home and found her husband in bed. He wasn't sick and he wasn't in bed with another woman. Her husband was having sex with her twin brother.

Mary Beth was now running the entire business empire. While wielding her executive powers, she had attempted, unsuccessfully, to contain her four wild girls who had been involved in drugs, and had slept with married men, teenage boys and teenage girls. Despite their escapades prior to their eighteenth birthdays, all of Mary Beth's daughters had made their debuts.

The remaining members filed into the room. Once the group of twenty-seven women (Trudy had not yet arrived) were seated, Bonita, gavel in hand, struggled from her seat and raised herself to her full height. With a crack of the tiny, gold gavel, (presented to her by the committee the previous year in appreciation of her outstanding work), Bonita brought the 1991 selection meeting of the Magnolia Ball Committee to order.

Total silence ensued.

"The meeting will come to order. Before we begin with the submission of names, I have a rather delicate matter that needs to be brought to your attention."

Celestine raised her hand and Bonita recognized her.

"Bonita, I hope I am not out of order, but I feel that this note I have received should be read to the committee before any other business is discussed." Celestine was the corresponding secretary, and, although it was not time for correspondence to be read, Bonita, out of deference for Celestine, allowed her to take the floor.

Celestine read,

"Dear Chairperson Roberts and Members of the Magnolia Ball Committee,

It is with a great deal of difficulty that I write this letter to all of you, my fellow committee members and my friends. Because of some unforeseen difficulties in Bill's business and personal problems that I am experiencing at the present time, I wish to ask for a leave-of-absence from the Magnolia Ball Committee until further notice. I hope it will not cause any hardship on the committee, and I ask that I may be reinstated at a later time. As you are all aware, this is the year for my daughter Sandy's name to be submitted, and I sincerely hope that my leave-of-absence will not adversely affect her being invited to make her debut.

Sincerely,
Trudy Waltham"

Celestine folded the letter and said, "I move that we accept this temporary resignation from Trudy and that we need no further discussion about it. Furthermore, I recommend that we do not let Trudy's current problems affect Sandy's invitation to make her debut."

Julia Bracer Mavis seconded the motion.

Bonita rose again and said, "Celestine, you asked to read a piece of correspondence. I am not entertaining motions at this time."

"I don't feel that Trudy's situation needs to be discussed, Celestine replied. She has 'resigned' for all intents and purposes, and I think we should respect her wishes. I'm sure Trudy will not be returning to the committee. However, I do not think that her letter should in any way affect her daughter, who is not responsible for whatever problems she may be having."

A general hubbub ensued as the committee members realized that there was something going on here and they were purposely being left out. Dixie Mavis raised her hand. Bonita recognized her. She said, "Obviously there's more to this letter than we are being told. I think it's incumbent upon you to let the committee know what's going on, Celestine."

"I read you the letter. She doesn't say what's going on, Dixie. She merely says that because of personal problems and financial difficulties, she wishes to take a leave-of-absence," Celestine answered.

"There's more to it, isn't there, Bonita?" Dixie asked.

Fifty-two individual eyeballs turned to Bonita.

"Yes, there is, and I think everyone here should be made aware of the facts," Bonita responded.

"Bonita, I don't think the facts are necessary in this case," Celestine pressed. "I have served on this committee for many years, and I think it is proper to accept the leave-of-absence and be done with it."

"Is she sick? Does she have some kind of disease?" Dixie asked. "I'd really like to know what's going on."

"What's going on is that Trudy has lied to us," Bonita stated. There was a collective gasp in the room.

"Bonita, I remind you that all of us have probably at one time or another embellished something, and I don't think we need to discuss this any further," Celestine cautioned.

Blanche, Bonita's shadow and right-hand (in her own mind), rose from her seat. "I agree with Dixie. Bonita has already explained this to me, but I think we all need to know what's going on. Tell everyone what Trudy has lied about, Bonita, and to whom she has lied."

Over Celestine's continued protestations, Bonita apprised the assemblage of Trudy's life story. An explosion erupted. Everyone now knew that Trudy wasn't what she had seemed. There were lots of "I thought so's," and "I never believed her story about her Louisville debut," and "A sharecropper's daughter!" and "That explains why she threw money around like she did; she never had any taste." The women were like buzzards. They had spotted the carcass; now they were circling and coming in to feed.

Bonita sat back in her chair with a tiny smile on her face. She watched and listened as the character assassination was completed. Celestine stared at the floor. She felt embarrassment and sorrow for her friend.

Once the fracas died down, Celestine rose and said, "Bonita, you will recall that there is a motion on the floor and it has been seconded. I'm calling the question."

"Very well, Celestine. A motion has been made to accept Trudy Waltham's request for a leave-of-absence and to disregard Trudy's deception when her daughter Sandy's name is presented to the committee," replied Bonita. "All in favor, please signify by saying 'Aye.'"

The vote was unanimous.

Bonita caught Blanche's eye and nodded to her. Blanche rose and said, "We have accepted her request for a leave-of-absence, but I think we should take another vote and remove her from the committee."

"Absolutely!" responded Adele, "Why, we can't have that kind of person on the committee! What if she decided she wanted to come back and serve next year or the year after that? Why, having someone like that on the committee would be a travesty. We are the society leaders of Dorchester County. All of us must be above and beyond reproach. My husband, the General, never allowed anyone who lied to be on his staff, I can tell you that, and I don't want to serve on a committee with anyone who has lied about their background. She made up the whole thing about her debut in Louisville. I just can't imagine anyone doing such a thing. Didn't she know we would eventually find out?"

"I agree, Adele," said Dixie, "Make a motion to remove her from the committee, and I'll second it."

"So moved," said Adele.

"Second," followed Dixie.

Celestine stood and said, "I cannot believe that you, my friends and supposedly Trudy's friends, would be so vindictive. Trudy Waltham is a good person. What has she ever done to any of you? Why do you want to do this? Isn't it enough to accept her request for a leave-of-absence? Do you think she would ever really try to come back to a committee meeting after what's happened here today?"

"Celestine, there is a motion on the floor," trilled Bonita. "All in favor signify by saying 'Aye.'"

And so Trudy Waltham was removed from the illustrious Magnolia Ball Committee. Celestine's plan had failed, for after speaking with Bonita the night before, she had visited Trudy and told her about the call. Celestine had actually heard every word that Bonita said. She had used Anthony as an excuse to pretend she hadn't heard her, as Celestine was wont to do when something unpleasant was said in her presence. Trudy had admitted everything to Celestine, and the two of them had come up with the letter requesting a leave-of-absence. They had hoped to keep Bonita from telling everyone what Rudy had revealed. Celestine's heart ached for Trudy.

"That bit of business being disposed of, we shall now begin with the submission of the names of the young ladies. Dee, will you collect them from the committee members, please?" said Bonita with a smug smile.

Dee circulated among the ladies and collected the slips of paper. She then passed them to Bonita. Bonita began to read each name. After she had read the approximately thirty-five names, she asked if anyone had anything they wished to say about any of the candidates. Various comments were made, some favorable and some not. These comments were recorded by Mary Beth.

Blanche stood and asked to be recognized.

"Yes, Blanche?" said Bonita.

"I know we voted to accept Trudy's request for a leave of absence and not to let it interfere with Sandy's invitation, but now that we have voted to remove Trudy from the committee. I don't think we should allow Sandy to make her debut," stated Blanche.

The majority of the ladies didn't agree with Blanche on this count, but they turned to see Bonita's reaction. What they didn't know was that

The Magnolia Ball

Bonita had explained to Blanche the night before that she not only wanted Trudy off the committee, but she also wanted Sandy's name removed from the list.

"What does Trudy's dismissal have to do with Sandy? Sandy's father was Doug Hibbert, a member of one of the best and oldest families in Dorchester County. Her stepfather is Bill Waltham, also a member of one of the oldest families here. It shouldn't be held against Sandy that her stepfather has fallen on hard times, and I don't think what Trudy did should be held against the child," Celestine said.

"How's it going to look when Trudy has been thrown off the committee for Sandy to make her debut?" mousy Nancy asked. Bonita had coached her, too.

"No one outside this room has to know that Trudy has been removed. All we have to say if it ever comes up is that Trudy requested a leave-of-absence," Celestine responded.

"But that would be lying," Dixie answered.

"Yes, I guess it would be lying, Dixie. And I'm sure that is something that no one in this room has ever done. Is it?" Celestine asked. Then Celestine did the inconceivable. She gathered her purse and Trudy's letter and walked to the locked door.

Bonita said, "What are you doing, Celestine? Where are you going? You know you can't leave the room until the meeting has been adjourned."

"What I know is that I cannot stay in a room with a group of hypocrites. I have never seen such vindictiveness, pettiness and nastiness in my life. I will not stay in this room, and I don't care whether the meeting is over or not. I resign from the committee, and you can accept it or not. I never want anything to do with this committee again for as long as I live!"

Celestine turned the lock on the door, opened it, and left. She did not close it behind her.

There was a stunned silence. Celestine was the granddaughter of the founder of the Magnolia Ball. She was a direct tie to the original event.

Whenever newspaper reporters from Savannah wrote an article about the Magnolia Ball, Celestine's name was mentioned. When an article had been published by the *New York Times* about the longest running debutante ball in the South, Celestine was the interviewee. She lived at Beechland, site of the first Magnolia Ball. She was the owner of the namesake magnolia tree. She was the hostess of the breakfast always held after the Ball, and the new queen was always photographed standing under that tree. Magnolia leaves from the original tree were still used in the Ball's decorations every year.

Bonita realized that she may have overstepped. The committee needed Celestine. She had never seen Celestine lose her composure, much less her temper, and she had never heard her say anything unkind about anyone. Celestine had denounced the entire committee. Bonita had to do something, and do it quickly.

"Ladies," she said as she banged her gavel. "Ladies, please be quiet. I'm sure that Celestine is simply overwrought. As soon as we have adjourned, I will personally call on her and see if we can't straighten this situation out. Is there any further business? If not, is there a motion to adjourn?" Bonita asked breathlessly.

The meeting was adjourned. Conversation erupted everywhere. No one knew what to do, but everyone knew that they had to convince Celestine to return to the committee.

Bonita conferred with her two secret cohorts, Blanche and Nancy, and told them that they would meet at her home the next afternoon to make the final selections, but the ladies weren't listening. All they could talk about was Celestine. What were they going to do without her? She was so much a part of the Ball. If they didn't have her, the Ball would lose a large part of its significance.

Bonita knew it would only be a matter of time before the ladies figured out that she had caused this situation by insisting Trudy be thrown off the committee. She had to change Celestine's mind! She felt something stirring within her that she had not experienced in fifty years—fear!

Part Two
The Debutantes

14

Patricia

Patricia Saxon moved to Dorchester County from Charleston, South Carolina, with her younger brother, Randall and her parents Biffy and Chucky Saxon. Everyone wondered why the parents had the "cutesy" names and the kids had the "formal" names. Patricia was entering eighth grade when the family moved to an old home that was built by a fish boat captain when Montiac reigned as the Menhaden fishing capital of the world.

Menhaden fish are not edible but are used for 'chum,' bait for bluefishing. The bluefish is an insatiable food fish that is common up and down the Atlantic Coast. In order to catch the delicious-tasting fish, fisherman spread ground Menhaden, chum, on the top of the water. Then with a slow-moving boat, they troll their hooks on top of the chum. The greedy bluefish bite the hooks while ravenously devouring the chum.

Menhaden are also used for oil. They give off a rather unpleasant odor when cooked and the factory created a horrible stench when the huge steamers were in use. In the early twenties, as now, the Menhaden fish were plentiful, and boats returned every night "deck-loaded," which means the boats were so full, they could not hold another fish. Millions of fish were brought in each night to the factory. Fish boat captains were paid by the number of fish they caught, and in years of bounty, the money flowed.

Montiac was only a mile from one of the factories, so the residents were quite accustomed to the horrid smell. When someone from out of town complained about the odor, many a Montiacan could be heard to say, "That's the smell of money."

Since there was no industry in Dorchester County other than working on the water and farming, the fish boat personnel were a large factor in the economy of the county. When fishing was good, life was good for everyone. Many fish boat captains made thousands of dollars during the six-month seasons. Five brothers, all captains, built huge houses along the road between Montiac and the water.

By the eighties, the brothers had passed on, and the houses were all put up for sale by various of their offspring. The Saxons bought one of the old homes, which had been palatial in its day, and set about renovating it with kitchen enlargements, panoramas of glass, bigger closets and more bathrooms. Chucky Saxon also went to one of the local boat yards and bought a thirty-foot sailboat that he docked at his waterfront property.

Chucky and Biffy had no known source of income. Supposedly, Chucky had been an office manager for a company in Charleston, South Carolina. But he and his wife were in their early forties when they moved to Dorchester County. So he must have done a lot of managing in a short period of time, people thought, or there was family money. Their neighbors wondered if maybe there were a money tree growing in the backyard, because the Saxons spent like it was going out of style.

Patricia was a pear-shaped girl with dirty blonde hair, hazel eyes and freckles. She was not particularly attractive, but when she was in the presence of her friends' parents, she cultivated a charming sense of confidence. She was very animated and somewhat reminiscent of Eddie Haskell on the old "Leave it to Beaver" Show. Patricia was so convincing that they all believed for awhile, anyway, that she was a sweet, genuine, well-reared young lady.

Everyone would eventually find out, however, (as her dates already knew), that sweet, little Patricia could suck the chrome off a trailer hitch or suck a golf ball through a garden hose. She began dating as soon as the school term began. She "went through just about every boy in Dorchester County faster than one could say, 'Pull your pants down.'"

She was both devious and manipulative. Other girls, whom she befriended, ended up in a great deal of trouble with their families. Patricia would convince them to sneak out of the house at night, lie to their parents about various things, and "borrow" the family car for joy riding. The fact that neither she nor any of her friends had drivers' licenses did not deter them. Patricia was from the city, and the country girls of Dorchester County were very impressed with her cosmopolitan ways. They also envied the fact that she had dates every weekend.

Her parents seemed, outwardly, to be very strict. However, they allowed Patricia to go out with anyone she chose. Patricia had a curfew, and heaven help her if she were one minute late, but her parents didn't seem to notice the disheveled manner in which she arrived home. As long as she was home by eleven o'clock, they were happy.

She soon got caught in several of her lies. Her parents, upon "seeing" the real Patricia, became genuinely concerned about their once sweet, innocent girl. Patricia's mother claimed that, until they moved to Dorchester County, she had been a little angel. Other parents found that difficult to believe. Patricia did make excellent grades, but after several of her escapades were found out, Chucky and Biffy decided to send her away to a boarding school. They felt she needed a more disciplined environment, away from the "juvenile delinquents" of Dorchester County. It would do her good to be surrounded by genteel, young ladies who would, certainly, set a good example for her. They looked for the very best school in the South.

Patricia, now in tenth grade, was sent to St. Elizabeth's School for Young Ladies in Atlanta. This exclusive and expensive boarding school had the reputation of accepting only young ladies from the finest of families. It also had an excellent academic department and its graduates could expect to attend the best colleges in the United States. The brochures for the elite school were impressive, emphasizing the structural environment and culture of the school. Though strict academically, St. Elizabeth's was not too exacting socially. Once the adolescents were "accepted" following their interviews, "St. E's" turned the little harlots loose. They had curfews, but were free to roam the streets of Atlanta. They did not have to introduce their escorts or dates to any authority figure.

Patricia did not waste any time finding the low-life district and proceeded to date every slimeball she could find. She also continued to give her dates the pleasure of her pear-shaped body. She was neither subjective nor selective and her repertoire consisted of males in all sizes, shapes, and colors.

One of these conquests, Dennis, was a ninth grade high school dropout, who for awhile worked part-time doing carpentry. Occasionally during that time, he smoked a little pot. After trying his hand at physical labor, he realized that the construction routine, where one had to arrive at work by six o'clock in the morning, was not for him. He preferred to sleep until noon and party until three or four o'clock in the morning.

His "happy weed" supplier was making four times more per week than what Dennis was making in construction. Even better, his business hours did not begin until three o'clock in the afternoon. Dennis immediately decided that the life of the small-time drug dealer was the one for him. He worked a week longer at the construction site where he earned enough money to buy his supplies and began peddling his wares.

Patricia particularly liked Dennis, because he always had money and was available to "play" at almost any hour of the day. She spent less and less time in classes and more and more time at his pad, which he shared with four other derelicts.

Dennis and his buddies lived in a rundown house they rented for two hundred fifty dollars a month on the seedy side of Atlanta. It was furnished with early attic and late Salvation Army furniture. The house was filthy—beer cans knee-high; ash trays teeming with stale butts; pans and dishes, with food permanently stuck to them in the kitchen sink; trash cans overflowing and dirty sheets matted on cots and beds. The front door was permanently ajar. There were no curtains on the windows, many of which were without panes, and no air conditioning, so the air was always thick and humid. In the front room, there was a color TV, a VCR, and a huge dartboard, which was painted on the living room wall.

Patricia loved the scene. It was so bohemian, so "in," so unlike anything she had ever experienced. As she told the girls at St. Elizabeth's, Dennis was such a man. He smelled like a man (probably because Dennis was not into showers, toothbrushes or deodorant) and she loved his lifestyle. She was then sixteen and Dennis was twenty-eight. Biffy would have had a stroke if she had known what her darling little girl was up to; she and Chucky shelled out eighteen thousand dollars per year for Patricia to be surrounded by girls from lovely homes who would set a good example.

Dennis was a generous guy. He shared his pot with Patricia. She found she could really relax and "get inside her head" when she got high. She loved how it made time stand still and how it made her laugh. When Patricia smoked, she thought everything was funny. The best thing about pot, in her opinion, was that it did not give her a hangover or headache. Also if some crisis occurred, it seemed she could snap right out of her high. Further justifying her drug use, she knew that pot was not addictive, so what could it hurt? Besides, cancer patients were smoking pot in hospices as therapy!

She altered her grooming habits to better fit in with Dennis' crowd. Where she had once taken good care of herself, she let her short hair grow and refused to style, or even comb, it. It hung in long, unattractive strings. She wore no makeup. She took to wearing the sloppiest clothes she could find. The less they coordinated, the better she felt. She often left school wearing an oversized, plaid shirt, contrasting plaid shorts, an old hat plopped on her head and combat boots with no socks.

Chucky and Biffy were quite concerned when Patricia arrived home from school for her Christmas vacation dressed like a bag lady. However, Patricia, blessed with the gift of gab and accustomed to lying whenever necessary, assured her parents that all of the girls at St. Elizabeth's dressed as she did. After all, it was a girls' school, so they did not need to impress anyone.

Patricia, however, was wise enough to clean up her act considerably while she was home with Chucky and Biffy. She wore some makeup, kept her hair clean, and wore decent clothes. She also had the courtesy to open the windows of her third-floor room late at night to exhale the marijuana smoke.

Patricia regaled her parents with stories of the other girls at her fancy school and told them what their fathers did for a living. Since the school only sent out grades at the end of the semester, she was also able to convince her parents that she was doing very well in her classes.

When her semester grades arrived, Biffy and Chucky were appalled. She had failed two courses, gotten a "D" in one, an incomplete in another, and a "C" in English. The Saxons made an appointment to meet with the Dean of Instruction and caught the first plane from Savannah to Atlanta. The dean, having been through this many times, assured the Saxons that this was not unusual in the first semester. She told them that St. Elizabeth's was a much more difficult school than Dorchester County High. Once Patricia adjusted to the new environment, her grades would certainly improve. She reminded them that Patricia would have a much better chance at being accepted to one of the better women's colleges with a diploma from St. Elizabeth's.

To the dean, the first priority was to keep Patricia at the school—and keep the eighteen thousand dollars per year tuition that her parents were paying. She promised Biffy and Chucky that Patricia would have weekly sessions with the guidance counselor. She would, personally, meet with Patricia, and she would arrange tutoring for her if necessary.

Patricia was aware that her parents were coming for the interview. That morning, she had taken special pains with her appearance. After the session with the dean, the Saxons met Patricia for lunch in the school cafeteria. She assured them that she would make progress. She had just about adjusted now to the more difficult curriculum. She knew that St. Elizabeth's was a much better school than the high school at home. The Governor of Georgia's daughter, who lived just down the hall from her, had gotten the same grades, and "Peachy," who had the highest average at her public high school in Warm Springs prior to coming to St. Elizabeth's, was also struggling. Biffy and Chucky returned home feeling better about their daughter and their investment in her education.

Patricia had bought herself another semester of playtime. She did, however, attend sessions with her guidance counselor. She met with the dean. She regularly reported that she thought she had adjusted, what a good school St. Elizabeth's was, how much harder it was than her public high school, and how she was trying. Patricia did spend more time in her classes. However, even though she was physically in the classroom, she was often high.

She continued her affair with Dennis and his "happy weed." Dennis soon introduced her to pot laced with PCP. Patricia had thought she loved plain marijuana, but it was nothing compared to this mixture. It made her feel like superwoman. She never felt hungry, sleepy, or tired. She adored it and smoked as often as Dennis would allow her. Dennis was doing quite well in his drug business and was quite generous. He allowed Patricia to smoke all of the marijuana with PCP she wanted. Patricia had always been quite adventurous sexually, but when she was smoking the new mixture, any inhibitions she may have had, disappeared. Dennis was having a great time with the teenager in his bed, and since he purchased the drugs at wholesale value, the cost was very little to him.

After Patricia became an aficionado of marijuana laced with PCP, Dennis, at a party one night, introduced her to pot laced with LSD. She had been in a particularly good mood when she smoked, and she had a delightful trip. She saw the most wonderful colors and lights. She watched the room dissolve, reappear, break into a million pieces, reassemble itself in a surrealistic manner, and then return again to normal. She had now found her favorite high.

Patricia began her rapid spiral downward into the netherworld of drug addiction. She was always willing to try anything new. Dennis asked her if she were ready for the ultimate high. Patricia was. Dennis heated the heroin in a spoon, tied off her arm, and injected it with heroin. She was almost immediately ill and threw up for what seemed like hours. Once the sickness was over, however, she was in ecstasy. Heroin was wonderful! She was so at peace and seemed to be floating. There were no problems, no tomorrow, only good things and good thoughts. Dennis was stingy with the heroin, though, and only shared it as a special treat on rare occasions.

Near the end of her tenth-grade year, Patricia realized her grades were not much better than they had been at the end of the first semester. If she wanted to continue her relationship with Dennis, she had to take drastic action. If she flunked out of school, she was going to have to return to "Dorksville" County. She wouldn't be able to see Dennis and share his wonderful drugs. Rather than buckle under and study, try to give up the drugs or ditch Dennis, Patricia convinced him it was time for them to marry.

She packed a few of her belongings and sneaked out of school after the dorm was closed for the evening. Patricia and Dennis took off for North Carolina, where they crossed the state line and went into the first justice of the peace they could find. Patricia, of course, lied about her age, but since North Carolina wasn't too strict about marriages, the JP didn't ask her too many questions.

They returned to Dennis' seedy apartment in Atlanta and got the other four derelicts to leave them alone for the night, where they celebrated their honeymoon through a haze of different mixtures of marijuana smoke, and finally a syringe of heroin. On the second day of the honeymoon, Patricia turned down a joint and asked for a heroin injection instead. Dennis refused, but gave Patricia all the joints he had on hand. She smoked most of them the same day.

Meanwhile, the head resident at St. Elizabeth's had realized that Patricia had not spent the night in the dorm. Rather than alarm her parents, the school set out to find her. They questioned her roommates and acquaintances, whose lips were sealed. It was a terrible thing to "rat" on a friend. However, one of Patricia's roommates called her at the apartment to tell her the school was looking for her, and that she better get back as quickly as she could and make up a good story.

Patricia, who had finished two joints prior to answering the phone, told her roommate that she wasn't afraid of anyone at the school, that she wasn't coming back, and that she and Dennis were married. She said she didn't care what the old biddies at St. Elizabeth's were doing. With that, Patricia promptly hung up on her friend and returned to her new husband and her new friends: the drugs.

Patricia's roommate kept quiet as far as the administration was concerned. Patricia was married! How cool! She told their friends; they got a vicarious thrill from Patricia's wild doings. Since none of the girls let the school know that they were aware of her whereabouts, the time came when the school had to notify Biffy and Chucky of Patricia's absence.

Chucky and Biffy, as expected, were absolutely distraught. They caught the first plane to Atlanta, hired private detectives, and began questioning the girls. They talked with the police and filed a missing person's report. After hours and hours of questioning, Patricia's roommate finally acquiesced and told them where Patricia was. She also revealed that Patricia was married to Dennis and was not planning to come back to school.

Chucky and Biffy had never heard of Dennis. They believed the roommate must be mistaken. They knew that Patricia would not throw her education to the wind and get married. They accompanied the police officer to the East Side of Atlanta, and as they went further and further into the ratty section of town, Biffy became more convinced that some mistake had been made. Her darling little girl could not possibly be in a place like this. The police car pulled up to Dennis' house. Biffy was almost ill as she sat in the back seat of the cruiser.

The parents and the police officer went to the door of the house and knocked. The knock could not be heard from the interior of the house because of the acid rock music blaring on the stereo. Finally, the officer pushed the door open, and they walked in.

Biffy was horrified at the filth and squalor. As she and the two men entered the house, she tried to step over the beer cans and the trash. She put her hand to her nose to try to block out the unpleasant smell of decaying food and body odors emanating from every corner. They walked down a long hallway and into a living room full of debris, dirty dishes, assorted articles of clothing, and a blaring television. The police officer turned off the TV and stereo.

In the ensuing silence, Biffy began to yell Patricia's name. When there was no response, she tore from room to room calling her child. On the second floor, Biffy threw open a bathroom door and there, in the corner, she saw Patricia lying on the floor with a piece of rubber tied around her arm, a syringe in her hand, and her eyes rolled back in her head. Biffy began screaming.

Chucky and the police officer entered the tiny bathroom. The officer called paramedics to the scene. Patricia was soon in an ambulance and on her way to the hospital. She had overdosed, but she survived.

The police located Dennis and arrested him for drug trafficking and contributing to the delinquency of a minor. Chucky and Biffy began the task of trying to straighten out their daughter's life. They had the marriage annulled. They took Patricia back home where they constantly watched her.

Later, they admitted her to Tucker's, a private mental institution in Richmond, Virginia, where Patricia entered a Narcotics Anonymous program for six months while a patient there. Once she was healthier, private tutors came to her room daily to assist her through tenth-grade classes.

The following year, Patricia was sent to a very strict school in South Carolina. Biffy and Chucky met with the headmistress and explained what had happened when Patricia was attending St. Elizabeth's. The headmistress was given explicit instructions that Patricia was not to go on dates and must be closely supervised. She remained at the school for four months until she bribed a maid to exchange clothes with her, walked out of the school, and disappeared for almost a year.

Throughout their ordeal in Atlanta, and even while Patricia was missing from South Carolina, Biffy and Chucky maintained a good front. They attended functions at the Country Club, and went to the old historic Episcopal Church for services every Sunday. When asked about Patricia, they responded that she was fine and doing quite well in school. No, she wouldn't be coming home for the summer. She had taken a position working with children in a Connecticut summer camp.

Patricia's parents, however, were frantic all of the time. They finally received a call about Patricia in 1990. She was in Seattle, Washington nearly dead from an untreated case of syphilis. Only because she realized she was dying had she allowed her current lover to call her parents and ask them to come see her.

Biffy and Chucky flew to Seattle, and emotionally broke down when they saw their daughter. They hired the best specialists on the West Coast, nursed Patricia back to health again, and brought her home.

Patricia was grateful to be alive. She asked her parents' forgiveness and promised she would never mess up again. She voluntarily enrolled in Narcotics Anonymous. She swore off all drugs, alcohol and sex and became the model daughter.

Tutors were again hired, and because of her remarkable aptitude, she received a GED at the same time her classmates were receiving their high school diplomas. She was accepted at a reasonably good college. The heroin addicted, promiscuous juvenile delinquent had her hair cut in an attractive style, wore makeup, went shopping with Biffy for an appropriate college freshman wardrobe, and went off to Hollins College in Lynchburg, Virginia.

In October of her freshman year, Patricia received an off-white, vellum envelope in her mailbox. She opened it. It was an invitation to make her debut at the 1991 Magnolia Ball in Dorchester County. Oh, how proud her parents would be!

15

Bill Waltham & Hunter Quarrels

Hunter Quarrels was quite surprised when the doorbell rang at ten o'clock. He and Lalique were not expecting business associates that night. Hunter went to the door, looked through the peephole and recognized Bill Waltham.

He opened the door. "Hello, Mr. Waltham, may I help you?" He did not hold the door open so that Bill could enter, but rather came out onto the front porch.

Bill said, "I'm sorry to trouble you so late, Mr. Quarrels, but I just thought I'd drop by and check on my property. You don't mind if I come in, do you?"

"Well, it is quite late, and my wife isn't dressed. I didn't realize there was a clause in our contract for you to come by and inspect your property unannounced. However, if you would like to set an appointment with us, I'm sure there would no problem. Everything is in tiptop shape. We're taking very good care of everything. We haven't finished furnishing the place yet, but everything's fine. We have no complaints, and as I said, if you wish to make an appointment with us, we'd be happy to have you come in and look around," Hunter said with a smile.

Realizing that the house inspection ploy was not going to work, Bill said, "Well, you see, Mr. Quarrels, I didn't come by only to inspect the property. I also came by because I am interested in your cellular telephone business, and as I'm looking at some new investments, I'm quite interested in what you're doing here. I thought I'd like to get in on the ground floor of your enterprise."

Hunter knew all about Waltham's financial difficulties. Waltham had to move from Walthome because he could no longer afford to live there. Hunter attempted to let Bill down gently.

"That's real nice that you're interested in investing in my cellular telephone business, but you see, Mr. Waltham, I've got all the investors I need now. Everything's all set up, and it's about ready to go. I'm unable to take anyone else in because the profits would be lessened for the other investors, and I have given my partners certain financial expectations. I'm afraid you're too late."

"I can't be too late. You don't understand. I have to get involved in your business," responded Bill.

It began to dawn on Hunter that he was in the presence of a desperate man, and there was always room for desperate men in his line of work. Hunter invited Bill in to discuss the "cellular telephone business."

Before the evening was over, Bill and Hunter had reached an agreement and shaken hands. Hunter was pleased with his new associate. Bill Waltham had many business acquaintances in the area, since he was a native—a part of the "good ol' boy" network—and knew where the money was.

Bill drove back to the carriage house feeling a little better about his financial situation. He did a fast two-step rationalization about the business in which he was about to become involved.

He put a false bounce in his step as he entered the house hale-and-hearty to tell Trudy that, before long, they would be back in the clover again. He entered to find Trudy passed out on the sofa. Her face was stained with tears and an empty vodka bottle was on its side in front of the test pattern on the TV.

16

Cinnamon

The owner of the Sweet Treat, Jordan Roget, had married a Dorchester County girl, Ellen James, in the nineteen fifties. They met in Massachusetts where she had taken a secretarial position. Ellen had been reared on a farm in upper Dorchester County and graduated from the upper county high school, (this was several years prior to consolidation of the county schools). After attending two years at a business college in Savannah, she went to Boston as the executive secretary for a large construction company.

In Boston, she met Jordan, whose family was the owner of a small French cafe where she and her co-workers sometimes ate. Jordan was handsome and dashing. Soon he and Ellen married and began to "bring forth." They had three sons and a daughter.

During Ellen's pregnancy with her daughter, she had an unending craving for cinnamon. She ate cinnamon bread, rice pudding, applesauce, cinnamon toast, and baked apples. She couldn't seem to get enough of the spice. When her dark-haired, blue-eyed little girl entered the world, Ellen took one look at her and said, "Hello, Cinnamon."

When Cinnamon was seven years old, both of Ellen's parents, who were elderly, became ill. Ellen and Jordan had recently sold the cafe that had been willed to Jordan by his deceased parents. So they left with the boys and Cinnamon, to take care of Ellen's parents in Dorchester County. Three years after they arrived, both of her parents passed on.

With the approval of Ellen's brothers and sisters, she and Jordan sold the homeplace and moved into town. They rented a house on one of the main streets of Montiac.

Jordan had thought the profits he made for the sale of the cafe would support them a long time. But with the medical bills that remained for Ellen's parents' illnesses and the ever-increasing cost of rearing four children, Jordan realized that he needed to get back into business. He took some of their profits, purchased a piece of land, and built a drive-in restaurant called the "Sweet Treat."

The Sweet Treat specialized in burgers, hot-dogs, custard, and sandwiches. It was an instant hit, especially with teenagers. Soon Jordan was making a great deal of money. An inveterate gambler, he saw a way to make even more. He became friendly with several of the wheeler-dealers in town. A "back room" was added to the small restaurant. Nightly gambling, namely poker, became a lucrative sideline business. Thousands of dollars changed hands several nights a week in the back room of the Sweet Treat.

Ellen got a job teaching typing at the county high school and occasionally helped Jordan at the restaurant. Cinnamon grew into a pretty and voluptuous teenager, who smoked, drank, necked, and made out in the back seats of various cars at the local drive-in movie on Friday and Saturday nights.

During Cinnamon's junior year, her high school hired a new band director, Herbert. He was a tall, good-looking young man fresh out of college. He took a room at Nana Grey's house, a few houses up the street from the Roget family rental home.

Nana Grey was an elderly lady who had been widowed for some thirty years, and she took in boarders for income. She was called "Nana" because she had become a grandmother at a very early age and didn't want to be called "grandmother," "grandma," or "granny." She had insisted that her little granddaughter call her "Nana," and the name stuck. Subsequent grandchildren called her "Nana," as did all of the neighborhood children, including Cinnamon.

Herbert began trying to excite the youth of Dorchester High School, now the consolidated county high school, about band practice, band concerts, and marching in parades. He

soon realized he was fighting an uphill battle. Band was not the most interesting of pastimes, it seemed, for the local teenagers.

Cinnamon, however, took special notice of Herbert. She would intentionally meet his eyes and then bat her long lashes at him. She joined the band and started playing the triangle. (The triangle is a relatively simple instrument. One usually only has to play **one** note per song, and it's traditionally close to the end of each selection.) She played, of course, specifically in order to spend more time with the band director. She always found an excuse to linger after band practice, and found many reasons to be out in her yard at times when she knew he would be passing by.on his way to Nana's.

Cinnamon's seduction was successful. Herbert had, in fact, noticed her voluptuous body, and soon Cinnamon and Herbert began a tempestuous relationship.

Her father, Jordan, was at the Sweet Treat every night, and Ellen, somewhat naive, was sure that Cinnamon and Herbert were only friends. Consequently, Cinnamon and Herbert spent numerous evenings in the living room while Ellen retired upstairs to her bedroom, to prepare lesson plans for the next day's classes.

Two of Cinnamon's older brothers were married, and the third was away at school, so she and Herbert had the living room to themselves. After the lesson plans, Ellen went to bed. Cinnamon's friends, faculty members at the high school, neighbors, and Nana Grey were all aware of the romance. Interestingly, when the liaison began, Cinnamon was not yet sixteen and, therefore, "jail bait." Fraternization between teachers and students obviously was not tolerated by the school administration, yet no one said a word. Regardless of the potential consequences,

Herbert and Cinnamon necked, petted, and fornicated regularly in the living room. Though most of her spare time was taken up with Herbert, Cinnamon did master the triangle perfectly and never missed a single cue when it was her turn to play her one note in any given song.

In March of her senior year in high school, Cinnamon missed her period. When she missed it again in April, she told Herbert of her problem. He responded by telling her that they must get rid of the baby immediately. She should understand that he could not marry her; if they were found out, he would lose his job.

Cinnamon had no choice but to go to her mother with her problem. Ellen did not act at all as one would expect. She simply told Cinnamon that she would "take care of it."

Ellen immediately, called her best friend Judith, who was a nurse for a local doctor. Judith had earlier confided in Ellen that she had been having an affair with the doctor for the past ten years. Ellen swore Judith to secrecy and then told her of Cinnamon's predicament. Judith was very understanding and divulged that her own daughter, Berniece, who was dating the doctor's son, was also pregnant. They were both too young to get married, and Dr. Ashcroft had plans for his son to go to medical school.

Judith explained that on Thursday night, after his regular office hours, Dr. Ashcroft was going to perform an abortion on Berniece. Judith was going to be involved in the proceeding. No one would ever know—not the doctor's wife, or Judith's husband. Judith was sure she could convince him to also take care of Cinnamon. Judith, Ellen, and especially Dr. Ashcroft seemed willing to overlook the fact that abortions were illegal.

The following Thursday night, Berniece had her surgery. After Judith had taken her home and made sure her daughter was comfortable, she called Ellen and told her to bring Cinnamon to the doctor's office. Ellen and Cinnamon arrived. Cinnamon was in the doctor's office for twenty-five minutes, and then Ellen took her home.

Interestingly enough, Berniece played the French horn in the band. Both Cinnamon and Berniece were unavailable for the spring parade the following Saturday. Once the bleeding stopped, however, both girls were back to their normal activities. Berniece continued to date the doctor's son, and Cinnamon continued to entertain Herbert while Ellen did her lesson plans upstairs. She was sure Cinnamon would not make the same mistake again.

Requirements for making one's debut at the Magnolia Ball included being enrolled at a college or university. Young ladies attending either community colleges or business schools were not eligible. In September of 1991, Cinnamon left for business school in Atlanta.

If a young lady didn't have the prescribed family background, occasionally the committee would issue an invitation provided the young lady had participated in numerous school and community activities and had performed well academically. Cinnamon had never excelled in academics or participated in any extracurricular activities except for playing the triangle and having a fling with the band director.

Cinnamon's family certainly did not measure up to the prerequisites for debuting at the Magnolia Ball. Her father simply owned a drive-in restaurant and was a "come-here." Her mother was merely a typing teacher and though she was a native and from an old family, it was not a prestigious one.

Cinnamon had an ace in the hole, however. Many of the socially powerful and prominent men, (who were married to socially powerful and prominent women), spent frequent evening hours gambling in the back room of the Sweet Treat. So, Cinnamon, who fulfilled none of the committee's criteria and who had aborted her first child, was pleasantly surprised when she received her invitation to debut at the upcoming Magnolia Ball.

17

Lynette

Ned Jennings worked with large machinery. He and his daddy owned a few bulldozers. They cleared some lots for people and did a little bushhogging of weeds and underbrush here and there; however, Ned dreamed of a lot more money than he made working with his father.

He had spent only one semester in college. He flunked out. During that brief period, however, he was introduced to life in the fast lane. He began a small, but very profitable, business selling marijuana to the local boys. On occasion, Ned went with his father to the Sweet Treat. While there, he learned to play poker. He found he had a natural affinity for card games and soon was a regular in the back room.

After getting to know many of the men who frequented the Sweet Treat, Ned realized that there was a much larger market for his business from the "gambling" clientele than the high school kids who wanted to buy the drug in small quantities. Ned made some business connections, and soon, his drug business grew to the point where he no longer needed to sit in the blistering sun on the bulldozer or risk mosquitoes and poison ivy as he bushhogged. Ned expanded his product line and began to sell cocaine. His business thrived.

As the money rolled in, he began to date a local girl, Lynette, who attended a girl's boarding school about eighty miles away. However, since the school was so close to her home, she was able to come home on weekends. On closed weekends, when the young ladies were not allowed to leave the school, Ned drove his Corvette to the school and sat in the parlor with Lynette.

The love affair flourished.as did Ned's business.

Soon he moved out of his family's home and into a small house at the end of a remote road leading out of Montiac. He bought a small house in an area known as "the jungle," with overgrown trees garbed in flowing gowns of Spanish moss. On weekends and school holidays, Ned and Lynette spent many wonderful hours in the tiny "jungle" house.

Lynette's family had come to Dorchester County ten years earlier. For the first few years, Frank and Hilda Karsh had no visible means of income. During the third year of their residency, however, they bought a huge tract of land and began to build a large and lovely, one-level brick home. Shortly after their home was built, Frank and Hilda bought another tract of land and built a factory where they processed peaches. They canned and pickled peaches, made peach cobbler, peach pies, peach cakes, peach sauces, and anything else one can think of to do with a peach.

After they built their home and factory, they began to spend money on a grand scale. It was nothing for Hilda to go shopping with a group of friends in Savannah and come back with a few diamond rings. She bought designer dresses, handmade boots, shoes, and lavish furnishings for her home. Frank bought Cadillacs, Lincolns, and a twin engined airplane.

Lynette was fairly tall with auburn hair and green eyes. She was built like a ceramic excretorium. Her thirty-six "D" breasts were in perfect proportion to her slim body. Ned was certainly not a rocket scientist, so he and Lynette were a perfect match. Her intellect wouldn't have filled the cup of a training bra. But he was a good-looking guy with He was broad shoulders. He had brown hair, blue eyes, dimples in his cheeks and chin, and a shit-eating grin that drove women wild.

Ned was well liked by most everyone except Tiny. Tiny and Ned once had been friends. Ned had cut Tiny in on his drug dealing at first, but Tiny wasn't always reliable and didn't always make deliveries on time. He had also allowed some of his friends to have their drugs on credit. Ned had severed their business relationship and Tiny had never gotten it.

He had enjoyed the easy money and little work. Tiny was determined to get back at Ned. However, Ned wasn't aware that Tiny harbored such hatred for him.

One night, Ned walked out of the Sweet Treat stuffing five hundred dollars in the pocket of his jeans. Tiny was waiting for him.

"So what's shakin', man?" asked Tiny.

"Hey, guy. Not much. Just got my biggest delivery ever coming in this weekend. That's all," responded Ned.

"No shit! What are you selling? Pot or coke?"

"Coke, man. Pot's nowhere. Now that I know all of the big boys in the county, I'm almost strictly into coke," answered Ned.

"You still aren't using, are you?"

"Hell, no. You think I'm stupid? I wouldn't touch that stuff. I do have a little problem though," confided Ned.

"What's that, my friend?" queried Tiny.

"It's Lynette," Ned answered. "She loves coke. Of course, she can't get any while she's at school, but she's on it almost all of the time when she's with me. I'm really concerned about her. She wants the stuff all the time on the weekends. I'm afraid she'll start wanting it during the week.too. She's beginning to act like a coke whore. She'll do anything, and I mean anything, to get me to give her the stuff when we're together."

"Man, that's rough. Maybe you should try to wean her off of it. Anyway, you got this big deal goin' down. Tell me about it."

"This Saturday night, I've got two kilos of fine stuff, uncut, comin' in, and I already got orders for most of it. I'm gonna cut it with aspirin, cuz the crash isn't as bad when the high wears off if it's cut with aspirin, plus, aspirin is so cheap. Ya know two kilos uncut is like six kilos once I cut it? At a hundred and ten dollars a gram, I'm gonna be able to retire.

You should see my customer list! It reads like a 'Who's Who in Dorchester County'!" bragged Ned.

"Saturday night, huh? Sounds great, man. I'll be thinking about you. Sorry our business deal didn't work out. I sure could use some of that bread," said Tiny.

"No hard feelings, Tiny. You understand why it didn't last, don't you? I mean, you can't be letting people have that stuff and pay you later. Once they've smoked it or snorted it, they'll never pay. Users are the pits. They're worthless, man."

"No, of course I don't have any hard feelings. I guess I wasn't cut out for that line of work. I appreciate the action you did throw my way. You and I are buddies, man. We've been friends for years. Hey, I gotta run. Hope everything works out with Lynette. Get her off the nose candy, man. See ya!" Tiny said as he headed back to his car.

"Good seeing you, man. Come around. You know I have my own place now, don't you?" yelled Ned.

"Yeah, you're living down in the jungle, aren't you?"

"Right. Last house at the end of the road. Come by, you hear?" Ned said.

"I will. I'll surprise you one of these nights," responded Tiny. He drove off.

Oh yeah, I'll surprise you all right, you shit, he thought as he headed down the main street of Montiac. "You haven't even begun to realize how big Saturday night is gonna to be for you, you motha'. You fucked with me, Ned. Me, your best friend, and you're gonna pay," he said aloud.

Tiny drove to the middle of town and pulled up to a pay phone across the street from the post office. He called the Narcotics Bureau in Savannah, and "dropped a dime" on his ex-best friend Ned.

Saturday morning Hilda was looking over her guest list and the seating arrangements for the huge dinner party she and Frank were having that evening at the country club. Lynette came running through the kitchen door.

The Magnolia Ball

"Hello, darling. I had no idea you were coming home this weekend. We're having a party tonight at the club. I'll just pencil you in at one of the tables. Where would you like to sit?" asked Hilda.

"Hi, Mom. Oh, I'm not planning on goin' to your party. Ned just picked me up this morning at school. We're gonna spend the day decorating his place and getting ready for a party he's havin' tonight. I hope you don't mind if I don't come," said Lynette, smiling.

"Well I'd love to have you there, but I understand you'd rather be with people your own age. Who's Ned having at his party? Friends of yours?"

"Yes. A whole bunch of girls are home from school this weekend, so it'll be a group of kids I know. Daughters and sons of your friends. 'Suitable people,'" teased Lynette.

"You know I'm not like that, dear. Have I ever given you any grief about your friends?"

"No, Mom, you haven't. You've been great and besides, I was just kidding. I'm gonna run to my room now and get some clothes. Since you and Dad will be at the club, is it all right if I stay at Ned's and get dressed there? I'll be home by my curfew at one o'clock," yelled Lynette as she started down the hall to her room.

"Of course. You know how much your father and I like Ned. We trust you, Lynnie. We've told you that over and over, haven't we?" responded Hilda as she followed Lynette down the hall.

Lynette stopped, turned, and walked to her mother. She gave her a hug and said, "Thanks, Mom. Now you go back to your party planning. I mean, I know how you are, everything has to be perfect," Lynette said with a big smile on her face.

Hilda returned to her list while Lynette rummaged through a suitcase at the back of her closet and got out the sheer black teddy she had bought at Frederick's of Hollywood last summer. She threw in the black garter belt, black fishnet stockings, and chocolate mousse-flavored feminine hygiene spray. Zipping the case, she ran back through the kitchen and told Hilda she'd see her later that night, and she hoped the party would be a smash.

"What are you going to wear, dear? Does it need to be pressed?"

"No, Mom. It's a casual party. I'm wearing jeans." Lynette raced out the door to the waiting Ned, who had taken the tee-tops out of the Corvette so Lynette's long, auburn hair could fly in the wind. She would look like Sheena, Queen of the Jungle, by the time they arrived at "the jungle."

Of course, Ned was not having a party. Girls from her school were not home for the weekend, and Ned and Lynette did not spend the day decorating. Ned's plans were to spend the day in bed, and while Lynette was interested in spending some of the time in bed (ergo her packed suitcase), she was also interested in decorating the inside of her nose with white powder. She asked Ned to let her snort two lines as soon as they arrived, but he told her it was still early. He persuaded her to wait. Lynette pouted and finally Ned gave in. It was a fair trade, however, for when Ned gave in, Lynette put out.

That evening, the socialites of Dorchester County moved from the Hibiscus Room at the Country Club, where they had consumed assorted hors d'oeuvres and cocktails, to the main dining room. They were ready for the feast of filet mignon and lobster tails, Duchess potatoes, salad Nicoise, Parkerhouse rolls, chilled Puligny Montrachet and 1978 Chateau Lafitte Rothschild Puilliac. Meanwhile, back in "the jungle," Ned was measuring and weighing grams of cocaine cut with aspirin. He placed them in plastic baggies for his customers. His shipment had arrived.

Lynette had by this time snorted about five lines up each nostril. She was practicing somersaults, splits and assorted other gymnastic moves in the nude. She was flying! Stereo music blared.

The doorbell rang. Ned told Lynette to go and put some clothes on, but Lynette said, "No, I don't want to put my clothes on. I feel so free this way. Besides, the human body, especially the female human body, and especially my female body, is an exquisite thing, don't you think, Neddy?"

Ned looked at her and admitted that he did, but he explained that the customer at the door would have to come in, because it was customary for the dealer to allow the customer to snort a line without charge. That way, the customer would know he was getting good stuff. "So you'll have to get dressed, Lynnie," said Ned.

"No, no, no! A thousand times no!" yelled Lynette. She suddenly jumped up, ran to the door and threw it open, all before Ned could intercept her. She looked right into the face of Four Eyes, two South Carolina state troopers and two narcotics agents. The five men pushed Lynette aside and headed for Ned, who had not moved a hair.

"Hello, gentlemen. May I help you? Is anything wrong?" he asked.

"What's that on the table in those bags, boy?" asked Four Eyes.

Lynette romped over to the table. "It's Comet. We're getting ready to clean the entire house," she said with exuberance and giggled.

One of the agents licked his finger and put it in the cocaine.

Ned asked, "Gentlemen, do any of you have a search warrant?"

The narcotics agent tasted a tiny amount of the powder, looked at Ned, reached into his inside jacket pocket and produced the search warrant. He said, "Yes sir, as a matter of fact, we do."

The second agent cuffed Ned. One of the state troopers read him his rights. The other state trooper cuffed Lynette. She began screaming and kicked at the officer.

"You take your filthy hands off of me! Do you know who I am? Do you know who my daddy is? Don't you touch me!"

After Four Eyes placed all of the drugs in a large bag, the group of seven started toward the door. At the door, Four Eyes stopped and asked the state trooper, "You're gonna let the gal put some clothes on, aren't you? Her daddy is a right important man, and he ain't gonna like her being arrested one bit, but he's gonna be *real* mad if she ain't got nothin' on."

The trooper turned to Lynette, "Where are your clothes? Get dressed."

"I don't want to get dressed," screamed Lynette, "I don't like clothes. I want to feel free, free, free! Don't you feel free without your clothes on?"

The officer saw Lynette's jeans on the floor. Her shirt was on a chair. He led her to the clothing, but Lynette refused to get dressed. The trooper took an afghan that was draped over the sofa and threw it over her. They headed for the county jail.

Later that evening, a waiter approached Frank's table and told him he had a phone call. Frank went into the bar. He picked up the phone and heard from the sheriff that Lynette was at the county jail being booked for "possession of cocaine with intent to distribute." The magistrate wasn't there yet, so he didn't know if bail would be set or not.

Frank returned to his table. Hilda asked who called. Frank told her that a little business matter had come up. He would to have to leave the club for a short time. He told her to continue entertaining their guests, not to make an issue of his absence, and to see that everyone had a good time. Frank headed over to another table where one of his guests, a local resident, the retired Chief Justice of the Supreme Court of South Carolina, Honorable Charles Bowen IV, was seated. He said, "Your Honor, may I have a word with you privately, please?"

The retired chief justice excused himself. He rose and went out into the hallway with Frank, who explained the situation. Justice Bowen, the fourth Charles Bowen in his family to be a judge, wielded a great deal of legal clout even though he no longer sat on the bench. He agreed to accompany Frank to the county jail.

A few years prior, Frank had been returning to Dorchester County from Hilton Head on a deserted back road late at night, when he had come upon a single car accident. A car was in the ditch on the side of the road. He stopped his car, got out and found an unconscious young lady reeking of alcohol at the wheel.

Frank immediately recognized her and knew she was not of drinking age. Rather than go to his car phone and request medical assistance, Frank, who had first-aid training, assessed the situation and realized that the young lady had suffered a bump on the head from hitting the steering wheel. She did not seem to have any other injuries. He took a bottle of Evian, which he always had with him when he drove any distance at all, and with his handkerchief, applied the water to her forehead and cheeks.

Within a few minutes, she regained consciousness and opened her eyes whereupon she began to ask questions. She was so drunk she didn't make much sense. Frank took her home.

On the way to her house, Frank called one of his factory employees who had a truck and told him to get her car out of the ditch. By the time Frank arrived home with the inebriated young lady, her father's car was safely off the highway and behind the house of Frank's faithful employee.

Chief Justice Bowen had been extremely grateful to Frank for finding his beloved Victoria, bringing her home, and hiding the car before anyone's prying eyes could spot it. No scandal ensued. No one found out the judge's under-age daughter had been drunk and wrecked his car. Justice Bowen owed Frank a favor. Frank was calling in his marker.

They went to the courthouse. The magistrate had arrived, and both Ned and Lynette had been locked up. Lynette was still partially in her afghan, since she still insisted on being "free, free, free!" which was a little difficult in the confinement of a jail cell. The other prisoners enjoyed watching Lynette and encouraged her freedom by suggesting she remove the afghan altogether. The magistrate had set Ned's bail at fifty thousand dollars and Lynette's at twenty-five thousand dollars. Frank was escorted by the bailiff to see Lynette while Justice Bowen went to have a talk with the magistrate. Within a short time, Lynette's bail was lifted, her cell unlocked, and she and Frank were on their way home.

Frank and Justice Bowen were back at the country club and the party within an hour after their departure. Hilda asked if everything was all right. Frank assured her that everything was fine.

Lynette did not return to school the next day. On Monday, she and Hilda went to Savannah and got photos taken. With Justice Bowen's help, a rush was put on their passports. On the following Friday, Lynette and Hilda left for a two-week trip to Europe. Frank had cleared the leave-of-absence with Lynette's school by claiming that the trip would be educational. After the tour, Lynette returned to school and graduated a month later.

The following October Ned went to trial. A circuit court judge sentenced him to twenty-five years in prison. Two weeks later, Lynette, a freshman at Savannah College of Art and Design, opened her invitation from the Magnolia Ball Committee and learned that she was to be presented to society in December. She quickly raced down the hall of her dormitory to her best friend Sherry's room. She read the invitation aloud. Then she read her latest letter from Ned, written from his cell in a maximum-security prison in Norfolk, Virginia.

18

Trudy and Bill Waltham

Bill got Trudy up to her bed and wondered what in the world could have upset her. She had drunk herself into a stupor, and Trudy was not ordinarily a big drinker. Bill expected she was having a late reaction to their financial problems. He hoped nothing else major had happened to their lives, which were rapidly falling apart.

At that moment, Bill remembered his earlier conversation with Quarrels, and he felt a little better. There was a chance to make big bucks there. Just this one deal, and Bill could take his money and reestablish himself financially in the community. He would then sever his dealings with Quarrels. Bill lay down beside Trudy and fell into a fitful sleep.

Early in the morning, Bill was awakened by Trudy's weeping. "What's the matter, honey?" he asked.

"Oh, the most horrible thing in the world has happened. I'm so sorry, Bill. We're going to have to move," answered Trudy.

"What are you talking about, having to move?"

"I'm going to have to move. I have to leave town. I'm going to go today," sobbed Trudy.

"Is this because of the mess I've made of the business? I've got good news, Trudy. I've gotten into the cellular telephone business with that fellow Quarrels. Everything's going to be okay. We'll be back in the money soon and we'll be able to move back to our house. It's going to be all right," purred Bill to the increasingly hysterical Trudy.

"No, nothing will ever be all right again. This doesn't have anything to do with our finances. This has to do with my life. My whole life is a lie, Bill."

"Trudy, I don't know what you're talking about. What do you mean your whole life is a lie?" he asked, confused.

Through her tears and with heaving sobs, Trudy told Bill her life story. She told him how Doug had tutored her with her grammar and social skills, about the lies she had fabricated about her family, and the truth about her brother Rudy. She told him how when he had been called to Bonita's house to fix the phone, Rudy told Bonita who she really was. She explained Bonita's phone calls to the members of the committee seeking to remove her, how Celestine had tried to help her, and about her letter to the committee asking for a leave-of-absence. Finally, she told Bill about the committee's vote to oust her from its membership.

When Trudy finished, Bill was in shock. He had first known Trudy as Doug's wife, and then had married her after both he and Trudy were widowed. Bill thought that everything he knew about Trudy was true. It took him several minutes to process what she told him, and after it had sunken in, Bill didn't have any idea what to do.

Trudy continued to sob, saying, "And now I know that Sandy won't be invited to make her debut. How will I ever explain this to her? I've allowed her to believe all of the lies about my life too. She will never understand why Doug wanted me to be someone I was not. What will we say to her when all of her friends are invited to make their debut and she isn't asked? How will I tell her that I am no longer a member of the committee? My god, Bill, what am I going to do?"

"I don't know, Trudy. I really don't know. Do you think you can talk to Bonita about this?" Bill asked.

"I know I can't. Celestine tried to talk to her at the committee meeting. She tried to keep Bonita from telling everyone the truth, but it didn't work. Blanche Givens kept insisting the committee members had a right to know what was going on, so Bonita told them everything. Celestine resigned from the committee because she was so upset about what happened. She's the only friend I have left in Dorchester County," wept Trudy.

"Then Celestine is the one you have to talk to."

"About what? What can she do? She's no longer on the committee."

"There has to be a way to get this all straightened out, Trudy. Give me some time. I'll figure out something."

Bill was trying to make Trudy feel better, but the fact was, he didn't have any idea how to straighten things out, or how to save the remnants of both of their reputations.

19

Bonita & Celestine

Bonita arose early the day after the committee meeting and placed a call to Celestine.

"I must talk to you, Celestine. Everyone on the committee is horrified that you have resigned. We all want you to reconsider. Do you have any time available today?" asked Bonita.

"I really don't see that we have anything to discuss, Bonita, but you are welcome to come over if you can come in the next few minutes. Anthony and I are getting ready to go riding."

"I'll be right there," answered Bonita.

Once Bonita and Celestine were seated in Celestine's enormous living room, Celestine said, "As I said, Bonita, I don't see that we have anything to discuss. I tried to get you to accept Trudy's request for a leave-of-absence and not make her stories about her past public knowledge, but you absolutely refused to do the decent thing. The woman is ruined in Dorchester County now. My only hope is that the committee will see fit to invite Sandy to make her debut. I don't feel the child should suffer because of what her mother did. What did Trudy's version of her past life do? Did it offend you? Did it offend anyone on the committee? She really didn't hurt anyone. I can understand why the other members may not want her to serve in a capacity where the debutantes are selected, since she certainly has less than an aristocratic background, but may I remind you of some of the escapades of girls that have been selected? I don't want to go into their private lives, but I'm sure you recall some of the embarrassing situations in which previous Magnolia Ball debutantes have found themselves.

"There are also members of our committee who don't always walk the straight-and-narrow. Again, I will not call any names, but I'm sure you are aware of some of the things that go on in some of the members' everyday affairs. We don't really know every background in detail. Not everyone who comes to live in Dorchester County comes from Spanish royalty, and has lived a life of luxury in the arms of an aristocratic family like you have," stated Celestine.

Bonita appeared to be deep in thought. She looked at Celestine, nodded and said, "What we really need to discuss, Celestine, is that you must rethink your resignation from the committee. Your great-grandfather began the Ball. Without you, we lose our direct link to the original Ball—your grandmother Celeste, the first Magnolia queen. You **must** reconsider," urged Bonita.

"Let me tell you about the first Ball, Bonita. My great-grandfather did not hold a debutante ball. My grandmother Celeste was the homeliest woman in six counties, and as she approached her eighteenth birthday, she was not married. My great-grandparents held that birthday ball to try to get her married off to someone. Now that's a scandal, isn't it?

"The fact that my great-grandparents only invited old maids or very young girls is the reason the Ball continued. Parents of those young girls watched as Celeste came down the staircase on her father's arm and witnessed eligible, young men vying for a dance with homely Celeste. Those parents continued the Ball in the hopes that they could marry off their less-than-perfect daughters.

"That is how the Ball started. We continue it with all the hoopla and homage paid to my great-grandparents and to my grandmother, as the original queen. Is that any less of a lie than what Trudy fabricated about her unfortunate life?"

"I never knew that your great-grandparents held the Ball to try to marry Celeste off," Bonita said.

"Well, that's why they had the Ball and it didn't work. Oh, a number of young men asked her to dance. She was the only one close to their ages, but none of them courted her and certainly did not marry her. Celeste wasn't married for another twelve years, and then to a much older man whose wife had died," answered Celestine.

"What's that, dear?" She turned to Anthony, perched next to her and dressed in a riding habit. "Not right now, Anthony. Mother is talking to Mrs. Roberts about the committee. And you know what, Anthony? You are very negligent of your manners today. You didn't speak to Mrs. Roberts when she entered. I think you owe her an apology, don't you?" Celestine chastised the doll.

In a squeaky voice, Celestine then said to Bonita, "I'm sorry, Mrs. Roberts. I was a very bad boy. My mother and I are getting ready to go riding, and I guess I'm just a little impatient today. Excuse me for my bad manners."

Bonita glanced at the doll and then turned back to Celestine. "As I was saying, regardless of how the Ball was started, it has become a tradition, and we need you on the committee, Celestine."

"Bonita, Anthony was speaking to you. Didn't you hear him?" asked Celestine.

"Celestine, this is a critical matter. I really don't feel like playing games with your doll today," Bonita responded, bristling.

Celestine rose and stood as if she were at attention. Her face was frozen. She stared at Bonita and informed her that Anthony was not a doll. He was her son. It was time for Bonita to leave. Celestine walked to the door and held it open.

Bonita began to apologize, but Celestine said, "Bonita, I have heard quite enough. I will now thank you to take you your leave."

As Bonita exited, Celestine, overcome with fury, slammed the door. Bonita stood looking at it. She wished she had spoken to the stupid doll. Her nerves were frayed. Bonita should have realized Celestine would get upset if she refused to talk to Anthony. Things were going from bad to worse.

20

Hunter's Game Plan

Within a few days after Trudy's confession to Bill, he became actively involved in Hunter Quarrels' business. He spent a great deal of time away from home each night, since Hunter met with most of his associates late in the evening.

One of the jobs Hunter assigned to Bill was to line up private yachts for transporting the product. Bill lost no time in setting up luncheon engagements and business dinners with his "good ol' boy" network. He met with many of his friends at various restaurants on Hunter's platinum American Express card. Bill learned quickly that many of his friends and former business associates were quite interested in the proposed deal and in making a fast buck.

He could be seen on any given night in one of Dorchester County's eateries with the likes of Chucky Saxon, father of Patricia; the husbands of committee members, Blanche Givens and Nancy Abrams; and committee member Dee Thomas' "husband" Chet. He also dined with Mary Beth Bracer's ex-husband; a town councilman of Montiac; a native attorney; a local doctor; and the owner of a wholesale supply house. Bill recruited Jordan Roget during one of his short visits to the Sweet Treat, for he no longer stayed in the back room for long, having no money with which to gamble.

He lined up his cronies, including Frank Karsh. They met with Hunter Quarrels in a business meeting rather than over a cocktail at one of their parties. More and more of Bill's associates began to attend evening meetings at Walthome. As the local cars approached the house, Four Eyes, the state boys, and the narcs from Savannah, who were alternating the stakeouts, took down license plate numbers and identified each person entering the house.

Continuing to monitor the phone at Walthome, the lawmen learned that Hunter was not in the cellular telephone business and did not intend to build a tower. Hunter Quarrels had selected Dorchester County and Walthome very carefully. He was a big-city boy and had underestimated the natives in believing they were neither bright nor observant.

Hunter was planning a colossal cocaine delivery to be made the night of December 28, 1991. Several private yachts owned by local citizens were to arrive at the mouth of the Savannah River that evening. The boats were to sail from Jeckyl Island to the river after offloading the cargo from a barge that would come up the intercoastal waterway from Florida with its nearly two billion dollars worth of contraband.

Hunter and the big boys in his organization planned to unload the coke onto the Quarrels' yacht, the *Diamond Jim*, on the river, where obviously there would be no "narcs" or "feds". The coke would then be brought into the creek, unloaded, and taken into Walthome. There the product would be cut, packaged, and transported to waiting cars. to be distributed to all points north from South Carolina to New York City.

Hunter's plan had been in the works for several months. The entire East Coast had been scanned and studied for the perfect location for the coke delivery. Dorchester County had been selected. The people visiting Walthome evenings with out-of-state license plates were a part of Hunter's arm of the Medellin Drug Cartel organization. Several had done time for drug trafficking, and they were aware that if caught, they would do time again. But each felt the money they stood to make from this deal was worth the risk. If they were caught, five or six years would not be too hard to take when there was close to thirty million dollars waiting on the outside once they were free. What they didn't know was that Hunter only planned to use one of them in this particular operation.

Dorchester County was not known to be a drug area. Heretofore, the river had not been policed for boats carrying drugs. Four Eyes and his boys were certainly not considered a threat.

Even when Lalique had questioned Hunter about the fifties and twenties in the briefcase and paying advance rent to Jimbo, Hunter had replied, "These people are stupid, Lalique. They don't know anything about what goes on in the real world. They're very isolated here. Don't worry about a thing. Just smile, take your exercises, make some acquaintances, and get us invited to some of the "in home" entertaining. You do that, and soon I'll find my man.

"We need an insider to introduce us to the big money here. It's been my experience, in little one-horse towns like this, the cops are there for one reason, and that's to protect the big boys in the area. We want to get some of those big boys involved, and when I find my man, he'll smooth the way to the head honchos. Then, if there should be a snag, those same big boys will bail us out, because the local posse won't be anxious to convict their own."

Each time Four Eyes monitored the phone lines and heard Hunter talking to someone in his organization about the stupidity of the people in Dorchester County, he slyly grinned. When he listened to Hunter joke about the ignorance of the local cops, he looked forward to the pleasure he would get the day he met Hunter Quarrels on his rented dock as he sailed the *Diamond Jim* into port with the huge drug cache aboard. Quarrels would see how much good it had done him to meet and deal with the honchos. Four Eyes planned to personally see that when Hunter Quarrels was convicted, the jailer threw away the key.

Hunter and Lalique continued socializing as more and more of what many considered the county's elite sold their moral turpitude for one big deal. They all figured this foray in the illegal drug trade was going to make them either wealthy or wealthier.

21

Darlene Entertains

Darlene was in a tizzy. Dr. and Mrs. Moreland were coming to visit for a week. That wouldn't have been so bad. They had visited Darlene and Joseph on several occasions, and although Darlene always suffered from nervous anxiety and heartburn the entire time her mother-in-law was in her home, she had learned to cope.

Why Darlene felt unsettled was that the Morelands were bringing another couple on their visit. They were traveling on their friends' yacht and were shortly planning to dock at Darlene's and Joseph's.

Mrs. Moreland had told Darlene for years about her best friend from college, Sissy, and her husband Portland Donnoghue, the newspaper-publishing magnate from California. In only three days, the four of them would sail into the river on the Donnoghue's one-hundred-seventy-five-foot yacht, complete with a staff of eight. Once they arrived, they would be staying at Darlene's and Joseph's house.

Darlene was a nervous wreck! She knew what to do, what to say, how to entertain, what to prepare and certainly didn't comment on lemon soup anymore. In fact, Darlene now owned twelve sterling silver finger bowls for her smaller dinner parties. But she had never entertained people of the Donnoghue's caliber.

Entertaining the tolerant Morelands was not really a big deal. Darlene had long ago learned how to ingratiate herself with the people of Dorchester County, so entertaining Joseph's parents was not horrific.

The Donnoghue's, however, were a different matter. They were extremely wealthy; Mr. Donnoghue was known all over the world, and had been entertained by royalty. So, to prepare for their arrival, Darlene prepared menus, hired caterers, planned cocktail parties, redecorated the guest bedroom and threw up about three times a day.

Celestine had also been a classmate of Deborah Moreland and of Sissy Donnoghue. Mrs. Moreland had specifically requested that, at some time during their visit, Darlene invite Celestine over for tea, a luncheon or dinner. Darlene decided to have a cocktail party the second night after their arrival. Her guest list would consist of many of the committee members and their husbands. Darlene had invited Celestine and Jamison to that function.

Two days hence, Darlene had a luncheon scheduled at the Crest for the three classmates. She planned to drive her mother-in-law and Sissy to Celestine's house, where she would meet Celestine and chauffeur them to the Crest and then gracefully excuse herself. She had arranged for the Crest limo to take Celestine back to her house and to return her houseguests to her home.

Darlene was proud of the itinerary she had arranged and had discussed it ad nauseum with Joseph. He assured her that he knew the Donnoghues; they were very nice people, and she did not have to go into apoplexy about their visit. Darlene knew Joseph was simply trying to make her feel better. He wasn't telling her the whole truth. Therefore, she continued to make her plans as if the Queen of England were preparing to make a personal call on her.

The two couples arrived, and the sight of the magnificent yacht nearly took Darlene's breath away. It was spectacular! Her mother-in-law had not exaggerated when she described it to Darlene.

Darlene and Joseph went down to the pier to meet their guests. For once, Joseph had been right. As soon as Darlene met the Donnoghues, she felt completely at ease. They were quite cordial and very down-to-earth.

Sissy Donnoqhue kept apologizing to Darlene and Joseph, "Now, we don't want to put either of you to any trouble. I've told Joe and Deborah that we can stay right here on the boat. We don't want to make ourselves unwelcome. A week is a long time to put up with houseguests you don't know. I know how much you want your folks here, they're family, but we don't wish to impose. You know the old saying about fish and guests? After three days, both of them start to smell. Now, we are going to stay on the boat and we can get together for lunch or cocktails or something," said Sissy with a smile.

Darlene was horrified to hear this after all of her preparations. The menus she had planned lay in wait, caterers were scheduled and she had paid a decorator a small fortune to redo the guest room. She would not hear of the Donnoghues staying on the yacht. "Absolutely not, Mrs. Donnoghue."

"Call me Sissy. 'Mrs. Donnoghue' makes me feel so old."

"Absolutely not, Sissy. Why, Joseph and I have been looking forward to your visit, and we want you to stay with us in our home. Your yacht is lovely, and I know how comfortable it must be, but we really want you to stay with us. It won't be any trouble at all. I haven't done anything out of the ordinary. You're going to have to take potluck and be treated as a member of the family. I'm sure we don't do things here in Dorchester County like you do on the West Coast, but we have a reputation for hospitality, and we'd be offended if you didn't stay with us," said Darlene. Darlene hoped the old saying about getting a black spot on one's tongue when a lie was told wasn't true, since she had told Sissy several in rapid succession. The fact of the matter was she plainly could not deal with all of her plans being upset.

Sissy magnanimously consented to her and Portland staying in Darlene's and Joseph's "humble" home.

Portland gave Joseph and Darlene a tour of the yacht. Darlene was speechless. Renoirs and Picassos hung on the silk moiré-covered walls of the staterooms. The dining room had a cherry table, inlaid with fourteen-carat gold, that seated sixteen people. A spiral staircase led from the salon to the lower deck, where Berber carpet covered the hallways leading to the staterooms. The galley was equipped with a sub-zero freezer, two wall ovens, two microwaves, a dishwasher, a three-compartment sink, a separate convection oven, a built-in Ronson appliance center and a marble floor. The head in the master suite had gold faucets, a bidet, a sunken tub and shower, a sauna and a Jacuzzi. Darlene couldn't believe the accouterments on the Donnoghue's yacht, the "Shangri-La." It was the most fantastic thing she had ever seen.

After the tour, two of the yacht's stewards transported the luggage to the Moreland's home, and Darlene escorted the Donnoghues to the newly decorated bedroom. Three black women from the catering company stood in readiness in the kitchen. Darlene hastily snapped orders for hors d'oeuvres to be served immediately. She hurried to her Florida room to make sure that the bartender was ready to serve any concoction her guests might desire.

Dr. and Mrs. Moreland were astounded by the elaborate preparations Darlene had made and the wait staff she had engaged. The Donnoghues, on the other hand, did not know that Joseph's house was not typically maintained in this manner, so they took everything in stride.

The following evening, twenty couples attended Darlene's cocktail party. They were all scions of Dorchester society, people Darlene hoped would impress her special guests. Several members of the committee attended, including Celestine and Bonita. Celestine was excited to see her college friends again, although she had seen Deborah Moreland a few times on her prior visits. It had been years, however, since Celestine had visited with Sissy.

Bonita was her usual, regal self and spent several minutes talking with Portland about California. She told him how she had lived in Los Angeles for several years while nursing her sick husband. She recounted how, early in her life, when she had recently arrived from Spain, she had tested for Hammond Productions and had made a few movies. Portland gave all of the appropriate responses. He was charming to Bonita as he was to all of the invitees.

The party was a smashing success, and everything went off without a hitch. As the last guests were leaving, Darlene reminded Celestine of the luncheon at the Crest with Sissy and her mother-in-law the following day.

Celestine gushed, "I can hardly wait. It's been so wonderful seeing my two best friends from college again. We had fantastic times together, and we have such beautiful memories. I'm really looking forward to the luncheon, Darlene, and I think you are just lovely to have thought of it. Your party was perfect, and you are too."

Darlene fell into bed that night exhausted but ecstatic. Celestine and Bonita were the two most important and socially prominent women in Dorchester County, and both had been at her party and had showered her with compliments. The Donnoghues had seemed quite impressed, and her mother-in-law seemed to be seeing her in a new light. Even though Darlene had been on the Magnolia Ball Committee for several years and had certainly been socially accepted, she felt her cocktail party had sealed her position in Dorchester society firmly in place.

She had entertained the closest people to royalty in America, and everything had been perfect. "You've come a long way, baby," Darlene said to herself, "From the ranch in Oklahoma and one semester of college at Podunk University to socializing with and entertaining the Donnoghues of California."

Meanwhile, as Portland and Sissy were getting ready to retire, Portland said to Sissy, "Did you meet Bonita Roberts, dear?"

"Yes, I did. She's the chairperson of the Magnolia Ball Committee, the one that selects the young ladies for the little debutante ball they have here. I think that's really cute, don't you, Portland, a debutante ball here in Dorchester County? According to Celestine, it's the longest-running ball in the South. Bonita chairs the committee. I take it from talking to Celestine that Bonita is, socially, a very important lady. Of course, Celestine's great-grandparents were the ones who started the Ball. When Celestine debuted, she invited me to attend, but that was when Mother and Father decided I had to go to Europe on the grand tour for the holidays."

"Did Bonita look or sound familiar to you?"

"No, did she to you, Portland?"

"I'm not sure. There's something about her though. She said she came to this country from Spain and made some movies for Hammond. She married and lived in LA for some years, but wasn't in the social scene because she had to nurse her sick husband. She didn't say what his name was, but after she was widowed, she married Joshua Roberts. I remember when she married Roberts; we ran an article about his marriage in some of the papers. You remember, he divorced his wife and remarried the next day or so?"

"Yes, I remember something about that. Was it Bonita he married?"

"Apparently so, but that's not what's puzzling me. There's just something about Bonita—her name, her voice or something—that makes me think I've met her somewhere before," responded Portland.

"I'm sure it will come to you. Are you ready for me to rub your neck?"

"Do you mind? It really hurts tonight, Sissy."

"I wouldn't have offered if I minded, silly," answered Sissy as she began to massage his neck, which had two, displaced vertebrae from a skiing accident Portland had suffered while on vacation in the Swiss Alps.

Two days later, Darlene loaded her guests into her car, stopped at Beechland for Celestine and drove to the Crest. As soon as the major domo seated the college friends, Darlene announced that when they were ready to leave, the Crest limousine would take them home.

Sissy insisted Darlene stay, but she said, "No, I really think it would be fun for the three of you to reminisce. I planned all along for the luncheon to include just you three. Now, you stay as long as you like. I've taken the liberty of ordering for you. C'iao."

She exited through the massive oak doors. Almost immediately, the sommelier arrived with a bottle of 1964 Dom Perignon. He opened it with a flourish and poured it into chilled flutes.

"Honestly, Deborah, you are certainly lucky. That Joseph is such a smart boy to have found Darlene. What a treasure! I know you must just love her to death," Sissy said as she raised her glass in a toast to her old college chums.

Deborah agreed with Sissy. Darlene really was being completely charming and very thoughtful. Deborah had never disliked Darlene; she simply had a difficult time forgetting her embarrassment when, in front of all of the elite of Bristol, Darlene had committed the faux pas about the "lemon soup." She thanked God daily that Sissy and Portland had been unable to attend the wedding. They had been on a trip to Monaco as the guests of Prince Rainier and Princess Grace.

Their luncheon consisted of cold, poached salmon, sautéed zucchini and fruit compote. The three old friends talked about old times. They caught up on their current lives, and laughed and giggled like they were teenagers.

At one point Sissy said to Celestine, "Deborah tells me that you're on the Magnolia Ball Committee. That's only fitting since your family started it. I remember when you made your debut and invited me to attend the Ball and your party, but I had to go to Europe with my parents."

"I'm not on the committee anymore," sighed Celestine.

"Why ever not?" asked Deborah.

"Oh, it's a long story, one that I certainly don't want to bore the two of you with, but I simply felt that I had to resign. I'm still the same idealist I was when we went to school together, I guess."

"What happened, Celestine?" pressed Sissy. "Your family originated the Ball. What could have made you decide to resign? You're not sick, are you?" Sissy insisted.

"No, of course not. A friend of mine had fabricated a little bit about her background, and she was on the committee at Bonita's invitation.

You remember Bonita, don't you? You met her at the cocktail party a few nights ago?"

Both ladies nodded.

"Well, my friend had fabricated some of her background, as I said, and Bonita found out about it. She called the committee members and had my friend thrown off the committee. When she phoned me prior to the meeting, I told her that I would not vote to remove my friend. I called my friend and told her what was going on. Together we came up with a plan. She wrote a letter to the committee requesting a leave-of-absence. She never intended to return as a committee member, because she knew Bonita would never allow it. Since I am, or was, the corresponding secretary of the committee, we thought if she sought a leave-of-absence and I read her letter at the committee meeting we could keep everyone from knowing that she had fabricated her background.

"Bonita wanted to let everyone know what my friend had done, but I think Bonita may have let it go if another committee member hadn't persisted in asking if there weren't more to the story. Consequently, Bonita told everyone at the meeting what my friend had done. When there was a motion to eject my friend from the committee, I just couldn't take it; I resigned.

"I cannot be associated with petty people like that. What my friend did was wrong, but it didn't cause anyone on the committee any harm. As I said, 'I'm sure we all have something in our closets that we would rather not have everyone know about.' The other thing that is so terrible is that my friend's daughter's name was placed in nomination. My friend was afraid her sins would be visited on her daughter. She is concerned that this scandal may keep her daughter from receiving an invitation. The girl is lovely—everything that a debutante should be—and knows absolutely nothing about what her mother did. She certainly should not be held responsible for her mother's actions. At any rate, my friend was expelled from the committee, and I resigned. The worst part of the whole thing is that I know her daughter will not, in fact, be invited to make her debut. The selection committee met and decided not to include her in the girls to be presented," Celestine explained.

"Who's on the selection committee, Celestine? Surely you are a part of that. You could demand she be invited." prodded Sissy.

"No, I can't. Bonita is the only one who knows who makes the selections. It's a secret even within the committee. Bonita asked me twice to serve on the selection committee, but I refused both times. I didn't want to sit with two or three other people whom I considered friends and hear them destroy a young lady's reputation with their tongues. Enough malicious gossip is spread by the entire committee when the nominations are made. I don't want to be exposed to all of that hearsay. If I don't hear it, then I don't have to deal with it. I can continue to feel the way I do about a person without being prejudiced by someone else and what they have heard or made up," said Celestine.

Sissy said, "There must be some way you can help your friend's daughter if you feel so strongly about it."

"I thought there was at first. I know that Bonita wants me to serve on the committee. It's true, my family did start the Ball. The namesake magnolia tree is in my front yard. I always hold the breakfast after the Ball at Beechland, and the queen's picture is taken in front of the tree for the *Montiac Minutes.*

"Bonita called me the day after I resigned to discuss my resignation. What I had planned to do was to blackmail her. Aren't I horrid? I had hoped that I could make a deal with her. I thought if she would convince the selection committee to allow my friend's daughter to make her debut, then I would come back on the committee."

"Didn't Bonita agree to that?" asked Deborah.

"I never suggested it to her," sighed Celestine.

"Why not?" asked Sissy.

"Because I was getting ready to go riding when she called and asked to come over to have a talk. Anthony was all dressed to go with me and was very impatient. Bonita arrived and didn't bother to speak to him.

She simply ignored him as if he weren't in the room. When Anthony politely interrupted to ask when our discussion was going to be over so we could go riding, I told him that he had been rude to interrupt, although he hadn't been at all. Anthony apologized to Bonita for interrupting, and Bonita again disregarded him. When I told Bonita that she had not responded to Anthony, she made an offensive statement about him. I was incensed and showed her to the door, and I have not spoken to her since," Celestine explained in a slightly raised voice.

"Who is Anthony?" asked Sissy.

"Why, Anthony is my son, Sissy," Celestine answered.

Sissy looked at Celestine rather strangely for a moment, as all three of the women were in their late sixties, and said, "Oh, then you adopted Anthony?"

"No, I didn't adopt Anthony. He's my son, Sissy."

"I'm really surprised. I had no idea that you had a son," commented Sissy.

"Well, we've finished lunch. Let's go to the front desk and call for the limousine and hurry to Beechland. You can meet Anthony," Celestine said.

"Yes, let's," said Sissy as she rose from the table.

Deborah said nothing. Darlene had already told her about Celestine's doll, but Deborah had not realized Celestine actually believed he was real. Deborah was quite concerned by Celestine's delusion.

Sissy spotted the doll as soon as they entered Celestine's house. He was wearing madras Bermudas, a red T-shirt, and tiny tasseled Weejuns. Celestine introduced them to Anthony and then talked in the high, squeaky voice she used for him. Deborah felt as if she had stepped into the twilight zone.

Sissy, however, thought it was a gas! She was delighted with Celestine's imagination. She wanted to see Anthony's wardrobe and she asked Anthony questions and regaled him with stories about his mother. Celestine was thrilled with Sissy's reaction, although all of her friends had always been nice to Anthony with the exception of Bonita.

As Sissy and Deborah settled into the back seat of the limousine to return to Darlene's, Deborah said, "I really think Celestine has lost it. She seemed so normal until she started talking about Anthony. She really believes that doll is her son."

"Oh, Deborah, I think it's cute. It's completely harmless, and of course Celestine knows Anthony is really a doll. She's merely pretending. She wanted a child for a long time. She has a firm grasp on reality. She's making believe. I noticed you didn't talk to Anthony very much," chided Sissy.

"Sissy Donnoghue, you're as wacky as she is,"
sighed Deborah.

"She's not wacky. She's coping with a situation that she can't accept—the fact that after years of trying to get pregnant and finally succeeding, her baby died at birth. I think it's perfectly harmless. Besides, I thought Anthony was cute," Sissy said with a wink.

"I don't know about you, Sissy, but most of all, I don't know about Celestine," said Deborah."

"Oh Deborah, loosen up! If I remember, you and I shared quite a few fantasies in our younger days, and I don't know about you, but I still fantasize every now and then. What's the harm?" asked Sissy.

"Fantasizing is one thing, Sissy. Losing touch with reality and believing that a stuffed doll is your son is quite another," Deborah insisted.

"Are you telling me that when Joseph Moreland, Sr. lowers himself over you, and you're pretending that Kevin Costner or Mel Gibson is making love to you, that you don't want to believe it's one of those handsome studs and not old Joseph?" teased Sissy.

Deborah reacted as if she had been slapped, "Why, that's not the same thing at all, you horrible woman!"

"It is, too!" said Sissy as she laughed and put her arm around her best friend's shoulder.

22

Sandy Hibbert

Sandy Hibbert did not resemble her mother Trudy in the least. She was a slender, willowy blonde with blue eyes and a lovely disposition. An excellent student, she won the DAR Essay Award, and was a National Honor Society student, a National Merit Scholar, president of her senior class and secretary of the student government at Dorchester High School. Listed in "Who's Who Among American High School Students," she had been accepted at the distinguished Sewanee, the University of the South, to which she had been awarded a full scholarship.

Sandy, unlike Trudy, was not smitten with Bill Waltham's money and, therefore, was not devastated when it was lost. She was popular with both sexes and dated a lot of nice boys from excellent homes and backgrounds. Sandy saw nothing wrong with a peck on the cheek or a little kiss with closed lips, but she did not neck, pet, or make out.

Sandy volunteered as a candy striper two afternoons a week at the local hospital. A Sunday school teacher at the old, historic Episcopal Church, she sang high soprano in the choir. She was a soloist with the Glee Club at school and a member of the Pep Squad. Serving as a library assistant and scorekeeper for the girls' basketball team took up any spare time she had left.

Sandy had attended the Magnolia Ball in her junior and senior years of high school as a page to help with the girls' presentations. She ran errands for committee members, and collected votes when the men cast their ballots for the selection of the queen. She generally served as a gofer and had enjoyed every minute of it as she looked forward to making her debut. The time was approaching when she would receive her invitation and she had already planned on whom she would invite to be her escort.

Two weeks after her freshman year at Sewanee began, Sandy met a delightful and handsome young man, Spence, from Mississippi. The two of them had hit it off immediately and had been dating since. Sandy had already hinted about all of the debutante doings during Christmas vacation, and Spence had shown interest, having had two sisters who'd made their debuts in Biloxi.

Sandy knew her mother and stepfather were having financial problems. However, Sandy had her mother's bent for sewing and had already selected the dress she planned to wear. She had a job waitressing in the dining hall at school to supplement her scholarship allowance, and she'd squirreled away two paychecks for her dress. By the time she began to make it, she would have sufficient funds to buy the beautiful, silk fabric. Since she already had an extensive wardrobe, she felt she would not need additional clothes for the other parties and activities during the debutante season.

The one thing Sandy didn't understand was why her mother had not attended any committee meetings since mid-summer. Whenever Sandy mentioned the committee or her debut, Trudy became quiet or began to cry. When Sandy asked her what was wrong, Trudy never wanted to discuss it. She guessed that Trudy must be going through "the change."

However, she was greatly concerned about her mother. Sandy hoped Trudy would get over whatever was troubling her and celebrate her selection with her. Trudy loved serving on the committee and everything that went with the Magnolia Ball. She had often told Sandy about her own debut in Louisville, Kentucky.

Sandy's older friends who had debuted had all received their invitations the second week in October. As she crossed off the days in

October, Sandy became more and more excited waiting for the heavy, off-white envelope. When it had not arrived by the end of October, she was not only puzzled, but she was also extremely disappointed. Obviously, there had been an oversight.

Thus far, a recovering drug addict, who had almost succumbed to syphilis, and a "come-here" whose father ran an illegal gambling joint had received invitations. A young lady who had screwed the high school band director for two years and had an illegal abortion, and a coke-snorting "come-here" nymphomaniac with a boyfriend doing twenty-five years in a maximum-security prison were to be presented to the social elite of Dorchester County. Sandy Hibbert, with a reputation and a soul as clean as an unused piece of fine, white stationery, however, had been excluded. Sandy was not to be presented at the Magnolia Ball. The girl was devastated and didn't understand why she was being shunned.

Sandy called her mother. She told her she had not received an invitation. Trudy tried to console her and said the Ball was not important. Sandy had accomplished so many things, and in a few years, this would mean nothing.

Sandy was even more confused after talking to her mother. She knew how Trudy really felt about the Ball. Something was very wrong, and somehow she knew that it had to be her fault. She, for reasons known only to the committee, had somehow shamed her family. Everyone she knew had been invited, and she had not. This was something she had planned on since she was eleven years old, something Trudy had always told her to expect, and now she had not been asked.

Shortly after Sandy hung up, Spence called. He asked her when the various deb functions were to take place, because he was getting ready to call his family in Mississippi, and he wanted to inform his parents when he would be in South Carolina. When would he escort Sandy to the parties and dinners? Sandy told Spence she wasn't going to make her debut. She was sorry she had asked him before the invitations were out. She hadn't been invited.

Spence couldn't believe it. Almost all she had talked about for the first month they had dated was the Magnolia Ball, and now she was telling him that she hadn't been invited.

He asked her why, and Sandy responded, "I don't know, Spence, but I must have done something terrible. I have to go now. It was really nice knowing you. Good-bye."

She walked down the hall and into her room. She didn't turn back to answer the ringing phone. She didn't have anything more to say to Spence. Both of her roommates were in class and wouldn't be back for several hours. She went into her closet and got six silk scarves, which she tied together with double knots. She stood up on the built-in bookcase, threw the scarves over a water pipe in the ceiling, and tied the end of the "rope" with a slipknot. Sandy got the chair from her desk, placed it under the scarves, fitted the slipknot around her neck and kicked the chair out from under her. In less than thirty seconds, she no longer cared about the Magnolia Ball. She was dead.

23

Celestine to the Rescue

Celestine visited Trudy Waltham as often as she could, but nothing she could do or say helped. Trudy was beside herself. She knew Bonita would see to it Sandy was not invited. Finally, because she was such a good person, and because she was so very worried about her friend Trudy, Celestine called on Trudy and told her what she was going to do. She would go to Bonita and promise to return to the committee if Bonita would see that Sandy was invited to make her debut.

"You would do that for me, Celestine?" asked Trudy.

"Yes, I will. I really don't want to serve with those women anymore, and particularly with Bonita, but I can't bear to stand by and watch you destroy yourself like this. I'm going to talk to Bonita tonight."

"But the invitations went out two weeks ago. How will you convince her to ask Sandy now?" wept Trudy.

"She'll invite her. She really wants me on that committee. She thinks I give it credibility, a link to the past and all that. And, of course, she wants me to have the traditional breakfast, and she wants the tree in the pictures for the newspaper. She'll have to think of some reason to explain to Sandy why her invitation is late. Has Sandy mentioned it?"

"I just got off the phone with her about fifteen minutes ago. She's really upset. I tried to make her feel better, but I know she wasn't convinced. She knows how much the committee and the Ball mean to me.

The poor child probably thinks it's something she's done. I haven't had the courage to confess to her about my past yet."

"And you shouldn't. Why does Sandy need to know? She's such a lovely girl. She shouldn't be penalized for something Bonita thinks is so horrible. What you did hurt no one," crooned Celestine. "Now, I'm going to Bonita's right now and I'll call you shortly. Then you can call Sandy. Her invitation will be mailed tomorrow. Tell her the zip code was left off, and it was returned or something. You can think of something to tell her."

"Oh, yes. Thank you, Celestine. How will I ever be able to repay you?" Trudy said.

"Put this all behind you. Hold your head up high. Start thinking about Sandy's debut. I want to give a party for her. We'll have to start planning it first thing tomorrow. Now, I'm going. I'll call you shortly." Celestine started for the door.

"I'll be waiting. Thank you so much."

Celestine drove from the carriage house to Creekside Farm. She didn't call Bonita. She wanted to use the element of surprise.

Hannah came to open the door when Celestine rang the bell. Bonita entered the parlor, and Celestine put her offer on the table. Bonita had no choice but to accept. Celestine asked to use the phone. She called Trudy. After thanking her profusely, Trudy placed a call to Sandy.

Sandy's roommates were returning from class. As they walked down the hall, the phone rang.

"Hello. Oh, hi Mrs. Waltham. Let me see if she's in. I'm on my way back from class and haven't gone into my room yet. Hold on. I'll go see."

The girl put the phone on the shelf, and the two girls walked to their room. As Betty went through the door, she opened her mouth to call to Sandy, but all that came out was a high-pitched scream. Trudy heard the commotion over the phone lines and thought how much fun it must be to live in a dorm at a good school, how happy Sandy must be there, and how elated she was going to be after Trudy told her the fantastic news.

Trudy held for what seemed like hours. She couldn't understand the delay. If Sandy weren't there, why didn't Betty come back to the phone? After waiting for seven or eight minutes someone came on the line, but it wasn't Sandy or Betty. It was the head resident of Sandy's dorm. She told Trudy there had been a horrible accident. Trudy and her husband needed to come right away.

Trudy and Bill Waltham went to the University of the South. When they were told what had happened, they went into a state of shock. Bill made arrangements to have Sandy's body sent to Montiac. Trudy was robot like. She ate, talked, drank coffee, smoked cigarettes, and carried on some semblance of conversation, but she really didn't know where she was, what she was doing, or what was happening around her. Her brain had ceased to function except on automatic. The loss of her only child was too harrowing and devastating to comprehend.

The Walthams returned to the carriage house. Friends and neighbors arrived almost immediately with food, gifts, and condolences. The phone rang incessantly. Trudy wrote down what everyone brought and thanked them for their kindness and generosity. She went to the funeral home with Bill and selected a beautiful, mauve casket with a pale pink, satin interior. She told Bill pink had been Sandy's favorite color. She went into Sandy's room and selected her burial clothes. She told the hairdresser how her child's hair was to be styled. She ordered the casket spray. She called the pallbearers and the retired minister who had performed her wedding ceremony to Sandy's father Doug to officiate at the service.

Trudy placed Sandy's National Honor Society hood across her breast. She went to the funeral home for the viewing and received the guests. She stood for hours and gazed at her beautiful daughter in the box, the pink lights focused on her. None of this was real. It was not happening. Trudy was unable to deal with any of it. It was as if she were watching it happen to someone else.

Bill tried to get through to her, as did Celestine, but nothing penetrated. Trudy went to the funeral and graveside. She didn't cry. She stared into space. She allowed herself to be hugged when the service was over. She returned to the carriage house and set out food and drinks for people who came after the service to pay their respects.

Celestine manned the door for those who came to the reception following Sandy's funeral. She was flabbergasted when she saw Alphonso step out of the Rolls Royce and help Bonita from the car. Bonita started up the walk. Celestine went outside and told her she shouldn't come in, but Bonita said she certainly couldn't understand why and crossed the threshold.

Trudy entered the living room as Bonita came through the front door. Maybe Bonita was just what Trudy needed, for when Trudy saw her, she went into a rage. She ran toward Bonita and began pummeling her chest screaming, "You killed my child! Just as surely as if you tied the rope around her neck, you killed her!" Trudy almost knocked Bonita over.

Bill ran to Trudy and grabbed her. He carried her off to the back of the house. Celestine called to Alphonso, who escorted Bonita out. Bonita didn't say a word; she was speechless.

Celestine walked them back to the car, where Bonita said, "What in the world is wrong with her? Why is she accusing me of killing her daughter?"

"Bonita, Sandy called Trudy the afternoon I came to talk to you about coming back on the committee. She told her mother she hadn't been invited. Sandy was planning on her debut for years. It was important to her. Trudy never confessed to Sandy what she'd done, or that she was no longer on the committee. I'm sure Sandy thought she was somehow responsible for not receiving an invitation. She was unable to live with the shame she thought she was causing her family."

"But she was going to get her invitation. I told you she would receive an invitation after you agreed to go back on the committee. Trudy knows that," sniffed Bonita.

"Bonita, Sandy knew when the invitations went out. All of her friends had already gotten theirs. Sandy did what she did because she wasn't invited," said Celestine.

"I see," murmured Bonita.

24

Ann Amelia

Ann Amelia was a brunette with naturally curly hair, blue eyes, and a few freckles across her nose. Her daddy, pronounced "deddy" in the South, was an attorney and a native of Dorchester County. Ann Amelia was a popular girl, but she always dated boys her own age or younger; she would have nothing to do with those who were older. When she dated, she preferred not to dance too closely and she did not like to have her hand held nor did she like to be hugged.

She seemed a normal girl in all other respects; however, she often awoke at night crying and sometimes screaming. Her mother had no idea when these night traumas were going to end. She had taken her to doctors up and down the East Coast, but no one could figure out what was causing the problem. One of the doctors suggested taking her to a psychiatrist, but when Mona had told Jason, her husband, he threw a fit. No daughter of his was going to a head shrinker! There was nothing wrong with her. Absolutely not!

It wouldn't have mattered if she had been taken to a psychiatrist. He or she couldn't have been able to find out what was causing the problem either, because she would never tell anyone. Ann Amelia was too humiliated and ashamed. After all, it was all her fault. Her father had told her so.

Ann Amelia's problem began when she was four years old. Her mother had gone out to play bridge with her lady friends. That evening, Jason gave Ann Amelia her bath, helped her into her "jammies" and put her to bed. He read her a story, tucked her in and bent to kiss her good night, when Ann Amelia said she had a stomachache.

"Mommy rubs my tummy when it hurts," she said to her "deddy."

"Oh, she does, does she? Well, then I guess I'll have to rub your tummy this time, cuz Mommy isn't at home."

"Okay," responded Ann Amelia as she threw off the covers.

Jason placed his large hand on her stomach and rubbed for a few minutes. "There, does it feel better now?" he asked.

"A little, but it still hurts."

"Why don't you pull up your pajama top and let me rub your skin. Maybe then you'll feel better," Jason said.

Ann Amelia pulled up her top and Jason rubbed her for a long time. All the while he told her how pretty she was, how much he loved her, and how "deddies" and their daughters had special feelings for each other. Jason ended up removing all of her clothes. He rubbed her all over. It felt good. Ann Amelia loved her "deddy."

From that night on, Jason put Ann Amelia to bed more often, and the rubs became more and more intimate. Sometimes Jason's "rubs" hurt Ann Amelia, but she never said so. She loved having her "deddy" all to herself.

As she got older, Jason's rubs became bolder, and by the time she was seven, her father was having intercourse with her. Ann Amelia didn't like deddy's "rubs" anymore, but she didn't want to hurt his feelings nor did she want her mother to know about their special times together, so she kept her mouth shut. She no longer wanted her father to come into her room, but he did more and more often. Ann Amelia didn't know of a way to make him stop.

When she was eleven and began sex education classes, she realized that what her deddy and she were doing or what her deddy was doing to her was not normal. It was called incest, and it was something horrible and disgusting. She tried to talk to her father one night when he came into her room, but he smelled of alcohol, and Ann Amelia knew she would be wasting her breath.

She dreaded going to bed. If her mother planned to leave the house at night, Ann Amelia feigned illnesses. Jason, however, always assured Mona he could handle everything. Even when Ann Amelia would tell Jason she had loads of homework to do, he insisted on their "special times."

At thirteen, she screamed at her father one night that what they were doing was wrong, that none of her friends' fathers had "special times," and that she didn't want them any longer. Jason became enraged and told her that none of her friends' fathers loved them like he loved her and that she had a filthy mind. What they were doing was not bad or dirty. He was her father, the man who protected and loved and provided for her. She was ungrateful and was not acting like his beautiful Ann Amelia.

There was no one she could talk to, certainly not her mother, any of her teachers, nor the old minister at the Episcopal Church. She tried to talk to her best friend. Speaking in the third person, she said she had read about it in a book. The friend was repulsed and told her she shouldn't be reading filthy books like that. Only low-class drunks did that to their own children. No one they knew had things like that happen to them.

At school, Ann Amelia's history teacher called on her in class, "Ann Amelia, I see where your father is representing the parents in the child-abuse case against the daycare center in Savannah."

"He is?" asked Ann Amelia, "I'm sorry, Mr. Smathers, my father doesn't discuss his cases with me."

"Of course not, but I read in the paper that your father was representing the parents, and I can only say that they are lucky to have such a fine gentleman on their side. What a horrid experience for those children. I'm glad your father is their attorney. No punishment is bad enough for the teachers who harmed those kids."

"I'll tell my father what you said," responded Ann Amelia.

She couldn't believe it. Her father was representing the parents against teachers accused of child abuse and sexual molestation.

That night at dinner, Ann Amelia said to her father, "Mr. Smathers said you were representing the parents in the child abuse case in Savannah. Are you?"

"Yes, I am."

"What did the teachers do to the children?" asked Ann Amelia.

"It's not something to be discussed at the dinner table, Ann Amelia."

"Why?"

Mona interrupted, "Because those awful teachers sexually took advantage of those young children. They did ghastly things to them. We are not going to talk about such deviant behavior during dinner."

"Why is it deviant behavior?" asked Ann Amelia.

"Ann Amelia, how can you ask such a question?" asked Mona. "Do you think it's all right for adults to have sexual relations with children?"

"No I don't. Do you, Deddy?"

"Of course not," said Jason.

"And that's why you're representing the parents of the children who were sexually abused, right?" asked Ann Amelia.

"Yes," responded Jason stonily.

"That's enough about this subject, Ann Amelia," Mona interjected, "Of course your father doesn't think it's all right for adults to have sex with children. Why all this sudden interest in adults having sex with children?"

"It's something we've never discussed. I wanted to know how Deddy felt about it, that's all."

Two nights later, when Jason came into Ann Amelia's room, she was sitting on her bed fully dressed.

"Aren't you a little late getting ready for bed, Ann Amelia?" asked Jason.

"Deddy, we have to talk. Why are you doing this to me? You said at the dinner table that it wasn't right. You're defending children who are just like me, who have been abused sexually by adults."

"It's not the same thing, Ann Amelia. I'm not abusing you. I love you. I've never hurt you, have I?" asked Jason.

"Yes, you have. I've told you. I don't want to have our special times anymore, Deddy. Please leave me alone. Please don't make me do it anymore. I can't do it anymore. I feel like I'm losing my mind. I love you, but I don't want you to do those things to me anymore," sobbed Ann Amelia.

"Now, now," said Jason. He sat on the bed next to her and began to massage her back. She jumped up.

"Don't touch me. Please, Deddy. I'm begging you. If you really love me, please stop this. I really can't take it anymore. I'm going to have to talk to someone if you don't stop."

Jason stood and looked down at his daughter. He was no longer her lover, but a strict martinet. "You will talk to no one about what we do. I forbid it. If you want any privileges at all, if you want any clothes at all, if you want to go out of this house, if you want me to love you, you'll forget about talking to anyone. Do I make myself clear?"

"Yes sir."

"Perhaps we will dispense with our special time tonight. You're very tired, I can tell. You're not acting like yourself," said Jason. He left the room.

Despite her threats, Ann Amelia's humiliation and shame continued. She was morose and continued to awaken in the night crying and screaming. In fact, her affliction became so acute that she no longer asked to go to slumber parties, to spend the night with friends, or to have anyone over. It was too embarrassing. She wanted to graduate and go to college so she could get away from deddy.

Jason won the case against the cruel teachers who had sexually abused the children at the daycare center. His picture was on the front page of the *Montiac Minutes*. Overnight, he was a local hero. Everyone was traumatized by the details of the case. Certainly, no one in Dorchester County did anything awful like that to children. Jason was asked to speak at church groups, at the Rotary Club and even at Ann Amelia's school.

Two weeks after he won his case, Ann Amelia graduated from the Dorchester County High School. She entered summer school at the University of South Carolina three weeks later after convincing Mona to let her go early so she would be adjusted when the regular semester began.

The following October, when Ann Amelia opened the white envelope and read the invitation to make her debut, her heart almost stopped. She'd have to spend time with deddy. How was she ever going to get out of this? She didn't want to be presented to society on her father's arm. He had introduced her to adulthood a long, long time ago.

25

Suzy

Suzy, Adele's daughter and General Dressler's step-daughter, was blessed with the same physical attributes of both her mother, "the former Miss Louisiana," and her handsome pilot father, Rod Callaway. Suzy was the spitting image of Grace Kelly. She was ten when her mother and the general had moved her and her brothers to Dorchester County. Suzy had loved living on the water and especially enjoyed the fresh air and sunshine enveloping the huge old house with its twenty-two rooms.

Suzy attended the local middle school and matured very quickly; she had quite a figure by the time she was in seventh grade. A boy, from a not-too-special family who lived down the road, thought Suzy was the hottest thing he had ever seen. Not that he had seen much in the flesh, but he had spent a great deal of time sneaking peeks at his older brother's girlie books. Suzy was built like those girls.

Mat was fifteen. He was definitely not a brain since he had to repeat fifth, sixth, and now seventh grade. However, he was a good-looking guy. He gave Suzy the rush. Before long, Suzy and Mat were walking home from the bus stop together via a grove of apple trees and stopping for a little hunting, pecking and pawing before going to their respective homes.

Events progressed rapidly. Before Suzy was thirteen, she had lost her virginity, having "lain among the apples" with Mat numerous times. Their interlude lasted through eighth grade. When Mat had to repeat that grade too, Suzy moved on to greener pastures and left the apple grove for good. She dated only one boy at a time, but she always provided her "steady" with sex.

Often, Suzy arrived at school with bruises, but no one really thought much about it. Once, she had been out of school for several days. When she returned, her face was black and blue, and her right eye was swollen almost shut. Suzy offered the old "I ran into a door" cliché, but with a twist. She said she had been chasing one of her younger brothers while horsing around, and as her brother slammed the bedroom door, she ran into it. Since Suzy's face was continually bruised, she gave the impression of being incredibly accident-prone.

Milicent Pritchard was at the high school one afternoon at an all-county faculty meeting. As she pulled her car into the parking lot, she saw Suzy getting ready to board the school bus. She called to her, so Suzy stopped to talk to her mother's friend and fellow committee member. Milicent commented on the large bruise on Suzy's temple, and Suzy told her the token story. Milicent chatted with Suzy for a few minutes and smiled as she entered the school. She thought about the children racing through the big, old house roughhousing. Suzy would have to be more careful, though, because her bruise looked nasty.

Milicent had only a half-hour from the time she arrived home from her faculty meeting until she had to attend a dinner meeting of the Magnolia Ball Committee. She took a quick shower, repaired her makeup and dressed for her meeting. As luck would have it, she sat beside Adele during dinner. As she was about to mention her visit with Suzy, she noticed Adele's bandaged hand.

"What happened to your hand, Adele?" asked Milicent.

"Oh, you know how my boys are. They're little monsters. The two of them were running through the house, and as I went to grab one, he ran through the door, pulled it shut and caught my hand in it," Adele answered.

Milicent expressed her sympathy and was about to mention Suzy's bruise when she bit her tongue. Suzy's door story and Adele's door stories were very much alike. Surely Adele's two boys didn't spend all their time running through doors and slamming them. Milicent started putting two and two together.

Suzy habitually said and did the right things when in the presence of adults. However, she had quite a different reputation among her peers. The girls all viewed her as a loose teenager, and her sexual feats were legion among the boys at school.

Her high school career continued with Suzy dating one boy at a time and pleasing him in any number of ways. She also continued to have "accidents." and finally confided to her only female friend Laura about Adele's heavy drinking and her mother hitting her on an almost daily basis. Suzy didn't know what to do about her abusive mother. She knew Adele was not happy with the general, who was many years her senior and not interested in socializing. The general preferred quiet evenings at home and going to bed early. Adele was still young. She loved going out to parties, which she had done frequently with her handsome first husband.

Frequently, Adele screamed at Suzy for no apparent reason. She would seemingly manufacture poor character traits with which to confront her daughter. Her latest concern was Suzy's lack of girlfriends.

"All I ever see come around here are boys sniffing like they know there's a bitch in heat somewhere. Why don't you have any girlfriends? I want you to bring some girls over."

After a few days passed, and Suzy had not had a girlfriend over, Adele would again start the inquisition. Usually before she would finish her tirade, she would smash her ringed hand across Suzy's beautiful face.

Suzy confided to Laura again. She said her mother wanted her to have girlfriends over. Laura had many friends. All of them wondered what Laura saw in Suzy, and why she associated with her. Laura told Suzy to ask her mother if she could have a slumber party.

"You get your mom to okay a slumber party, and I'll get a bunch of girls there," Laura whispered during study hall.

"How will you get them there? They hate me. You're my only friend," said Suzy.

"You get the permission and I'll get them there," promised Laura.

That afternoon, Suzy asked Adele if she might have a slumber party the following weekend. Adele was drinking her five o'clock cocktails, even though it was only three-thirty.

"Oh, you don't have a hot date this Saturday night? Wanna spend your time with girls, do you?" Adele snarled.

"Mother, you've been goading me to have girls over. I'm only trying to make you happy. Will it be all right if I have a slumber party?"

"It'll be fine. How many girls are you going to invite? Do you think any of them will come? Where are you going to import them from, Suzy?"

"I'm not going to import them from anywhere, Mother. I'm going to invite about six or seven girls from school who are friends of mine,," said Suzy.

"Six or seven. You have six or seven girlfriends at school? Why haven't I ever seen them?"

"I didn't know you were so anxious for me to bring girlfriends home. Besides, the house is always full with my bratty brothers' friends. Now that I know it's important to you, I want to have them over for a slumber party, okay?" said Suzy with a smile.

"All right. I'll plan a special dinner."

"Mother, don't go to a lot of bother. I think slumber parties here are very casual. We could have fried chicken or pizza or something like that. Don't make a big deal out of it. I don't want to put you to any trouble," Suzy said.

"Now you're telling me how to entertain. Do you think I never went to a slumber party? Do you think I don't know how things are done? You listen to me, young lady. I'm going to plan the menu. I'm sure that some of those girls have never had the opportunity to be in a home of this caliber and have never been exposed to a fine dinner. You leave everything to me," Adele stated emphatically.

Suzy thanked her mother and went to her room. She didn't really care about the girls at her school too much except for Laura, but she certainly didn't want any of them to come to her home and have a horrible time. She was worried Adele would ruin it by trying to show off.

Laura fulfilled her promise. She told Suzy six of her friends were planning to come over Saturday afternoon. With the two of them, there would be eight in all. Laura suggested that maybe they could sleep in the large room on the third floor. The playroom would be like a dormitory. With the television and the billiards table, they could stay up and be entertained all night. Suzy said she would check with her mother, but she was sure it would be fine.

Suzy entered the house after school and called to Adele. After calling several times and receiving no response, she went looking for her mother and found her in bed.

"Mother. Mother!" said Suzy.

After several shakes Adele finally responded, "Whadda ya want? I'm trying ta take a nap."

Suzy knew Adele had been out for cocktails and lunch, or to one of her ladies' functions, followed by more cocktails. She wasn't taking a nap; she had simply passed out. Suzy left the bedroom and later that evening, approached Adele again. She told her there would be seven girls coming, so with her eight in all, and they would like to sleep in the third floor play room.

"Absolutely not. They can't sleep in the playroom. There are no beds. Where in the world would they sleep?"

"On the floor, Mother. Each girl will bring a sleeping bag."

"A sleeping bag. We have eight bedrooms in this house. Why in the world would we want or expect anyone to bring a sleeping bag? No, we'll put two girls in each of the four back bedrooms"

"Mother, I think the purpose of a slumber party is for everyone to be together. The girls don't want to be separated."

"Well, I won't hear of it. You'll have plenty of time to be together during and after dinner. Now, we've discussed this enough. I need to think about the dinner menu and the entertainment afterward."

"Entertainment? What kind of entertainment, Mother? We can all go up into the play room and watch TV or play billiards or just gossip. We don't need entertainment."

"I'll take care of all of this, Suzy. Some culture would be good for the girls. Now, I'll plan some entertainment they'll all love. You just leave everything to me."

Suzy went to Laura the next day at school and said, "We've got to call this party off. My mother is planning some kind of fancy dinner and cultural entertainment and wants two girls to sleep in each of the four back bedrooms. This is going to be a disaster. No one is going to have fun. They'll hate me more than ever. I only wanted to have some girls over so she'd get off my back, but I don't want to be the laughing stock of the entire school."

"You won't be, Suzy. Lots of moms have tried to organize slumber parties. Everyone will put up with it. As soon as your parents go to bed, we'll get up and meet. No one ever goes to sleep at any of these things. At Koko's slumber party, we sneaked out of the house and walked into town and ran down Main Street in our baby doll pajamas. We ducked behind stores and into alleyways whenever a car came.

"At another party, we sneaked out and walked three miles to this boy's house, where he had five friends over. They sneaked out, too, and we went down on the waterfront and lit a bonfire and partied all night long. The parents never found out. So don't worry. We'll let your mother think we're paired off and in the guestrooms, and then we'll do whatever we want. Everything will be fine," Laura assured her.

Suzy felt better but was still very leery about the whole situation. Even in her wildest nightmares, she couldn't imagine how disastrous her slumber party was going to be.

Laura and her six friends arrived Saturday afternoon. All wore shorts or Bermudas and carried overnight bags. A few had sleeping bags in tow. Some brought Coca-Cola and bags of chips. Adele was at the front door with Suzy to greet them.

"Oh, you girls didn't have to bring any snacks. We have plenty to eat, and as for those sleeping bags, you just leave them right out here on the porch," Adele said. "You'll each have your own bed. We have four guestrooms, so it will work out perfectly. There's plenty of room here. No one will be crowded. Now, Suzy will show each of you to your room. I'm sure you'll all want to freshen up a bit. Then I'd like for all of you to come down to the first floor parlor after changing. We'll have refreshments there prior to dinner. Dinner will be served at six sharp in the dining room. Please be on time. Oh, yes, we dress for dinner. Suzy will tell you what's appropriate." Adele turned and walked toward the kitchen.

Koko, one of Laura's friends, looked at Suzy and said, "Wow, your mother is a gas! Separate beds, freshen up, the parlor for refreshments, dressing for dinner. She's kidding, right?"

Suzy looked down and in a very low voice said, "No, I'm afraid she's not. I'm really sorry. I've tried all day to explain to her what a slumber party is, but she just doesn't listen."

Laura giggled. "Hey, no problem. Remember what I told you, Suzy? We'll humor your mother, and when bedtime rolls around, we'll really party. Now, what's the proper attire for dinner?"

"She'll want us to wear skirts," sighed Suzy.

Cinnamon piped up, "No one brought a skirt. What are we going to do?"

Suzy smiled and said, "I guess we're all going to go up to my room and find something to wear."

She ran up the huge mahogany staircase. The other seven girls clamored behind her, shrieking and laughing. Suzy showed everyone to their rooms. Each of them put their belongings on a bed (in case Adele checked up on them). Then they all gathered in Suzy's room. They had a great time trying to fit Suzy's petite, size-six clothes on various body sizes. After several minutes and lots of laughter, everyone was dressed, although the clothes weren't necessarily suitable.

Suzy led the procession to the parlor, where Adele's maid had set out trays with glasses and a bowl of punch. On a glass tray were small toast rounds with smoked salmon and capers and crackers with caviar.

Koko started laughing, "Wow, what is this stuff?"

Adele looked down her nose at Koko and said, "That's smoked salmon, and this is caviar, and here we have a nice refreshing punch."

The girls each took some punch and a few tried some of the hors d'oeuvres. Everyone was on edge, and Suzy was mortified. Adele served herself punch, took one of each canapé and sat in her blue velvet chair, whereupon she began to question each girl as to who she was, where she lived and what her father did. This question-and-answer period seemed to last for eons. When she had finished with her inquiries, Adele rose and announced that dinner would be served in exactly twenty-five minutes in the dining room. Suggesting that the ladies might want to use this time to repair their hair or makeup, she reminded them they would be expected in the dining room five minutes before six. There they would find their place cards at the table and be seated.

Adele went into the kitchen, and Suzy began apologizing again. Now that the pressure was off, the girls laughed and assured her it was okay. If nothing else, it certainly was a new experience. Some of them even told Suzy how beautiful her mother was. They heard she was once Miss Louisiana. Where was her crown and trophy? Did she have any pictures of her mother winning the title? Suzy felt better. Maybe this party would turn out all right.

The girls promptly entered the dining room and could not believe what they saw. The table was set with ten pieces of flatware per place setting, place cards, candles, china and crystal. Everyone went to her designated chair, and a few sat down. Suzy remained standing and advised them to stand until her mother entered the dining room and took her place. Everyone stood. Adele, who had changed into a flowing organza dress, entered the dining room and nodded to each girl. As she stood at her chair, she inspected the table and sat down. Suzy then sat and the seven girls followed suit.

"Where's General Dressler?" asked Cinnamon.

"The General will not be joining us for dinner this evening. He's taking his dinner in his room. This is a girl party, right?" answered Adele.

Yes, it is a girl party, Mother, thought Suzy. *Girls, not mothers, what are you doing here?*

"Aunt" Emma, the old, black maid began serving the meal. (Older, black people in the south are referred to by the title "aunt" or "uncle" when they reach the age of about sixty-five, therefore, Emma was called "Aunt" by all whites who knew her.) First Aunt Emma served consommé. It was obvious from what remained on the cleared plates that it was not a big hit. Next came the watercress salad. The girls were having a difficult time not laughing. Their taste buds had not progressed much past pizza, fried chicken and steak, and so far, some of them had never before seen the food they were being served.

The dinner continued; things went from bad to worse. When the main course of sweet breads arrived, one of the girls inquired as to what they were. As Adele responded to her question, several girls were ready to rush into the powder room and throw up. Apparently, they hadn't reached the thymus gland in their biology books yet. They thought it was something dirty. Dessert was eventually served, and the baked Alaska flambeau was a success. Suzy could not believe how much her mother was trying to make an impression. What was wrong with her? Aunt Emma cleared the dessert plates and brought coffee. None of the girls cared for any; Adele proceeded to give a lecture about coffee's digestive attributes after a heavy meal.

The entire evening was beyond funny. All of the girls wanted to escape. Adele finished her coffee and announced it was time to refresh themselves. She would expect them in the drawing room at eight. She arose from the table and exited into the hallway.

"What the hell is going on, Suzy?" asked Koko. "You got us into this, Laura. We're doing this as a favor to you, but you didn't tell us we were going to be in a torture chamber. I'm calling my mother to come get me. To think that I gave up a date with Charlie to come to this three-ring circus!"

"Come on, Koko. Think of it as an adventure. Don't call your mother. Remember, soon this will be over, and we can really have a good time. You promised to do this for me," wheedled Laura. She turned and smiled at Suzy.

Cinnamon laughed. "Yeah, let's go with the flow. Hey, we have seven minutes to go refresh ourselves. Let's see, we've been here for three-and-a-half hours or so, and we've freshened up twice, and now we get to freshen ourselves again. That's pretty much free time, ladies. So, let's refresh and retire to the drawing room."

Cinnamon's light banter eased the friction. Everyone trudged down the hallway to the living room.

Adele, who had changed from her organza dress, was now attired in a lavender, satin dressing gown trimmed with white fur. She stood in the living room with only one light burning and it was focused on her like a spotlight in the otherwise darkened room.

"Welcome to all of you. Please take a seat," said Adele.

When a few of the girls opted for the floor, Adele corrected them and told them to sit on the furniture. The girls arose and sat on various settees and chairs. Adele reached for a book on the table beside her and said, "I am now going to read to you several selections from my favorite poetess, Edna St. Vincent Malay."

She proceeded to read for the next two hours, stopping only to find a new selection or to take a sip of "water." The longer Adele read, the more slurred her words became until she was barely comprehensible. Finally, she fell back into her chair and said, "Now, I'm gonna read one more of my favorite poems to you. I just need to find it. Where is it?"

She riffled through the book. Unable to find the poem, she threw the book on the table. "I'm tired of reading anyway. You all probably don't understand a thing about any of it. What are you all sitting around her staring at me for? Go to bed. You know where your rooms are. Get outta here."

No one moved. Everyone was embarrassed and didn't know what to do. At last, Cinnamon rose and said, "Well, girls, you heard Mrs. Dressler. Let's go up to bed. Thank you very much for reading to us, Mrs. Dressler. It was very inspiring. Good night."

Cinnamon left and the other girls followed her. No one spoke until they were upstairs. When the last girl had entered Suzy's room, Cinnamon shut the door. Everyone burst into gales of laughter while Suzy was almost in tears.

"Hey, it's okay, Suzy. My old lady drinks too," said Koko. "She doesn't read poetry, though, and she's never served me sheep balls, but, hey, different strokes for different folks!"

Laura said, "She didn't serve us sheep balls; she served us the sheep's thymus gland."

"Same difference," Koko giggled. "A gland is a gland is a gland."

Everyone laughed. Suzy shrugged and joined in with the rest of them.

Adele staggered up the stairs and told everyone to be quiet. She banged on Suzy's door and said, "Is everyone in their assigned rooms?"

"Yes, Mother. Good night."

Adele's footsteps were heard retreating down the hall. Everyone started talking and laughing again when suddenly the door burst open! There stood Adele. She looked crazed.

She came across the room in a flash and screamed at Suzy, "You lied to me, you little bitch. I do everything I can for you. I have your scuzzy little low-class friends over here and try to serve them a decent meal and expose them to some culture, and then you lie to me."

Suzy tried to move out of the way, but she wasn't fast enough. Adele's right hand, with the huge, diamond ring, hit her with a backhand. It tore into Suzy's eyeball.

Blood was everywhere. The girls screamed. Adele told all of them to shut up and go to their rooms. She left. Laura ran to Suzy and tried to see what damage had been done, but Suzy wouldn't take her hand away from her eye.

"We have to call a doctor, Suzy. You're bleeding really bad," said Laura.

"No, we can't. She'll really be angry if you do. Oh, it hurts," cried Suzy.

The girls didn't know what to do. They all wanted to get out of the house, but they were sorry for Suzy and didn't want to desert her. Some of them were beginning to understand the reason for Suzy's constant bruised condition.

Cinnamon went downstairs and phoned her mother. She very calmly told her what had happened, and Ellen called Dr. Ashcroft.

Within half an hour, there was a knock on the door. Cinnamon opened the door and escorted the doctor to Suzy's room. He told Suzy she would have to go to the hospital immediately because surgery was needed to repair her eye. Dr. Ashcroft then told Laura to awaken the Dresslers.

Suzy told him she had fallen and hit her eye on the corner of her nightstand. When her parents entered the room, Suzy quickly related to her mother the story she had told the doctor. Adele immediately went into a tirade for the benefit of her husband and the doctor—about how Suzy had to be more careful, how clumsy she was, what this would do to her face, and how she was going to have a scar. Adele rushed to Suzy and began to cuddle and hold her.

None of the girls could believe what they were seeing. Unfortunately for Adele, Ellen had told Dr. Ashcroft exactly what Cinnamon had reported. Suzy and her parents followed him to the hospital. The girls called their parents to collect them and proceeded to tell them exactly what had happened on the way to their respective homes.

Suzy's eye was saved. Dr. Ashcroft questioned Adele alone, who swore it was an accident. This had never happened before. It would never happen again. Her husband must never know that she had just a little too much to drink. The doctor let it go. He wrote his report that Suzy had fallen. Three days later, Suzy was released, and Adelle and the General drove her home.

Suzy completed the last two years of high school. During that time, she kept her distance from her mother. Although Adele threw a few punches, she was very careful and tried to stay away from Suzy. The General had asked Adele a lot of questions and had been very suspicious about Suzy's eye, especially since Suzy had so often been bruised. Adele had convinced him that Suzy was exceptionally clumsy, but she realized that if her daughter turned up with one more injury, General Dressler was going to take action. For her own self-preservation, she tried to avoid contact with her daughter.

Suzy left for the University of Miami the September after she graduated from high school. She dated the first college man she met and got pregnant, and the young man did the honorable thing and married her. He was a senior and wanted to finish school before they told his parents. Her new husband was the only reason Suzy remained in school. Of course, the baby was due in April, and graduation wasn't until May, so she would have to leave school before her freshman year was over. But Bobby got a healthy allowance from his parents, and he planned to get an apartment for the last few months of school. Once she had the baby and he graduated, he would introduce his parents to his new wife and grandchild.

Suzy received her invitation to make her debut at the Magnolia Ball. She had no intention of debuting nor was she planning on going home for the holidays. She was never going back to Adele's house again.

26

The Uninvited

Numerous young girls received invitations that October. Among them was Shannon, daughter of the owner of the Crest. Her invitation was a foregone conclusion. Daughters of various members of the committee, as were several "come-heres," whose families had only been on the scene for a short time, were also invited. No one knew much about the backgrounds of these daughters of the latter group, but their families had money or at least the appearance of it.

Several girls were also invited who had never lived in Dorchester County, but whose mothers or fathers had lived there at one time. There were also those who had an "in" with someone on the committee and managed to get their names on the invitation list.

One of the more comic invitees, compliments of Blanche Givens and Nancy Abrams, was the daughter of a "come-here" hardware store-owner. He had married a local girl who barely finished eighth grade. Her parents were unable to read and eked out a living making lawn furniture. John, the "come-here," and Joan, the local, had two daughters. Both were unattractive and obese.

Mandy, the older, received an invitation. People in the know were sure she was invited as payment of a debt. (John ran a bookie joint in back of his store.) Nevertheless, fat Mandy was going to be presented. It would promise to be quite a sight to see gaunt, wrinkled, almost illiterate Joan her mother, all decked out in a gown. The grandparents, who could neither read nor write, would also be at the festivities. Someone had certainly sneaked Mandy past Bonita. She was sure to be appalled.

A girl who was not invited was the daughter of a local orthodontist, Dr. Short. He had lived and worked in the area for about four years. Unlike most doctors and dentists however, he did not play golf, had not joined the country club, and rarely socialized. Therefore, his daughter, Bettine, was not invited. Dr. Short, a member of the Sons of the American Revolution and one long on heritage and family name, was so enraged, he sold his practice and his home and moved north.

Antoinette Haskins had made her debut in the late fifties, and she was from an excellent family. However, a few months after her presentation, she became pregnant by the garbage truck driver who made twice-a-week stops at her parents' stately home. Antoinette and her husband now owned the trash hauling operation and two hundred dumpsters, but their daughter, Margaret, did not receive an invitation.

Antoinette was terribly hurt, disappointed and angry. Her husband took it right in stride, not really understanding what all the fuss was about.

Candace Murphy wasn't invited either, and no one knew why. Although her parents weren't really in the social scene, they were good people. Both were from old Southern families—aristocratic stock. Candace's father had put his brothers and sisters through school after their father's death. He was a welder, owned his own business, bought everything for cash, drove a new car every year, and lived in one of the largest homes in Montiac.

Candace was a good student. She was involved in school activities and although she liked to have a good time, she neither drank nor smoked. She did enjoy necking, but she certainly never went "all the way." Candace, an honor student from Dorchester High School, was attending the University of Virginia, one of the foremost schools in the South. Someone on the committee must have had it in for either her or her parents since she was not included in the debutante list while all her friends in her social set received invitations.

27

Adele and Suzy

Adele threw a fit after Suzy's call from the University of Miami two days before Thanksgiving holiday. Suzy told Adele she wouldn't be coming home.

"What do you mean you're not coming home?" Adele screamed. "It's Thanksgiving. You haven't been home since you left for school. You most certainly are coming home. You know that on Saturday you have to be at the club for the debutante tea."

"I'm not coming home for the holiday, and I'm not going to the debutante tea, the debutante parties, or the Magnolia Ball. I'm not making my debut, Mother. What does being presented and being a debutante have to do with the world today? Most of the girls here in school have no idea what a debutante or a debut is. When I mentioned a debutante ball, they thought I was talking about a "coming out" party, like the Hispanic girls have when they turn fifteen. It's like what the Jewish girls do at "sweet sixteen" parties. Debuts and debutantes are a thing of the past. I don't like all that nonsense. You're the one who likes to show off, not me," bristled Suzy.

Adele could not believe her ears. Suzy had never spoken to her like this. Suzy certainly must be aware how important the committee and Ball were to her mother.

Adele reached for the bottle of vodka and poured herself a healthy shot. She said, "I don't want to hear about Hispanics and 'sweet-sixteen's.'

You get on that plane tomorrow night and you fly into Savannah. The General and I will pick you up," ordered a furious Adele.

"I'm not getting on the plane, Mother, and I'm not coming home. As a matter of fact, I don't have a plane ticket."

"What do you mean you don't have a plane ticket? The General mailed it himself two weeks ago. Are you telling me that you never received it in the mail?" Adele asked, thinking quickly about calling a travel agency to buy a last-minute ticket.

"I got it in the mail and I took it to the airline office and got a refund. I got your money back and I've already spent it."

"Why did you do such a stupid thing? We are going to have a terrible time getting a ticket now. Do you know how full the planes are at Thanksgiving?"

"I did it because I was never planning to come home. I'm not coming for Thanksgiving, and I'm not coming for Christmas, New Year's, Ground Hog's Day, Valentine's Day, Easter, Mother's Day, Memorial Day, or any other day. I never intend to set foot in your house again. Good bye, Mother." Suzy hung up.

Adele went into a frenzy. She screamed and threw objects all over the room. General Dressler hurried in and asked what had happened.

Adele calmed down long enough to tell him about her conversation with Suzy, and the General called his many years of military service and experience into action. He told Adele he would handle the situation.

He immediately placed a call to Suzy's dormitory and asked her for a full explanation of her actions and why she had put her mother into such a state. Suzy told her stepfather about how Adele had abused her for years. She related the true story about what happened to her eye at the slumber party. "Mother is an alcoholic, General. You play golf or watch the stock market reports on television, so you never know what was happening in her life. Beside the fact that I don't intend to come home, I'm married and I'm pregnant and I'm very much in love with my husband. I'm not coming home again. Thank you, sir, for your kindness to me and to my brothers. Goodbye," and she hung up on him.

General Dressler walked over to Adele, who was pacing, and put his arms around her. He steered her across the polar bearskin rug to the bed and sat down with her. He told her about Suzy's pregnancy and marriage.

When he finished, Adele's only concern was the committee and how ridiculous she would look, since she was a member, when her own daughter refused the invitation. What was she going to tell people? How would she be able to explain Suzy's refusal to be presented? What would she say? She did not voice concern over her daughter's marriage nor did she question who Suzy's husband was. Not a thought seemed to be given to the fact that her eighteen-year-old daughter was married and pregnant.

General Dressler attempted to address the child abuse issue. Adele refused to discuss it. Her only concern was, "Tell me, how I am going to be able to hold my head up in Dorchester County when Suzy refuses to make her debut?"

The next day, Adele felt somewhat better, having spent the major part of the night trying to come up with a plausible story. Since Suzy had excelled in French in high school and had expressed a desire to attend the Sorbonne in Paris when she'd first entered the University of Miami, Adele came up with a plan. She thought she could convince people that Suzy was doing so well in French she was selected to go to the Sorbonne early and had to leave prior to Thanksgiving break. She was sure her status on the committee would allow Suzy to be asked again next year. Although Suzy probably wouldn't make her debut then, either, Adele could at least buy time. She convinced herself this explanation would work. Adele poured herself a stiff drink, took a deep breath and called Celestine.

Celestine, who always thought the best about everyone and who didn't suspect ulterior motives, told Adele how pleased she was for Suzy. She and the General must be so proud of such a bright daughter. While she knew they were going to miss Suzy over the upcoming holidays, she was sure the other committee members would be as delighted as she that one of their Dorchester High School graduates was doing so well. Of course, Suzy would be invited to debut the following season.

Adele hung up. She was delighted. It was only as she descended the staircase for breakfast that she realized with horror that in only six months she was to be a grandmother. Even though she had no intention of ever seeing Suzy or the little bastard, the fact remained that she would be a grandmother. Thank God no one in Dorchester County would know!

Adele headed for the dining room and poured herself a glass of orange juice from the pitcher on the sideboard. Crossing to the doorway to look out, she saw the General return from his morning walk. As he fetched the newspaper from the box at the end of the lane, she hurried to the dining room and peeked into the kitchen where Aunt Emma was bent over the stove checking on the homemade cinnamon rolls. Adele had just enough time to go to the bar, uncap the vodka, and pour a double shot into her morning juice.

28

Ann Amelia & Jason

Ann Amelia called Mona a few days after her invitation arrived. "Mommy, I received an invitation to debut at the Magnolia Ball."

"I know, dear. Isn't that exciting?"

"Not especially. I don't want to be presented. Please tell me that I don't have to do it."

Mona could not believe what she was hearing.

"Why, of course you have to make your debut, Ann Amelia. Why on earth would you not wish to be presented? It's an honor. Poor Sandy Hibbert killed herself because she wasn't invited. How could you think of refusing? Do you know what that would do to Deddy? Why, he's so excited he can hardly stand it. He keeps talking about his little girl being presented to society. He's already ordered a new Yves St. Laurent tux and wants to give the dinner after the rehearsal. You know, it's usually done by a whole group of parents, but Deddy said he wants the three of us to give the entire party. Nothing is too good for his little girl. Now, why in heaven would you want to break your Deddy's heart?"

"I don't want to break his heart. I just don't want to be presented. I think it's kind of silly. There are so many girls whose fathers are out of work, and we're in the middle of a recession. It seems wasteful to spend all that money on clothes and parties and a white gown for nothing. I mean, why present me to the society of Dorchester County? I've known everyone in society since I was little. I don't need a formal presentation to them. Please, Mommy, I really don't want to do this," whined Ann Amelia.

"I'll tell you what I'm going to do, Ann Amelia. I'm not going to mention this phone call to your father. He doesn't need this upset. You must get all of this nonsense right out of your head. Your father is the foremost attorney in the county, and you will be making your debut at the Magnolia Ball on the twenty-eighth of December on his arm. You will glide down the steps in a designer gown. You will look beautiful and have a smile on your face, and you will not break your father's heart. Do you understand me, darling?"

"Yes, Mommy."

"Good, then we'll pick you up at the Savannah Airport Wednesday night. I'll keep my part of the bargain and won't say a word about this to your father, and I expect you to do your part. I do not want to hear the merest mention of your not wanting to be presented again. Remember. Smile, smile, smile! Millions of girls would kill to be in your shoes. You live in a lovely home, and have a deddy who absolutely worships the ground on which his daughter walks. Good-bye, dear. See you Wednesday," said Mona as she hung up, pleased with herself for solving a crisis and protecting her dear, sweet Jason and his beautiful relationship with his "little girl."

29

The Parties

Thanksgiving holidays were at hand. The girls to be presented at the 1991 Magnolia Ball arrived in Montiac on Wednesday night. Their first big debutante function was to be on Saturday. The invitees and their mothers were to be the guests of the Magnolia Ball Committee for a luncheon. Afterwards, publicity shots would be taken for the front page of the *Montiac Minutes.*

The event called for skirts, blouses, sweaters or suits, and heels. Each debutante was given a nametag. Introductions were made. The rubber-chicken luncheon was served. People chattered. The reporter posed the girls for group shots and took photographs.

Following the luncheon, Bonita gave a welcoming speech. She briefly alluded to Sandy Waltham, who was to have been presented but had tragically died at the end of October. She then asked the girls about their individual parties. Bonita nodded happily when she heard that one of the girls' parents was planning to give a party alone. She did not approve of the plebeian style of several sets of parents collaborating together on a function. She thought this practice, which had arisen in the past five years or so, was common. When a girl responded she was participating in a group given function, Bonita showed her dissatisfaction.

Patricia Saxon, drug addict, sex maniac and former syphilis carrier, announced she and her mother would entertain at a Victorian tea at their home on Friday, the sixteenth of December, at four o'clock. Before she sat down, Patricia complimented Mrs. Roberts on her lovely dress and accessories. Bonita beamed. A few of the other debutantes gave each other the eye as if to say, "Same old Patricia. Always a brown-noser."

Cinnamon rose. She announced that her father would clear out the back room of the Sweet Treat for a sock hop. They would provide burgers, custard, dogs, sandwiches and soft drinks. (An expensive party, for there would be no gambling that night.) Bonita was not enthralled, but asked Mary Beth to duly note Cinnamon's party for inclusion in the forthcoming article for the paper.

Lynette was going to give a masked ball at the Crest.

Committee members and their spouses were to be included. Bonita loved that idea. She thought the Karshes had such class.

When Ann Amelia's name was called, she rose, reluctantly, and said that her parents would like to give the dinner following the rehearsal. Bonita was elated since for the past several seasons several families had jointly hosted that party. She was glad such a good caliber of girls had been selected this year. There weren't going to be any of those groupie affairs, for which Bonita was greatly relieved.

Shannon of the Crest Resort family invited everyone to a dinner-dance cruise on the family's private yacht, which the Kirkhams had bought in the name of the hotel as a tax write-off. It was an ancient boat filled with quality copies of art and polished teak and mahogany furniture. Although gaudy, it was the biggest yacht in South Carolina, so everyone oohed and ahhed at the invitation.

Mandy stood. She said her grandpaw and grandmaw were gonna give her party and they were gonna go out and tong some oysters and clams and roast'em out in their backyard on the grill. Everyone should come real casual cuz her grandpaw and grandmaw were just folks, and there wasn't any indoor plumbin'.

Bonita reached for her little black lace fan, even though it was chilly. She forgot to make sure Mary Beth made a notation. A few of the debutantes snickered, but Mandy smiled at everyone and plopped her massive body back in her chair. She was quite pleased with herself.

The remainder of the girls made their announcements. Bonita reminded everyone of the annual breakfast at Beechland following the Ball, when the queen would be photographed in front of the magnolia tree. She then gave a brief synopsis of the Ball's origin, the standard version, however, not the one Celestine had recently related to her. Bonita concluded the luncheon, and the young ladies and their mothers left the club. The 1991 Magnolia Debutante Ball Season had officially begun!

30

Patricia's Victorian Tea

Patricia Saxon's Victorian tea was the first party of the season It was held at the old fish captain's home, where Chucky, Biffy, Patricia, and Randall resided.

Biffy had never attended a high tea, but she read about one in a Barbara Cartland romance novel and thought it would set just the proper tone for Patricia and her forthcoming debut. She bought every etiquette book she could find, and her tea table looked exactly like the one in the **Emily Post Book of Etiquette.** She asked two of her closest friends to pour. The book said that those who poured were especially invited prior to the event by the hostess. The pourers were counted on to be gracious to everyone under any and all circumstances. Biffy had selected two of her yacht club friends, Patti and Louise.

The two "pourers to be" arrived at Biffy's house for lunch in early December to go over their duties. Biffy explained to them what they were to say and what the appropriate attire would be, and how they were to act. She began her lesson with a role-playing scene.

She said, "Now Louise and Patti, it is perfectly acceptable for a total stranger to walk up to the tea table and say, 'May I have a cup of tea?'" (Interesting, Biffy thought. If one is at a tea, wouldn't it stand to reason one would walk up to the tea table and want a cup of tea? But it is gratifying to know if one walks up to the tea table at a tea, it is perfectly all right for one to ask for a cup of tea. Further if everyone at the tea was invited, how could one account for a total stranger walking up to the tea table?).

Biffy continued, "Now your response, ladies, should be a very enthusiastic 'Certainly! Do you take it strong or weak?' If the guest wants it strong, then you deluge it with boiling water. You watch the recipient's reaction and check to see if she nods or gives an indication as to whether she prefers cream, lemon, or sugar." (Maybe, Biffy thought, it would make more sense if one of the "pourers" **asked** the guest what she wished in her tea. Not, however, according to Emily.)

"On the other hand," Biffy continued, "Perhaps the guest will prefer chocolate. The chocolate will be at the other end of the table." (That's interesting. If the chocolate is at one end and the tea is at the other, why would the guest go to the tea end of the table and say, 'May I have a cup of tea?' if what she preferred was a cup of chocolate? But then, Biffy asked herself, who was she to question Emily Post.)

"The hostess pouring the chocolate should answer in the same manner as the tea hostess by responding, 'Certainly!'" tutored Biffy. "If you are very busy and pouring for a lot of people at once, all you have to do is smile as you pass the guest her tea. But if there is no one around, it is incumbent upon you to make some pleasant remarks, such as, 'How nice of you. I have been feeling neglected at my end of the table. Everyone today seems to prefer tea.'"

Biffy went on to explain the proper setup for tea. She told Louise and Patti the only table would be the tea table. People would sit downstairs taking their tea and/or chocolate.

"You know, of course, tea tables are only provided in public tea rooms, never in one's home."

Biffy studied her book carefully. On the day of the tea, she had her table properly prepared. A cloth had first been placed on the table and was hanging exactly one half yard over the edge on all sides. Her cloth, which she purchased in Savannah, was the conventional white linen cloth, the only one absolutely suitable for tea. It had the exactly the prescribed amount of needlework and lace.

The day of the party Biffy placed on the cloth a sterling silver tray large enough to hold everything except the plates of food. The kettle was placed on the tray. A spirit lamp set under the kettle to keep the water hot. The lamp would be lighted after the kettle was placed on its stand—but not before, because Emily had warned, in her book, that a terrible accident might occur if the lamp were lighted beforehand. Additionally, on the tray, there was an empty teapot, a caddie of tea, a tea strainer, a slop bowl, a cream pitcher, a sugar bowl, and a glass dish with slices of lemons.

Next to her tea tray were stacked cups and saucers and small, matching tea plates. The napkins measured exactly twelve inches square and were hemstitched to match the tea cloth. They were folded on each of the tea plates like the filling in a cake. Each guest was expected to lift her plate with the napkin. On the table surrounding the tea tray were additional plates for small cakes, sandwiches, and hot bread.

The sandwiches were made by buttering the end of a loaf of not-too-fresh bread, spreading on a filling, and then cutting off the prepared slice as thinly as possible—no thicker than an eighth of an inch. The sandwiches were filled with jam. The second slice of bread was placed on top, the crust was cut off to leave a new square, and that square was cut diagonally to form two, triangular sandwiches. Biffy also had Irene's Catering Service make a plate of sandwiches cut with cookie cutters. Additionally, she was serving gingerbread, crumpets and hot biscuits, which were split open and buttered.

Even though Biffy was sure that all of this was correct according to Emily, she felt she should have more food. It looked very sparse to her, but Emily said that no nuts, candies, cinnamon, cloves, pickles, etc. were to be served. Therefore, because Biffy wasn't going to do something improper, she ruefully chose not to serve anything else.

Everything was in splendid readiness for the high tea when Biffy and Patricia came down the stairs into the foyer. Biffy had purchased matching, red velvet dresses with white, eyelet pinafores for her and Patricia to wear in their hostess roles. Each of them wore opaque hose and smart, red Pappagallo flats. They were nauseatingly cute. Randall and Chucky had been banished, and the ladies of the house were ready to receive. The doorbell rang and various committee members, debutantes, and their mothers entered the foyer to attend the tea party.

Mandy was the first to head for the tea table. "What're you serving?" she asked Louise.

Louise, who had only been prompted with "certainly," responded, "Certainly. How do you take it?"

"Take what?" said Mandy. "I didn't take anything."

"How do you take your tea?" Louise asked.

"I don't know. I've never taken tea anywhere," Mandy laughed.

Louise, realizing that she must try to save this situation, said, "Would you care for some tea?"

"Sure."

"What would you like in it?" asked Louise.

"Ice," said Mandy. "I don't want any hot tea. We always drink iced tea with sugar in it, don't we, Mama?"

"She's right about that," said Joan. "We drinks iced tea every night at our house, summer and winter. Always put lots of sugar in it, too. We makes sun tea sometimes in the summer. You ever had that? It's right good. I'll have an iced tea with sugar, too."

Louise didn't have a clue what to do. Biffy hadn't covered any off-the-wall requests. Louise looked at Mandy and Joan and said, "Excuse me for a moment, please."

She hurried into the foyer, took Biffy aside and said, "I have two orders for iced tea with sugar in it. What am I going to do?"

"You must have misunderstood, dear. This is a tea. We're not serving iced tea with sugar."

"You better explain that to Mandy and her mother, because that's what they both want."

Biffy was horrified! But she recalled Emily's advice that one should always try to make guests feel comfortable in one's home. She quickly entered the kitchen and told Irene to prepare two large iced teas with sugar, and to get them out to Louise, **pronto!**

Other young ladies entered the dining room and made their way to the tea table. Most of the debutantes opted for hot chocolate, while the mothers and the committee members took tea. Celestine was duly impressed with Biffy's tea table and Bonita was effusive with her compliments. Irene and two of her helpers came out to pass the tiny sandwiches, the hot breads and cake.

Mandy sat on one of the settees. She balanced her napkin and jam knife across her little tea plate on her generous lap. When Irene passed the sandwich tray, Mandy took six. Even Irene rolled her eyes at that one. Mandy, however, had not read Emily and did not know that tea sandwiches were not made to satiate one's hunger. Mandy only knew she was hungry, as usual. She was at a party and had come to eat. She loaded up on the biscuits and the cakes and even went back for seconds and thirds. It was truly embarrassing for everyone. However, Mandy and Joan were unaware of their lack of social graces or their faux pas. They had the most fun of anyone.

Little groups gathered for dull conversation. Everything was very subdued. Biffy thought it was an immense success, except for Mandy and her mother. Risking Bonita's wrath, Biffy was so bold as to ask Bonita how Mandy had ever been selected. Bonita confided that, frankly, she didn't know. One had certainly been put over on the selection committee, but they didn't know how to tactfully get out of including her. Bonita assured Biffy, however, that she would personally call Joan and John and meet with the family. She would teach them acceptable behavior for the Ball. (*Good luck, Bonita,* Biffy thought. *Talk about making a purse from a sow's ear.*)

The tea ended promptly at six o'clock as was "customary." Everyone enthusiastically thanked Biffy and Patricia and took their leave. Biffy glowed. What a lovely party!

As each of the girls got into her respective automobiles with her mothers, almost each and every one of them said, "What a bore. I hope the other parties are better than this one." Each mother, except for Joan, tried to explain to her daughter that teas were very acceptable social engagements for ladies. Biffy had given a proper tea, and she, the respective daughter, might be expected to give one at some time, especially if she married a man on his way up the corporate ladder.

Everyone was gearing up for the big dinner cruise on the Crest Hotel's yacht, *Annabelle*, the following evening. Shannon's party was expected to be a blast.

31

Shannon's Dinner Cruise

Shannon and her parents were on the *Annabelle* ready to receive their cruise guests. Shannon was in a black velvet, off-the-shoulder dress that was much too old for her, but she felt it made her look elegant and more mature than her eighteen years. Sarah, her mother, had attired herself in a column of gold and looked like a sparkler, since she was so thin that she was about the same size as one. Her afternoon had been spent in "Tresses," where the hair stylist had sprayed gold highlights into her hair and then applied gold glitter to the spray. The glitter also adhered to the cream eye shadow covering her eyelids.

Sarah's color scheme for the party was gold (naturally,) and, therefore, everything had to be coordinated. The flatware was gold, the plates were gold, and the goblets were gold, as were tablecloths, serving trays and napkins. It was really too much, but Sarah was partial to gold. She felt it was elegance personified. The affair had set Sarah back financially, but what was Alex's money for other than to spend on extravagance? Sarah shared Dolly Levi's of Thornton Wilder's **The Matchmaker's** attitude that *money was like manure.* It wasn't worth anything unless it was spread all over the place, causing young things to grow.

The ramp on which to board the yacht from the pier was covered with gold sculpted carpet. Golden ropes were on either side of the walkway for the guests to grasp for their ascent.

Shannon's escort was the son of a Menhaden Fisheries' executive from Greenville. The boy's father had been in trouble in his hometown. At seventeen the father ran away to Montiac and obtained a job sweeping up chum in the fish factory. A nice looking, talented young man from a bad background, he reacted to the people at the factory like a stray dog. He responded to their love and concern for him and rose from a floor sweeper to a member of the crew, then to first mate, and on to captain. Eventually, he ascended the corporate ladder into administration and was now second in command of the largest Menhaden fishing plant on the East Coast.

Brant, like his father, was a nice looking young man who had inherited his father's penchant for getting into trouble, but he had neither his father's talents nor his ambition. Unfortunately, in the long term, for him, not only was his father an executive making a handsome salary, but his mother was also from a very wealthy family, and whenever Brant got into trouble, his parents paid off the owners of whatever property he had destroyed. He was chastised, grounded for a few days, and then allowed to continue his escapades, therefore, he did not have a reason to change his mischievous ways.

Brant's first adventure had occurred when he was only six years old. He took a bucket of sand and dumped it into the gas tank of a neighbor's large yacht therefore ruining the engine. The cost was thirty-five thousand dollars! Daddy rescued him and paid for a new engine in the yacht. And so it continued. When Brant tore up several motel rooms where he and his friends were partying on a New Year's Eve, the other boys were charged and went to court. Brant, the ringleader, was released, since his father arrived with his amply stuffed wallet in time to appease the motel owner and to convince him not to hold Brant responsible.

The young ladies boarded the yacht with their escorts and were definitely in a party mood. Not one to try to mix with the youngsters, Sarah left them on their own after they were received. The yacht's chef had prepared shrimp cocktails, steak, baked potatoes, salad, green beans, home-baked bread, and chocolate nut sundaes for dessert. Before the yacht set sail, guests gathered in the main salon where there were soft drinks, chips, dip, pretzels and punch.

Shannon had told Brant about the agenda and menu before the big night, so Brant and a few of his friends who were escorting other debutantes were already prepared to "fix up" the punch. Brant looked around and made sure Shannon's parents were not close by, quickly pulled the flask out of his inside jacket pocket and emptied a fifth of tequila into the punchbowl. He gave the signal to two of his friends who had also "borrowed" spirits from their parents' liquor cabinets, and they sauntered over to the punchbowl and poured the contents of their flasks into the punch. One added vodka, and the other emptied his flask of gin. Everyone received word to pass on the soft drinks, but to try the punch; it was delicious! Brant knew they would be safe, because Sarah's parents were being served cocktails by the ship's steward. They wouldn't be imbibing the punch. The bowl was quickly emptied, and when the steward appeared with a second batch Brant again gave the signal. That punch was quickly "doctored" also.

Everyone was having a wonderful time. The hilarity escalated rapidly. By the time dinner was served, all of the young people were in highly charged spirits.

Since Sarah was so cosmopolitan and wealthy that she often felt above the law, she had decided to serve wine with dinner, although none of the guests were of age. Her rationalization, which she explained to her husband, was that they were at sea, so the state's laws regarding minor drinking did not apply. Besides, they weren't selling alcohol to the kids, they were giving it to them, and what could one glass of wine hurt? The wine served with dinner was red, and as the crimson liquid hit the already saturated stomachs of some of the minors, quite a few of the debutantes and their dates became too high, and some were very close to being ill.

After dinner, when the dancing began, Brant and his two closest friends excused themselves to go to the head to smoke a joint. On the way back to the dining room, one served as a lookout to make sure the stewards were still clearing from the dinner, while Brant and his other friend raided the liquor supply below deck. While Sarah and Alex were having after-dinner liqueurs on the aft deck and smiling at the children, they were unaware that what was being swigged in the main salon made their drinks look like water.

Several of the young ladies had removed their shoes for dancing. As the liquor took effect, their inhibitions disappeared. The dancing became increasingly risqué. Skirts flipped higher and higher into the air. Body movements became more and more provocative. At one point, Cinnamon pulled her skirt up, took off her black half-slip, pulled it over her head and wore it around her neck. All of the guys cheered and yelled, "Take it all off!"

Even though it was December and a chilly night, the kids quickly became very warm from the dancing and the liquor. They all wanted to go out on the deck of the yacht. Shannon had entertained at many parties, and the guests knew the Kirkhams were cool and didn't check too often on what was happening. Most of the guests left the main salon by the side door and headed for the forward deck to cool off. It was only a matter of time before someone was going to slip and fall or get pushed. "Pushed" was the order of the day, and soon Cal, one of Brant's friends, was overboard.

Shannon ran to the back of the yacht and notified her father, who hurriedly called the captain over the intercom to tell him that one of the guests was in the water. The captain slowed the boat and turned around. A steward held a pole out into the water to assist Cal to the ladder that was attached to the back of the yacht. Other than being a little cold, Cal said it had really been fun. Sarah instructed a steward to take Cal below and get him some dry clothes.

The Magnolia Ball

A few of the guests decided to go with him, since the staterooms below had been off-limits prior to Cal's mishap. About ten of the guests went with Cal, and as the steward supplied him with heated towels and deck hand's clothing, the other guests explored the staterooms by jumping on the beds, flushing the heads, and turning on the water faucets, televisions and radios. They went wild.

It wasn't long before things were completely out of hand. The time was ripe for destruction to set in. Pictures were ripped from the wall and thrown. Bedclothes were taken off beds, and drawers were ransacked. Water was poured on Oriental carpets. Drapes were pulled down. Havoc reigned. After about a half hour of tearing everything up, the group of ten smoothed their clothing, the girls combed their hair and reapplied their lipstick, and all of them retired to the main salon for more dancing. The stewards didn't think to check the staterooms at that point. After all, these were debutantes and their escorts; they were guests of their boss.

The yacht sailed back to the pier approximately four hours after it had left its mooring. Shannon and her parents stood next to the ramp to say good night. After the last had departed, Shannon and Sarah returned to the salon to get their wraps. Shannon, who didn't feel very well and hoped she could get up to her room quickly once they were home, thanked her parents for the lovely party.

An hour later, while Shannon was in the bathroom of her bedroom suite, the phone rang. Shortly after, Shannon heard her father's thunderous voice summoning her downstairs.

"I'll be right down," she called as she swirled some mouthwash in her mouth, dried her face, combed her hair, and went to see what was wrong.

Her father told her about the destruction on the yacht and wanted to know who was responsible.

"I don't have any idea, Dad," Shannon replied.

Although she didn't tell her father, she was sure Brant was involved. What was his thing about tearing everything up? He did it all the time at parties and usually got away with it, because none of his friends told on him.

Alex Kirkham described the destruction to Shannon as it had been reported to him by the captain of the *Annabelle*. Shannon began to cry and told her father how very sorry she was, but she stuck to her guns and told him she had no idea who had done such a thing. She knew her father had insurance, and the yacht was owned by the hotel. It was only money and there was plenty of it to clean up the damage. All she wanted was to go upstairs to her bathroom to pay homage once again to the marble throne.

32

The Sock Hop, Masked Ball and Oyster Roast

The next night Cinnamon's sock hop was held in the back room of the Sweet Treat. It went off without a hitch. The kids really seemed to have a good time, and since Jordan and Ellen were on the premises and wouldn't allow the kids to leave, there was no drinking or pot smoking until after the affair was over. Then everyone went to the cove, a necking spot, and had a real party.

Affair number four was Lynette's masked ball at the Crest. Preparations had been going on for days in planning the costumes. Mandy was the absolute funniest of all. Her two hundred and fifty pounds were stuffed into a short dress with mountains of crinolines, and her hair was curled in tight, little springs. On her feet were little lace socks and black patent-leather Mary Jane shoes, for Mandy was dressed as Shirley Temple, complete with an all-day sucker. She ran around all night singing, "On the Good Ship, Lollipop" to anyone who would listen. She hadn't been able to get a date for this function, nor any others. So, wherein an escort was necessary, she was accompanied by her cousin, Elvis.

Elvis wore sideburns down to his chin, his hair slicked back in a DA, and had three tattoos on each arm. Elvis had dropped out of school after seventh grade, and went to work at the local bowling alley setting pins until they got an automatic pin setter. Later, he ran the fountain, and now was a short-order cook.

Elvis had given a great deal of thought to his costume. He wore skin-tight, white pants, white cowboy boots, and a white shirt open to his waist revealing yet another tattoo on his hairless chest. He wore a red, silk neck scarf and a guitar attached to a strap over his shoulder. He had, of course, come as Elvis Presley. "I'm just a hunka, hunka burning love," written in black magic marker, emblazoned the back of his shirt.

Shannon, with her million-dollar figure, was dressed in a flesh-colored body suit to which she had attached colored feathers. Feathered stiletto heels complemented her ensemble and a hood festooned with feathers completed it. (She seemed to be a sort of bird, although no one knew what kind, since she had feathers of every color.) She looked good though; the body suit clung to every curve. Brant arrived dressed in black jeans, white T-shirt with one sleeve rolled over a pack of Marlboros, and hair slicked back in a pomade, white socks and loafers. Supposedly, he was a juvenile delinquent. Apparently, Brant, like Elvis, didn't understand that at a costume party, one is supposed to be disguised.

Cinnamon and her date were beatniks. Ann Amelia and her escort arrived as Rhett Butler and Scarlet O'Hara. There were clowns, princesses, Cinderellas, Lone Rangers, Batmen and Batwomen and maharajas. The debutantes' parents were also present, and Adele came dressed as a beauty queen complete with her "Miss Louisiana" crown and banner. She had eliminated the 1945 date, however. General Dressler was in his dress uniform, apparently "disguised" as the escort of the beauty queen.

Celestine and Jamison came as Lady and the Tramp, complete with papier-mâché' heads of the collie and the mutt. Anthony was also there with his little papier-mâché' head. Celestine introduced him to everyone as Scamp, offspring of Lady and the Tramp.

Darlene came as a Gypsy princess, and Jonathan was a bullfighter. Chet was dressed as a doctor in whites complete with stethoscope. Dee was attired with stuffing to amplify various bodily parts, and introduced herself as "Nurse Goodbody." Milicent wore a wig with a bun, granny glasses, and old ladies comfort shoes, a long black skirt, and a high-necked, white blouse and carried a ruler in her hand. Such originality. Milicent was "incognito" as a schoolteacher.

Bonita, however, stole the show. She came in yards of white, transparent chiffon trimmed in silver sequins. On top of her bleached-blonde head, she wore a tiara and in her hand she carried a wand which she waved over everyone constantly. She also sprinkled everyone with fairy dust (silver glitter) and granted them any wish they desired. Bonita was Glenda, the good witch of the North. She tittered and pirouetted around as if she were petite. Everyone agreed that she looked and acted like a complete ninny.

Several other parties and luncheons filled the next week, but then, all too soon, it was time for Mandy's oyster and clam roast in her grandmaw's and grandpaw's backyard. Bonita really did not want to attend that function, but it was expected she be present at all the activities where the committee was included. She also hoped to get Mandy's parents aside for a little talk, so that they would have some clue about how to conduct themselves at the Ball.

Bonita was yet to figure out how Mandy had been selected since her name had not been mentioned at the selection meeting. When she questioned Blanche and Nancy, her chosen ones, they both denied having had anything to do with Mandy's invitation. It was a mystery, but it would certainly not happen again. The committee had tried to invent some tactful way to rescind Mandy's invitation but had finally decided to grin and bear it.

Bonita wore a warm dress and mink coat with mink-lined boots, hat and gloves. She summoned Alphonso to drive her to a stretch of road beyond the town of Montiac known as the "Back Alley." The name was given to the area because of the people who lived there. One thing was for sure, no one from the Back Alley had ever been presented at the

Magnolia Ball before, and certainly none of Dorchester County's socialites had ever attended a party there.

Bonita could see the lights long before they arrived at the shoddy house. Mandy's grandpaw was well known for one thing in Dorchester County: he had more Christmas lights than anyone else in the state and every year he bought more. His house and lights had been featured on the front page of the *Montiac Minutes* and also in the Savannah newspaper. Santa and all of his reindeer in lights pranced across the roof. Every tree in the yard was draped with tiny bulbs. Each bush was covered with them. The entire house was edged in strings of lights. There were twinkling lights around the fence, strung on either side of the driveway and outlining every window and doorway of the tiny house. There were even large blue lights strung along the foundation.

Bonita gasped when she saw what Grandpaw had added to his light menagerie this year. Six foot high, white lights were mounted across the top of the house above Santa and the prancing reindeer. The new addition was a flashing sign above the entourage that read, "Happy Birthday, Jesus!"

Alphonso turned around from the front seat and said, 'Well, Ms. Bonita, it's all right if I dies and goes to heaven now, cuz after seeing that sign, I knows I has seen it all."

Bonita sighed and began to gather her bulk to get out of the car. She was already not having a good time.

Grandmaw and Grandpaw were on hand to greet everyone. Grandpaw had on his oilslicker, black pants and oystering boots. Oysters were unappetizingly displayed in the bed of a beat-up, dirty pickup truck. Six grills were fired up where Elvis dumped the mollusks. A wooden table was garnished with oyster knives, butter, vinegar and saltine crackers. Coolers were filled with beer. There were no plates or chairs, only flaming grills and what seemed like a ton of oysters and clams in the back of the truck all amidst what appeared to be more Christmas lights ablaze than lit up Fifth Avenue in New York City.

Grandpaw walked up to Bonita and said, "Hey, Ms. Roberts, glad you could come." When Bonita extended her gloved hand, he slapped a cool can of Pabst into it and said, "Merry Christmas." He continued on to greet a carload of arriving guests.

Bonita reached for a handkerchief in her purse to wipe off the foam that had splashed on her mink. She picked her way over to several other committee members who were standing together gawking at the decorations.

Bonita had not eaten before coming to the function and, although she loved Oysters Rockefeller, she had never eaten a roasted oyster and did not have a clue how to open one. Once everyone arrived, Grandpaw whistled and yelled that the food was ready. The guests proceeded to the large, wooden table. Grandpaw took his oyster knife out of his oilslicker pocket, and pointed out the location of the oyster's "mouth" and demonstrated how to open the shell. He cut the muscle, held the shell up to his lips and sucked the oyster out. Bonita thought she was going to be ill.

"Now, I likes mine jest the way they is, but there's butter and vinegar if you wants to dip'em first. Elvis, show'em how to do that."

Elvis reached in his pocket for his oyster knife. Bonita wondered if an oyster knife were something these plebeians carried on their person on a regular basis. She didn't think it was a personal item, since there were many of them on the table, but Grandpaw and Elvis each seemed to have his own. Elvis repeated the demonstration of where the oyster's mouth was. He opened the shell, cut the muscle, plunged his knife into the oyster, dipped it into a bowl of vinegar, and ate it off the oyster knife.

"That's all there is to it. Dig in," said Elvis.

Bonita noticed that there were only two large bowls of butter and two large bowls of vinegar on the dirty table. She watched as Grandmaw reached in her apron and took out her personal oyster knife and started the process. Grandmaw dredged her oyster through the butter and plopped it into her mouth. Elvis had shucked another by then and dipped his in the same bowl of butter Grandmaw had used.

If Grandmaw, Grandpaw and Elvis had sacrificed a goat at this point, Bonita couldn't have been any more shocked. She backed away from the table and, unseen, hurried back to her car. Fortunately, she had told Alphonso to wait. A few late guests were surprised as they drove up to see Bonita hanging out of the side of the car with Alphonso holding her head. She threw up all over a boxwood decorated with twinkling lights and mechanized Santa's elves hammering away on little toy trucks.

33

Hunter & Lalique

Hunter threw the yellow Ferrari into park, hopped out of the car, slammed the door and started for the front door to Walthome. He didn't realize Lalique was still in the car until he heard her door shut.

"What's the matter with you, Hunter?" she asked as she followed him.

"What's the matter with me? Have you taken leave of your senses? Where have we just come from? A funeral! Whose funeral was it? Sandy Hibbert's. Doesn't that mean anything to you?" yelled Hunter.

"It means that some stupid young girl had her hopes set on this ridiculous debutante business that these country bumpkins put so much stock in, and because her mother lied about her aristocratic background, the girl wasn't asked and she killed herself. A tragedy. Sad, but stupid," answered Lalique.

"That's all?"

"What else?" questioned Lalique.

"I can't believe that you can find your way around sometimes, Lalique. What did I look for from the first day we settled here in 'Hooterville?'"

"You looked for one of the locals to introduce you to potential 'business' partners in the area."

"Right. And did I find my boy through your social contacts and all of those boring home cocktail parties and dinners to which you got us invited?" Hunter queried.

"No. You lucked into him. Bill Waltham came to his former front door, which is now yours, and asked to be cut in on the deal."

"Very, very good, Lalique. Now, I ask you again, does the funeral we very recently attended make any more sense to you now as to why I may be a little concerned?"

"Oh, you mean because Sandy Hibbert was Bill Waltham's stepdaughter?" purred Lalique.

"Exactly! Give the lady a hundred dollars; she said the magic word."

"I still don't understand what you're talking about."

"Well, this may seem very strange to you, Lalique, especially after seeing Trudy Waltham, but for some reason known only to him and God Almighty, Bill Waltham is in love with Trudy. Trudy is obviously upset; her only daughter is dead, killed herself, and I'm sure Trudy feels a great deal of responsibility for her death. Trudy and her lies are the reason the selection committee didn't invite her daughter to debut and the reason Sandy draped the scarves around the water pipe," explained Hunter.

"Yeah? So?" questioned Lalique.

"I cannot fathom that you are so dense. Do you think Bill Waltham is going to be able to concentrate on our deal? No, he's going to be consoling his wife. When is the deal supposed to go down? On the twenty-eighth of December, planned purposely to be at the same time as the frigging Magnolia Ball. In case you forget, we checked on this place months ago. We were aware of the Magnolia Ball before we ever drove into this dark hole. Since the reason the kid killed herself is because of the Ball, do you think Bill Waltham is going to be able to leave Trudy that night? I think not."

"He already told you he wasn't going to be able to be here for the drop. He told you that before his stepdaughter killed herself. Since he thought she was going to be debuting he said it would look funny if he weren't at the Ball, didn't he?" asked Lalique.

"Yeah, but his being at the Ball would be fine. He'd have a phone and be able to contact us. Now he'll have to stay at home with Trudy. Some of the locals aren't going to be here for the actual drop because they have to be at the Ball, which will provide a good cover. I don't care who does it or how that stuff gets off loaded, but it's got to get into this house, and it's got to get in here fast. Bill was supposed to coordinate all of the 'good ol' boy' network, and now he'll be sitting at home playing nursemaid to Trudy," stated Hunter.

"Maybe not. He's completely broke. He'll probably think of something to tell her so he can get out that night."

"You are totally hopeless. Nothing phases you, does it? If you weren't so damned gorgeous, I'd send you down the road," smirked Hunter.

"I doubt it," smiled Lalique, as she passed in front of Hunter, put the key in the lock, opened the door, stepped into the center hall and out of her black, sheath dress, all in one motion. She wore absolutely nothing underneath it.

When Hunter looked at her fantastic body, standing there with nothing on but her black pumps, he forgot his anger about Bill Waltham and the drug drop. Lalique had that effect on him from the first he laid eyes on her.

After several hours of lovemaking on the cold, slate foyer floor, Hunter was spent. He leaned up on one elbow and reached for his jacket that lay in a heap on the floor. Fumbling through his pockets, he retrieved a cigarette.

As he lit up he said, "Well, I'm going to have to figure out a way to call Waltham and see what he's going to be able to do for us, if he's in or out. Maybe he's got a backup who can handle his part of the deal. What excuse could I use to call over there tonight? I mean they've only shortly gotten back from the damned funeral."

Lalique languidly rolled over on her stomach and said, "Well, I guess you could check to make sure the dinner I had sent to their house arrived."

"You sent a dinner to the house?" asked Hunter.

"Yes. I called the Crest and ordered dinner for Trudy and Bill and had it delivered to the carriage house. It should have gotten there about fifteen minutes ago."

"Why did you do that? I already sent about two-hundred dollars worth of flowers to the funeral, plus a plant to the house," Hunter said.

"Because to anyone who knows anything about anything, in the South, it's customary to send or take food to the home of the bereaved. You people from the Bronx know nothing about nothing," teased Lalique.

"Anyway, I take it all back. You are a genius. Yes, that's a perfectly good reason to call, especially if Trudy answers the phone. I'll call Bill to make sure their dinner has arrived."

Hunter stood, grabbed his clothes, and headed for the bedroom phone.

"Bill? Hunter Quarrels. Lalique and I wanted to offer our condolences again and to have you give our sympathy to Trudy. By the way, we ordered dinner from the Crest for the two of you for this evening. I want to make sure it arrived."

"Yes, it did. Thanks, Hunter. That was very thoughtful of you. Both Trudy and I really appreciate your kindness. Your spray of flowers at the funeral was absolutely lovely, and thank you for the beautiful plant too. You've both really done too much," responded Bill.

"No problem. Anything we can do to help. Say, Bill, I don't want to put any pressure on you or anything, but I'm sure you are aware that our business deal is to take place on Magnolia Ball night. I know that will be a bad time for you, and that night will be an especially difficult time for your wife, but can we talk about the logistics of the deal?" Hunter pressed.

"Of course. I'm sure you know that I won't be able to be physically present for the actual deal on the twenty-eighth. As you say, that's going to be a particularly difficult time for Trudy; however, I can certainly spring loose in the next few days for a little meet. It shouldn't take too long, do you think?" Bill answered.

"Should be able to run through everything in about an hour. Do you have someone in the wings to kind of take over your part in this thing, Bill?"

"I haven't actually asked anyone yet, but I've been thinking about it since Sandy's accident, and soon I'll have a name for you. I have someone in mind. I only need to speak with him," said Bill.

"That'll be fine. I know you'll make sure it's someone trustworthy. You know, everything has to go like clockwork."

"It will, my friend. It will. Take it from me. We live down here in the country, but these old boys are smart as whips. Everything will be smooth as silk. Where shall we meet?"

"How about here? Eight o'clock? Tomorrow night?" asked Hunter.

"You got it. I'll be there tomorrow night at eight and yeah, that'll give me plenty of time to meet with my people. Gotta run now, Hunter. Doorbell is ringing. More people coming over to console Trudy. She's not doing well at all, you know?"

"I know, it must be very difficult for her, Bill. Again, you have my deepest sympathy and I hope the two of you enjoy your dinner," Hunter finished and hung up the phone.

"Well, you certainly are the height of sensitivity, 'deepest sympathy and enjoy your dinner' in the same breath," yawned Lalique.

"How the hell am I supposed to know what to say? I don't give a damn about Bill Waltham and I certainly don't give a damn about his dead step-daughter."

"That's my Hunter. The only person he cares about in the whole world is himself," Lalique said as she stood up to go to the bathroom.

Hunter leaped across the room and grabbed her in his arms.

"No, there's one more person I care about. Who's that?" Hunter questioned.

"I don't have any idea. Who is that, Hunter?"

Hunter didn't answer. He buried his head between her breasts and lowered her to the floor and demonstrated for her and to her who the other person was. Lalique spread her legs and thought how she would have to wear a full length leotard for her exercise class tomorrow, for between the bruises from the slate floor and the rug burn from the carpet, she was truly going to be a mess by morning.

34

Ann Amelia & Jason

Ann Amelia was relieved. She was still wary, but since her father had first begun molesting her, this was the longest time she had ever gone without being pawed and petted She pleaded too much schoolwork for most of the semester at college, so her first visit home had been Thanksgiving break.

Since the beginning of school, she had dreaded the five days at home, but mercifully her father was on a case out of town when her mother met her at the Savannah Airport Thanksgiving Eve. Later that evening, before her father returned, her mother's sister, brother-in-law, and her two female cousins arrived to spend the holiday. The guests remained through the weekend. She made sure no occasion had arisen where she and her father were alone for even a moment, although he did, one time, try to entice her to go to the store with him. She insisted her cousins accompany them. Other than that, her father left her alone.

On the Saturday after Thanksgiving she and her mother had attended the Magnolia Ball Debutante tea. Although she certainly wasn't looking forward to the upcoming events the following month, she was hoping that perhaps there would be so much activity her father wouldn't have a chance to get near.

Once again on the plane home now for the Christmas holidays, Ann Amelia was praying her nightmare was finally over. Maybe her father wouldn't bother her anymore. As she walked off the plane and into the airport, she hesitated for just an instant. Her mother wasn't there.

"Hi, sugar! How's Deddy's little girl?" her father said as he briskly walked toward her enveloping her in a bear hug.

She felt herself immediately tense as he touched her, but said, "Fine, Deddy, how are you?"

Her father released her, and they walked to baggage claim together. He kept up a line of chatter about the activities in Montiac and why her mother had been unable to come to the airport. After the luggage was collected, they walked to the car. Her fear was palpable. She was close to paralysis.

There were so many abandoned roads and turnoffs along the route from Savannah to Montiac. At each turnoff, she feared her father would swerve off the road and want to show his little girl "how much he loved her." She was surprised, however, because her father didn't veer to the right or left during the entire drive, and he did not reach out for her, hold her hand, or even ask her to move closer to him. He made no suggestive remarks nor did he look at her in the "special way."

The Cadillac pulled into the driveway just after her mother's Mercedes arrived. Mona rushed over to Ann Amelia, hugged her, and exclaimed about how good she looked. Deddy was left to bring in the luggage as mother and daughter entered the house.

"Tomorrow, we're going to buy your dress," her mother gushed.

"Oh, I don't need a new dress, Mommy. I can wear my graduation dress."

Her mother wouldn't hear of it. The next day they would buy the most gorgeous, expensive gown in all of Georgia, Florida and the Carolinas combined. And they did. The gown was absolutely exquisite and cost almost twenty-five hundred dollars.

For the next two weeks, Ann Amelia attended parties, teas, and luncheons, sometimes accompanied by her mother, sometimes by both parents, but mostly by her escort, Tom, a local boy who was certainly not a romantic interest. They had been friends since early childhood and shared a comfortable relationship. Tom was from a good family and he was an excellent dancer. A good-looking young man, he was popular with young and old alike. Best of all, Ann Amelia's father liked him, therefore he didn't get angry when she went out with him.

To her complete surprise, Ann Amelia was enjoying herself. Even though she had fought this "deb thing" at first, she was having fun. Her father hadn't bothered her at all, and for the first time since she could remember, her life seemed to be almost normal. She was even beginning to relax at night.

The night before the rehearsal for the ball, when no other functions had been planned, Ann Amelia and her parents spent a quiet evening at home. Mona suggested Ann Amelia try on her ball gown and let her father see her in it.

She didn't want to and said, "Oh, why don't we let Deddy wait, and then it'll be a surprise?"

Jason countered, "No, Ann Amelia, I'd like to have you try on that gown. After your mother told me what it cost, I'd like to make sure I'm getting my money's worth."

Reluctantly, Ann Amelia went upstairs to her room to try on the dress. She pulled on a pair of panty hose. Removing the Merry Widow corset from her lingerie drawer, she called to her mother to come up and help her. There was no way she could fasten all of those hooks and eyes.

Mona assisted her in getting into the long-lined bra. After Ann Amelia removed the clear, plastic cover from the lovely dress, her mother helped her slip the scoop-necked satin gown over her head. It was truly beautiful and fit her perfectly accenting her small waist and showing off her pretty shoulders and back. Mona had suggested earlier that Ann Amelia wear her hair in a French twist for her debut.

"Now, put your hair up so Deddy can get the full effect while I get your heels."

Ann Amelia dutifully put her hair up with a few pins.

Her mother backed out of the room telling her how stunning she looked and said, "Now, I'll get Deddy and we'll stand in the foyer so you can make your entrance down the staircase."

Ann Amelia waited a few minutes until she heard her mother's call. Then she exited her room and started down the stairway. The gown was fitted with just a slight fullness to the skirt. Though Ann Amelia had been a little nervous about her exposed cleavage, Mona had told her that she was eighteen now and didn't need to be so modest.

She was about halfway down the steps when the look in her father's eyes registered. He had that horrible look he always had when he wanted to show her "how much he loved her."

She stopped and put her hand against the wall.

"What's the matter?" her mother asked.

"I suddenly don't feel well. I'm going to go take the dress off. I feel like I might throw up."

"You couldn't have gotten sick that quickly," her father grumbled. "Come on down here and let me have a look at you."

"No, Deddy, I really feel sick," she said as she started to turn to go toward her room.

"Come down here this instant!" her father yelled.

"Jason, what is the matter with you?" asked Mona. "She said she feels ill."

"She doesn't feel ill at all. She's ungrateful. I've spent all that money on a dress and she doesn't care. She didn't want to try it on in the first place. Now she's complaining that she's sick. That's nonsense! Get down here right now, young lady!"

Ann Amelia turned and started down the steps. As she reached the bottom step, the phone rang.

Mona reached for the telephone on the foyer table. "Hello. Yes. Oh my goodness! Why, of course, I'll be right over." She replaced the receiver and said, "That was Mrs. Webster. She fell in her kitchen and has cut her hand pretty badly. I'm going over to see if I can help her."

Mrs. Webster was an elderly lady who lived two doors away. She had a maid all day but refused to have help in the house at night. Sometimes when she needed aid, she called Mona.

Mona went to the foyer closet to get a jacket. Ann Amelia started up the steps.

"I'll get out of this dress and go with you, Mommy."

"Oh, there's no need, and you said you weren't feeling well. I'll be back shortly." With that, her mother was out the door.

Ann Amelia continued up the stairs at a rapid pace, but Jason came behind her taking the steps three at a time. He grabbed her by the wrist and turned her toward him.

"Now, you don't have to go and take that lovely dress off. I've hardly gotten a good look at you in it."

"You'll get a good look in two nights, Deddy. I really want to take the dress off. I don't feel well. I'm not kidding."

"Very well," he said and released her arm.

She turned and slowly continued up the steps moving cautiously toward her room. As she tried to shut her door, he was in the doorway.

"I know you don't want anything to happen to that lovely dress, and since you needed your mother to help you into it, I'm sure you'll need your deddy to help you out of it."

"No, I don't, Deddy. It'll only take a minute. Please go back downstairs. I'll be right down."

"No, I insist. I'm going to help you out of your dress."

He reached for the zipper. As he grabbed for it, she pulled away, and the dress ripped.

Jason went ballistic, "Now look what's you've done! How are you going to explain this to your mother? Why didn't you stand still?"

Ann Amelia had all she could take. She turned and screamed at him, "I didn't **do** anything! You did it! Why can't you leave me alone? Get out of my room! Other fathers don't try to undress their eighteen-year-old daughters. Leave me alone! Get away from me! You're perverted!"

Her father looked at her for a split second in stunned silence. Then he moved toward her, grabbed the front of the dress and ripped it away in one rapid movement. She was so frightened she couldn't move. She stood stock still completely bewildered. Little was left of her gorgeous gown. Jason plunged his hand down the front of the Merry Widow and tried to pull it off. Galvanized, she began to push, kick, and scream. He took her arm and bent it behind her back. He pushed her over to the bed, where he threw her down and began to pull and rip at the hooks and eyes. Ann Amelia screamed and kicked and tried to get out of his grasp.

With the noise and the thrashing about, neither of them heard the front door open or Mona running up the stairs. She opened Ann Amelia's bedroom door just as Jason unzipped his fly and prepared to enter his writhing daughter from the rear.

Mona screamed. Jason jerked around to see his wife's stricken face. He hastily straightened himself up, turned his back on Mona, zipped his trousers and walked out of the room. Mona rushed to her daughter and held her as they both sobbed.

Jason went down the grand stairway. He got his jacket from the foyer closet, crossed to the mudroom door and went into the garage. He started the Cadillac and sped down the driveway. He had no idea where he was going, but he knew life as he knew it was over. Mona would never forgive him. There would be a divorce. Any kind of relationship with Ann Amelia was out of the question. His only hope was somehow keeping Mona and Ann Amelia from revealing his sickness to society. One thing he knew for sure was that Mona's silence, if he could get it, was going to be expensive. She loved her creature comforts. Perhaps a large enough settlement could guarantee she would keep quiet.

When Mona had stopped sobbing uncontrollably and had caught her breath, she gently asked Ann Amelia what had happened. Kept stored inside of her since she was a little girl, the horrors Jason had inflicted upon her since childhood tumbled out She told her mother everything. Mona was traumatized not only because of what had happened to her baby, but also because she had never suspected a thing.

She helped Ann Amelia remove the Merry Widow and bathed her face and put her to bed. She sat down next to her daughter and very practically began to deal with the situation at hand.

"First of all, we have to worry about the next few days. Early in the morning we have to get another dress. This one is definitely not repairable."

"Mommy, I don't care about the dress or the Ball. I don't want to make my debut, especially now. I never really did. I'll call Tom. He'll understand when I tell him I've changed my mind."

"Darling, I'm sure Tom would understand, but all of Montiac won't. Now, you're going to make your debut. You're going to stand up straight and tall and you're going to look splendid. We'll get another dress tomorrow."

"No! I don't want to ever have anything to do with my father again!"

"Who said anything about your father? He won't be coming back here, I promise. Your father has forfeited any right to have anything to do with you or me. I'll call your Uncle Jack in Houston, and he'll fly out and present you."

"How are you going to explain any of this to him?"

"I don't know yet, but he's my brother, and something will come to me."

"Mommy, please! I don't want to do this."

"You must, dear. The Magnolia Ball has been a part of life in this family for generations. You're made of sturdy stock. It'll all be over in two more days. We'll get through this and then I'll deal with Jason."

Mona bent over and kissed her daughter softly on the cheek. She told her how much she loved her and gave her the universal mother's promise that "everything would be all right." Ann Amelia sighed and told her mother she loved her too. Mona picked up the ruined dress. She crossed to the door and turned back to look again at her child. Switching out the light, she soundlessly closed the door.

Jason continued driving aimlessly. Before he realized where he was headed, he had turned into the Sweet Treat. He entered the back room. By the end of the evening, Jason, through Jordan Roget, had found a way to make a lot of money fast. If everything went as the plan had been laid out to him, it could well be enough to keep Mona's mouth zipped. After all, what did he have to lose?

35

Celestine, Sissy & Anthony

The afternoon of the Ball, as Celestine was making her final preparations for the festivities, the telephone rang. She was pleasantly surprised to hear Sissy Donnoghue's voice on the other end. Sissy asked about Anthony, and Celestine bubbled.

"Oh, Anthony's fine, dear. How sweet of you to ask. He's taking a little nap at the moment. The Ball is tonight and Jamison and I always take him. He's gotten a new tux for this year with a plaid cummerbund and bow tie. He told me that plain black just isn't 'in' anymore."

"That's so cute, Celestine. I do hope that Portland and I get to attend that Ball of yours one of these years before I die. We're on our way out, but I wanted to call and tell you something. Portland has been going out of his mind ever since we were there last summer trying to remember how he knew Bonita Roberts. He did some checking and then contacted Hammond Studios and finally was able to get some old reels of those 'B' films Bonita made back before God was born. As soon as Portland saw Bonita on the screen, he remembered where he had seen her. He met Bonita about thirty years ago at a convention where one of his associates was escorting her. Portland said that Bonita was quite attractive then, and very attentive to his business associate, but Portland knew that the man was married. At a propitious time, he asked his friend what was going on. The business associate confided that he was one of

Bonita's regular clients, and that she charged one thousand dollars an hour for her services. Are you getting my drift, Celestine?"

There was a long silence on Celestine's end of the phone before she whispered, "You mean she was a prostitute?"

"That's exactly what I mean. She lived at the Beverly Wilshire and worked for Enrique Dubra, a pimp. Portland called his old friend and he told Portland that Bonita had been the highest priced call girl in Los Angeles for over thirty years. She lived in one of the cottages at the hotel. He also said, 'What a woman!' The old fool was getting excited just talking about her. Portland's friend didn't know what ever happened to her but said he would love to see her and be with her just one more time. I don't think Portland told him what she looks like now, but can you believe it? That woman who stirred up such a ruckus about your friend Trudy making up her background did exactly the same thing, only worse. Wouldn't everyone in Dorchester County just die if they knew about old Bonita?"

"Yes, they certainly would. Oh, this is very unnerving, Sissy," Celestine replied.

"Have I done the wrong thing by telling you, Celestine? I certainly thought you should know."

"Well, I don't know if I should know or not. If I had never known—oh well, Bonita's secret is safe with me. I certainly won't tell anyone. It is horrid of her to have done what she did to Trudy, though, and to be so high-and-mighty about it when she's done the same thing. Only she's covering up a lifetime of sin, not one of poverty."

"Anyway, Portland did fill his friend in on where Bonita lives and what she's doing now. The friend got a big laugh out of it and said to Portland, 'Leave it to Bonita to fool everyone. She never made it big on the screen, but she is a damned good actress.'"

"She certainly is. Thank you for the information, Sissy, but I won't do anything with it. At least now Portland can stop worrying about where he saw her."

"That's true. It really was bothering him. He never forgets a face, and ravaged though hers is, he knew that he had seen her somewhere. Oh, here he is now. We have to run, Celestine. I hope the Ball is the best ever. Love you, dear. I'll call again soon. Bye."

"Bye, Sissy," said Celestine as she dropped the receiver into its cradle. She crossed the great room and went up the stairs.

At the nursery, she stuck her head in the door and said, "Well, I see that my fine young man has awakened from his nap. Did you sleep well, sweetheart? Come into mother's room while I start preparing for my bath. I have to tell you about that mean old Bonita Roberts who wouldn't speak to you the day you and mother were going riding."

Celestine picked Anthony up from his bed and lovingly carried him into her room. She proceeded to regale Anthony with the entire story Sissy related to her on the phone.

36

Izonia & Hannah

Celestine's maid, Izonia, had been with her since she had been a child, just as Queenie had served Vivian Bauer back in the early thirties. Izonia was one of twelve children. Her ancestors were owned by the Beecham family prior to the War Between the States, known as and still referred to in "Dixie" as the "War of Northern Aggression." Izonia's great grandparents had worked the land surrounding Beechland, where Izonia lived her entire life. Her mother was the maid to Margarine, Celestine's mother. Izonia and Celestine had played together as children, since Izonia and her family had lived in one of the many dependencies at Beechland.

One of many functions Izonia performed for Celestine was shopping, a chore Celestine loathed. Since Izonia did all the cooking, it made sense for her to purchase the ingredients. Since she was a trusted servant, she had an account at the local bank in her name, into which Jamison made monthly deposits for running the household. Each Thursday morning at ten o'clock she left Beechland in the Piersall's chauffeur-driven Jaguar sedan to purchase the weekly supplies.

There were two grocery stores in Montiac. One was a Safeway and one was locally owned. The shopping area of the town also provided the home of the Bauer Butcher Shop and the Farmer's Market, where during one of her forays into town, Izonia made the acquaintance of Hannah, Bonita's maid, who was also shopping. Alphonso stood beside the maroon Rolls Royce. The two women were both at the Farmer's Market inspecting the first cantaloupes of the season.

As Hannah put a melon to her nose, Izonia said, "What you doing?"

Hannah replied, "I'm sniffing the melon to see if it's ripe."

Izonia said, "Where you from, gal?"

"California originally," Hannah answered with a smile.

"These here melons is locally grown. Maybe you have to smell California melons, but these here you have to thump. Let me show you," Izonia said as she took the melon from Hannah and gave it several thumps. "Were you going to buy this one?" Izonia asked after she had finished her thumping.

"I was thinking about it. It has a nice, ripe smell to it," Hannah answered.

"Well it ain't ripe yet, honey. That melon'd have to sit for another four days before it'd be fit to eat."

"How can you tell by thumping?" Hannah asked.

Izonia picked up another melon and thumped it with her knuckle near the top. "Hear that? That hollow sound. That means the melon is ready to eat right now."

Hannah picked up a melon and thumped it, but it didn't sound the same as Izonia's melon had. She tried several more and finally found one that made the hollow sound. She passed it to Izonia, who in turn thumped it and said, "Now you got yourself a good melon."

Hannah laughed. She took a sniff of the melon. "It don't smell too ripe," she said.

Izonia responded, "Have you been having good luck with your sniffing method, sugar?"

"Not really," Hannah admitted.

The two introduced themselves. When they found out for whom each worked, they had a good laugh, since they were employed by the two leaders of Dorchester County society. Their mistresses were friendly with each other, or at least they had been before the Trudy Waltham scandal and Sandy Hibbert's death.

The maids struck up a conversation; a friendship began. They exchanged phone calls, recipes and visits on their days off. Izonia regaled Hannah with stories of Miss Celestine and Anthony. She told Hannah she almost believed Anthony was a real person herself and had caught herself talking to him when no one was around. She told about when Miss Celestine left and didn't take Anthony, she usually left him in the kitchen with her. Laughing, she told about the time she had been trying a new recipe and, after tasting it several times herself, had asked Anthony to taste it and tell her what he thought. She caught herself, embarrassed, and laughed out loud.

"Now Miss Celestine, she had a great sadness in her life," Izonia told Hannah and she related to her how Miss Celestine had been unable to get pregnant for so many years. "Finally, she had a beautiful, little baby boy with the cord wrapped around his neck. That was how she took to that doll. And now she calls Anthony her son. I don't think there's no harm in it though. Miss Celestine is the kindest, warmest, most thoughtful lady in the world, and I think she wanted that baby so bad both for her and Mr. Jamison that she just couldn't deal with the fact that her baby died, so Anthony took his place in her mind. She's made him all kinds of clothes. He's got more get-ups than most real folks, and she slicks his hair up when he goes to the Ball. He looks real cute in his little tuxedo with a rosebud in the lapel. I think Anthony's good for Miss Celestine, and he don't cause no harm, 'cept sometimes I think some of her friends think she's a little tetched in the head. But she's just as sane as anyone I've ever known. Miss Celestine don't like gossip. She won't allow no gossip in her house except from Anthony. Every once in a while he 'says' something that Miss Celestine wouldn't never allow no one else to say."

"Doesn't she do the talking for him?" Hannah asked.

"Sure she do. In a high, squeaky voice."

"Then she is doin' the gossipin' if she talks for the doll," Hannah reasoned.

"No, you don't understand. Miss Celestine don't ever gossip. The only reason she lets Anthony get away with it is because she loves him so much and thinks he's so cute."

Hannah shook her head and thought how she hoped she got the chance to meet this Anthony, because Izonia, although she denied it, seemed to think he was a real person too.

Hannah then told Izonia about Creekside Farm and some of the goings-on there, but she certainly never divulged Bonita's occupation in California or her extracurricular relationship with Alphonso. She did describe Bonita's ridiculous master bath and some of the ludicrous at-home outfits in which she attired her ever-expanding bulk. But Hannah spoke kindly of Bonita. She loved her just as much as Izonia loved Celestine. In short, the two women enjoyed each other's company immensely and became good friends.

Part Three

The Ball and the Drug Delivery

37

Bill's Network

Bill Waltham worked hard for Hunter Quarrels to arrange for partners in the "cellular phone business" deal and to set up the distribution centers for the product. He had used the "good ol' boy" network to recruit some of his cronies. Chet Thomas was the first contact he made. Although Chet and Dee lived well, it was most recently due to Dee's inheritance from her father, who died several months earlier. At the time Bill approached him, Chet was rapidly depleting the inheritance and was anxious to get in on anything that would make him rich again—the sooner, the better.

Frank Karsh was financially secure but was always eager to make more money to keep Hilda in baubles. He was in, too.

Jordan Roget didn't have to be asked. Chet mentioned to him that he was working on a deal with Bill Waltham, so Jordan approached Bill and told him he wanted in also. Chucky Saxon, with no known source of income but a high-flying lifestyle, was also interested. When Bill spoke with him about the plan, Chucky agreed immediately.

Waltham was extremely careful about the contacts he made and thought long and hard before he approached each person. Patrick Abrams had been a "for sure," as his gambling debts were legendary. Although John, the hardware store owner, wasn't really in Bill's social circle, though he had heard Mandy was "debbing," Bill knew the local bookie would want to be involved.

Many of the players were cast. The stage was set and the big "cellular phone deal" was to go down the same night as the Magnolia Ball.

Early December, Hunter and Lalique began taking nightly sails on the *Diamond Jim,* no small feat on the sixty-five foot sloop. Each night after sunset the two set out and sailed out of Nassa's Creek and into the mouth of the Savannah River heading for the Atlantic Ocean. Various adaptations had been made to the vessel, allowing the two of them to handle the large craft without the necessity of a crew. Hunter had some difficulty convincing Lalique of the importance of making the nightly journeys, for Dorchester County's Southern climes often turned raw in the winter months, particularly as the sun withdrew earlier and earlier with each passing day. Lalique was definitely not excited about having to bundle up every evening, board the boat and sail into the chilling wind. Hunter insisted, however, because he didn't want to arouse any suspicion when the *Diamond Jim* left its moorings on the night of the Ball.

The first week in December, Taylor, Hunter's friend from Pennsylvania (who had earlier been stopped by Charlie, the Montiac town cop, for speeding), was standing in a deserted airfield near Bogota, Colombia. He watched carefully as the last load of cargo was placed in the bay of a DC-3.

Taylor had called Hunter as soon as he returned to Pennsylvania and informed him about his brush with Charlie. Hunter was incensed at Taylor's stupidity and recklessness. He told him he was never to come to Dorchester County again. Taylor had been involved with Hunter on several other deals and had never made a mistake, but Hunter wanted to make sure Taylor didn't create any problems for him now. He waited to hear from the authorities about the speeding charge and Taylor's ultimate escape from Charlie, but several months passed with no reference being made to the incident. When an occasion arose, Hunter casually mentioned the encounter to Four Eyes, who admitted Charlie had told him about stopping Taylor. But Four Eyes hadn't seemed concerned, so

Hunter was satisfied. He had made the right decision to select Dorchester County for his biggest job yet—these people were so dense!

Taylor phoned Hunter and confirmed that the product was aboard the plane. Then he gave the pilot the signal to take off. The DC-3 roared down the runway and took off for its flight to a small grass strip between Key West and Marathon, Florida. There, two more of Hunter's lieutenants would meet the plane and pay some locals to offload its cargo onto a barge harbored at a little retreat called Rainbow Bend, near mile marker fifty-eight on Route One. Two tugboats would push the barge to Jeckyl Island, Georgia, up the inland waterway arriving on the twenty-second of December. There, three private yachts belonging to prominent Dorchesterians would await the cargo. The yachts, once loaded, would set sail and arrive at the mouth of the Savannah River at precisely six o'clock at night to rendezvous with the *Diamond Jim* on the scheduled date.

Hunter spent hours briefing Bill Waltham and his men on exactly what had to be accomplished on the big night. Mitch, ex-husband of Mary Beth Bracer, and Chet Thomas were to accompany Hunter and Lalique on the *Diamond Jim*. It had been outfitted with a hoist so that the stacked pallets of cargo could be unloaded expeditiously from the holds of the three yachts and placed on the *Diamond Jim*. The sail would take thirty minutes each way. Hunter decided to also use the hoist to remove the cargo from the hold of his boat onto the dock. There was, however, the problem of transporting sixty thousand pounds of cocaine from the dock, up a thirty-foot bank, and into the great room of Walthome.

Bill had come up with a solution. In October, he suggested to Hunter to apply for a permit to build a larger dock at Walthome to accommodate the *Diamond Jim*. Since Bill Waltham owned the property, he'd give Hunter his permission. There wouldn't be a problem obtaining the permit. Once the permit was granted, construction could be set to start after the first of the new year, although Hunter had no intention of building a dock.

In order to build a dock, new pilings had to be sunken in the creek bottom. This was accomplished with a crane. Hunter made arrangements with a local construction company, to have the crane in place so work could begin promptly after the first of the year. The crane was on its barge in Nassa's Creek, where it would never be used for sinking pilings, but awaited its part in the transfer of the cargo. Chet Thomas knew how to operate it. Once the *Diamond Jim* landed with the cocaine, Chet would man the crane, remove the pallets from the hold, swing them over the bank, and deposit them on a conveyor belt. Electrically powered, a simple flip of a switch would deliver the cocaine to the great room. There, the rest of Bill's boys could stack the bags until morning, where they would await the next phase of the plan.

The removal of the cargo from the *Diamond Jim* to the great room was scheduled to take no longer than one hour. The time planned for the complete operation would take two hours and forty-five minutes. Those men involved in the deal, who were fathers of young ladies being presented at the Ball, would not be involved in the return sail. They would have to be at the club for the beginning festivities at six o'clock, just when the transfer was to begin. The plan was brilliant!

Four Eyes and his boys thought so, too.

38

Blanche and Nancy

Blanche Givens called Nancy Abrams in a panic.

"Nancy, Bonita has just left here and she's in a rage. She went to Mandy's oyster roast last night and was horrified at the girl's grandparents and their tacky Christmas decorations. She's furious and wants to know how Mandy was selected."

"You didn't tell her, did you?" asked Nancy.

"Of course I didn't tell her, but how long do you think it's going to take her to figure it out? For God's sake, Nancy, you and I are the 'chosen ones,' and we addressed the invitations. I told you this would never fly."

"Blanche, are you my best friend in the entire world?"

"Yes."

"Have I gone to the wall for you on the damned committee and other times too?"

"Yes, Nancy, you have, but I think…"

"I can't help what you think. Patrick owes that damned John tons of money because of the stupid bets he's made, and John is willing to forgive ten thousand dollars of it if Mandy makes her debut. Now, you and I discussed all of this a long time ago. We weighed the pros and cons and decided we could pull it off. Don't back out on me now."

"I must have taken leave of my senses. We're going to get caught. Bonita will figure it out soon enough, and then your husband is going to be in worse trouble when Bonita demands Mandy's invitation rescinded."

"You don't think she'd do that, do you? I mean, the write-up has been in the *Montiac Minutes*. Mandy has already given her deb party, such as it was."

"I think Bonita's capable of anything right now. I've never seen her so distressed. She wasn't as upset about Trudy's lies as she is about this Mandy situation. If only Bonita hadn't gone to the party! But she did, and she says that Mandy will make a sham of the whole affair. She referred to her as poor, white trash. What are we going to do?"

"We're going to deny, deny, deny! What else can we do?"

"What are we going to say when Bonita starts her 'Spanish Inquisition?' You know how carefully we're supposed to guard those invitations. Are we going to say that somehow someone stole one from us?"

"That might work, Blanche," Nancy replied.

"Have you lost your mind? She'd really go into orbit then."

"More than she is now? Maybe we could say that we addressed them together at the Crest or somewhere, somewhere public, and I had to go to the ladies' room, and someone must have taken one and sent it to Mandy. Or how about, we were at the Crest and one of the waiters hit our table, and the invitations fell onto the floor, and when he helped us pick them up, maybe one got misplaced? Do you think that would work?"

"No, Nancy. I don't think anything will work. Bonita is going to figure it out, and Trudy is not going to be the only one dismissed from the committee. In addition, Mandy's invitation will be recalled and Patrick's debt is going to be tripled. John will be so enraged that he'll probably have Patrick's kneecaps broken, or worse."

"There must be something we can do. What if I went to Bonita and told her the truth? Do you think that would work, Blanche?"

"Nancy, have you completely lost it? Bonita is from Spanish royalty. She takes this debutante business very seriously, probably even more seriously than we do. She would never understand how we could jeopardize the Magnolia Ball and the integrity of the committee over some personal problem, especially one dealing with what Bonita would consider a very small amount of money."

"Then what are we going to do?" cried Nancy.

"I don't know. I really don't know. I'll try to think of something and call you back. You try thinking too, but think of something realistic. We can't tell Bonita the truth or the waiter story. I'll call you after awhile," said Blanche and rung off.

Nancy hit the button on the speakerphone, put her head down on her folded arms and cried.

39

The Ball's Progression

Since the early nineteen hundreds, the Magnolia Ball has been divided into three segments. Traditionally for twenty years prior, during the first segment, the debutantes, their parents and escorts, a tightly controlled guest list, the committee members and their spouses all met at the local country club for cocktails and dinner. Afterwards, the girls were introduced by Bonita on the arms of both their fathers, or their designated presenters, and their escorts. The fathers and their daughters danced one dance which was followed by another which the debutantes were expected to share with their escorts. The formal presentation of the debutantes of the season, the second segment, took place later at the Ball.

Once at the Ball, everyone danced, drank and socialized. Bonita then, customarily, made a short welcoming speech. Another short speech by Celestine concerning the history and the greatness of the Magnolia Ball followed. The season's debutantes were then formally presented, afterwhich they performed the "German," a traditional and fairly complicated figure, with their escorts.

The men at the Ball were subsequently given ballots on which they wrote the name of one of the debutantes. The ballot constituted each gentleman's vote for the new Queen of the Magnolia Realm. The votes were tallied and, supposedly, the girl with the most votes was crowned queen by the visiting dignitary. The dignitary first orated extolling the virtues of America, the South, Dorchester County, motherhood, apple pie, and the lovely ladies presented that evening. Prior to being crowned, the newly elected queen selected two debutantes to serve as her ladies in waiting. Everyone in Montiac knew the choice of the queen was political, and each year everyone in the county could pretty much determine who the new queen would be.

In 1991, everyone knew that Shannon Kirkham would walk away with the crown. Her father, after all, was the wealthiest father this year and wielded the most influence of any of the other dads. In addition, the accountant who "counted" the ballots each year worked for Alex Kirkham and was on his personal payroll. Shannon's victory was not only assured, it was guaranteed.

Following her crowning, the queen was presented with a white rose bouquet. It was donated by the same, lucky florist selected to provide the decorations and replaced the queen's red roses she had carried earlier when presented to society. The scepter, donated by Appleby's Jewelers and used from year to year, was placed in her hand. Lights flashed as a multitude of pictures were taken including those for the next edition of the *Montiac Minutes*.

A two-hour intermission followed, at which time most of the party-goers left the high school gymnasium. (Newcomers to Dorchester County found it most amusing that this, the zenith of society events, was held in the high school gym with exposed rafters, sweat stains, and stale aromas left over from athletic events. Nonetheless, local florists vied for the privilege of trying to transform the odiferous arena into a winter wonderland each year for the big event.) The chosen florist did the decorations gratis in hopes of recognition and future sales from the "powers-that-were", and for the honor of having their business name in the *Montiac Minutes* as the decorator of the moment.

Intermission parties were another highly toted social event. Anywhere from twenty to thirty parties in various homes took place during the two-hour recess.

The Magnolia Ball

Once the Ball resumed, approximately half of the guests returned. The other half were usually too inebriated to do anything other than go home or pass out at whatever intermission party they had attended. The second half of the Ball, the third segment, consisted of dancing, congratulating the debutantes and the queen, picture-taking and people-watching.

40

Dr. James Nyland

Dr. James Nyland, who had provided Darlene with magic diet pills to lose weight when she had first moved to the area, had come to Dorchester County in the late seventies to rent the medical building once belonging to Dr. Fent. Dr. Fent had been the local doctor in Hanover until eight years prior. One Wednesday afternoon he closed his office and took his Piper Cub out for a short flight. He never returned. It was not known whether he crashed or whether he continued flying for parts unknown. Neither he nor his plane had ever been seen or heard of again.

Nyland, his homely wife Dina, and their two, snotty-nosed kids had arrived in Montiac in the dead of winter in 1977. Nyland was driving a battered, old blue Pontiac pulling a U-Haul trailer, which contained all of his and his family's worldly possessions.

The doctor had come to Dorchester County to open his first practice. After finishing his residency, he was not drafted by any large metropolitan hospitals, so he checked around and contacted Mrs. Fent, widow or abandoned wife of Dr. Fent. They reached an agreement, whereby Jim Nyland could rent Dr. Fent's medical building and all of the equipment.

Unlike most newcomers to the County, Jim Nyland bypassed Waterfront Galore and all of the other real estate offices on his route into Montiac and stopped his car in front of the only men's shop on the Main Street. Mr. Cummings, the owner, greeted Nyland as he entered and asked if he could be of service. The doctor introduced himself and told Mr. Cummings he was going to open a family practice in the building once owned by Dr. Fent in Hanover. Cummings welcomed him to the community, and Nyland asked him if he knew of any houses or apartments for rent.

It happened that, in his spare time, Mr. Cummings bought small, "fixer-upper" houses. He renovated and sold them at huge profits. Mr. Cummings had recently finished one of his projects. Although he had always sold houses in the past, he agreed to rent this one if the new doctor were willing to sign a year's lease.

Jim agreed. He then asked Mr. Cummings a question, which Cummings thought a mite strange for a doctor. He related to his wife that evening that the new doctor had asked him, "How much money do you think I can make here?"

Mr. Cummings took Jim and his family to see the little house in which he had put second-hand appliances, a new linoleum kitchen floor and inexpensive carpet. To the new paint job, he had added an arbor to make the house larger and more modern. Dr. Nyland and his family moved their meager belongings into the house that evening.

The next day Dr. Nyland and Dina went to the medical building and began cleaning it. They worked for a week sprucing up the old building. They purchased artificial plants and some second-hand chairs for the reception area. Jim hired a woman to be his nurse, receptionist and assistant and hung out his shingle. He donned his white lab coat and waited for his first patient to arrive. He waited for three months and not one sick person, pregnant woman or even a drug salesman darkened his door.

There were two local doctors in the nearby town of Montiac, and another in the upper end of the county. Since Dr. Fent's disappearance, the citizens of Hanover had traveled the four miles to Montiac for all of their medical needs. If surgery were required or something serious was wrong with them, they traveled to Savannah to one of the hospitals. Dorchester County did not have a hospital. The local doctors could deliver babies, tape a sprained ankle, set a broken bone, administer a shot of morphine to a heart attack victim, stitch up a cut and write prescriptions. They also made house calls. Many a Dorchesterian had succumbed to a heart attack or given birth in the back of the local Rescue Squad wagon on the way to Savannah.

Because Dr. Fent had been gone for so many years, the locals had grown accustomed to going to Montiac for their doctoring. They saw no reason to change their habits at this point. Therefore, Dr. Nyland had no patients.

Dina Nyland joined the local woman's club, enrolled the children in public school, signed up to be a room mother, and volunteered two mornings a week at the local library. She became acquainted with some of the women and heard a number of them bemoan their fate at being overweight. The next time Jim complained about having no patients and getting further into debt, Dina mentioned the many women fretting about their girth. Jim suggested that the next time they complained, she should mention to them that her husband could possibly help them.

At her first opportunity, Dina did just that and shortly Jim was seeing patients and writing prescriptions for diet pills. He gave the ladies a diuretic shot on the first visit, which caused them to lose three or four pounds overnight. Even though they gained it again in the next few days, Jim told them he was helping them to get started on their way to sveltedom. Cunningly, he only prescribed fifteen diet pills each visit, so the women came faithfully every two weeks for a new prescription and therefore another bill. His practice was booming.

The diet pill industry wasn't as regulated in the late seventies as it is today. The Dorchester matrons were "speeding" through their days. Their husbands, while enjoying their new slimmer wives, were in the market for earmuffs because the women talked, talked and talked all day long. If no one was around to talk to or they had exhausted all of their friends on the phone, they were perfectly happy to talk to their reflections in a mirror. The women were delighted with their new shapes. Besides, they had energy to do all of the housework and the cooking and still felt like partying at night! Dr. Nyland became the favorite doctor of the ladies in Dorchester County.

When the year's contract on the rental house ran out, Jim and Dina bought a brick house on the water and moved to a nicer section of the County. The old blue Pontiac was relegated to the junk heap and the doctor purchased himself a Mercedes and a BMW for Dina. Expensive, designer furniture was acquired for the new house. The earth the swimming pool would occupy was excavated. Dr. Nyland began taking flying lessons. The kids were transferred from the public school and matriculated at the Country Day School. As his practice continued to flourish, and the Dorchester County ladies' bodies continued to diminish, the Nylands made application to and were accepted as members of the local country club. Both immersed themselves in golf lessons. Soon they were entering club tournaments and becoming entrenched in the social scene. Within a few months, Jim joined the Lion's Club. Before long he was elbow-to-elbow with the movers and shakers of his new hometown.

Jim Nyland had attended two years at a community college in Montana and had then transferred to Montana State University. He did well enough to be accepted to the medical school at the University of Maryland, where he barely graduated. Jim was in the bottom ten percent of his medical school class. He did his internship and residency at a two-bit hospital in New York City. The small, under-funded hospital was so desperate for doctors they would have taken practically anyone who could walk, talk and breathe simultaneously.

The aspiring doctor had managed somehow to get through both his internship and his residency. Two nights after his graduation from med. school he made love to Dina and three months later she informed him of her pregnancy. The "almost a doctor" felt obligated to marry her, therefore burdening himself with a wife while he was interning and on twenty-four hour call three days a week. Six months later, his child was born and ten months later, Dina brought forth a second child. Over the years of drudgery, filled with long hours at the hospital and little sleep, where potential failure daily stared him in the face, Jim barely managed to fulfill the minimum requirements to become a full-fledged doctor and found his way to Hanover, South Carolina.

As he began to move in the upper social circles, Jim started talking to many of them about the need for a local hospital. Everyone agreed. A meeting was held. Studies were made. Money was raised. A site in Montiac was selected. The property was purchased by a syndicate comprised of resident businessmen. The negotiators for the group manipulated the owners of the chosen property into believing they would personally be responsible for Dorchester County not having a hospital if they did not sell. So sell they did, and at a very reasonable price. The first spadeful of earth was turned with dignitaries on hand, including the Governor of the State of South Carolina. Construction on the Dorchester Hospital had begun.

Dr. Nyland placed ads in newspapers and medical journals and began to interview and to hire professional staff and administrators. Within two years the citizens of Dorchester County no longer had to travel to Savannah, but could now tend to their sick and give birth to the young in their hometown. Their offspring would be true natives—bred, born and reared in South Carolina. Surgery was also performed. Heart attack victims could be monitored, and only the most serious of trauma patients had to be airlifted in the Nightingale helicopter to a Savannah Hospital.

New professionals flocked to the area. The Realtors were in heaven. "Spec" homes were being built. Apartment complexes sprang up, seemingly overnight, and farmers were beating a path to the board of supervisors' monthly meetings to obtain permission to subdivide tracts of their land to sell to the newcomers. Jim Nyland was a local hero. It only seemed fitting to the local community leaders that, since Jim had been the only one with the idea and the know-how to facilitate the creation of a hospital in their county, he should be the Chief of Staff.

Jim's own practice had grown so much that, with his new duties at the hospital, he soon took in three partners. Dina continued to volunteer at the library. She baked cookies for school functions, attended her monthly woman's club meetings and cared for her home and children.

The one thing Dina didn't care for, however, was Dina. She was too skinny. She had faded green eyes, lack-luster brown hair, a large mouth, and a more than generous number of big, brown freckles on her face. She did not have a flair for fashion. Most often she was seen in cotton house dresses unless she was on the golf course, at which time she attired her less-than-desirable body in baggy Bermuda shorts and an oversized T-shirt.

Jim was not a bad looking man, but certainly he was not movie star handsome. However, with his new lofty position he visited Mr. Cummings at the men's shop and was outfitted properly. He had his hair cut and styled, bi-weekly, at Tresses and he often made comments to Dina encouraging her to spruce up her appearance. His urging to fix herself up, however, seemed to fall on deaf ears, which stuck out of her head at an unattractive angle.

41

Corey Tarry

Corey Tarry had come to Montiac from a neighboring county at the age of nineteen to find fame and fortune. She had worked as a waitress, a typist, a pet groomer, and had attempted to sell real estate. She dated the produce man at the local supermarket, a couple of plumbers and electricians, and one college student. (That is, until his parents found out.) Although Corey hadn't found her fortune, she had a modicum of fame; whomever she dated, she also bedded.

Perhaps the one adventure for which Corey was best known occurred when she had been in Dorchester County for about four years. She was on her way to dinner at a waterfront restaurant and was flagged down by a man on the side of the road. The fellow was from somewhere up north, and he had rented a cottage in the area for the weekend. After unpacking his car, he had planned to go into town for groceries, but his car failed to start. Since the cottage had no telephone, he had gone out onto the highway to flag down a car. Corey stopped and he asked her if she would mind taking him to a phone. She agreed and drove him to the nearest country store where he called one of the local service stations. She returned him to the cottage.

He invited her in for a drink, and she accepted. After a short while, however, she explained she had to leave because her girlfriend was waiting for her at the restaurant. The fellow asked her to come by after dinner. Four of his friends were joining him for the weekend to fish. Corey said she'd see. A few hours later, she and her friend were back at the cottage with the five men. Neither Corey nor her friend, nor any of the men left the cottage again until the following Monday. Corey had a wonderful time, apparently, because she entertained many of her acquaintances with tales of her escapades that weekend and, of course, those who were told the story passed the word.

Frustrated by her lack of immediate success in any of the positions she had held, she turned to selling cosmetics and became the local Mary Kay distributor. Her route was from Hanover to the Savannah River. She did quite well. Many of the wives of the watermen had never been exposed to cosmetics. Corey was patient and attentive to her ignorant customers. She did complete makeovers on their wrinkled, haggard and sun-damaged faces, and they, in turn, regularly gave her their household money.

One Saturday afternoon, one of the best days to sell her wares (Corey had discovered many of the women along her route had small children, and on Saturdays, the husbands were at home and could baby-sit while Corey did her makeup demonstrations), Corey set out with her cosmetics kit. She pulled into the Nylands' driveway. Corey had seen Dina on a few occasions and thought she would be the perfect candidate for a makeover. Also, Corey needed to expand her base of sales, because she really wanted to win the pink Cadillac for her division, which would be awarded at the Mary Kay annual sales meeting in Atlanta in five months.

She checked her makeup in the rearview mirror, grabbed her cosmetics kit and exited the car. When she rang the doorbell, Dr. Nyland answered and informed her that Dina was not at home. Corey commented on the lovely home, and after a few more pleasantries, Jim invited her in for a glass of iced tea. They sat on the patio near the site of the soon-to-be-completed swimming pool. Corey made appropriate remarks about the lovely landscaping, the perfect view, and anything else she could think of to ingratiate herself with the young and reasonably attractive doctor.

Everything was seemingly above-board. After twenty minutes, Corey gave Jim a brochure for Dina and told him her name and phone number were on the back of it and to please ask Dina to give her a call. Jim said he certainly would, and Corey took her leave to continue her route for the rest of the afternoon.

Several weeks passed, and Jim found himself more than once thinking about the buxom, auburn-curled, brown-eyed, sexy Corey Tarry. When Dina was suddenly called out of town to tend to her sick mother in Montana, Jim waited only a few days before he unlocked the desk drawer in his study. He extracted the Mary Kay brochure, which he had never given to Dina. He called Corey.

When she answered, Jim said, "Corey, this is Jim Nyland."

"Hello, Dr. Nyland."

"I'm not calling about the cosmetics."

"You're not?"

"No, I'm calling to see if maybe you and I could get together this evening. I hope you're not offended."

"Offended? Of course not, Dr. Nyland," giggled Corey.

"Please call me Jim."

"Well, Jim, what would you like to do?" Corey purred.

"I'd like to see you and talk to you, but we can't meet here. My wife is out of town, but my children are here with the au pair," Jim explained.

"You can come here if you'd like," Corey answered.

"Do you live alone?"

"No, I have a roommate. She's an obstetrics nurse at the hospital, but she has to work until six tomorrow morning, so I'll be here all alone."

"What time shall I come, Corey?"

"How about right now? Let me give you directions."

Corey was thrilled! This man was not a plumber, an electrician or a produce man. He was a doctor—a professional! She didn't give a thought to the fact that he was also married.

Jim told the au pair he was going to make a house call. He jumped in his Mercedes and took off for Corey's apartment. The "one night stand" turned into a full-fledged affair. They saw each other at every opportunity.

Often, when Jim was meeting or socializing with his social peers, one or the other of them would boast about a sexual conquest. Before long, Jim was openly describing the pleasures Corey provided him and told his cronies about his affair. Now the men, although they typically confided in each other about their little flings, went home and told their wives about Jim Nyland and Corey Tarry. Corey told her roommate what was going on, and several times the roommate made little comments about Dr. Nyland and Corey on her shifts at the hospital. Before long everyone in Dorchester County knew about Jim and Corey—everyone, that is, but Dina.

Although Jim never drank when he was on call, he did drink quite a bit when he was off duty. At several social functions he had become rowdy and had even, at one time, "streaked" on a bicycle at a private party. That, coupled with his rather open affair with Corey, was making some people nervous. Jim had turned out to be an excellent doctor, even though his medical school record left a great deal to be desired. He had, on at least two occasions, saved people's lives when there had been very little hope of their survival.

The three doctors whom Nyland brought in as partners in his family practice were growing increasingly concerned about his spreading harmful reputation. After several private meetings, they asked Jim to leave the partnership. He was outraged and told them the practice was his. *He* had brought them into it.

Although a good doctor and an able administrator in his role as Chief of Staff, Jim was not a very astute businessman. When he recruited the other doctors into the partnership, he had sold each of them twenty-five percent of the corporation rather than retaining fifty-one percent for himself; therefore, he controlled one vote. Consequently, he was ousted from the practice that he had started, staffed, built up, and expanded. The business leaders who had opened their bucket mouths were now getting pressure from their wives to do something about Jim Nyland remaining as Chief of Staff. The women wanted to make sure Nyland was punished for his behavior, probably so their husbands wouldn't get the idea that they themselves could "wander" and get away with it. The wives continued the pressure until the hospital board called a special meeting and Jim Nyland was removed from his position at the hospital he had established.

Dina, of course, learned the truth and immediately filed for divorce. Within three days of the final decree, Jim and Corey were married at the old, historic Episcopal Church. They hopped into her new pink Cadillac, compliments of Mary Kay Cosmetics for Corey had been named Saleswoman of the Year in South Carolina's Fifth Division. Miami was their destination. Once there, they boarded a cruise ship for a two-week honeymoon to Trinidad and Tobago.

Jim had sold his portion of the practice to the other doctors for top dollar. When they returned from their honeymoon, Jim and Corey moved into a rental townhouse on the golf course of the country club, and Jim opened a new family practice. While he once again waited for patients, Corey packed up all of her cosmetic samples and returned them to Mary Kay for a refund. She retired from the working world, since she was now a doctor's wife. There was no time for work as she began her search for the Nyland dream home and spent most of her days riding hither and yon with first one real estate agent and then another.

Finally, she found the "perfect" house where no improvements would have to be made, or so she told Jim. Jim's new practice hadn't taken off yet, but he managed the down payment on the house. He and Corey moved into the eleven-room English Tudor on Ballad's Creek.

Within days, Corey had carpenters there to gut the house, build partitions, add rooms and alter the foyer. Meanwhile, she shopped for new furniture, window treatments, Oriental carpets, linens, china, silverware and crystal. She spent money as if it were water. Jim tried to talk to her about their financial situation, but Corey would simply smile, go to the bar and fix him a drink. Kneeling at his feet, she would remove his shoes and suck his toes while working her way up to treat him to numerous sexual favors. With Corey's head buried in his lap, Jim seemed to keep forgetting that bankruptcy was rearing its ugly head right outside his door.

At his office waiting for new patients, Jim constantly worried about Corey's extravagant habits. Along with all of Corey's spending, he was also paying Dina alimony and child support. Still no patients came until Hunter Quarrels entered the office. He had slipped on the wooden stairs going down to the dock where the *Diamond Jim* was moored at Walthome. As a result, he had a nasty sprained ankle and a large gash on his left leg. While Jim was stitching the gash and taping the ankle, he and Hunter chatted.

"How's your business going? Cellular phones, isn't it?" asked Jim.

"It's coming along quite well. I should be putting the final deal together soon," responded Hunter.

"Maybe I could get involved. I'm really looking for a way to supplement my income. You know, I pay alimony and child support now along with all of my other bills?"

Before answering, Hunter cogitated about what he knew about Nyland. Lalique, for all of her working out at ModBod, had been Nyland's patient. While the other women had kept their little magic diet pills secret from their husbands, Lalique had not only told Hunter about the pills, but had also shared them with him. Hunter knew that even though the distribution of diet pills was exactly illegal, it wasn't entirely on the up-and-up. He also knew about Jim's recent loss of his partnership and his position as Chief of Staff, and of his divorce from Dina and marriage to Corey, whose spending habits were common knowledge. Hunter decided he had found another business associate. Hunter had always had a sixth sense about whom he could and could not trust.

"I'm not really in the cellular telephone business, Jim. I sell something much more lucrative than that," Hunter said with a wink.

He explained a little about his business to Nyland and offered to let him become a partner. By the time Jim was adjusting Hunter's crutches for him to leave the office, he and Hunter had reached an understanding.

42

Hunter

Hunter was a multimillionaire. He was an alumnus of Harvard Business School and a very intelligent man. When he graduated and was hired by a large firm on Wall Street in New York City, he quickly found he did not like either the claustrophobic confines of an office or a nine-to-five job. He worked diligently and hard scrimping and saving until he had a sizable amount of money. Then he went into the drug business.

He did well and soon caught the attention of some of the higher-ups in the Medellin Cartel who needed and wanted smart dealers and distributors in the United States. Hunter was originally approached by Escobar himself while on vacation in Colombia, and very soon he was the head of his own organization in the states and making more money than he ever dreamed possible. He had been involved with the cartel for twelve years and had pulled off some of the biggest drug deals in North America. He never got caught, or as far as he or anyone in the cartel knew, even drew any suspicion. He always planned very carefully, and his selection of assistants had always proved to be excellent. The cartel was very pleased with Hunter Quarrels and his ability to move their product. Thus, Hunter was able to convince the cartel to go along with this latest deal; the shipment of thirty thousand tons of raw cocaine.

Hunter further convinced the cartel, because of his loyalty over the years, to allow him to distribute this megashipment and delay payment for two weeks. The cartel did not usually operate in this manner, but

Hunter had always proven himself to be reliable and they wanted to sell this shipment and have it distributed.. Hunter had carefully and methodically scouted the country until he decided on Dorchester County. He convinced the members of the cartel he could not only pull off this shipment, but also many more in the little community before moving on. Hunter told the cartel everything, with the exception of his use of local people.

He was only using one person from his prior organization, the unfortunate Taylor who had been stopped by Charlie. Taylor was to be in Bogota to oversee the loading of the shipment to Marathon. He was to fly to Marathon to make sure the removal of the cargo from the plane to the barge went smoothly. From then on, Hunter's own people, who were not involved with the cartel, would take over. That was how he could promise them so much money for one drug deal. Each person involved stood to make from ten to thirty million dollars on this one drop since the cargo, once cut, would be worth close to two billion dollars on the street. Hunter had no intention of paying the cartel for the drug.

About six months prior to his arrival in Montiac, Hunter obtained a passport and other documents under a false name. It was really an easy procedure. He merely went to Boston, looked through the periodicals' file in the local library and found the name of someone who had passed away at the age of twenty. He sent to the Bureau of Vital Statistics for that person's birth certificate and became Harvey Wayne Chase. In order to try out his new credentials, Hunter traveled to Spain with his new passport. While there, he purchased a small island off its coast and made arrangements to have a house built and a small runway constructed. Once the drugs were distributed and Hunter had his money, which would be in the neighborhood of seventy-five million dollars, he planned to hop on his privately chartered jet and fly to Spain where plastic surgeons stood ready to change his physiognomy. Then he would get back on the jet and fly to his private island. The numbered Swiss bank accounts in which he would deposit his newly acquired money had already been opened. He told no one of his plan, not even Lalique.

Hunter wanted out of the drug business. This was to be his last deal. He was smart, however, and knew one didn't go to the drug cartel and tell them one was tendering one's resignation. One also did not retire from the drug business, at least not when one was at the level of the organization Hunter had attained. It was well known that when the powers within the cartel were ready for a person to retire, he retired. However, the cartel did not hold a cocktail dinner party and present the "retiree" with a gold wrist watch for his years of faithful service. They usually rewarded someone for whom they no longer had a purpose or a need with a small piece of lead placed behind the left ear, fired from a thirty-eight special.

43

Rehearsal for the Ball

There was one day remaining before the Magnolia Ball. At the high school gym, the debutantes and their parents, the escorts and the committee members finished the rehearsal of the figure to be performed at the Ball on the following evening. It had been a grueling night of intricate steps, giggles, Bonita's incessant chirping on a small golden whistle which she wore around her neck on a velvet cord, and about twenty repetitions of the complicated figure. At last the committee agreed the young ladies and their escorts were sufficiently proficient in the "German."

Everyone scrambled into Mrs. Jerkin's algebra classroom, which would officially become the coat-and hatcheck room the next evening. They headed to their automobiles for the drive to the Crest, where Ann Amelia and her mother were hosting the rehearsal party.

Several girls had asked Ann Amelia where her father was. Mona had quickly offered the excuse that Jason was suffering from a terrible case of bronchitis and was unable to attend. She only hoped he would be able to be in attendance the next evening. Mona's brother had been summoned and was at the rehearsal to present Ann Amelia. He was also hosting the rehearsal dinner and dance with Mona and Ann Amelia that evening.

Mona had indeed hustled Ann Amelia to Savannah that morning and purchased another silk gown for her to wear to the Ball. The second dress was even more beautiful than the first. But nothing could make Ann Amelia feel better. Her whole world had fallen apart. However, she knew how important this whole "debutante thing" was to her mother, so she was determined to get through it somehow, but she wasn't sure how she was going to be able to make it.

    Mona, however, was the picture of composure. To look at her, no one would guess that anything untoward had occurred, much less suspect that she had walked in on her respected attorney husband as he attempted to sodomize their only daughter. Ann Amelia hurt for her mother, but she was also proud of her. She bit her lip with new resolve. She would get through this whole charade for her mother's sake.

44

More "Come-Heres"

The day of the Ball dawned a cold, blustery gray day. Shortly after, two black Fords stopped in Montiac at the Gas 'N Go and filled up. The teenage boy on duty went out to service the cars. There were four men in each, all strangers dressed in flannel shirts, jeans and docksiders. The boy, an honor student at the local high school, noticed the men were trying to dress like the "bubbas" of Dorchester County. However, they had close-cropped haircuts, were clean-shaven, and they weren't wearing the de rigeour baseball caps. He also noticed they had uncalloused hands and clean fingernails. Also, not a single one of them had a "chaw" in his mouth, so they certainly weren't "bubbas."

As Mike, the gas station attendant, opened the gas tank of the lead car, he noticed the federal license plate. He turned and saw that the second car was also federally tagged. The driver of the first handed him a credit card, so Mike went into the station to write up the charge slip. He chuckled as he looked at the name on the credit card; it read "Federal Bureau of Investigation." Mike hoped the feds weren't attempting to come into Montiac undercover.

Once their cars had been serviced, the eight FBI agents headed for the Dorchester Grand and checked into four rooms, two men in each. The bellhop collected their luggage—eight briefcases and eight tuxedos—and carried them to the proper rooms.

The Magnolia Ball

Once in their rooms, Steve, the head agent, contacted Four Eyes and told him the team was in Montiac. Four Eyes assured him all arrangements had been made. They were to report to the gym that night at eight o'clock, where they would be met by one of the Dorchester deputies who would introduce them to the crew at the high school as security men hired by the Magnolia Ball Committee. Steve and his men walked across the street and ordered a Southern style breakfast. Everyone in the restaurant turned and looked, speculating about the strangers.

45

The Deal Countdown Begins

Frank Karsh and James Nyland left Dorchester County on December 21, in their yachts. They headed for Karsh's private estate on Jeckyl Island in Georgia. Hilda Karsh and Corey Nyland were quite put out by their husbands' sudden desire to go boating so close to Christmas and right in the middle of the debutante season.

Hilda chastised Frank and told him how much Lynette was counting on him to present her at the Ball, but Frank assured both of them he would be back in time for the deb festivities on the twenty-eighth of December. He also assured them he didn't have to be at the rehearsal, having already presented his two older daughters at previous Magnolia Balls. Frank and Jim convinced their respective wives there was a new marina near the Karsh estate which performed excellent work hauling and scraping boats at a very reasonable price. They said that was the reason for their trip to Georgia. The marina was closing for two months at the end of December, hence the timeliness of the trip. The yachts would then be ready for early cruising on the Savannah River in March and April.

Corey was quite distressed. This was the first debutante season where she would be attending the dinner and Ball as an invited guest, since she was now a doctor's wife. She had been present at a few of the dinners preceding the Ball in the past when she had been a waitress at the country club. However, this year she had received an engraved invitation with the magnolia branch on the cover. She made James swear he would be back in time to escort her that evening. He promised he would not only be back for the Ball, but he would also make up for missing their first Christmas together by taking her on a Caribbean cruise in January.

Chucky Saxon also incurred the wrath of his wife and daughter by accompanying the other two men with his sailing vessel. Chucky took along George Givens and Patrick Abrams to help crew. However, Chucky was flying back to Savannah the morning of the rehearsal to be on hand for the deb functions. Patrick and George would sail the *Saxony* back to the Savannah River with the cargo. Chucky, Patrick, George, Jim and Frank were rendezvousing with the barge that had steadily been on its way from Marathon, Florida, since early December.

The barge, pushed along its way by two tugboats, was loaded with six-hundred, one-hundred-pound burlap bags marked "confectioner's sugar." So far, the barge had not hit any snags, even when the Coast Guard had boarded the vessel to make an inspection. Everything looked in order. The proper number of life jackets were on board and a holding tank was on each of the tugs for waste material. A permit for hauling the "sugar," and a bill of lading from the Sucrito Sugar Company of Colombia were in their proper place. Of course, there really were bags of confectioner's sugar on the barge, too. They had been carefully placed on top of and surrounding the rest of the cargo.

The five men had met with Hunter and Bill and agreed to take the yachts to meet the barge, get the cargo loaded onto them and sail back to the mouth of the river. Only Patrick and George would be able to assist with the unloading of the product, since Chucky had to fly back before the yachts sailed, and Frank and Jim had to meet their wives for the Ball. Hunter and Bill agreed that this would pose no problem. They had made arrangements for other of their assistants to be on hand to help the shipment in its transfer from the *Diamond Jim* to the great room of Walthome. Frank already alerted Hawkins, one of his faithful peach factory workers, to pick him up from his yacht in a speedboat and then shuttle him to Walthome where a waiting car would whisk him and Jim to the country club by six o'clock.

Four Eyes and his posse were ready. They engaged the assistance of several of the Menhaden fish spotters to carefully watch and report the progress of the barge up the inland waterway.

Fish spotters are private airplane pilots who fly small, single-engine planes, usually Cessnas. They fly over the waters from dawn until dusk looking for large schools of Menhaden fish. When they spot a school, they radio the boats, which move to the area as quickly as possible and set their nets, catching entire schools of the commercial fish at one time.

Since everyone on the eastern coast of the United States is accustomed to seeing the spotters in the air during fishing season, no one gave their presence a second thought. Every day the spotters flew on their rounds and reported to Four Eyes the progress of the shipment on its journey to the mouth of the Savannah River. The two spotters didn't know what the barge carried, but they had an idea. However, they kept quiet. They liked the intrigue. Also, they both had been charged with DUI's within the past year and were anxious to help the local authorities in any way they could, in case they might need a little favor themselves in the future.

When Frank Karsh, James Nyland and Chucky Saxon set sail, Four Eyes also asked the spotters to keep him posted on their whereabouts and their ultimate destination, since the Jeckyl Island estate's exact location was a closely guarded secret. The spotters were happy to comply.

Everything was going as planned. The young ladies had their gowns and the many parties were in progress. The barge was on its way from Florida. The yachts had left to meet the barge on Jeckyl Island and Hunter and his network were ready to offload and distribute the product. Four Eyes was all set with his network of local, state and federal boys to make sure not one gram of cocaine made it out of the great room of Walthome unless it was removed by a law enforcement official.

The Magnolia Ball

Four Eyes had grown more excited each day. This "bust" was going to be so sweet. No one would ever make fun of him again. He was even considering running for Mayor of Montiac in the next election rather than sheriff. Sitting in a nice office all day with occasional outings to cut ribbons and kiss babies would be a lot easier than stakeouts and cruising around in the squad car looking for speeders. He always worried about the very real possibility that he might someday get shot.

Jordan Roget was to escort his daughter, Cinnamon. John, the owner of the hardware store with the bookie operation in the back room, would escort Mandy. They would not begin their involvement in the plan until after the Magnolia Ball had concluded. Chet Thomas left home early, before the Ball, to accompany Hunter and Lalique on the *Diamond Jim* and help with the unloading. Mary Beth Bracer's ex-husband, the ex-college professor Mitch, did the same.

With George Givens, Patrick Abrams, Chet, Lalique, Jason and himself, Hunter figured the entire exchange could be made in under an hour. Chet, George and Patrick could be back in time to meet their wives for the Ball, set to begin promptly at nine o'clock. By that time, the cargo would be safely inside Walthome, and the cutting and distribution process would wait until the festivities were over. Then the product would be loaded into private vehicles, distributed and sold all the way to New York City. Within days everyone involved would be rich, and Hunter would be on his way to Spain.

The plan was faultless, and Dorchester County was the perfect place to execute it. So far no one was at all suspicious or concerned about Hunter or Lalique, the goings and comings at Walthome, or of the *Diamond Jim*. Hunter was about to pull off the biggest drug deal of the century and screw the Medellin Cartel at the same time. He planned to pop a bottle of Dom Perignon after the cargo was safely inside the house. He would drink a toast to the lovely, young ladies and offer them a thank you for keeping all of the county mounties and the state smoky bears busy with traffic control and security at their dippy, coming-out party.

46

The Delivery

The night of the Ball Hunter and Lalique boarded the *Diamond Jim* with Mitch and Chet just as most of the debs and the committee members were putting on their last touch of lipstick or patting their hairdos for the third or fourth time. It was exactly five o'clock p.m. Lalique noticed a small wooden boat called a "skiff" near the opposite shore of Nassa's Creek but since they were a common sight on the creek, she didn't think it was important, so she didn't mention it to Hunter. Lalique figured the little skiff had loosened from its mooring and simply floated away from its dock.

This particular skiff had not floated off, however, but had been put in the water early that morning around the cove from Walthome. Four Eyes and his deputies had put the skiff in the perfect position from which to videotape the entire unloading of the *Diamond Jim* when it returned with its cache.

The *Diamond Jim* reached the mouth of the Savannah River just past five thirty that evening. The three yachts were waiting. As soon as Hunter maneuvered the sloop and anchored, Frank Karsh and Jim Nyland, resplendent in evening clothes, jumped aboard. Hunter told them the speedboat just entering the mouth of the river would take them back to Walthome immediately. Frank's peach factory worker killed the engine of the speedboat and came alongside the *Diamond Jim*. Frank and Jim climbed aboard.

The Magnolia Ball

Frank yelled, "Get us to Walthome as fast as you can!"

"Yes sir," responded Hawkins.

Hawkins surely thought these rich folks were fools. He didn't know why anyone would be out here at the mouth of the river on a cold night like this, and especially when Mr. Karsh had to escort Miss Lynette to that Magnolia thing in only twenty minutes. Hawkins gunned the outboard and they arrived at Walthome in less than five minutes. The three men ran the length of the dock to the front of the house. They jumped into the car, with Hawkins at the wheel, and sped to the club to meet their respective wives and Frank's daughter.

47

The Ball

The country club staff was ready. The clubhouse was lavishly decorated. The waiters, trays in hand, were attired in their tuxedos. The kitchen staff had prepared a feast of shrimp cocktail, cold cucumber soup, prime rib, Duchess potatoes, spinach soufflé, Parker House rolls, Caesar Salad, and Crepes Suzette for dessert. The valet parking attendants were at their stations. The orchestra was tuned up and had began their first medley. The club manager walked through the clubhouse making his last minute inspection, turned to his staff standing at the ready and with a wink said, "Let the games begin!" He threw open the massive front doors and welcomed the first arrivals.

The committee members and their spouses arrived. The young ladies with their parents and their escorts followed.

Nancy Abrams and Blanche Givens entered together and tried to squeeze past Bonita quickly, which was very difficult given the size of both Blanche and Bonita. Bonita wouldn't allow it, however, and called to them. The two dutifully walked over to her.

Bonita said, "I know that one or both of you sent an invitation to that disgusting Mandy. I've had so much on my mind with the Trudy thing and Celestine's resignation and reinstatement and then the unfortunate death of Sandy that I haven't been able to give Mandy much thought until today. However, when I really considered it, I came to the conclusion that one or both of you are the only ones who could have sent her an invitation, since we three are the ones who made the final selections, and you two addressed the invitations. Now which one of you did it?" queried Bonita.

Both Nancy and Blanche looked down at the floor and neither responded.

Bonita said, "I asked you a question."

Blanche looked up at Nancy and Bonita and made a snap decision. She decided to save her own skin and said, "Well, Bonita, Nancy did it, but she had a very good reason and I'm sure when you hear the whole story, you'll understand."

Nancy stared at Blanche in horror. "Blanche, you're supposed to be my friend. What are you doing to me?" wept Nancy.

"She figured it out, Nancy. She knows one of us did it. Do you expect me to take the blame for you?" said Blanche loudly.

Bonita shushed her and said, "We do not want to cause a scene here. The damage has been done. I only hope she and her ridiculous family do not embarrass themselves or the committee too much. There is no sufficient reason to explain what you have done, Nancy. You have violated a sacred trust. I have placed my utmost faith in you over the years, and you have made this year's presentation take on comic overtones. What could have possessed you? Whatever it was doesn't matter, and I don't even want to know. My first order of business in the new year will be to remove you and your insipid daughters from the committee."

Blanche put her arm around Nancy's now convulsing shoulders and said, "Oh, Nance, I'm so sorry."

"And as for you, Blanche, I'm sure you were aware of this from the very start. You should have come to me with this information long before this evening. I have no choice but to also remove you from the committee."

"But, Bonita, I didn't send Mandy the invitation," wailed Blanche.

"Perhaps not, but you knew about it and didn't do anything to stop it. Now we're not going to discuss this anymore. People are arriving. For heaven's sake, Nancy, pull yourself together. Go into the powder room and fix your face," commanded Bonita.

Nancy made a little movement toward the door and said, "No, Bonita, I'm going home. I can't stay here now."

"You most certainly will stay here. I will have nothing else causing problems here tonight. Now you do as I say. Fix your face and take your seat at the head table. Do it now!" Bonita hissed.

Nancy, with Blanche waddling behind, headed for the powder room to repair her jaundiced face. Bonita turned and with a big smile received the Kirkhams and their lovely daughter, Shannon. Shannon had chosen for her debut an Oscar de la Renta original of white satin with a strapless bodice and flesh-colored net. It was appliquéd with tiny rhinestones covering the sheer sleeves and top of the gown.

Only after the Kirkhams moved on, Bonita realized both Nancy and Blanche had been alone. Where in the world were their husbands?

Dee was the next to arrive. She wore a silver, tea-length sheath slit on the side, with one shoulder exposed. The other arm was fully encased in lame'.

"Hello, Bonita. My, the club looks lovely, doesn't it? I'm so sorry Chet is unable to be here. He had an important business matter come up right as we were about to leave the house, but he was already dressed and said he would be able to join us later at the Ball."

Bonita was not happy. Something wasn't right. The committee members' husbands had always escorted their wives to the dinner prior to the Ball. Bonita didn't have time to continue thinking about Chet's absence as, just then, the Bracer contingent arrived.

Julia Bracer Mavis might have all the money in the world, but she looked like a street person. Although Bonita recognized the apparition that Julia wore as a Dior, it was older than Noah and looked as if it had been through the flood with him, after which Julia had kept it stored in the bottom of the laundry hamper. The gray, chiffon column was wrinkled beyond belief. Julia had put her gray hair, usually in a ponytail, on top of her head and fastened it with a brilliant and very expensive diamond clip. However, the clip was not positioned to cover the dimestore scrunchy that held the original ponytail. Four black bobby pins vividly stood out in her yellowing gray hair.

Bonita was absolutely horrified by Julia's attire, but she managed to hide her disdain. She tried to remember that the truly wealthy could usually get away with almost anything, notwithstanding the fact that Julia was a permanent resident of "La La Land." Julia's ancient husband tagged along behind her in his equally ancient tails and black riding boots. What a sight!

Bonita, on the other hand, had spared no expense in her gown for the gala. She had found a few open days between Thanksgiving and Christmas to fly to New York and visit the showrooms. She had found exactly the right dress. Her three hundred plus pounds were entirely covered with black this year; black was slenderizing, the designer's models had assured her.

The fabric was beaded by hand from collar, which stood up behind her head a-la-Count Dracula's cape, to hem. At Tresses, the stylist had arranged her bleached mop of straw into a maze of curls atop her head where she had placed a Spanish onyx-bejeweled comb, an "heirloom" from Bonita's family. She was quite a vision with her fluorescent blue eyeshadow, her black eyeliner, her pale, pink lipstick, and her onyx and diamond chandelier-sized drop earrings, another family "heirloom" no doubt.

Darlene and Joseph Moreland entered next. Cute little Darlene was in a peach creation. It was long and flowing in the back but street-length in the front, perhaps to emphasize the peach-colored, high-heeled sandal shoes. True to form, Darlene always took advantage of showing off her pretty feet.

Patricia Saxon arrived with her parents and escort. Biffy wore an elegant, green velvet gown with a portrait neckline and matching green shoes. She looked wonderful.

However, Patricia seemed to have taken a page from Julia Bracer Mavis' book. Her dress, which may have once been white, was now a dingy yellow. It had obviously been professionally dry-cleaned, but it still had wrinkles. The fitted bodice came down to a vee in both the front and the back, and the chiffon skirt billowed out. It was a most unfortunate dress for pear-shaped Patricia.

Biffy cooed compliments to Bonita about how marvelous she looked. She told her Patricia was wearing the same gown her grandmother had worn when she had made her debut in Mobile, Alabama, forty years before. Bonita commented on how important tradition was and what a lovely idea. She felt pity (as much as she could muster for anyone) for Patricia, who definitely did not look happy about the gown. Chucky, who kept glancing at his watch, finally terminated the conversation with Bonita by suggesting it was time to take their seats.

Frank seemed a little out of breath as he entered with Hilda and Lynette. Lynette was escorted by her cousin from Cincinnati. The three of them had waited in the parking lot of the club for Frank to arrive so that all of them could enter together. Lynette wore a white jersey dress that was completely unsuitable for a debutante ball.

Bonita realized that next year she was going to have to sit down with the selected girls and their mothers and explain to them the proper attire for a young lady being presented to society. She had certainly thought that those selected would know what to wear. Lynette's dress looked as if it had been painted on her and it was entirely too low-cut. The girl's breasts were obscene. Bonita spoke to them quickly and moved them on into the main dining room. She watched Lynette walk away and wondered how in God's name she was going to perform the figure when she could hardly walk in that tight dress.

Cinnamon, Ellen, and Jordan Roget entered next. Cinnamon looked very nice in a white taffeta dress with a peplum at the waist, a tastefully modest scoop neck and short, puffed sleeves. Following the Rogets were Adele and the General. Bonita had graciously accepted Adele's story about Suzy's admission to the Sorbonne, but she didn't believe it for a minute. Milicent Pritchard had told Bonita that Suzy was not an excellent student, but it really made no difference. Adele was truly a beautiful woman, had excellent taste, was married to a retired general, and had voted the "right" way about Trudy. Bonita extended her plump, diamond-bedecked hand to Adele, who was glamorous in a red sequined jacket and a full-length, black crepe skirt with red sequined shoes and purse to match.

Adele leaned into Bonita and whispered, "That Mandy is just coming up the walk. I think you're going to be very surprised."

Bonita held her breath. This was the moment she had been dreading. What would that horrid girl and her horrid family wear?

As John, Joan and Mandy approached, Bonita was shocked almost beyond words! John was dressed in formal attire, rented, she was certain, but he looked presentable. The gaunt, scrawny Joan looked fantastic. She was almost pretty. Her stringy hair had been woven into a beautiful French knot with wisps of curls framing her normally horsy-looking face. She wore a plain long skirt of pink velvet with a silk jacket tastefully appliquéd with pearls. Her shoes and matching shoulder evening purse were pink also, just a shade darker than the dress, and made an excellent contrast.

Bonita was more than pleasantly surprised, but then reminded herself she had not seen the "debutante" yet. She surreptitiously peered around John and Joan to catch a glimpse of Mandy, but Grandmaw and Grandpaw were next in line. Again, the tux was surely rented, but Grandpaw looked presentable too, and if he had that horrid oyster knife with him, he had somehow managed to conceal it. Grandmaw wore an ivory lace, floor-length gown that didn't look too gauche. She had obviously spent some time at the hairdresser's or with someone who knew how to wield a comb that day. The four of them stepped aside, and Mandy entered.

Bonita gasped! Mandy looked beautiful. Electrolysis must have been performed on her face, because the one disgusting eyebrow was now separated into two, distinct, beautifully shaped and plucked brows. Her normally patchy skin tones were all smoothed into one—a glowing peach complexion. Her blue eyes glittered under the individually applied fake lashes. Her dishwater colored hair was now a vibrant, chestnut brown and had been styled into a loose pageboy. Her white peau de soie gown had wide straps and fell straight from the bodice, thus drawing attention away from her shapelessness. Across the front of the dress and trailing behind was flowing chiffon that billowed around her just enough to make her seem graceful. Her long white gloves, single strand of pearls and pearl-stud earrings were perfect.

Bonita was greatly relieved. Spying movement out of the corner of her eye, she turned to see Blanche and Nancy peering around the corner of one of the sitting rooms. Bonita gave them the tiniest hint of a smile and a nod as she passed Mandy and her entourage into the dining room. She wasn't even too put off as Elvis passed her and said, "Hey, Ms. Roberts. Great looking get-up you got on." At least he, too, was dressed appropriately, but he still had those horrible sideburns and that greasy, slicked-back haircut. Fortunately, though, he had come *sans* guitar.

Blanche and Nancy had also seen the Karsh family arrive. Blanche made her way over to them and chatted for a few moments before asking Frank where Patrick and George were, since they had accompanied him to Jeckyl Island.

"Oh, those guys were really great. Since we arrived here with only a few minutes to spare, they said they would 'batten down the hatches' and secure the boat. They asked me to tell you as soon as I arrived that they had given me their solemn word they would meet you at the Ball. Forgive me for not coming right over, but Hilda and Lynette haven't finished reading me the 'riot act' for making them so nervous by arriving at the last possible minute," Frank said charmingly.

The Magnolia Ball

Blanche and Nancy engaged in small talk with Hilda and Lynette for a few moments and then moved to another grouping, but not before Blanche said, "My heavens, did you see that child's dress? She's all but falling out of it! Frank and Hilda look so chic, but that Lynette looks like a slut."

"Well you know she was involved with that boy who was dealing cocaine. I heard the sheriff took her to the jail completely nude. Oh, hello, Biffy, and look at Patricia. So this is your grandmother's debutante dress. Tradition is so important, isn't it?"

As Blanche and Nancy spoke with Biffy and Patricia, Chucky excused himself and went over to Frank where he said, "Good evening, ladies, Frank. Frank, if you don't mind and if the ladies will excuse us for just an instant, I'd like to have a word with you."

"Certainly. Excuse me, ladies. I'll be right back."

"Well, how's it going?" asked Chucky.

"Just like clockwork. Smooth sailing all the way. We arrived at the mouth of the river about forty-five minutes ahead of schedule, and Hunter was there right on time with Hawkins close behind to get Jim and me here for the festivities. Chet, Mitch, Patrick, George, Hunter and Lalique are taking care of everything else. The other fellows should be finished a little before nine, and then they're going to meet their wives at the Ball. Everything's perfect. Just a few more days and the money will be rolling in."

Chucky reached for a handkerchief in his pocket and patted his forehead, where there was a great deal of perspiration.

Frank said, "You need to calm down, Chucky. It's about thirty-one degrees outside and you're perspiring."

"I can't help it. I thought this was a great idea. I still do, and everything seems to be going as planned, but I'm a nervous wreck."

"Relax, my friend. Just keep thinking of all those lovely, shiny bills. Listen, I've got to get back to Hilda. I'm still in the doghouse for my trip to the island."

"All right. Thanks. See you later," responded Chucky.

Bonita glanced at her diamond watch and realized that it was almost time for dinner to be served. Just then the Jamisons arrived. Celestine looked perfect, as she always did. She wore a purple gown that covered one shoulder and resembled something befitting a Greek goddess. Of course, she had Anthony in her arms. He was in his tiny tux and a plaid cummerbund and bow tie.

Celestine approached Bonita, held Anthony up, and squeaked, "Good evening, Mrs. Roberts. You certainly do look pretty this evening. May I kiss your hand?"

Bonita, determined not to upset Celestine again, extended her hand to Anthony, which Celestine took and held while she bobbed Anthony's head down to touch it.

Bonita said, "Why thank you, Anthony, and may I say that you look very handsome yourself? I especially like your colorful cummerbund and tie."

Celestine beamed and said, "Well, Anthony, I guess you were right. You told mother that black cummerbunds weren't 'in' among the young set, didn't you?" Celestine then turned to Bonita and said, "How is everything going?"

"Oh, absolutely fine. Mandy turned up looking smashing, and the only thing I am concerned about is that some of the committee members are here without their husbands. Also, Ann Amelia's father Jason won't be here to present her. He's suffering from severe bronchitis. That's such a shame. It's obvious how much he loves Ann Amelia, and then to miss this important evening in her life."

Celestine agreed and then said that maybe the committee members' husbands were sick too, since there was a lot of flu going around. Celestine, Anthony and Jamison took their seats. As the last guests entered the dining room, Bonita glanced into the gold French mirror and touched her hair. She turned to the left and to the right to admire herself, and regally entered the main dining room to officially begin the 1991 Magnolia Ball.

48

Eight O'clock-December 28, 1991

At eight o'clock, when the first part of the evening had concluded at the country club, the various BMW's, Jaguars, Cadillacs, Mercedes and one Rolls Royce (Bonita's), were brought by the valets to the club entrance. They would transport their owners to the high school gym, where the official Ball would take place.

The *Diamond Jim* sailed into view and proceeded to its dock at Walthome. Four Eyes and his men were on alert. As soon as the boat was spotted, Four Eyes radioed to the deputy in the skiff. The deputy engaged the infrared light and began taping. Hunter maneuvered the large sloop into the slip beside the dock and cut the engine. Chet jumped off the yacht onto the dock and leapt onto a waiting Boston whaler. He piloted it to the barge and crane sitting in the creek. Patrick and George, meanwhile, removed the cover from the hold while Lalique went to the house to open the door of the great room. She would turn on the conveyor belt once the crane had placed the first pallet on it. Mitch left the boat to follow Lalique and help unload the conveyor belt into the great room, where Jason was supposed to be waiting for them. As Lalique and Mitch entered, they were both amazed to see Bill Waltham there.

Mitch said, "Well, I sure am surprised to see you here, Bill. I didn't think you'd be able to get away tonight, of all nights."

"I felt I had to be here. I told Trudy that I needed to get out and drive around a little. I've stuck pretty close to her since Sandy's death, and she was real understanding. She even agreed I should get out. I know tonight is going to be real difficult for her, but the way things are going, I should be back home in an hour."

"You can count on it. This is one smooth operation. George, Chet and Patrick have to meet their wives at the Ball in about an hour, so I'm sure you'll be home shortly."

The three men watched as Lalique switched on the conveyor belt. The first pallet started into the great room. The team worked together like a "well-oiled" machine. As the last pallet was offloaded, it seemed as if the sun came up. There was light everywhere—floodlights from the other side of the creek, from the end of the dock, even from the little skiff that Lalique had chosen to ignore.

Jason and Bill went to one of the numerous sliding glass doors surrounding the great room to look out.

"What the hell is going on?" Jason said to no one in particular as a loud voice was heard over a bullhorn.

"This is the Sheriff of Dorchester County. All of you are under arrest. Put your hands over your heads and come out of the house. We have each and every one of you covered with automatic weapons. Do not make any sudden movements, or we will shoot on the spot."

Hunter was on the dock when this announcement came. He leapt into the air and did a surface dive into the chilly water of Nassa's Creek. Bullets riddled the water, but Hunter didn't come up. Bill, still in the great room, immediately headed for a screened porch connected to the room, which from the outside of the house didn't appear to have a door.

Bill had lived at Walthome for years and he knew a way out. He also knew how to work his way down the side of the hill to the highway and freedom. Quickly, he entered the side porch at a run, opened the camouflaged door, and jumped onto the soft ground to begin his trek down the hill to the highway. Just as Bill hit the ground, two FBI agents grabbed him from behind.

One of them said, "Going somewhere, Mr. Waltham?"

Chet slipped out of the crane's seat and sidled his way across the barge behind the crane to the Boston whaler, which he intended to use to make his getaway. He stepped into the boat where a waiting agent greeted him with a gun pointed in his face and a pair of shiny, new handcuffs. It was exactly eight forty-five.

49

Before the Main Event

Several of the debutantes and their parents returned to their homes to freshen up before going to the Ball. Some went to friends' homes for a toddy prior to the main event. Shortly before nine o'clock, they entered the high school gym.

The FBI agents had left the Dorchester Grand at ten minutes to eight. They were at their stations covering various entrances and exits of the high school.

Trudy was sitting alone in the small living room of the carriage house, drinking vodka and staring at a picture of Sandy. Tears slowly ran down her cheeks. The doorbell rang. She went to the door, and there stood Rudy.

"Hulloo, Tru-u-di. I wazza comin' down da rudd anna I seen Billy drivin' by anna I taught you wazza probly by youself, so I decides to come anna tell youse I wazza sorry 'bout youse 'lil gel."

Trudy looked at Rudy for a moment and didn't move. Then she walked to him, embraced him and said, "Thank you, Rudy. I don't know of anyone I would be happier to see tonight. It was very kind of you to come, especially after all I did to you. Your speech has really improved a great deal. Won't you come in?"

Rudy moved into the little living room, removed his baseball cap and said, "I's been agoin to adult ed at ta high school in the nights."

Trudy smiled at him.

50

The Second Segment of the Ball

The girls were herded up by Blanche and Nancy as they entered the high school and gathered backstage. There they were to stay until introduced by Bonita. They would then make an entrance onto the stage, and each young lady's presenter would meet her and assist her down the stairs from the stage to the main floor. There each would be met by her escort and where both gentlemen would walk her to the end of the room to wait for the other debutantes before beginning the figure.

Bonita went backstage and rather ungracefully managed to climb the steps and plant herself in the wings. When she gave the signal to Dee Thomas, Dee would wave to the orchestra to play the trumpet fanfare for Bonita's entrance. There were special pink gels Bonita insisted the winning floral designer of the year place in the light bars, with one mounted, pink-gelled fresnel spotlight to cloak her in its flattering light. She would make her opening remarks under it before the official presentation of the debutantes of the 1991 season.

Dee, Blanche, and Nancy had things well under control backstage, but they were all fit to be tied. None of their husbands had arrived yet. All were beyond angry. The husbands weren't yet late enough to cause apprehension, but Chucky Saxon and Frank Karsh were feeling acute anxiety. The others should have arrived by now. Once in the main gym where the fathers and other presenters were lined up, Frank, Chucky, Jordan, John and Jim Nyland were in a close knot. This was much to

Darlene's chagrin, as she continued trying to get them to take their places in line so they would be in the proper order for the presentation.

Every time she separated them, within a few minutes the five were back in a knot. They talked in hushed tones with worried expressions. They looked at their Rolexes or the main entrance to "Fairyland," this year's Ball theme. Once more, Darlene insisted they get into their positions. The fanfare sounded, and Bonita made her grand entrance.

"Welcome, ladies, gentlemen, debutantes, escorts, parents and socialites of Dorchester County to this, the ninety-ninth annual Magnolia Ball, the longest continually held debutante ball in the South."

More fanfare from the trumpets followed.

"Before we begin this year's presentations and the introduction of the governor of our fair state, our guest speaker for the evening, I would like to ask for a moment of silence in memory of Sandy Hibbert. Sandy was to be presented here this evening, but she tragically passed away in early November. Will all of you please bow your heads?"

Once the moment had passed, Bonita resumed.

"Thank you. And now I take great pleasure in presenting to you Celestine Piersall, granddaughter of the first Magnolia Queen and resident of Beechland, site of the first Ball held in 1892. Celestine, would you please come up and say a few words, dear?"

Celestine walked over to the steps leading to the stage and began her ascent, as she had done every year since she herself had made her debut. Anthony was with her. She had always brought him to the Ball since his "birth," but she had never brought him on stage when she made her opening remarks as the direct link to the original Ball and queen.

Once the applause had died down, Celestine began, "I want to thank all of you for being here this evening. We are very fortunate to have lovely, young ladies who will be presented tonight, and I know all of you—excuse me—what is it, Anthony? No, dear, you can't talk now. Mother is busy welcoming everyone to the Ball. Now you promised me you would be good if I let you come up with me. Forgive me, gentlefolk.

Now where was I? Anthony, I'm going to have to ask your father to come and get you if you don't stop interrupting me. I apologize for my son, Anthony. I can't imagine why he is acting this way."

The guests were becoming very uncomfortable. A few of the younger crowd giggled and snickered. Jamison stepped out into the hallway. He had always humored Celestine with her doll, but she was really going too far this time. Maybe the strain of the committee and Sandy's death had been too much for her. Celestine's fellow committee members and friends were embarrassed for her.

By this time Celestine had her ear pressed to Anthony's tiny mouth. "Well, the little fellow is very persuasive and he tells me there is something that he absolutely must tell you. I hope you will indulge us while I allow my son Anthony to speak to you for a moment. All right, Anthony, what is it that you are simply bursting to say?"

Celestine held Anthony up to the microphone and began speaking in her high-pitched Anthony voice.

"I want to tell everyone about mean, old Bonita. Today my mother received a phone call from her college friend Sissy, and while my mother was getting dressed for the Ball, she told me everything Miss Sissy said, but my mother said she would never tell another soul. Mrs. Roberts has been to my home several times, and almost every time she comes, she upsets my wonderful mother. She's not a nice lady, and I think all of you need to know the truth about her.

Bonita is not a member of Spanish royalty and wasn't taking care of any sick husband out in California. Bonita Roberts is a Mexican, and she is from a poor sharecropper's family in Texas. When she was young, she was scouted by a director from Hollywood, and he took her there to make movies, but she wasn't any good, so he gave her a plane ticket home. Bonita didn't want to go back to Texas and poverty, so she moved into the Beverly Wilshire until she could figure out what to do. She met a man named Enrique there who was a pimp, and he hired Bonita. She worked as a prostitute for over thirty years right out of her cottage at the hotel. She charged one-thousand dollars an hour. Mr. Roberts was one of her clients, and he married her. They lived in New York 'til Mr. Roberts had a stroke, and then they moved here.

"Bonita is a complete phony, and all this time all of you thought she was so classy and well-bred. You've allowed her to ruin girls' lives because you thought she knew everything about the debutante business. Well, she didn't know anything about it until she moved here. She's always rude when she comes to my house and never speaks to me, but Sandy Hibbert was real nice. She and her momma always talked to me. Mrs. Roberts is the reason Sandy's dead. Sandy killed herself cuz Mrs. Roberts wouldn't let her make her debut. She wanted to punish Mrs. Waltham for making up her background. Isn't that funny? Mrs. Roberts wanting to punish someone for doing exactly what she had done?" Celestine paused in her squeaky voice and looked at Anthony and then in the high-pitched voice she said, "Thank you, mother, that's what I wanted to say. I'm finished now."

During Anthony's tirade, Bonita had been signaling to Dee to kill the microphone and to the orchestra to play and to the light technician at the other end of the gym to kill the lights. But everyone was mesmerized by what Anthony was "saying," and no one obeyed Bonita's orders. The assemblage had moved closer to the stage as Celestine squeaked in her high-pitched, "Anthony" voice.

When "he" had finished, Celestine said, "Anthony, you have been a very naughty boy. Mother told you not to repeat anything she said to you about Mrs. Roberts," and with that Celestine excused herself and exited to the backstage area.

Bonita stood there in the center of the stage. She tried to compose herself and made a tentative step toward the microphone when she fainted. Dee finally broke out of her trance and signaled to the orchestra to play. The crowd erupted. Everyone spoke at once. No one went to Bonita's assistance until Adele ascended the stairs, took Bonita's notes from her outstretched hand, and asked Dee to arrange to have her removed. She took the microphone and said, "The debutantes to be presented at the 1991 Magnolia Ball shall begin with Cinnamon of the House of Roget."

Jordan moved to the bottom of the stage steps as Cinnamon walked primly to its center. She descended the stairs to her father's uplifted hand. At that instant, a commotion started in the school hallway. Four Eyes burst onto the stage from the wings as Bonita was carted off. He signaled to the orchestra to cease, took the microphone from Adele and announced, "All of the entrances and exits to the school have been secured. We are here to make arrests. Tonight, thirty-thousand tons of cocaine were transferred from three privately owned yachts onto the *Diamond Jim* and moved to Walthome. Mrs. Thomas, Mrs. Given and Mrs. Abrams, in case you're wondering where your husbands are, they've been placed under arrest for their part in the cocaine deal. Your ex-husband has been arrested too, Ms. Mary Beth. Mr. Waltham and Mr. Jason Honeycutt are also in the county jail by this time."

Silence enveloped the gym. An FBI agent moved over to Jordan Roget, removed his arm from his daughter and handcuffed him.

Cinnamon screamed, "What are you doing? There must be some mistake. My father isn't involved in any cocaine deal. Tell them, Daddy. Let him go! Mother, don't let them arrest Daddy!"

The FBI agent led Jordan away as another agent handcuffed Frank Karsh. Hilda and Lynette simultaneously burst into tears.

Corey said to Jim, "Well, I never. This is the most shocking thing that's ever happened. Can you believe all of this, Jim?"

Corey turned to where Jim had been standing and saw him flattened against a twinkling, lollipop wreath against the wall. Corey started toward him but was intercepted by a state trooper. He handcuffed her husband. The remaining state troopers rounded up Chucky Saxon and John.

Four Eyes spoke again. "I'm real sorry about this, folks, and I'm sorry to ruin the evening for you little gals. You all look real pretty, but being an elected representative of the people, I got a job to do."

Four Eyes and the law enforcement officers marched all of the detainees out the front door to waiting police cars and transported them to the jail. Everyone had been accounted for except Hunter. The state police divers were looking for his body, and the Rescue Squad already had boats and grappling hooks dragging for him. Lalique was arrested and locked up, too. She was the most exciting thing that had happened to inmates at the jail since Four Eyes had brought Lynette Karsh in with nothing on but an afghan.

Neither Hunter nor his body was ever found. The yellow Ferrari was later sold at public auction and purchased by, of all people, Jimbo Taylor, real estate magnate.

51

After the Ball

Dorchester County had been exposed. The very old, very social, very political county and many of its prominent citizens were splashed all over the front of every newspaper in the country, including the *Montiac Minutes*. The oldest continuing debutante ball in the South was no more. No young ladies were presented to society on December 28, 1991, in Montiac. No new queen was crowned. There was no breakfast served at Beechland nor were pictures taken of a new queen under the old magnolia tree.

Strangely enough, for the first time in its long history, the following summer the gorgeous old tree failed to bloom. Specialists were called in from all over the South by Jamison but none of them were able to figure out what was ailing the hardwood. It finally withered and died. The Magnolia Ball became a memory. It has not been held again.

An era ended. The Magnolia Ball Committee was dissolved. Although she did sometimes allow Rudy to visit her, Trudy remained a recluse, and Bonita became one. Darlene had an affair with an oysterman who jump-started her car one day as she left Tresses. Dee was murdered on a dark, country road after leaving a Labor Day Party she had attended alone, since Chet was in prison. Her murder has not yet been solved. Joshua Roberts, Bonita's husband, finally passed away. Bonita had him cremated and held no funeral or memorial service, nor did she place an obituary in the *Montiac Minutes*.

The Magnolia Ball

Adele lies at home bedridden, a victim of liver failure. She does not have much longer to live, but Suzy has refused to see her, even though the General has beseeched her to come to visit several times. Milicent was finally forced to enter a retirement home. Nancy Abrams had to go and live four months each year with each of her three, beautiful sisters'-in-law and their families, since Patrick had gambled away everything they had prior to his incarceration. Blanche Givens went to work as a checker in the local supermarket to help make ends meet.

Cinnamon got pregnant in January of 1992 and was married, unhappily, to—of all people—a high school band director. She settled in Maryland, where she gave birth six months after the wedding. Two years later, the band director left her, filed for divorce, and married one of his students. Suzy divorced her husband and is now married to number two.

Four Eyes was awarded several medals and was invited to the governor's mansion for a special dinner and celebration in his honor. He has already announced his candidacy for Mayor of Montiac in the forthcoming election.

Biffy and Patricia Saxon closed up the old sea captain's house, took Randall and moved away. No one knows where. Joan is diligently attempting to run the hardware store while John does his time, but it's hard to place a bet in Montiac these days because Joan has closed the bookie operation. Mary Beth of the Bracer tribe spoke kindly of Mitch. "After all, he is my children's father," she explained, "Perhaps when he is released, I should give him a larger monthly allowance. I hadn't realized that he needed more money."

Hilda Karsh has added new products to the peach factory's line and is doing quite well running the company. Lynette is counting the months until Ned is released from prison so they can get married. Corey Nyland had to sell the dream home, but she still drives the pink Cadillac. She was fortunate that she had done so well as a Mary Kay distributor, because Mary Kay took her back. They were able to send her the very same cosmetics sample kit she had returned to them only a short time before.

Ann Amelia, after a hiatus from college, is back at school now in her senior year and seems well adjusted. Mona married a doctor, whose wife had recently died, after he resettled in Montiac to practice at the new hospital.

Jamison persuaded Celestine to take a trip around the world and to leave Anthony at home with Izonia. Celestine wrote to him every day. Jamison also made arrangements for Anthony to disappear during their absence.

When they returned from the trip and Anthony wasn't to be found, Celestine went into a catatonic state and had to be hospitalized in Westbrook in Richmond, Virginia. Jamison retrieved Anthony and took him to visit Celestine.

At first she remained silent, but when Jamison prepared to leave and reached for Anthony, whom he had placed on Celestine's lap, she suddenly asked Jamison where he was taking her son. Jamison immediately rang the bell for a nurse, who in turn called Celestine's psychiatrist. After several sessions he declared her absolutely sane. He explained to Jamison that Celestine was a good person with impeccable morals. Anthony had become her avenue to occasionally say those things she needed to say but could not because of her irreproachable ethics. Jamison was greatly relieved. He took Celestine and Anthony home. It's rumored in Dorchester County that Jamison now converses with Anthony occasionally.

Julia Bracer Mavis returned from the Kentucky Thoroughbred Auction with three new horses. The ancient editor of the *Montiac Minutes*, the Dorchester County Bible, passed away, and he and the newspaper were "put to bed" for the last time.

Jimbo Taylor patented his funnel/fork and became a millionaire overnight. He and Lillie Mae retired to Miami Beach, Florida.

52

Farewell Bonita

The small plane landed on the runway at Creekside Farm. Alphonso ran out to meet it. The pilot opened the window and handed him a square, white box.

"Thank you, sir," said Alphonso.

"No problem," answered the pilot, "The pay was certainly worth the trip."

"Yes sir," Alphonso responded as he moved away so the pilot could turn the plane around and get into position for take off.

The black servant walked back to the front of the mansion with the box. Bonita came out the massive, double front doors. The last Mayflower moving van was heading down the long lane as she turned the key in the lock.

"Well, it arrived just in time, didn't it, Alphonso?"

"Yes'm."

He held the door of the Rolls open for Bonita. Hannah, the maid, was already in the front seat. Alphonso saw Bonita in and walked around to the driver's door. He drove slowly down the long driveway in case Ms. Bonita wanted to take a last, long look, but she never glanced back. As the big car neared Montiac, Bonita reminded Alphonso to stop at the cemetery.

"I remembers, ma'am, but don't you want me to do whatever needs doing? It's awful cold out there today."

"No, Alphonso. I want to do this myself."

Alphonso pulled the car in at the old, historic Episcopal Church and stopped at the entrance to the cemetery. He jumped out, opened Bonita's door, and offered her his arm.

"You wait, Alphonso. I'll be right back."

Bonita walked amongst the headstones until she came to Sandy's final resting-place. She knelt with great difficulty and opened the box. She removed a perfect, hothouse magnolia blossom and placed it on Sandy's grave.

"Sandy, it's me. Bonita Roberts. Today is December 28, 1992, the day we always held the Ball. There won't be one this year, Sandy, or any other year, I don't imagine. I'm sorry. You should have been asked to make your debut last year, and you should have been the queen. You had everything to live for and I ruined it for you, didn't I? I hope you can forgive me," Bonita whispered as tears streaked down her heavily made-up face.

She rose, smoothed her dress and coat, took out her lace hanky and blotted her tears.

Alphonso opened the car door and returned to the driver's seat. "Where to, Ms. Bonita? We knows we's moving, but you ain't told us where we's going."

"We're going to Tennessee, Alphonso. I've read about a lovely, little town there just outside of Memphis. Right now, they only have a small cotillion, but I'm sure after we're settled I can convince the powers-that-be to make the small party into a much larger ball, don't you think? I've never been to Tennessee, but from the brochures I've received from the Chamber of Commerce, I think we're all going to like it there very much. I wonder if magnolia trees grow in Tennessee? It would be so nice for the cotillion to become a large debutante ball, and "Magnolia Ball" has such a nice ring to it. I can see the article in the local newspaper now, 'Bonita Roberts, formerly of Spain, California and New York and a recent arrival here in our fair community, will chair the first Magnolia Ball Committee to select the debutantes for 1993 in Spencer, Tennessee.'

The Magnolia Ball

Remember now, Alphonso and Hannah, we're not going to mention Dorchester County, Montiac, South Carolina, the Magnolia Ball, or any of the recent unpleasantness to any of our new friends."

Both servants nodded their heads, but Hannah's big, brown eyes rolled. Bonita ignored her and settled in for the ride with a pleased expression on her face. The Rolls drove through the center of Montiac and had to stop for both lights, but Bonita did not look up from her map of Tennessee. She had new worlds to conquer.

Epilogue

A few weeks after arriving in Tennessee, Hannah placed a call to her friend Izonia.

"I told you before we left that I'd give you a call, but you gotta promise not to tell Miss Celestine or no one else where we are, cuz Miss Bonita'd have a fit."

"I ain't going to tell no one. I'm just so glad to hear from you, gal. I really misses you,' answered Izonia.

"I miss you too. And I don't like this here Tennessee one bit, but we got a real nice house and Miss Bonita seems happy. She's already out meetin' everybody. I reckon before long she'll have the folks here organized and be having a Magnolia Ball in Spencer, Tennessee."

"I hope that don't work out. It sure caused a lot of problems here."

"How's Miss Celestine?"

"Oh, she's doing fine now that Anthony's back. Everything is real good with her and Mr. Jamison."

"And how's Anthony?" Hannah asked.

"He's jest fine; he's sittin' right here in the kitchen with me now. Miss Celestine's at one of her meetings, so I'm 'Anthony-sitting,'" responded Izonia.

"Tell him I said hello."

"I'll do that. So you're in Spencer, Tennessee, huh?" asked Izonia.

"Yes, and I guess this is where we's gonna stay. I don't reckon I'll ever see you again, because I don't ever leave Miss Bonita for more than a day at the time."

"Yeah, but we can still call each other every now and then. Can I write to you?" asked Izonia.

"No, I don't think that would be a good idea. Then Miss Bonita'd know I told you where we was. She don't want no one from Dorchester County knowing our whereabouts. And I think you better not call me either. Just let me call you."

"All right. I won't say a word, and I'll just wait for your calls. You will call me now and then, won't you?"

"You know I will, Izonia. You been a wonderful friend to me. Gotta go. I love you. Bye."

"Bye, Hannah," sighed Izonia.

She hung up the phone and crossed to the stove. As she stirred the bouillabaisse she was preparing for dinner, she turned and looked at Anthony sitting in a chair near the kitchen table.

"You know who that was, Anthony? That was my friend Hannah who works for Mrs. Roberts. You remember Hannah, don't you? She was so wanting to meet you, and she finally got to when Mr. Jamison and Miss Celestine went 'round the world, and you stayed here with me. Do you 'member her? Alphonso brought her over here to visit me and to meet you. They was in that big maroon car. Well, they's livin' in Spencer, Tennessee, now, but Mrs. Roberts don't want no one to know that, so don't you go tellin', you hear?'"

Maybe it was just the way the rays of the sun reflected in Anthony's large blue, glass eyes, but Izonia could have sworn he winked.

About the Author

*R*ebecca Tebbs Nunn graduated from Mary Washington College of the University of Virginia with a BA in Dramatic Arts and Speech. She has taught drama on the high school and college levels, acted in stage productions, performed in numerous television and radio commercials and directed at dinner theatres in Maryland and Virginia. She lives in Raleigh, North Carolina, and Kilmarnock, Virginia, with her husband, Spike, a retired commerical airline pilot and her two Shelties, Mikey and Cluny.